## Praise for

'Arne Dahl is one of the t...
crime ...
**Mark Bi...**

'Arne Dahl is possibly the most thoughtful and playful
contemporary Nordic crime writer. He also happens to be one
of the most thrilling'
**Ian Rankin**

'Brilliant visceral writing with terrific pace, this book grips you
like a vice from the very first line and never lets you go'
**Peter James**

'Arne Dahl has created a school of his own within the Swedish
crime writing tradition. He combines global intrigue with
intelligence, suspense, and genuine literary quality'
**Lars Kepler**

'There's no one in Nordic crime right now who's better
than Arne Dahl'
**Jyllands-Posten**

'It's not for nothing Arne Dahl is known as the master of plots ...
The suspense is borderline unbearable ... One of Sweden's
most read-worthy and rebellious crime writers'
**Norra Skåne**

# Praise for Arne Dahl

'Arne Dahl is one of the true greats of Scandinavian
crime fiction'
— Mark Billingham

# ARNE DAHL

Arne Dahl is a multi-award-winning author, critic and editor. Dahl is the creator of the bestselling Intercrime series, which was made into a BBC TV series. His books have sold over three million copies and have been translated into 32 languages. Arne Dahl was awarded the prestigious European Crime Fiction Star Award (Ripper Award) in 2018.

ALSO BY ARNE DAHL

# ARNE DAHL

# YOU ARE NEXT

Translated from the Swedish
by Ian Giles

**VINTAGE**

1 3 5 7 9 10 8 6 4 2

Vintage is part of the Penguin Random House group of companies
whose addresses can be found at global.penguinrandomhouse.com

Penguin
Random House
UK

First published in Vintage in 2023
First published by Harvill Secker in 2022
First published with the title *Mittvatten* in Sweden by Albert Bonniers
Förlag (by agreement with Salomonsson Agency) in 2018

Copyright © Arne Dahl 2022
Translation copyright © Ian Giles 2022

Arne Dahl has asserted their right to be identified as the author of this
Work in accordance with the Copyright, Designs and Patents Act 1988

penguin.co.uk/vintage

Printed and bound in Great Britain by Clays Ltd, Elcograf S.p.A.

The authorised representative in the EEA is Penguin Random House
Ireland, Morrison Chambers, 32 Nassau Street, Dublin D02 YH68

A CIP catalogue record for this book is available from the British Library

ISBN 9781529111477

Penguin Random House is committed to a sustainable future
for our business, our readers and our planet. This book is made
from Forest Stewardship Council® certified paper.

MIX
Paper | Supporting
responsible forestry
FSC® C018179

# YOU ARE NEXT

I

# 1

The corridor reposed in darkness. Nevertheless, Berger could make out a winged insect crawling slowly across the ceiling. He followed it with his gaze for a long time. Only when he stopped looking did he realise that it was a bee.

The sole source of light in the corridor was the small circle at eye level on the closed door between him and the other man. The two of them were pressed against the ice-cold concrete wall on either side of the door, each with a firearm raised. In the almost non-existent light, the older man fixed his steely grey gaze on Berger and nodded distinctly. Without letting go of his weapon, Berger produced something that looked like a magnifying glass. Soundlessly, he placed it against the peephole and looked into it.

The perspective was distorted, but the interior of the flat was fully discernible. A hallway led onto a living room. Straight ahead in the first hint of a November dawn, it seemed as if a pair of gigantic eagles were swooping in towards the large windows of the room. As if moving in slow motion, the distortion brought them closer and closer – black silhouettes that appeared for a moment to be soaring on thermal currents directly outside the

3

windows. Then the eagles assumed human contours as they stood still, their feet firmly anchored. One of them raised its hands and showed ten fingers, then nine, eight. Berger thrust the object akin to a magnifier back into his pocket and yanked out the skeleton key. He inserted it into the lock as quietly as he could, but it still rattled disquietingly as he fumbled for invisible tags, spikes. Six, five, four. It wasn't taking hold – for the first time in years, the skeleton key wasn't taking hold. Three, two. He finally had a bite and heard the click as the key did its job. Weapon raised, he opened the front door. At the exact same moment, the two black-clad figures kicked their way in through the balcony door, each with a small sub-machine gun raised to the shooting position. They silently ducked to the left-hand side of the flat. Berger crept to the right, weapon raised, not making a sound.

The rest of the living room materialised: a woodburner and tiled fireplace surround, sofa, reading chair, drinks trolley. A hefty book on the side table beside the armchair. Without holstering his pistol, Berger went over. Now he could see a pair of spectacles on top of the book – they were absurdly thick. And the volume in question was the complete works of Shakespeare, in English.

Not touching anything, Berger raised his gaze. There was just a single picture on the wall – a piece of landscape photography. The bewitching gleam of sunset playing across a hillside covered in cypress and pine trees, a couple of white houses, a few donkeys with their heads bowed, a column of beehives set on terraces climbing the hill and a bed of butter-yellow flowers that extended across the bottom until it reached the glittering sea. Far away, a large cliff expanded into the water. Berger thought he recognised Gibraltar.

He returned to the book, crouching, scrutinising the glasses, noting the bookmark protruding from between the thin pages. But he touched nothing.

'Here,' shouted a muffled voice.

Berger stood up and turned round. The older man was watching him from the hallway. His close-cut hair was reminiscent of iron filings around a magnet. His name was August Steen and he was Head of the Intelligence Unit at the Security Service.

Berger and Steen headed towards the voice, passing through the kitchen and into a corridor. Fragments of a conversation were drifting out of one of the far rooms. Berger went in.

The sub-machine guns were slung over the shoulders of the black-clad figures. With a degree of scepticism, Berger contemplated August Steen's external resource duo.

'Flat secured,' said Roy Grahn.

'But this is where she was,' said Kent Döös, gesturing with his hand towards the obvious soundproofing on the walls of the windowless room.

Berger looked around. It was a completely anonymous room – the very opposite of the cosiness found beyond its walls. The absence of any trace of chains, leather straps or drip stands didn't mean that those kinds of things hadn't been present or that drugs hadn't been used. All that was present was silent emptiness.

The living room had had more to say.

Berger squatted beside the crumpled sheets on the unmade bed. He looked at the pillow and made out at least three long black strands of hair in the slowly gathering dawn light.

'Our friend isn't exactly making much attempt to cover his tracks,' he said.

'Why would he?' said August Steen. 'All he needs to conceal is where he's taken her.'

Berger heard a faint buzzing. He looked up towards the

ceiling. A bee flew across the room. The same bee? He followed it through the kitchen and back into the living room. He stopped by the armchair and put on gloves. He moved the spectacles off the book. Then he opened the book to where the bookmark had been left. It was held in place with a clip onto the page.

*Hamlet*. Act Three. The bookmark touched upon the world's most famous literary phrase.

*To be, or not to be . . .*

Berger went over to the photograph on the wall and contemplated it. Saw the sea, the cliff, the flowers. Saw the beehives climbing up the hillside.

Saw the beehives.

The bee buzzed again. It sounded different – the sound had doubled. Berger looked up. There were two of them in the corner of the ceiling now.

Did bees hang on until late November? In Sweden?

*To be, or not to be . . .*

'He's a beekeeper,' said Berger.

Kent and Roy looked at him disdainfully, while Steen maintained an air of neutrality.

'What?' Roy said at last. 'In here?'

'Hardly,' said Berger.

'It's a trend, isn't it?' said Kent. 'Beehives on roofs?'

'Bloody hell,' Roy said.

Steen frowned. Then he said: 'There are three ways up to the roof. The stairwell, the fire stairs and via the balconies. Grahn, can you climb up another two storeys?'

Roy glanced at the balcony where two ropes were hanging down from the storey above. He nodded.

'Döös, take the fire stairs,' Steen continued. 'Berger, the main stairwell. I'll try to find a view. Coordinate before action. Report your location. Await orders from me. Hop to it.'

Roy headed back out onto the balcony, while Berger and Kent tumbled out of the front door. Kent went one way, while Berger turned on the light and headed along the corridor. He reached the stairwell and spotted a bee crawling along the wall.

There were two options. Either the bees were fugitives or they were tasters – clues. If they were fugitives, then the perpetrator might very well be up there with his kidnap victim, completely unprepared. But it was probably more likely that he was drawing them up onto the roof for a reason.

Regardless, they had to go up. There was no turning back. There were no other police who could be brought in – this was absolutely top secret. Berger wasn't even sure exactly how much Kent and Roy knew. He watched the bee for a few seconds in its seemingly aimless meander across the wall.

Then he set off upwards.

The grubby, fluorescent-lit stairwell terminated at a sturdy steel door with a handle on the inside. Berger pulled out his walkie-talkie and reported his location. It crackled and then Roy's voice emanated from it:

'Also in position.'

Another crackle, then August Steen said: 'Have a view from the adjacent property. There is indeed a small, low structure on the roof in the north-east corner. Closest to you, Grahn, maybe five metres away. However, the door is on your side, Berger. Twenty metres from you. Döös, it's ten metres from the fire stairs on the far side.'

'Roger that,' said Roy. 'Kent?'

'These fire stairs are a mess,' Kent panted. 'Give me a couple of minutes and I'll report back.'

Silence descended.

The fluorescent lighting in the stairwell went out. Darkness consumed Berger. In the silence, a buzzing could be heard. There was a luminous red button in the darkness, signifying the light switch. He reached for it. The light stuttered back into life. The bee buzzed onwards, remaining invisible.

Everything was about the waiting.

The unbearable waiting.

This waiting summoned the memory of a darkened motel room, little more than a strip of light penetrating from the roaring motorway outside. Berger had slipped in, clutching his pathetic carrier bag in one hand, filled with sandwiches and drinking yogurt from the petrol station, and he had just about settled into the armchair before he realised there was someone there. His heart leapt into his throat and then August Steen spoke.

'Is this what you call staying under the radar?'

The seconds crawled past in the stairwell. Berger ran his hand over his chest, the contours of the bulletproof vest almost as familiar as those of his own ribs.

The motel room continued to impose upon his mind. Berger now on the bed, breathing heavily, his gaze now fixed on Steen in the armchair.

'We think we've located where Carsten is holding Aisha,' said Steen. 'Be ready early tomorrow morning.'

Berger slowly shook his head and looked around the depressing motel room.

'What the fuck am I doing here?' he said.

'You're Sweden's most wanted man,' said Steen. 'You're keeping your head down – that's what you're doing.'

'And you're one of the top brass in the Security Service,' said Berger. 'I'm not and never have been in the Security Service. Why would you help me?'

'We're helping each other,' said Steen.

The bee continued to hum on its way around the stairwell, but it failed to disperse the memory of the nocturnal scene.

Berger had stared through the darkness at August Steen, who eventually felt compelled to continue.

'You're part of my team now, Sam. I'm going to need you – for real – just as soon as we find out more about what's going on. You'll have to sit tight for the time being. We're sorting out a safe house for you. But I need you tomorrow morning.'

'What the hell is it that's "going on"? Some kind of terrorist attack?'

'The worst act of terrorism ever –'

'Yeah, yeah. I know. The worst act of terrorism in all of Sweden's history. But I know fuck all about it. I can't stand the Security Service's bloody hush-hush around everything.'

Steen sighed audibly and leaned back in the moth-eaten armchair.

'Carsten was my deputy for several years – one of the pillars of the Security Service. Then it turned out he was the mole – the treasonous traitor – in our organisation, the one I had spent a long time looking for. He kidnapped Aisha Pachachi for the same reason that he murdered your colleague and friend, Sylvia Andersson . . . To smoke out my most vital asset – Aisha's father, Ali Pachachi, the man behind the network. In short, he's abducted Aisha to silence Ali.'

There, on the bed in the drab motel room, Berger felt reluctant, no matter how much his police instincts were beginning to come back to life.

'Because Ali is on the brink of finding out where, when and how the worst act of terrorism ever in the history of Sweden is going to take place?'

'Yes.' Steen nodded. 'My assessment is that an international terrorist organisation needs to silence Ali, which is why they've bought Carsten. Presumably we're dealing with Islamic State, but that remains unconfirmed.'

Berger looked around the disheartening motel room, but there was nothing to fix his gaze on. Nothing other than the shunned Head of Intelligence of the Security Service.

'And you're saying that it's Carsten who's left me in the shit right now?' said Berger. 'Made me Sweden's most wanted man? "Ex-cop sought for murder of suspect." Shot a killer using my old service weapon. Why the fuck has he done that?'

Steen shook his head.

'It's a little unclear,' he said. 'But he has some kind of emotional tie to Molly Blom. He was watching her up in the interior. His reports had an odd overtone – one that only became apparent to me after the fact, when I read them in one go. He referred to you as the man and the woman, but using symbols.'

'Symbols?'

'Like this,' said August Steen, producing a pen and drawing on the back of a newspaper.

Berger saw two symbols – ♂ and ♀ – and frowned.

'♂ was you, Sam, and ♀ was Molly.'

'The Molly who's in a coma and carrying my child,' Berger said grimly, shaking his head.

Steen hoisted himself forward in the shabby armchair and placed a hand on Berger's knee, which was a little unexpected.

'We've got one big advantage over Carsten,' he said, using a voice that Berger had never heard before. 'He is undeniably a very dangerous man – we could probably go so far as to call him a well-trained professional killer – but he's very close to going blind. He has an escalated variant of RP – the eye disease retinitis pigmentosa. And tomorrow morning is our best chance of catching him. I need you with me, Sam.'

*I need you with me, Sam*, Berger thought to himself in the nondescript stairwell of the block of flats, faced with the equally nondescript door during a wait that increasingly felt eternal. He returned with full force to the present and noticed his unsecured weapon – it was trembling with an oddly regular rhythm that was presumably somehow related to his heartbeat.

His only hope was that Carsten was on the verge of blindness.

All he could hear was the buzzing of an invisible bee. It kept going, going, going, in a complete monotone.

Then the walkie-talkie crackled.

'In position,' said Kent's voice.

'Right then,' said Steen. 'Three, two, one.'

Berger pushed the door open and looked out. Something supposedly akin to dawn was spreading its faint glow across the rooftops. The scene was still in a state of semi-darkness. Twenty metres to his right was the small building, which looked like a squat lump of concrete. Diagonally ahead of him he saw Kent emerge from the fire stairs and start towards the building. At the same moment, Roy hauled himself up his rope and rolled over the small parapet.

Berger ran. He was present and not present; he saw everything as if it were from a strange, distorted distance, as he waited for the volleys of shots.

Roy got there first, Kent not far behind him, Berger arriving last. He saw Roy raise his foot, kick down the door and vanish inside. Kent also reached it, arms and legs all over the place. He too dived into the building.

Berger was close now. He felt a powerful stab of pain at his throat, as if a silent weapon had been fired. He slowed down, touching his neck, at which point his hand was also stung. He had almost reached the wide-open door when Kent staggered out of the building. He was writhing wildly and oddly. He flailed, his service weapon flying off in an arc. Kent fell to his knees, threw himself forward and rolled around. The sound of buzzing was even louder. Berger began to be filled with pain – a gnawing pain that spread through his body, burning into his limbs.

At that point, a figure emerged from the structure. It looked like an animal – a bear on its hind legs. The figure raised its arms as if in prayer, but they weren't arms – they were paws. Mitts. They appeared to be covered in thick, lumpy fur. The rest of the body was the same, rotund – seemingly woolly – but there was a face, white as a sheet, visible on the bearlike figure. A face with a staring gaze, its mouth wide open but silent. And the buzzing got louder and louder until Berger finally realised what he was looking at.

The face was Roy's and his entire body was covered in bees.

Roy staggered towards the edge of the roof, past the rope anchor point, taking the heavy, peculiar steps of someone on the lunar surface. He clambered onto the small parapet separating the roof from the abyss. Berger heard himself shout with someone else's voice:

'For Christ's sake, stop.'

But Roy just carried on, up onto the wall, as if driven by a power altogether different from that of his own volition. Finally, he took the irreversible step over the edge.

It was as if he were hovering. For a brief moment that seemed never-ending, amid humming that was rising to a cacophony, Roy's body seemed to float in the boundless air, as if the force of gravity had been completely switched off, as if there were no longer any up or down. And as if responding to an order, the bees let go, shooting up from the body like an inverse maelstrom.

Berger looked into Roy's eyes in that moment. What he saw was death. He was looking straight at death. And then Roy fell.

Berger heard himself bellow. He staggered in that direction, the pain which had been suspended for several seconds returning with full force. Kent stopped rolling on the roof, got up and brushed his body feverishly. Together, they staggered towards the edge of the roof. From which Roy had just fallen.

Just before they reached the edge, Berger turned his head and saw a huge plume of bees gushing out of the wide-open door and forming the darkest of clouds above the dimly lit city.

Berger and Kent exchanged a glance. Kent removed a bee from his pale cheek and nodded. They looked over the edge.

Roy's shattered body was lying in the car park some thirty metres below.

He'd hit a car – half of him was still on the bonnet.

The sound that Kent emitted was inhuman.

'Berger!' the walkie-talkie yelled. 'Paramedics en route. Secure the building.'

Berger got up slowly from beside Kent, who was collapsed on the roof. Berger removed the bees from all exposed parts of himself. He felt a queer intoxication spreading through his body. He moved unsteadily towards the small building. He pressed himself against the concrete wall, glanced inside quickly, then stepped back to his position. There was no one inside – no concealed spaces. There were at least six open beehives. Only a few bees remained, sluggishly buzzing away. He judged it possible to go inside and took a firmer grip of his weapon.

He waved his hand in front of him to ward off the final bees, chasing them out. Then he looked around the space. Apart from the beehives, there was just a table and a chair. Aisha hadn't been held captive in here – no, Carsten's aim had been to entice them up here. To harm them? To kill them? Hardly. Carsten was not a sadist. Mad as a hatter, sure. Traitor to his country, absolutely. Uninhibited, definitely. But he was rational. That meant there was another reason why he had led them here.

Floor, ceiling, walls – nothing. An altogether unremarkable

space. That meant it had to be something inside the beehives or on the table. And Berger had no intention of rooting around inside the beehives – he'd had enough close encounters already.

Only now did he spot that a number of bees were lingering on the table. They were more placid than the rest of their kin, creeping around in a set shape – rectangular, a few inches wide. Berger used the butt of his newly issued Security Service gun to remove the bees from the surface. There was a piece of paper left. He didn't dare touch it, but he saw that it was glazed with something sweet and sticky. Something the bees would like.

It looked like a small envelope. The kind that usually contained greetings cards. He left it lying there. Left it in spite of all his instincts, so that it could be handled by the Security Service's forensic team. Then he spotted the closed drawer under the tabletop. He crouched and began very carefully to open it.

The blast was beyond all imagining. The force that threw him backwards even more so. The shock was total, the pain disorientating. His vision went black.

All that was left was a single, floating thought in the neverending nothingness:

*What a fucking way to die.*

Then nothing but darkness.

He wasn't sure whether he was alive until he opened his eyes and found himself looking into an icy grey gaze framed by close-cut metallic grey hair.

'The perfect spy is admittedly a castrated spy,' said August Steen, 'but there's no need for it to occur quite so dramatically.'

'What?' Berger panted.

'If you hadn't been crouching, you would have had your cock shot off.'

Berger looked down at his bulletproof vest. Where the bullet had hit him was clearly visible – right in the heart.

'Jesus Christ,' he said.

Steen proffered him a hand which he took, and he was pulled to his feet in a cascading series of painful jolts, before being led to the open drawer. Inside the remains of the shot-off front was a pistol fixed in place with steel thread wrapped around the trigger. Berger recognised the weapon immediately. It was a Sig Sauer P226. Presumably Berger's own former service weapon. There was a tiny handwritten note taped to the barrel. It was short and sweet:

'*Boom!*'

'Carsten is after you, Sam,' said Steen. 'Now we need to make you invisible, for real.'

Berger glanced at the small envelope one last time, let out a deep sigh and stumbled towards the door. Steen caught up with him and held him upright.

Approaching slowly, looking almost unreal in the pale grey of the November sky, was an air ambulance.

# 2

His senses were out of kilter. Everything was swaying. The sound of the approaching helicopter increasingly resembled the buzzing of an enormous bee.

Berger was sitting on the roof, all sorts of pain sweeping through the fibres of his being, and he felt unable to distinguish between body and soul.

He saw August Steen produce a roll of gauze from a bag without understanding why. He saw it being unrolled and coming closer to him.

'You'll have to go in the chopper,' said Steen, starting to wrap his head. 'And since you're Sweden's most wanted man, you most definitely don't want to be seen.'

The downdraughts from the landing helicopter swept across both of them. As if in a strange form of slow motion, Berger watched Steen drop the gauze and the gusts unfurl it so that it fluttered like a long banner before Steen let go and allowed it to sail across the Tensta rooftops. He pulled out another on which he retained a firmer grip, managing to wrap Berger's head. Then he said:

'You keep your cool. I'll pick you up from the Southern Hospital.'

After that, Berger was ignored. He curled up in the corner of the helicopter, feeling airsick, with his chest aching from the shots and variously located bee stings. Nevertheless, he was still easily in the best shape out of the patients contained in the cramped space.

The two halves of Roy Grahn's ragged body were covered in a bloodied blanket. Kent Döös was conscious enough to moan, the moaning occasionally rising to downright roars of both sorrow and pain. A paramedic appeared to be painting portraits in the air with a syringe filled with morphine that he had not yet been able to administer.

Berger seemed to recollect similar scenes from various war movies. He was overwhelmed by nausea and was on the brink of vomiting copiously straight into his head bandages by the time he found a window to look through.

The sight of water had always placated his guts. He saw the water's surface below, but it took a while for him to recognise the waters of Ulvundasjön, then the Tranebergsbron bridge, then the island of Lilla Essingen. Then Reimersholme, the Liljeholmsbron bridge, Årstaviken bay. The water was under the helicopter all the way to a roof with a circle and a plus sign and a large H at its centre. The helicopter landed on the letter without making any obvious attempt to reduce its speed.

Then everything happened quickly.

The doors opened. Roy's stretcher was trundled away and disappeared. Kent, whose burly body had finally submitted to the morphine, was conveyed across the helipad of the Southern Hospital.

Berger was left behind.

While the pilot jumped out and the rotor blades meekly ceased to rotate, Berger crouched there in his corner – his head completely covered in bandages. Eventually, a white-clad man peered inside and waved him over, and together they walked into the large hospital. His guardian didn't look his way even once.

In keeping with his reception, Berger was left seated in a corner of Casualty, behind drawn curtains, for a duration that he stopped monitoring after a while. A lot of time passed. Incomprehensible time. Hour elapsed into hour until he no longer had any grasp of them.

He set about feeling his way through his body. Most painful was the gunshot – the point where the Kevlar had stopped the bullet from the Sig Sauer P226 – but he questioned whether his rib was damaged. The poison from the bee stings was harder to assess, but that didn't seem enough to warrant admission. That meant August Steen had put him there for another reason. Perhaps because it was the safest place for him to wait. Were they sorting out a safe house for him? Were his things being moved there from home? Had they been to his house? Was the Security Service going through his place while he sat here like a vegetable?

He hadn't been home in a very long time. Although it was probably more that it *felt* like a very long time. It had barely been a month. Probably not even that.

The hours continued to trickle between his fingers. He tried to think and to settle the free flight of his thoughts.

If Carsten had rigged up the beehive house to take down Sam Berger, then was he truly safe here? Getting into the casualty department at the Southern Hospital before putting a couple of silenced rounds into a weakened patient behind protective curtains would be a straightforward task. It would probably be a while before anyone even noticed it had happened.

At that moment, the curtains were pulled apart.

For a moment Berger saw Carsten – his screwed-up, unreadable eyes behind those thick lenses; he saw the pistol raised, he saw the barely perceptible smile that would be the very last thing that Sam Berger took with him to the land of the dead.

But it wasn't Carsten who entered. Nor was it a doctor. It was the man whose close-cut hair reminded him of iron filings around a magnet.

'Let's go,' August Steen said curtly.

They left. Berger said nothing. Nor did Steen.

In a secluded corner of the Southern Hospital's car park, they got into the car before Steen set a course southwards out of the city. It was only as dusk began to set in that Berger realised how long he'd spent waiting for a doctor who never came. Who had never intended to come.

As they were passing Haninge, Steen finally spoke.

'That bastard murdered Roy.'

Berger could feel himself stiffly staring dead ahead. He saw the body floating there, contrary to reason, shrouded in bees. Then he saw the body in two down in the car park.

Carsten was not a man to be toyed with.

And he was definitely out to get Sam Berger.

Apparently Steen wanted to talk.

'Apologies for the delay,' he said.

Berger laughed, though he was not exactly bubbling over with joy.

'I had to expedite matters,' Steen continued. 'This was the quickest I could manage.'

'Where are we going?' Berger asked.

'You'll have to drive a motorboat,' said Steen.

Berger stared at him.

'I know you can do it. I know you like water. I know that many of your childhood summers were spent in the Stockholm archipelago.'

'You know more than I do,' Berger muttered.

'The sight of water calms you,' said Steen.

Berger shook his head.

'Don't worry, it's simple. Modern navigation systems practically do all the work for you.'

'And I'm just supposed to sit there, am I? In some isolated safe house?'

'The assignment I have for you is extremely important.'

'And I take it you don't intend to tell me any more than the fact that it's related to "the worst act of terrorism in all of Sweden's history"?'

'I can't right now,' said August Steen. 'But for the time being, you must stay out of sight at all costs. *Properly* under the radar. That means this will be the only time you use the boat. You can never use it again, except in absolute emergencies. The navigation app will lead you to a boathouse – you're to take the boat inside and moor it up there.'

'A boathouse?' Berger exclaimed.

'A real boathouse,' said Steen, stony-faced. 'The kind you drive a boat into. You drive it in, moor it up, then you wait. There are plenty of goodies in the little cottage there; there's a secure internet connection and lots of books. Consider it paid holiday. Do you have any hobbies?'

Berger wasn't staring at him, but was staring into space.

'Clocks,' he said at last. 'Clockwork.'

August Steen chuckled.

Then they said nothing more during the drive. They arrived on the outskirts of Nynäshamn, drove through the centre of Nynäshamn, exited through the outskirts on the other side of Nynäshamn. It felt like the end of the Earth.

The visitors' harbour was inhospitable. Presumably it was the friendly, glowing lights on the nearby islands that made the sea leading up to them seem so black. So merciless. And the fact that they were alone that made the world around them appear so desolate.

They ambled along the jetty, the boats moored there floating on the water as if cradled by darkness itself. It was dry, thank goodness. And not particularly windy either. The only thing that felt frightening was the darkness. That, and the simple fact that Sam Berger hadn't driven a boat in a very long time.

They stopped. Steen passed Berger an iPad. Berger took it and looked down at the dark screen. Steen swept a finger across it and a map appeared.

'Straightforward GPS navigation,' said Steen. 'The route avoids every single reef, I promise you.'

'You've tried it then?'

'A chopper will deliver your things from home. There will shortly be four large moving boxes outside the cottage.'

'And what are you going to do? What's the Security Service going to do? Find Carsten before he finds me?'

'Don't flatter yourself,' said Steen. 'You're not that important. But yes, of course we're going to catch him – the investigation is already in full swing. But we're primarily looking to apprehend him so that we can free Aisha Pachachi and thus deal with Ali Pachachi's difficult problem. As long as Aisha is a hostage, he won't talk. And the only person in the whole wide world who knows where Ali is located is me. Until now, our mole has been waiting for Ali to make contact – presumably to offer to exchange places with his daughter. Now Carsten seems to have entered a more active phase – he's going to find Ali Pachachi by himself. Obviously the clue that led us to the trap in Tensta was planted. He wanted us there. He wanted to mock us.'

'You catch Carsten, get the information from Pachachi, I act on that information? Is that the play? And that brings us to the question: why me?'

'Do you really want to have this discussion right now?' Steen asked. 'You've had a whole car journey to talk about this.'

'Yes, I want to know. Otherwise there's not a fucking chance I'm getting in that boat.'

'And what are you going to do instead? Hide in another boat-house? Flee the country?'

'Why? Why me?'

August Steen sighed and led him over to a powerful but compact boat with a big outboard motor attached.

'You've got a special skill that will be of the utmost importance when the time comes,' Steen said eventually.

'A special skill? Me?'

'And you didn't answer the question,' said Steen, passing Berger his Security Service-issued pistol and ammunition. 'It was serious.'

'Which bloody question?' Berger said, taking the gun.

'Do you have any hobbies?'

# 3

He broke through the surface of the water just as the ice was setting. In the course of his flight, he saw from the corner of his eye segments of the smooth surface changing sheen in the light. It was as if he was seeing in the matter of a split second the individual liquid atoms reaching out to unfamiliar oxygen atoms and forming a most delicate crust.

That was when he broke it.

The shock of the cold followed just as expected, but theory is one thing and practice quite another. He was overwhelmed. The icy cold pressed the tight wetsuit against his shocked skin. The waters of the archipelago embraced him as if they wanted to freeze him and keep him for an afterworld that would contemplate in surprise the equally surprised prehistoric being inside a block of ice. Scientists would thaw him out in laboratory conditions and he would – without that look of astonishment disappearing – sail into the zero-gravity atmosphere of the artificial planet that had long ago replaced the devastated Earth.

That peculiar image had a calming effect. What was more, his first movement was actually reminiscent of a spacewalk. He sucked in the pressurised air from the diving bottle greedily, felt the pain in his ribcage where a bullet had been stopped not long ago, and seemed to recollect why he had quit this intrepid hobby in the first place.

A hand brushing the side of a huge blue-and-yellow-striped fish with kiss-me lips had summoned up the hobby *diving*. That gilded memory had subverted the fifteen years that had passed since Sam Berger had last put a rubber mouthpiece between his teeth, on a magical diving holiday on the Indonesian island of Lombok. It had erased all manner of factors that had made him abruptly consign his diving bottles to the back of a cupboard upon his return, while providing him with ill preparation for the cold shock of the Baltic waters.

Once he finally stopped being distracted, a strange world hove into sight.

The water had looked dark from up above – like jumping straight into a bucket of tar. It had been a grey, overcast morning – pretty typical for the first day of December – and he hadn't exactly been expecting to see much down here on the more or less dead Baltic seabed. But the light that was filtering down, broken as it was by the slowly growing sheet of ice, nonetheless revealed a world of greys and greens permeated by furrowed rock formations and various billowing seaweed branches that actually touched him. A small, colourless shoal of fish darted past as he kicked his way through water that could be no more than five degrees. He felt again the fascination of visiting the hidden part of the Earth's surface – the biggest and most secret part. He felt his reborn being coming back to life as the seabed changed in character and became smoother and more barren. And fell away, for there was no doubt about it, he was swimming into deeper waters.

He was cautious, ensuring he planned each move in advance, always keeping his gaze fixed on the more distant elements of his field of vision – just as he had when learning to drive a car. It was surely no more than five or six metres away, and then, suddenly, he could no longer see the bottom up ahead. It simply vanished. He stopped, floated, observed. Then he finned forward, floating closer. It really was as if the small inland sea's bottom had disappeared and been replaced with a precipice.

He was at the edge now. It felt strange: it was a cliff that couldn't be fallen off.

This was Sweden – the Stockholm archipelago. Everything was safe and familiar, and suddenly there was this abyss leading down to something entirely unknown. He realised he needed to stay away.

But as was so often the case when one knew one ought to stay away, he moved closer.

He glided out above the chasm, looked up, looked down. He saw nothing. He waited. He felt a gentle current against his right thigh, nothing more. Then he made one careful movement downwards.

At first he didn't understand what it was – little more than a vague change of state. His face felt a little colder, that was it. Then he realised that it was not just cold, it was wet too. The ends of his moustache caught inside the diving mask bobbed slowly, like strands of seaweed on the seabed.

The mask had leaked.

But such insight didn't register – it had an altogether different impact. His body flailed in panic, chaos jolted straight through his soul, shattering it. He felt himself floundering into empty nothingness.

In the pure chill.

By means unknown, his senses returned to him. He stopped struggling. He confined the panic. The mask needed emptying – clearing a mask was one of the first things you learned as a diver.

He tried to remember the procedure. Then he pressed the top of the mask to his face while looking up and exhaling through his nose. He repeated this a couple of times, and finally the mask was more or less empty. He tried not to sigh in relief.

Then he looked around. He looked down, he looked up, he looked to his left, he looked to his right. Except there was no up, no down, no here, no there. There was no direction whatsoever. And he realised where he was.

He was in the mid-water.

There was no gravity, no lift. There were no bearings. There were no reference points. His next movement might just as well lead him straight down into the abyss as it would up to the surface, or out to sea.

Sam Berger remained lying there, floating in the great nothingness, each movement potentially taking him closer to death.

He was fully disorientated.

He could see no surface, no bottom, and there was nothing to visually indicate which way was up and which way was down.

There was nothing to hold on to.

It was as if he were floating in the middle of the global ocean. As if he had been fully lost in the empty, desolate and infinite expanse of space.

But he had managed to clear his mask. It had only been a few seconds ago that he had managed to pull himself together and put his experience to use.

The bubbles from his breathing drifted wildly around him. He continued to spin for a while in the gaping void. Then something occurred to him – something as unfamiliar as a thought took root.

Air was his route home.

He settled down in the great nothingness, lying stock-still. He held his breath for a while until the space around him was devoid of any bubbles. Then he exhaled hard.

The flurry of bubbles suddenly assumed a clear direction.

Seemingly down his body. He turned over and watched the stream of bubbles float downwards.

What he had perceived to be downwards.

It was actually upwards.

He exhaled again, heavily, and set off in pursuit of the bubbles.

Upwards.

He emerged from the abyss and was once again able to discern the seabed and realised that he was on his way home after all.

He settled for a moment on the bare rock and cleared his mask again.

Mid-water.

He had forgotten about mid-water – the feeling when all the laws of nature disappeared. He had been there before – just after the encounter with the big blue-and-yellow-striped fish. And he had allowed the good memory to hide the bad.

In the harbour on Lombok, he had sworn never to dive again.

He wasn't good at learning from his mistakes.

As he finned towards the cottage on the small island off Landsort, he swore never to dive again.

# 4

Sam Berger contemplated the water. The air temperature had once again climbed above freezing, and the thin layer of ice he had broken that morning when emerging from the mid-water was almost completely gone. He tracked a small floating chunk of ice with his gaze as it melted before his very eyes.

He looked up into the grey skies. They offered a merciless light. No illumination, no joy. A grey gaze filled with schadenfreude that indicated there was almost six months of the same still to follow.

His gaze traced the outermost islets of the archipelago. Beyond those there was nothing but open sea – all the way south to Gotland.

Time was so strange. Everything was pure anticipation. He hadn't been on this desolate island long, but the restlessness had already begun to eat away at him.

He turned on his heel and set off back to the cottage. Halfway up, he came to a halt and glanced down towards the jetty. It wasn't visible. The camouflage was practically perfect. And the boathouse a little further away with the speedboat he had driven here through the archipelago night wasn't visible at all.

The same was true of the cottage. Tree branches – seemingly nonchalantly arranged – covered the moss-covered roof, and in the unlikely event that an unexpected visitor caught sight of the front door, they would have the impression that whatever was behind it was both small and dilapidated.

It was an illusion. A deliberate and professionally implemented illusion. Berger opened the door and passed the wine racks. In accordance with his tastes, the extensive collection had been supplemented with a few bottles of first-rate single malt. He made his way through the room with its ideal temperature and darkness before reaching the large living room. He thought of it as the large living room, but honestly he had no idea how to define the room he was now surveying. The completely unexpected space, the sofa, the dining table, the desk. A kitchen island suddenly appearing round the corner. A fully equipped bathroom with sauna. The kind of fisherman's-cottage-sanitised-with-luxury-on-a-desolate-island that would have sold for tens of millions of kronor on the open market.

But neither the cottage nor the island had the slightest thing to do with the open market. On the contrary. It was not the first Security Service safe house that Berger had visited, but it was definitely the most pleasant. And his assignment was to wait.

He ambled through the living room, over to the wall by the desk. Next to a large map of the Stockholm archipelago was a whiteboard. On it were lots of pieces of paper in random groups – they were obviously subordinate to the centre of the board.

At the centre of the board was a photograph.

A clean-cut, unsentimental school photo of a smiling, dark-haired girl. Aisha Pachachi. The symbol of Sam Berger's failure. The only one of the seven kidnapped girls that he and Molly Blom hadn't managed to free.

Seven minus one.

She would legally be an adult before long.

Of course, Berger realised that the Security Service was in the full throes of a major manhunt – even had he been permitted to contribute his own efforts, they would have been negligible. Nevertheless, it was frustrating to just sit here like some sort of resource on standby. 'Properly under the radar', as August Steen had put it.

Aisha Pachachi. Snatched once by the man who was supposed to be protecting her. Then snatched a second time by a Security Service mole – a deadly man by the name of Carsten, whom everyone was now hunting.

That was the situation.

With a grimace, Berger averted his gaze from Aisha's photograph. Instead, it fell on the only things in the big living room that were not in meticulous order: the four oversized moving boxes containing a hotchpotch of stuff. The grimace remained on his face, transitioning into distaste. The mere thought of Steen's confidants – who were no longer the erstwhile duo of Kent and Roy – rifling through the drawers of his home turned his stomach. At the same time, he understood it. Sam Berger was Sweden's most wanted man and it was clearly out of the question for him to return home to Ploggatan in Stockholm's Södermalm. Regardless, he couldn't help picturing a coarse hand in the bottom drawer, casting aside children's and women's clothing without an ounce of respect just to find Sam Berger's underpants. As expected, all sorts of rubbish had come along from the decidedly untidy closet. He glanced grimly at the closest box. Obviously he needed a yellow bicycle helmet, two remote controls, a box of drawing pins, a couple of old school yearbooks, a fabric anaconda, a broken badminton racket and selection of pages that had come loose from Freja's self-help paperback. Yes – obviously he needed these here on this desert island.

He had barely touched the boxes since the helicopter had lowered them onto the island. He had carried them inside, opened them, been overcome by reluctance and left them where they stood. Instead, he had opened the bag he'd brought with him from the interior – the one that had made it through both previous cases.

Admittedly, the first thing he had pulled out had been the box of watches. It was standing there in front of him on the desk, along with both the magnifier and the case opener. On a cloth lay his Rolex Oyster Perpetual Datejust from 1957. Its insides were exposed, like those of a dissected animal. Within, he glimpsed the perfectly coordinated constellation of interacting small cogs and pinions. But out here on the island, time felt as if it were passing more slowly than usual – as if every second were significantly more protracted than in the real world. The world where he was not relentlessly still, not unsparingly lonely.

The second thing he had pulled out of the bag was the school photograph of Aisha Pachachi. He had affixed it to the centre of the whiteboard. Then he had unpacked the computer and Molly Blom's entire gamut of gadgetry, comprising mysterious boxes and cables, routers and hubs – all the things that in the best of worlds would give him the same undetectable access to the Security Service's network that she'd had at her disposal in her capacity as an undercover cop. Before she'd been beaten to a pulp and cut by a madman.

Not now.

Don't think about it now. It was enough that it consumed his nights and ruined his sleep. Not now too.

He was not even one per cent clear how Molly's cybersecurity kit actually worked. Defying his 'benefactor' August Steen by attempting to connect to the Security Service's internal network and starting to drill down into the various security levels with the utmost secrecy was a big risk. He would have to proceed with very small, very cautious steps. He had all her passwords – it ought to be possible. If nothing else, it was a way to cure his restlessness.

It was off the charts. The restlessness was incurable. It wasn't personal, it wasn't private. It was a case of professional restlessness, and that could only be satisfied through work. And in spite of everything, this was a form of work. Even if it was progressing with ant-sized steps.

Whatever it was that August Steen was *saving* him for, just sitting there on standby while slowly being drained of energy was unbearable. That wasn't his actual assignment. Sam Berger didn't leave assignments half done – not even six-sevenths done.

His assignment was to find Aisha Pachachi.

That meant he needed to know more about Carsten. And there was still some way to go in that respect.

The fact was that he didn't know a thing about him.

Except for images. Unerasable images. The image of Sylvia with the black sock rammed down her throat. The image of the killer from the interior who had been killed with three gunshots right to the heart. The image of Roy's seemingly woolly body floating in nothingness, as if gravity had disappeared.

None of those images would ever disappear. Not until Sam Berger himself died.

He was consumed by fury – a gigantic, hard, explosive fury. He needed to take down Carsten.

He really did.

He observed his right hand. It was trembling. It was trembling with fury. He pressed it down with his left, holding it fast. He put everything into trying to sober up and think clearly.

If Carsten had managed to rise to the position of August Steen's right-hand man, he must have had a long career at the Security Service. Which meant the Service had indubitably turned him inside out – doubtless they knew him through and through. Yet he had managed to deceive them all. Steen had been on the hunt for a mole for the best part of a year without success, even though the mole was right in front of him. Granted, that matched the Carsten that Berger had met, albeit in haste – he was both intelligent and resourceful. And presumably a little bit unhinged – otherwise he would never have allowed himself to be bought by a foreign power. And not just any old foreign power, but the worst imaginable – the once powerful and now subsiding caliphate.

Well, Carsten was clever, resourceful, crazy, spineless, greedy, on the brink of blindness – and had apparently, during the recent weeks of surveillance, become just a little infatuated with Molly Blom.

But none of this was new to the Security Service. Steen had told Berger this himself. This was data that a large, well-oiled machine was already processing. Berger had nothing of his own to add, no new information, no angle that the Service had missed. No matter how much he delved into his own depths, he could not find a perspective where he – the ex-cop wanted for the murder of a suspect – could honestly say he held any advantage over the Security Service.

Except possibly that he had nothing to lose.

Everything had already been lost.

He sat down at the desk, touched the laptop trackpad with his hand and realised that the ongoing search was still ongoing. It was one step en route into the Security System networks – something about finding an open port. Molly had tried to explain, but as usual he had only listened with one ear, in some kind of absurd belief that she would always be there and would always handle the technicalities.

But he had let her down. A pair of sick serial killers had wrenched her from him, and he had let it happen.

He had let it happen.

No.

Not now.

It would seek him out when he fell asleep anyway.

His gaze returned to the scrolling symbols on the laptop display. Restlessness overcame him. Would he have to go outside again, back down to the jetty to stare at Landsort's outer archipelago, where he would find nothing to fix his gaze on? At any rate, the thing he *wasn't* going to do amid this hopeless wait was to pull on his wetsuit and cast himself into the ice-cold water. That hobby had had its day.

Then it dawned on him he could check online. He had already activated the anonymous proxy network. Apparently, there were a number of CCTV cameras on the island that could be activated at any moment, and those would override what was going on right now on the screen.

He opened a new Google tab and went through his borderline mechanical routine for searches – the one that he had done on a daily basis for years without turning up any results. First he searched for 'Freja Babineaux'. As usual, nothing. It was as if his ex-partner had gone underground with her new husband in Paris. She was presumably, he reflected with a bitter-sweet sensation, back to being a housewife without a life of her own. Then he searched for 'Marcus Babineaux'. Despite the fact that this also failed to provide any useful results, he never considered the possibility of not searching for Marcus's twin brother, ten minutes his junior. He tapped in 'Oscar Babineaux'.

His twin sons.

The lights of his life – the lights that shone by their absence, and even more strongly at that. The polar star. The still point of the turning world. What everything hinged upon.

Then something came up. A Facebook profile. Oscar Babineaux, Paris.

And the profile photo did indeed depict his younger son. An incredibly upgraded version of him, anyway. Eleven years old and, judging by the photo, a fully fledged hip-hop artist. Berger instinctively took screenshots of everything on the page, which wasn't a lot. It had been created a few days earlier, and there were only two posts with a few comments beneath them – all in French. Oscar had scraped together twelve friends, and all the comments came from these individuals. The first post expressed sorrow at the big terrorist attack in Paris that had occurred while Sam Berger had been lying unconscious up in Lapland, and the brief comments underneath were mostly sad emojis. The more recent post consisted of a photograph taken in a messy boys' room. Someone was lying under a duvet in the lower bunk of a bunk bed, both hands outstretched and fingers in a V-shape. Protruding from under the duvet were their feet – the toes were also in a V-shape.

Berger started. A lump formed in his throat. He reached out with a hand and gently caressed the cold laptop display. That was *his* gesture – Sam-the-dad's exaggerated gesture of great joy. Neither of the twins quite had that ability in them – they'd both had to work hard to manage true separation of their two biggest toes, while at the same time folding away the rest. The result was a pretty weird foot. Then you had to get under the covers – for example after a win in a video game – and stick out both your arms and legs, hands and feet.

Then you formed four V-shapes.

The only comment under the photo was '14–8', which was

presumably some result or other. One of the twins had probably beaten the other in a game, but just who was under that duvet disclosing their not-entirely-unspoilt-by-schadenfreude pleasure, it was impossible to tell.

Sam Berger chose to interpret it as a sign. His twins – who had effectively disappeared for the last three years, consumed by the big city that was Paris – were communicating with their traitor of a father. The father who had without any objection let their mother Freja have sole custody – who, despite being a policeman, had failed to explore whether they were happy in their new home with their new French stepfather Jean Babineaux. The father who had acted on the basis of the dubious mantra that *no news was good news* and instead cultivated and refined his own sense of abandonment.

It was as if Sam Berger had matured by a couple of decades in just a few weeks.

That very moment, he decided to join Facebook. While he sat there pondering whether to use his real name or some kind of code name that would only be understood by the twins, the computer let out a chime. He swapped windows. The scrolling search had stopped and it was now flashing affirmatively from the screen; he had at least taken another step into Molly Blom's advanced system.

Molly.

Who was carrying Sam's child.

No, not now. Wait until tonight. Leave that shit to mature, to rise, to putrefy, to take shape as new nightmares.

He gingerly activated the next step in the log-in process. A new search began.

Then he switched back to Facebook. At least he now knew how to combat the nightmares: with four V-signs.

36

# 5

The first time the night nurse heard the sound, she let it be. Admittedly, she did look up from her Spanish grammar, but the verb *hacer* kept her at her desk – its conjugation was on the verge of driving her mad. Anyway, it *couldn't* have been a window – if there was one thing that was certain in this department, it was that the windows were properly locked. People recovering after being anaesthetised and undergoing long periods of unconsciousness weren't quite themselves, to put it mildly. If they were given the opportunity to hurl themselves out of a second-floor window then wakefulness might be no more than a confusing interval between one long sleep and the next.

Like life itself, the night nurse thought to herself, shivering in the winter night. December had just arrived and December always felt more palatable than November, all things considered. But then came January, February, March, April – which were all much easier to deal with in Lanzarote.

*Hago*, she wrote. *Haces. Hace. Hacemos* . . .

Then she heard it again, and this time the sound was unmistakable – replete with rattling windowpane and all. The night nurse put down her pen and pricked up her ears.

All she heard was silence.

She stood up. The noise surely had to have come from one of the three or four closest rooms – one of the six-bed wards or perhaps one of the singles.

Had she been afraid of ghosts, she wouldn't have chosen this occupation. The same went for the fear of loneliness. She had chosen the job because it reminded her of a fireman's existence. Or indeed that of the national SWAT team. Or why not the army, for that matter? The sense of anticipation, calm, solitude, boundless opportunities for self-improvement. But constantly being on one's toes, ready to deploy at the first hint of an alert. That was in her nature.

However, with time that capacity had been put on ice. The marker of a successful night shift nowadays was not having to deploy at all and being left to study Spanish. Which, despite *hacer*, was very much a piece of cake when compared to Hebrew or Korean.

But now it was time. A window opening and closing was no trivial matter in a department like this.

The night nurse set off. She noticed that the security guard by the locked door not only had earphones discreetly in his ears, but was in fact also asleep – there was something about his posture that suggested he might tumble to the floor at any moment. In a way that was for the best – she wanted to deal with this on her own. Hopefully he would wake up if she screamed bloody murder.

She opened the door of the nearest six-bed ward. All the beds were occupied, all the patients seemingly lifeless as usual. And all the windows were just as tightly closed and locked as usual.

The next room was an empty single, normally used for the most critical patients.

The third room was another single. The window here was

also firmly shut, and the patient was in a state that might be permanent, as was becoming increasingly apparent. The night nurse had just begun to close the door ready to move on to the other six-bedder when she spotted something through the crack without knowing what it was. By the faint illumination of the night light the respirator was operating with the same deep, heavy breaths as usual, but there was something else. Something that was different.

The drip stand.

The tube was fluttering as if an imperceptible breeze was blowing through the room. But there was nothing.

The night nurse opened the door again and stepped inside. She went over to the bed and looked down at the patient. She was lying still under the covers – all that was visible of her were two heavily bandaged arms that had far too many cuts to them, and some frizzy hair that had once had the structure of a page-boy haircut. The brown was increasingly shedding on the pillow, revealing the underlying blonde. The nurse reached for the moving tube, inspected it, gently squeezed the infusion bag mounted into the stand, then tapped the regulator with her nail.

Everything seemed normal.

Then she went over to the window and looked out at the first harsh winter's night of December. She looked straight across the Årstaviken bay, the trembling lights over by the quay at Liljeholmskajen not quite able to match the dense darkness. She touched the window. It was just as tightly closed as ever; it had no handle and was just as impossible to open from the inside as the outside. She cast her gaze down along the facade of the Southern Hospital, but the view soon faded into the dark of the night.

And there were no signs that the window had been touched. It needed a special key to open it, and that was kept at the porter's reception.

But the night nurse *had* heard *something*. The drip tube *had* been swaying in a way that would hardly have been possible without interference.

She returned slowly and thoughtfully to the foot of the bed. She picked up the patient notes and read. Molly Blom. First month of pregnancy. Foetus seemingly unharmed. The night nurse returned the journal and glided up to the head of the bed. She scrutinised the now-still tube. No, she'd imagined it. There hadn't been anyone here; it was impossible. And definitely not through the window. The department was suitably secured – after all, it was a high-risk setting. And no matter how much the security guard at the door listened to music and dozed off, he would never have let an intruder past.

The only possibility was that one of the other patients had woken and stumbled into the wrong room. But then the alarm should have gone off. And how that was connected with a locked window being opened and closed she couldn't fathom.

No, she'd imagined it.

Then her eye was caught by the nightstand. There was something there, leaning against a mug. A piece of paper? Hmm, more like a small envelope. As if it contained some kind of greetings card.

The night nurse picked it up, turning it over and over. It was blank. And sealed.

It might very well have been there before. It might have been left over from a bouquet that had wilted by now and been consigned to oblivion. But she hadn't seen it before. On her night rounds, she had wiped down the nightstand, and there hadn't been any envelope there then. She was certain of it.

She gently squeezed the drip bag again. There were no signs that anything might have happened to it.

But the tube *had* been swaying.

The night nurse stood there for a while with the small envelope in her hand. Was it enough to justify raising the alarm? Set the cat among the pigeons throughout the clinic, be interviewed by the dozing security guard and his unpleasant colleagues and have the window noises explained away as imagining things? Be met with scepticism by the clinic management, who were about to announce their plans for staffing reductions – just when she'd secured a contract at the private clinic in Lanzarote?

Nope, she'd imagined it.

She had most definitely imagined it.

She slipped the envelope into her pocket, and as she returned to the corridor – where the security guard was by now slumped very close to the floor – she was already thinking about that rather odd conjugation, *hacéis*.

# 6

On the wall behind the man in his suit was a row of framed photographs of other men in suits. She found it fascinating that only men had been tasked with overseeing the moral status of the long arm of the law.

'Superintendent Rosenkvist,' the man said tersely. 'A little concentration, please.'

'I *have* been concentrating,' said Desiré Rosenkvist, sometimes known as Deer. *I've been concentrating for two days while Chief Superintendent Eskilsson's men – obviously they were men – have questioned me with the utmost thoroughness.*

'And now we're trying to come to a conclusion,' said the chief superintendent doggedly. 'So I'd be grateful if you could tear yourself away from my predecessors' appealing mugs, the like of which have never been seen before.'

Deer pointed to the *mug* at the end of the row – a mug with a red blotch on his cheek – and said:

'He gave a series of lectures on Internal Affairs when I was at the police academy. My final year.'

Chief Superintendent Leif Eskilsson turned round, followed Deer's index finger and nodded with a degree of interest.

'Ah yes, Hjelm,' he muttered. 'Any good?'

'As I remember it, he painted us a comprehensive picture of why the police should remain in a constant state of reflection about their relationship to the monopoly on violence. So yes.'

Eskilsson nodded and said:

'Of course, he's otherwise one of our black sheep . . .'

'Oh really?' said Deer.

'He moved on to the Security Service to assume duties of an undisclosed nature. Then he went to Europe under even less clear circumstances. Now he's some sort of high-ranking EU bigwig. But I'm sure you know the story . . .'

'Not really,' said Deer.

'But that's not what we're concentrating on right now,' Eskilsson said, pulling his chair closer to the desk with a highly deliberate scraping sound. 'Our conclusion is. Above all, I'm curious to know your conclusions, Superintendent Rosenkvist. What's your appraisal of your escapades in the interior?'

Deer sat in silence for a while. She was thinking, while at the same time carefully weighing up her every word. Eventually, she said: 'They went as well as was humanly possible.'

Eskilsson looked at her sceptically.

'Rumour has it that you single-handedly unmasked a hitherto unknown serial killer, found a large number of hitherto unknown victims and actively contributed to neutralising said serial killer. However, that rumour disregards many contradictory and downright irregular circumstances.'

Deer met his gaze without averting her eyes.

'I hope that it's been clear through the course of all the long interviews that some deviations from regulations were necessary. Otherwise we wouldn't have stood a chance.'

'You say "we",' Eskilsson said, nodding. 'And that's what's so worrying about this whole affair. The circumstances around you combining forces with your dismissed ex-colleague Sam Berger remain shrouded in darkness.'

'That is because the Security Service is a separate body,' said Deer, 'with their own internal investigation to conduct. There came a point where I needed their help, and I needed Berger for a very specific and previously explained reason. To find Molly Blom.'

'The murderer was laid to rest last Sunday,' Eskilsson interrupted. 'They say the church was eerily deserted.'

Deer nodded.

'I really hope it was,' she said.

Eskilsson shook his head and said: 'Rarely has the Swedish police been hit by a PR blow of the magnitude that struck when it emerged that Berger killed the perpetrator in cold blood. You have to understand the burden being shouldered by the Special Investigations Department at present. By me.'

'Is that your way of apologising for a two-day grilling by your toughest detectives?'

'Not an apology,' said Eskilsson. 'An explanation. And thank goodness Press Communications seem to have managed to find the right angle with their emphasis on the *ex* in ex-cop. The media is now depicting him as a thug who was kicked off the force for gross negligence. Fortunately not all the guilt has landed on us.'

'Wouldn't it have been better to concentrate the interviews on where Berger might be, instead of covering every last detail of our hunt for the serial killer?'

'You have to look at the bigger picture.'

'The bigger picture?' Deer exclaimed. 'Surely catching Berger is the biggest bloody picture of all? If you really do believe that a cold-blooded killer ex-cop is on the loose out there?'

'Naturally it's one of our priorities,' said Chief Superintendent

Eskilsson, shuffling straight a bundle of papers that was presumably a printout of the mercilessly long round of questioning Deer had undergone.

She sat still, thinking to herself. She surveyed the long, homogeneous row of Internal Affairs chiefs – the department now known as Special Investigations – and she felt slightly nauseous.

'So what sentence are we looking at?' she asked finally.

Eskilsson wrinkled his nose.

'It's not up to us to pass sentence,' he said. 'But if your story is straight, then the misconduct on your part can generally be regarded as insignificant. Justified and/or insignificant. Superintendent Rosenkvist may return to active duty.'

Deer's gaze glided down from the row of besuited portraits and when it reached Eskilsson she could almost make out a frame around his torso.

'Is that all then?' she said.

'We're satisfied for the time being, yes. Should it be necessary to seek further details then of course we'll be in touch.'

She stood up and remained in that spot for a brief moment, contemplating Eskilsson, before she turned on her heel and headed for the door, expecting to be stopped for some final words of wisdom.

And she was.

Behind her, Eskilsson said: 'Superintendent Conny Landin at the National Operations Department says feel free to take the rest of this week off. And the next week. Ten days' extra holiday. I don't think I need quote the remainder of his message . . .'

Deer turned quickly and replied: 'Yes. Yes, I'd like you to do that.'

Chief Superintendent Eskilsson looked disapproving – downright displeased in fact – but he still picked up the sheet of paper and spoke.

'These are Landin's words. You're to receive ten days' paid leave for, and I quote, "one of the finest individual police efforts in Sweden in the modern era". End quote. As you'll be aware, Landin isn't one for nuance and subtlety . . .'

As Deer turned away and went out into the corridor, she could feel the wide smile on her face. It remained in place all the way to the lift, where a higher ranking officer she knew only by sight nodded encouragingly at her. Enough was enough.

She emerged onto Polhemsgatan, which was as bleak as usual. It was a pale and austere day which seemed to be teetering at freezing point. She felt completely exhausted. She'd obviously been expecting a proper interview – but a whole legion of bastards from Internal Affairs relieving each other for a full forty-eight hours?

And all without breaking her.

More or less all of her long statement was one big fat lie. But it was a thoroughly prepared, convincing, consistent and wholly cohesive lie. There was far too much from the case in the interior that could never see the light of day. If it did, Superintendent Desiré Rosenkvist would not only be an ex-superintendent, but probably also an ex full stop.

But the result was no lie. The result was without doubt 'one of the finest individual police efforts in Sweden in the modern era'. She sent up an astonished thank you to Conny Landin. There was just one thing that wasn't true – it wasn't individual. A trio had been behind it, with Deer just the support act. The ones who had really solved the case were Molly Blom and Sam Berger.

Of course she'd been asked during questioning where Berger might be. But there had been something listless about those questions – especially compared with the other ones focused on the details. At the time, in the heat of battle, it had simply seemed strange, but just now in Eskilsson's office she'd received confirmation of the pattern.

Apprehending Sam Berger was 'naturally one of our priorities'.

This had been uttered by a man whose mission in life and very calling was putting away bent coppers, ex- or not, guilty or not.

No. It didn't add up. Chief Superintendent Leif Eskilsson would never have used that reasoning. Which meant he wasn't the one doing the reasoning. Which meant orders were coming from somewhere else. And what was the smallest common denominator to everything that had happened over the past few months?

There wasn't much more to it than that. On Sunday 25 October at 10.14, Deer and her then boss Sam Berger had embarked on a raid at a secluded house in Märsta – and events had snowballed from that. In fact, they were still rolling along inside it.

She shook her head and crossed Kronobergsparken, making for Fridhemsplan to catch the number 3 bus. The one that went all the way to the Southern Hospital.

In the absence of any next of kin, Deer had taken it upon herself to visit Molly Blom. She had done so every day since it had happened. Even during those two days of suffocating questioning she had been granted dispensation to pay her a visit.

It was so strange seeing Molly lying there with a haircut and colour that weren't hers. It was Deer's own style and colour – even if the former was dishevelled and the latter had by this point started to fade away.

Deer sat with Molly Blom to get things off her chest. The fact that the listener had to be unconscious in order for her to open up wasn't a good sign. But on the other hand, double-dealing wasn't a good approach to life.

She saw the bus in the distance. She ran. She missed it.

For a brief moment, she stood there as if caught in a vacuum. Then her brain focused and everything became very clear.

The smallest common denominator to everything that had happened in the last month was the Security Service. Only they had enough muscle to hold back a heavy like Eskilsson.

Deer had seen Sam. He'd suddenly turned up at Molly's bedside. That hadn't been more than four days ago. At the time he had quite clearly protested his innocence in the matter of the murdered serial killer. Someone had framed him, using his old service weapon. And Deer had believed him. In this rotten world of double-dealing, it was necessary to have someone to believe in, and she didn't have anyone better than Sam to believe in.

Someone had framed Sam Berger for the murder of the man he'd been hunting throughout those intense weeks in the interior. Then the Security Service had put a lid on it, ensuring that Berger – currently Sweden's most written-about man – wasn't pursued for real.

Something listless.

Why?

Deer's first conclusion was that it couldn't be a good thing.

Her second was that she needed to find Sam Berger.

At that moment another number 3 turned up. They ran frequently.

After all, she had ten days.

# 7

The articulated bus bent itself double as it rounded the corner off Ringvägen, then it straightened out again and glided slowly up the hill towards the hospital. The Southern Hospital was a long-term building site, and this December morning of mixed shades of grey was the same as any other December morning. The bus navigated to the main entrance with precision steering and dispensed a steady stream of passengers at the door.

One of them was an unremarkable woman in early middle age. That was precisely what the reflection in the glass doors depicted. Deer had already exited before realising that it had been herself she'd seen.

After wandering the impenetrable corridors for a while, she ended up in a lift with a corpse. Even though the corpse was meant to be getting out, the two porters in white were so absorbed in their loud conversation that the doors managed to close again before they realised they'd arrived. Deer had to press herself against the wall of the lift while the men a little irreverently wheeled the trolley out. There was a forearm protruding from under the lumpy sheet, and the dead fingertips brushed her abdomen. A peculiar, icy-cold feeling spread throughout her body.

The lift reached the right floor, her body temperature normalised and as Deer wound her way along the colour-coded floor she also made her way further into her own soul. Once she reached a certain depth, she could admit that it wasn't just conscientiousness that brought her back to the Southern Hospital daily. She was also hoping to be the first person there when Molly Blom woke up. There were still too many questions unanswered, and if anyone had the answers it was Molly.

What exactly had she and Sam Berger been up to in the interior?

Deer rang the bell at the entrance to the department. The security guard sitting just inside the door rose ceremoniously and scrutinised her through the window.

Not many years ago, it would have been a police officer sitting there ensuring that no unauthorised persons gained access to Molly Blom – and indeed that she didn't escape. Deer wondered whether half-dozing security guards really were more cost-efficient.

After a little too long, the security guard opened the door and scanned her police ID.

'Everything under control?' she asked.

The security guard shrugged, hastily scrawled something in the notebook hanging on the wall behind him, sat down again and returned to his mobile phone. She committed him to memory, nothing more than that, then ambled along the empty corridor to Molly Blom's door. It was shut, so she opened it.

Blom wasn't in her bed.

Deer's first reaction was one of spontaneous joy. Molly was up and about; her time in a coma was at an end.

Her second was unease. The feeling that something was wrong. And it was a palpably stronger reaction.

Deer looked around the small single room. Apart from the bed, the respirator, the nightstand and the window, there was a drip stand. She followed the tube via the regulator down towards the cannula. There was something odd about the way the long needle was lying there. It was in a small patch of blood in the middle of the sheet, and the bloodstain was in turn framed by a much bigger stain left by a colourless fluid. Upon closer inspection, the blood formed a spatter, and there were the torn remains of surgical tape around the needle. Deer doubted that the staff would leave the bed in this state – unless it had been a real emergency. A life-saving manoeuvre perhaps.

The needle had without doubt been *torn* out of Molly Blom's arm.

There was one more thing in the room – another door.

Deer went over to it and slowly opened it, to find a toilet. The scent of antiseptic drifted from the darkness within, and as the fluorescent tube flickered to life with the utmost languor, she began to make out a figure. It was a female form, slowly being summoned through the faint flashing of light.

The woman was sitting on the toilet. The body was draped in classic hospital garb, the head leaning forwards so that the brown shoulder-length hair tumbled down over her face like a waterfall. Her arms were slack at her sides, the forearms bare. There was a large, bruised needle mark visible at the crook of her left arm. But not a hint of blood.

Deer took a step closer, not breathing. She couldn't. There was something about this sight that was off – something she only understood once she was right beside the woman.

The arms were whiter than the hospital clothes.

Her arms were chalk white.

'Molly,' Deer hissed.

She gulped hard. Then she sank to her knees. As if it had a life of its own, she watched her own hand as it approached the woman's head.

The dead woman's head.

Ever so slowly, she brushed the shock of hair aside. She met the gaze looking back at her, although it wasn't a gaze that could be met. It was visible – the blue eyes were there to be looked into – but there was no one on the other side.

Molly Blom was dead.

She really was dead.

Existence entered a deep freeze. It remained in that state much too long. But then a brain cell stirred. Deer wasn't even certain that it took place in *her* brain, but that brain cell triggered several others, and together they began to interpret the shape of the face. Something didn't add up.

She got the better of herself, brushing aside the dead woman's hair properly and tilting her neck up – rigor mortis had not yet fully set in – so that she could look at the face.

Admittedly, she had seen far too many dead bodies in her life and she was well aware of how death changed people's appearance, how the face could assume a completely new state. But still . . .

No, this was not Molly Blom. It wasn't.

She let the woman's head fall back to her chest, ensuring with the utmost care that the deceased didn't fall off the toilet seat. Then she stood up and thought.

She thought in depth.

She returned to the single room again, looking at the bed with the yanked-out drip lying in the bloodstain. Then she made for the corridor.

She ran towards Reception. There were no staff anywhere to be seen. For a moment, it felt as if the world had been abandoned. It was not until she opened a fourth door revealing a ward with six beds that she found a nurse sorting out an empty bed. Deer opened her mouth to shout at her, then she stopped herself and looked at the empty, freshly made-up bed.

'Who was there before?' she managed to squeeze out of herself, a little arbitrarily.

'Who's asking?' the nurse replied in a practised tone.

Deer produced her police ID and held it up.

'Police. It's about Molly Blom in room 4. She's missing.'

'Missing?' the nurse said with great scepticism.

'Instead, there's a dead woman sitting on her toilet. So let me repeat: who was in that bed?'

The nurse checked herself and met Deer's gaze with the kind-but-cynical acuity common to all healthcare personnel.

'Hanna,' she said at last. 'Hanna Dunberg.'

'And she's dead? When did she die? What does she look like?'

'Like a dead person.'

'Cut the crap,' Deer said coolly. 'Just tell me.'

The nurse put a sheet down on the bed and crossed her arms:

'Hanna died an hour ago; it wasn't at all unexpected. She was in the late stages of breast cancer. The doctor came and declared her dead, and we put her on a gurney in the corridor to be picked up by the staff from the mortuary. After a while they came and got her.'

Deer rapidly digested this information, staring at the ceiling.

A strange, icy-cold sensation spread through her body.

'Bloody hell!' she shouted, rushing into the corridor. She ran past the security guard who barely did more than look up from his mobile, and found the stairs next to the lift. She hurled herself down the stairs, emerged in the corridor on the bottom floor and yelled at a man in a white doctor's coat:

'Where the hell is the mortuary?'

'Building 4,' the doctor said, pointing with the measured calm of a physician.

She followed his hand and ran on, ever deeper into the labyrinth. She found a sign directing her to building 4 and followed it. She dashed here and there. She found the mortuary. The door was ajar. In the corridor there was an empty trolley; the sheet appeared to have been dropped on the floor. A man in white emerged from a door, stopped and scratched his head. Deer recognised him from the lift. Another man dressed like him appeared from another room and she saw them exchange glances.

'This is nuts,' one of them said.

Deer ran up to them, shouting: 'Where's the nearest exit?'

They looked at her for a while, as if she were from outer space. Eventually, the first one pointed down the corridor.

'There's an emergency exit at the end of the corridor, but –'

She abandoned him, running in the direction he'd indicated, reaching the end of the corridor. As he'd said, there was an emergency exit there, and the door was ajar. She went outside, emerging into a rear courtyard with a staircase which she took three steps at a time before finding herself back at the point where the hill up to the hospital doubled back on itself. By the main entrance, she could see a number 3 bus departing. She ran, ran some more, even faster. She had almost caught up with the bus when it began to accelerate away from her. She shouted and bellowed, but the bus driver just kept going. The last thing Deer saw before she stopped was the gaze through the back window of the bus. Blue eyes, not entirely clear, but still clear enough under that brown pageboy haircut that was showing its blonde roots.

Molly Blom's gaze.

Then the number 3 turned onto Ringvägen and disappeared from sight.

# 8

A world that slides into being. How odd.

Pieces of the jigsaw put together. Synapses out of practice making themselves felt, finding old connections. A lost world being resurrected, piece by piece, segment by segment.

In the beginning, all was chaos. Waking up happened very suddenly. Disparate impressions called for professional insight; the rest would have to keep. Comprehension, context, memories – all were subordinate to instinct. Even consciousness itself had to wait.

It caught up with her after a few stops. That was when she realised she was starting to draw attention. She waited as long as she could, allowing her newly awakened brain cells to summon a map of Stockholm, trying to produce a plan of action, optimise a transit route. In the meantime, the voices around her rose and fell. By now the bus was fairly busy, but the seats around her remained empty. Since she could make out fragments of conversation, language must also have returned to her. They said she might be dangerous, could have escaped from the psych ward, ought perhaps to be detained. She didn't have much time to play with.

The bus stopped. She pushed her way through the increasingly agitated mass of commuters, got off, and immediately felt the cold eating into her through the sole of her foot. She slipped into a backstreet with far fewer people, glanced at a shop window and stopped. She saw herself and she could go no further.

Molly Blom looked like a fallen angel.

The fluttering white hospital gown, her bare feet, her bandaged arms, the face pale as a corpse, hair dyed the wrong colour. What was more, it had begun to snow. It was like being in a distorted nativity scene. The archangel Gabriel as a cross-dresser.

This would not do. It had to be remedied. She hoped her internal map had fallen into place correctly.

At any rate, one of Stockholm's most hyped cafes was on this street, just as she remembered it to be. She glanced quickly through the window. Within, things were rather disorderly – it was lunchtime, and there weren't enough seats for everyone so people were reserving seats and then fetching food from a fair-sized buffet. No one paid her any attention as she sidled inside and slipped her hand into an abandoned designer coat. She returned to the street, pressing herself against the wall so as to be invisible from within, and extracted a wad of cash from the thick wallet. Then she threw the wallet towards the cafe entrance before leaving.

The goth shop was a couple of blocks away. They were cold blocks. The advantage was that no one cared about her in there: at least three of the customers were in weirder get-ups than she was. She found the shop's least eye-catching outfit, including a pair of shoes with chunky soles, and made her way to a cubicle where she changed before emerging to allow the blasé till assistant to scan the tags Molly had removed. Then she exited onto the street, threw her hospital clothes in a bin and set a course for the phone shop.

She bought two pay-as-you-go phones: cheap, childish models – one in red and another in blue. She switched on the red one, wrote a short message and received an unexpectedly prompt reply.

*Woken up. What's new? M.B.*

*Most gratifying. The plan is back in play. Retain phone.*

She smiled grimly – she might be brain-damaged but she wasn't a child.

She switched on the blue phone and called a number.

She agreed a time and location.

She tossed the phone into a skip and shoved the crushed SIM card right up an exhaust pipe.

She had important stuff to do.

The plan was back on.


A setback.

She was just waiting for the setback. It had to be coming. She had woken up so abruptly and acted with such immediacy – and then just carried on with her day at top speed. She had no idea how damaged the capillaries in her brain were, how much of a beating her heart had taken. Not until now had she allowed herself the time to remember what had actually happened during those fateful days in the interior.

She was sitting in a pitch-black space remembering another pitch-black space. Out on the waters of Riddarfjärden, the odd illuminated boat passed by – otherwise there was only darkness.

She needed to remember the nature of the injury – that was it. It was entirely rational; she needed a chance to prevent any setbacks.

The problem was that every such attempt resulted in completely different memories. Out of the darkness a heavy metal chair slowly came into sight, a concrete floor, icy cold, mouldy damp, the sour stench of a cellar, ties around her arms and legs. A plush sofa covered in plastic, a couple of figures barely perceptible in the dark, engrossed in some mad pantomime. And her arms.

No, she had to stop and detach her consciousness. She checked the time on the childish red mobile phone. The minutes were dragging their heels.

Her arms.

No, no. Not her arms.

But yes, actually. It was rational. It could be rationalised. Blows to the arms, no matter how hard they were, left very few people in a coma. Knives, however . . . knives slowly sinking into the skin, cutting it open. Blood spattering, flowing.

A body being drained of blood.

That was probably it. Serious blood loss, lack of oxygen to the brain, unpredictable consequences. Even a respirator.

All of a sudden he was there. She didn't have time to react. She ought to have had time – she cursed herself. Never again would she be the underdog.

Never again.

The man was half concealed by a door, taking her in. A boat sailed past, illuminating his face like a bolt of lightning. His expression was quizzical, but she couldn't tell whether he was armed. When he saw that she had spotted him, his expression relaxed and he nodded to her.

'Intriguing outfit.'

'You got it?' she asked, her heart racing.

'But what do *you* have for *me*, Molly?' he asked, with an over-dramatic gesture.

'What does it look like I've got?'

He nodded, the faint residual light from the receding boat

making his shadow nod its way along the wardrobe. Was the light just being slow? Wasn't light the fastest thing known to humankind?

'An explanation would be interesting,' he said.

'All in good time,' she said.

A pause settled on them. There was no light left in the room – she *couldn't* see him nod again. Yet there was no doubt that he did. An entirely different sense told her that.

'Fancy you still having this flat,' he said. 'All the monologues I heard here . . .'

'It was sweet,' she said. 'Short but sweet.'

'I had no idea it was still around. I should have known about it.'

'It's a refuge,' she said.

'Wasn't that the case back then too?' he said. 'In our day?'

'It's a final outpost.'

'Why don't you have any weapons here?' he said, seemingly genuinely interested.

'It's not that kind of outpost,' she said. 'On the contrary.'

She heard him laugh, although it wasn't the slightest bit ironic, as she had expected. The subsequent pause was about him looking for the right words, nothing more. She waited.

Eventually he spoke.

'I'm happy on so many levels to see you alive, Molly. You have no idea.'

'What do you know about it?' she asked.

'You know where I work,' he said, appearing to shrug.

She watched the barely visible shadow before replying.

'You barely had anything to do with the case.'

'You know I work for August Steen,' he said. 'What else do you know?'

'That I woke up this morning. That I've been in a coma. That

I was kidnapped and tortured. That's all I know. What do you mean?'

The man nodded for a while. Then he aimed a pistol right at Molly Blom's chest.

He turned it with a slick movement of his hand and passed it to her.

'Thanks,' she said, accepting it.

He slowly pulled his fine leather glove up and began to move back into the shadows.

A boat slipped past somewhere out on Riddarfjärden, its lights briefly reflected in his thick glasses.

'How's the vision doing?' she asked.

'I'm hoping to get help with that soon,' said Carsten, and vanished.

# 9

The crevice in the rocks wasn't much bigger than the boat. Even though he could barely make it out in the darkness, it was as if it were custom-made – cut from the rock itself. Carsten drove in. The camouflage was hanging at the ready from the branches of the trees. All it took was one simple hand movement and everything was covered.

He stood there for a while, looking around. Seeing. Seeing enough. For once, he appreciated not being able to see anything much. The boat had effectively been swallowed up by the forest and sea. He set off.

It was a journey through a purer time. Being twenty-six and realising that the moment had passed. That it had been there but disappeared again. Just gone.

A flash of cast-away meaning in life.

Molly.

Here. These steps. The exact same steps, right here. In another life. A far better life.

The two of them.

Ah, the smoothness of the steps: he felt the verve, the elasticity of his legs. His entire being was a marvel of smoothness; all those years of training were still inside him – the entire acrobatic and juggling programme from circus school. But everything had to work. Everything. Including his eyes.

Every chain had its weakest link. His chain was so strong but the weakest link was so disproportionately weak. He was strengthening it now – that was what he was doing. He was fully occupied with the task. The chain had to be salvaged. The strong chain of his life.

There was one other element of disruption. Perhaps by now it had been eradicated. Hopefully. But even the most precise plans had factors of uncertainty, and in this case they were unusually high. But damn it, surely that arsehole August Steen would take ♂ to Tensta? He really did love having absolute power over his staff. Frightened personnel on the run were very much his thing. And Steen would certainly get himself to safety before dispatching his brain-dead henchmen, Roy and Kent. If Carsten knew Steen at all, ♂ would be the third man. By then, his beloved bees would have finished their work. The shed on the roof would be emptied. The hour of revenge would be almost upon them.

Revenge for what had happened in the interior. For ♂ taking possession of ♀.

He had arrived. The sea wasn't visible beneath the cliff edge; the odd reflection of light was the only thing that distinguished it from the expansive darkness of the sky. As he moved down the rock, he sensed a change in the air – a concentration. Something was afoot. A storm was gathering somewhere at sea; it was suddenly so palpable. He stepped onto the ground by the cottage, pushed the thick glasses up towards his forehead and headed inside.

Darkness. The cottage. Such anxious breathing. So anxious after two and a half years. He went over to the fireplace, adjusted the double portrait on the mantelpiece and looked up at the bewitching glow of the sunset. He was back there again – by that gentle hillside. Just like he had been during his sick leave. Three tough years of undercover work. Really tough. He'd infiltrated the Albanian mafia, run their awful trade in sex slaves, been forced to take drugs to survive. The big raid, altogether successful. Except he had hit the wall. Heavy detox. Cold turkey. So he'd caught a flight at random to somewhere in the world – anywhere that was warm.

He'd ended up there. By the hillside. He's walking there now. A young man who has come through hell, who was seemingly born on this hill. Who is strolling around with his umbilical cord unsevered and the caul still around his head, down the sun-drenched hillside covered in cypress and pine, past a couple of white houses, some donkeys with their heads bowed, a row of beehives on terraces up the hill, an expanse of butter-yellow flowers running down to the glittering sea. Far beyond, the Rock of Gibraltar extends into the water.

The beehives. The sign *Se vende*. The buzzing. Getting close to the bees and understanding them – understanding their community. He bought them, pitched a tent nearby and lived with them. He looked up at the villa with its two terraces, one facing the sea. Like heaven – an unattainable dream. Sometimes, he saw people on the big terrace – people drinking white wine from glasses with condensation on them. People laughing and smiling.

People in love. People who loved.

He stayed in his tent on the hillside among the bees, lived there until he was healthy and strong once again. Returned. Resumed his position – never again undercover. August Steen let him back into the warmth of the Security Service.

He returned every year. Stayed with his bees. Remembered the meaning with increasing clarity. The meaning of life. And that it belonged in the past.

Returned to literature, to the mutual literary idol of their youth. She had taught him to read – she and no one else. Now he expanded his repertoire, ending up with Shakespeare and staying there. He read. He read a lot in the absence of life. He got the impression he was reading his eyes to pieces.

His vision began to deteriorate. To hell with it – surely it was no big deal. Eventually, he dragged himself to the doctor. Got the diagnosis. The eye doctor's frown, all the professional waffle, and the unexpected comment: 'Try to live in the present.'

That was what Carsten remembered afterwards. Nothing else about RP – retinitis pigmentosa – no facts. Just that.

'Try to live in the present.'

Easier said than done. He was Security Service, and he realised his days there were numbered. An agent with impaired vision was a retired agent.

He returned to his hillside. To his bees. Why not simply roll around on his back, bare his stomach, accept his death sentence? He could just stay here with his bees, letting them take his soul and fly away with it.

Slowly reconciling himself with his inescapable fate.

Then that sight. Like an echo of the past.

The sign *Se vende* again. But this time a little higher up the hill. Beside the villa. There wasn't anyone on the big terrace any more. No one in love, no one loving. Just the sign swaying gently in the sea breeze.

*Se vende.* For sale.

Unattainable now too. But a vibrating sense of hope. A heaven that was suddenly within reach. With the right means.

With enough money.

But who was it who had once taught him to see? Here, right here, on this island, in this cottage? They'd said: 'I don't know what kind of drawers he likes,' and he'd said: 'None, I think.'

And picturing that moment, when the two of them realised they had no underwear. Just seeing that. Right here.

He'd so clearly seen a star-shaped birthmark just below a right breast.

Which ♂ had absolutely, definitely also seen.

But ♂ was dead now. So he hadn't seen the star-shaped birthmark just under the right breast.

And the contact. An event that looked like a thought. It wasn't the first time that he had been made into a target, but it was the first time it encompassed an authentic promise for the future. To gaze out across the sea from the unattainable terrace, blind but seeing. To see with someone else's eyes.

Those that had taught him to see.

Carsten looked down from the gaudy landscape photo. The landscape of meaning. His eye was caught by the other photograph. It was a wedding photo of two beaming young people. He picked it up, inspecting it carefully. Then he took out a pen, a thick orange marker. With great care, he drew a circle around one of the four eyes. He contemplated the result. Then he drew around the next one, then the next and the one after that. Eventually, there were fiery circles around all four eyes.

They belonged together. All four of them.

He put the picture back on the mantelpiece and looked at it from a distance. It made a very distinct impression.

These four eyes. No others.

Anyone else who tries to get involved dies.

They were gunned down in a house in the interior. They were picked up and dragged away by his bees. They got their cocks shot off.

How simple. Carsten lay there with his belly bared. Then he saw the sign and everything became possible again. He's going to win.

Carsten is going to win.

No one is going to stand in his way. Least of all ♂. Least of all Sam Berger. Misery personified.

Castrated Sam Berger.

♂ without his arrows.

Carsten took a few steps. He followed the anxious breathing. So anxious after two and a half years. He opened the bedroom door.

The first thing he saw was the teddy bear. The shabby, dusty teddy whose name he still hadn't learned. It had slipped away from her, and was lying halfway off the edge of the bed, propped against the tube from the drip. He went over, listened to her breathing, grasped the teddy and set it against Aisha's cheek.

Then he sat down and contemplated her.

They didn't have any real contact. Sometimes he thought the years of captivity had turned Aisha's brain to mush. No one could cope with isolation for that long without going mad. Sometimes he was less certain; sometimes he thought she was looking at him covertly while he talked.

He pulled out his big knife. He held it against Aisha's cheek. Deep in her unconsciousness, she felt the chill of the blade. Something in her quailed in response.

You can see, Carsten thought to himself, moving the knife closer to her eye. You can see, Aisha. And it's not fair.

I could hollow out your eye right now.

# 10

Despite the darkness, Sam Berger could see the sky becoming overcast. Between the sparsely scattered islands in the far south of Stockholm's archipelago, the brittle layer of ice had expanded. That was where he saw the final twinkles of the stars vanishing. At the point where the archipelago ended.

The storm didn't emanate from within the archipelago, it came from the open sea.

If he focused his gaze as much as he could, he was able – with a small dose of imagination – to make out the sweeping light of Landsort lighthouse in the distance. Although right now his outermost field of vision was shrouded in something that was definitely an approaching storm. It was coming from the southeast and the Landsort Deep – the deepest point in the Baltic. Over the years, this chasm half a kilometre in depth had been used as a dumping ground for everything from radioactive waste to spent ammunition and scrap cars, and it was as if the storm were rising directly from this contaminated abyss.

Berger craned his neck and saw it getting closer. He was an inveterate city dweller and had never really understood what the sky *gathering* meant.

Now he understood.

It was time to get indoors.

The moving boxes were still untouched in the centre of the floor of the big living room. Aisha Pachachi's photograph continued to loom above the desk from its spot at the centre of the whiteboard. He passed it all by, through the kitchen and reaching the bedroom. The window faced the sea. He stood there for a while. It was a fascinating spectacle, seeing the storm drawing closer through the darkness and how it seemed to whip up the sea, illuminating it, turning it white metre by metre. When it hurled its first thick volley of snow against the windowpane, it was as if he were looking straight into his innermost self.

It was the nightmares crashing over him. Molly Blom, who left a blood trail in the chalk-white snow that was much too long. Molly Blom in a coma with his baby inside her. Molly Blom, who probably didn't even know herself – might never find out – that she was going to be a mother. At the same time, here was Sam Berger on the run from everyone and everything, and the only person he could trust was the one he trusted least of all – August Steen, Head of the Intelligence Unit at the Security Service. Whose bagman Carsten had not only turned out to be a mole in the Service, a real quisling, but had also abducted Aisha Pachachi, snatching the girl out of the hands of her last kidnapper. Carsten, who had managed to lure his pursuers to the shabby flat in Tensta and unleashed a swarm of deadly bees on them with the greatest precision. There was obviously some kind of sick symbolism there, some ancient idea about the bee's relationship to the soul and to the death of the soul, but that wasn't anything Berger cared about right now. All he saw was Roy's bee-covered body appearing to float in nothingness, and then the bees suddenly letting go.

*To be, or not to be.*

Sam Berger pictured Roy's body split in two before him and felt the fury growing within. As if watching from the ceiling of that shed on the roof, he saw the drawer in the table explode and himself cast backwards, and the fury grew even more.

He was going to get Carsten – that much was certain.

Carsten wouldn't win. There was no chance.

He turned his back to the storm and passed through the kitchen before settling down at the desk, contemplating the dark screen of the computer, touching his chest and seeing how the bruise was doing and being reminded of the exact contours of the mark. He really hoped that the tension in his chest originated from the bullet that had been stopped by the Kevlar rather than self-pity. Self-pity was easy. It was the only way out. Suddenly having all the time in the world opened the floodgates for dwelling on the same things over and over. He couldn't end up there – he couldn't lose himself in perpetual circular reasoning.

His brain knew that, but his heart did as it pleased.

It generally possessed an altogether different form of wisdom.

Hence the job: police work, logical, rational. Hence continuing to try and get into the unassailable Security Service network and trying to get to the bottom of who Carsten really was.

But when he swept his fingertips across the trackpad, it was still running – that search that he would never really understand. And he would never know quite how many footprints it left in its wake. And whose they were. But it was Molly's procedure; he was following her expertise as best he could. It would just have to keep going.

He'd have to trust her.

Instead, he went to Facebook. In the end, he had created an account using an untraceable name, but now that he searched for Oscar Babineaux, he could find no trace of his younger son.

For a long time he thought he might have made a mistake or that he simply didn't understand how it worked, but it gradually began to dawn on him that the account had been deleted. And as usual, there was no sign of the rest of the Babineaux family.

Just how easy was it to delete a Facebook account? Weren't there hordes of people trying to take down the profiles of deceased loved ones without any joy? He clicked on the screenshots of Oscar's harmless profile. He couldn't find a single credible reason why it might be gone.

Of course, it could be completely innocent. Maybe Facebook had changed its policy, or Oscar had changed his mind, received too many spam messages, got bored, not been allowed to borrow the computer enough, got sick of all that crap. The primary characteristic of eleven-year-olds was that of inconstancy. He might think the toes flashing a V were ugly.

The twins' sign to their father.

He had to let go of it. There was no immediate solution. Anyway, he was late to the party. If he'd really wanted contact with his twin boys, he should have kindled it years before.

The pressure across his chest increased. He closed everything that could possibly remind him of the disasters of the past and went to check his encrypted email.

He hadn't checked it since he'd arrived on the island. Who would be sending emails to his secret address? But there was actually a message from an unknown sender. When he examined it in closer detail, he realised it was from a forensic specialist at the Security Service notifying him that she'd been ordered to forward the results from the investigation of the crime scene in Tensta.

The flat was full of DNA belonging to both Carsten and Aisha. He really hadn't made any effort to cover his tracks. Up on the roof in the shed, however, there were only traces of

Carsten – notwithstanding an infinite quantity of bee DNA. Aisha had clearly never been up there.

What the email didn't divulge were details of Carsten's identity. There was no social security number, no surname, nothing that took Berger even a step closer to the mole. He sensed August Steen's ill-disguised guiding hand in the background. Berger noted that the specialist didn't address him by name. Presumably she didn't even know whom she was emailing. Steen was keeping him both top secret and isolated.

The detailed account of what had been found in the apiary on the roof did include a couple of interesting points. The pistol that had been rigged up in the drawer really was Sam Berger's old service weapon – his very own Sig Sauer P226, the one that had been used in the killing of the murderer for which Berger was now wanted. The note taped to it with the word 'Boom!' hadn't offered anything else. The steel thread had been applied so that the gun would be fired at 'hip height' when the drawer was opened, as the specialist had put it a little prudishly.

Why? Granted, Carsten had led them up to the roof and into the bee house. He knew who was coming: there wasn't really a choice in the matter. Steen was after him, and it was pretty obvious that Steen would have Kent and Roy playing the battering rams. But Berger?

Could Carsten really know that August Steen would bring in Sam Berger?

And if so, how?

And how could Steen be so bloody sure from the off that the shot from the drawer meant that Carsten was after Berger in particular? There was a logic to Kent and Roy going in first – perhaps Carsten had set things up so that there were enough bees for two, while the third man on the scene was probably going to be the one who headed into the mostly vacated apiary to open the drawer. But in that case he had to know that Berger, a wanted man, would be included in a top-secret raid carried out by the Security Service. That *he* would be the third man. How the hell could he?

What was more, Steen knew that Carsten had known.

Berger couldn't make any sense out of it. But he was relieved that he'd crouched to open the drawer.

It had been a long time since he'd hated with the kind of *purity* that he hated Carsten.

That bastard had tried to shoot his cock off, and that in turn was surely to do with Molly Blom. It was some kind of sick jealousy that Berger couldn't wrap his head around. How could Carsten know anything about his and Molly's relationship? Whatever it was . . .

There was one thing left. The little envelope that the bees had been gluttonously crawling over had been covered in nectar, bees' favourite treat. Inside the envelope had been a letter – a congratulatory card, really. The forensic specialist wrote: '*On the front of the card there's just one thing – the number 1 written in ballpoint pen and then circled. On the back there is handwriting using the same ballpoint.*' And it had said two things on the reverse – both written carefully, almost pedantically by hand.

The first thing was: '*Some say the bee stings: but I say, 'tis the bee's wax; for I did but seal once to a thing, and I was never mine own man since.*'

Berger stared blankly at the text – both the handwritten version and his correspondent's transcription. What the hell was this?

After googling, it transpired that Shakespeare often mentioned bees in his works. In fact, he knew more about bees than most of his peers. In *Henry V*, there's a long monologue about the organisation of bee society, while *Henry VI Part II* sees rebel leader Jack Cade utter those words about bee stings and bee's wax.

If read in context, it was apparently to do with contracts – signed agreements. The legal pacts of the sixteenth century were sealed with bee's wax. Compared with the sting of a contract, a bee sting was nothing, because once a contract had been sealed you were never free again.

This was starting to make sense. Was Carsten using his bees to say this was nothing compared to the contract that I've signed? A pact with the devil? Or Islamic State? Or was he referring to something else – a contract with the Security Service, or perhaps August Steen?

Carsten certainly didn't feel free. He was no longer his own man.

The forensic specialist added laconically: *'We've also examined the bee's wax. There's nothing there.'*

Not literally I suppose, Berger thought to himself.

What was this? Why was Carsten pointing to an agreement that he seemed to regret? Did he want to say that he had no choice?

Berger left that question hanging in the air.

The second thing on the back of Carsten's note in the small, nectar-soaked envelope said: *'like the Andalusian girls'*.

That was it.

Berger's thoughts returned to the picture on the wall in Carsten's flat. The photograph of the beehives on the hillside terraces, the donkeys, the flowers. And the Rock of Gibraltar. Wasn't that in Andalusia? Was it a coincidence?

Did Carsten have ties to Andalusia?

Which Andalusian girls was he talking about?

At that moment, something happened on the computer – something that Berger wasn't responsible for. The wallpaper was suddenly replaced by a new window with an image depicting a shoreline in darkness. Up in the corner shone the number 2. CCTV camera 2. Of the five cameras on this island, number 2 was the second closest. Number 1 was just outside the front door. The storm was whistling across the computer screen, but he could still make out something akin to a white bow cutting through the frenzied water.

Could it be a big seabird? A swan? But it had surfed out of shot before the camera caught a glimpse of it.

In the best case.

Worst case, he had an intruder on the island.

He scrutinised the screen. What sort of intruder would be capable of leaving that kind of trail in the stormy waters? Not a human one, at any rate.

Then a bird hopped into shot for a few seconds before disappearing again. He guessed it was an eider.

Only when he saw the eider did he realise that he had been holding his breath since the CCTV image had appeared. His deep exhalation almost made him miss the chime from the computer.

The eternal search had reached its end. Carefully, he clicked OK and the Security Service intranet appeared before his eyes. He wouldn't make it all the way through the different layers of security, but he would get a fair way in. At the very least, he could start laying out the mysterious jigsaw that was Carsten.

Start the process of getting him.

Berger really did hope he would have the opportunity to kill Carsten, not that he would ever say as much aloud.

There was another chime. He closed his eyes and grimaced. Please, no error messages, no being forced to start over with another search lasting days. The thing he feared most was that restlessness would force him back into the depths of the sea.

Into the mid-water.

But it wasn't an error message. The chime came from an email, but this time it was from an anonymous sender. It contained no text whatsoever – only a file. There was much to suggest it was a video. He took a chance and clicked on it. A message appeared asserting that the file was encrypted.

Berger paused for thought.

Then he returned to a previous email from August Steen with the basic instructions for his stay on the island. Among many other things was an encryption key intended for, quote, 'solely classified communications between you and me, Sam'. If the video file could be decrypted then it was without doubt from the Head of the Intelligence Unit. 'For your eyes only.'

With a degree of scepticism, Berger dragged the video file to the decryption program and saw it slowly come into view.

# 11

It crackles. A picture is slowly trying to take shape but remains fragmented, a mosaic, a jigsaw in which the pieces are in flight, dancing freely. It is a mad, confused, spasmodic interaction between pixels that attract and repel each other. It is like an infinite disturbance.

But then something happens. Slowly, the jigsaw pieces begin to gather together and as the crackling dissipates, they find their places. Eventually, the spectacle comes to resemble a picture.

Darkness reigns. There is little other than background light. Gradually, the camera stabilises. There is a brick wall with the contours of mould outbreaks on it, a sturdy chair back corroded with rust. Nothing else. Except, suddenly, the side of a person who bends forward and then withdraws, seemingly sucked backwards as if by an invisible rubber band and deposited on the chair with a crash. The face is out of focus at first – focus is on the wall behind what is increasingly identifiable as a man. But then it is adjusted.

And the face becomes strangely clear in the dark. Down to the smallest wrinkle. The close-cut hair is reminiscent of iron filings around a magnet. The distinctive gaze is fixed on the camera. Distinct but different. There is certainly fear contained in it, worry, the jitters. It is a gaze that says a fixed and stable world has unexpectedly fallen apart. It is a surprised look, the look of a man who could never have expected anything like this. It is the astonished look of the hastily dethroned authority.

*Then a voice speaks.*

*A voice that is also distinct but different.*

'*I managed to free my hands,*' August Steen says hoarsely. '*But my feet won't budge. Micro camera with 4G, always on me, well hidden. Reception in here is terrible, and the film can only be sent in small pack-ets, one by one, as they wait for a weak, weak signal in optimised conditions to find its way in. Not to mention the pale light trickling in from an unknown location. But I'm going to try and film everything in one take. Everything I have to say. Everything I have to say to you, Sam Berger. Only to you. Because I have no idea how long I've got left.*'

*The Head of the Security Service Intelligence Unit seems to take a deep breath. Then he leans forward a little and begins.*

'*I don't know who got me, but it was a pro. I left police headquarters for a late lunch, then everything is a blank until I woke up in this cellar, strapped to this chair, my ankles cuffed and my wrists bound, a hood over my head. And not a soul here. I haven't seen a single person yet, nor heard a sound. And I've no idea where I am.*

'*Now you know the premise. I'm going to keep things as brief as I can.*

'*April '76, before you were born, Sam. Nightclub by Slussen in Stockholm. I was twenty-four, it was my first major assignment for the Service. I'd pulled off a successful wiretap – I had a valuable cassette tape. I confronted the suspect in the gents.*

'*I put my cards on the table. With backup from two steady chaps, I got straight to the point.*

'"*Nils Gundersen,*" *I said. "Mercenary in Lebanon. I have a tape.*"

'*He just looked at me, hard and sharp as flint.*

'"*Tape?*" *he said.*

'"*Cassette tape,*" *I said. "You and the alleged Albanian arms dealer Isli Vrapi. You're not exactly talking about stuff that's legal.*"

'*Gundersen fixed his gaze on me and spoke in Swedish that sug-gested he was a polyglot. "Since we're talking I assume you want something?*"

' "Your private army is growing," I said. "It's the right time to grow in the Middle East. You're making a success of things in the undergrowth between contract killer and genocidal maniac."

'My theatrical pause didn't elicit any reaction. I carried on. "You can keep doing everything you do, no matter who the fuck hires you. All you have to do is report back, month on month. Straight to me. Otherwise the tape gets played to the wrong ears."

'Nils Gundersen was silent. He slowly began to nod.

'I had recruited him.

'Gundersen turned out to be a fabulous resource on the ground in the Middle East. As long as he delivered, he was free to go about his dirty business. I reported directly and only to the Head of the Security Service; my reports received the highest level of security classification and were buried in the deepest archives. Only I knew about our most important asset in the Arab world.

'The age of jihad hadn't yet begun. When it arrived after the war in Afghanistan, I was the one who was in possession of all material information. Thanks to Gundersen, I rose quickly through the ranks. I've been offered the top job at the Service on three occasions. Each time I've declined. I've had more power as things stand. I've had greater opportunities to protect Sweden from the position I've been in. Until today. Today I don't have a position at all. Today I'm closer to death than power.

'There were a whole bunch of freelancers in the Afghan Freedom Front, contracted by the CIA. One of them was Nils Gundersen, who by this stage had a big and impressive army of international mercenaries. It was at this time that he solidified the contacts that would be of crucial importance to Sweden. Not to mention the entire Western world.

'In his next spell in Iraq, Nils Gundersen grew close to one of the leading experts in Islam – a professor and imam in Baghdad. At the time, this man led a relatively powerful movement seeking to modernise

Islam. For him, the future of divinity hinged on successfully moving away from the literal, medieval, authoritarian version of Islam. The professor had a long-standing network in place across more or less the entire Muslim world that was keeping its eyes open for all tendencies towards militant Islamism. However, the situation became increasingly critical, his life was in danger and he was the subject of constant death threats, which became particularly serious during the closing stages of the Gulf War. If the professor was to survive, he had to leave the country – and bring with him his knowledge and networks.

'Gundersen realised what a gold mine this man was. He set up a secure, anonymous escape route and provided the professor and his wife with false identities. It was of the utmost importance that there was not a single trace that might lead to their new home country.

'It was a success. Right until a month or so ago, I was the only one who knew that the professor was holed up in a shabby sixties flat on Stupvägen in the Helenelund neighbourhood of Sollentuna, and that he went by the name of Ali Pachachi.

'Now all sorts of people – the wrong people – know, thanks to a mole in the Service. A mole by the name of Carsten.

'When I received indications that there was a spy in the very innermost inner sanctum, even before we'd had it confirmed, I erased all documents from the Security Service archive and extracted the Pachachis from Sollentuna.

'I'm the only person in the world who knows where they are.

'If it is Carsten who's got me – and surely it must be – then he'll use every method at his disposal to make me talk. And I know exactly which methods he has at his disposal.

'But I won't talk, Sam.

'I won't talk.'

# 12

Deer had forgotten the code to the main door. Or it had been changed.

Regardless of which it was, it hinted at how long it had been since she had last tapped the digits into the keypad by the door on Ploggatan in Stockholm's Södermalm.

She bided her time. Dusk had set in. The small side street was desolate. A malignant storm had just blown in from the southern archipelago. Winter was arriving in the capital.

The question was whether it was worth waiting for a neighbour either being forced out into the storm or seeking shelter from it. At any rate, there was no one nearby.

After thirty seconds of agonising, Deer pulled the lock pick from her pocket and gave the door her full attention. She could feel how rusty she was when it came to routine police work.

The police work she had been involved in lately had been the very opposite of routine.

Eventually, the door opened. Naturally, she immediately encountered a neighbour in the stairwell and the young man's gaze suspiciously took in the lock pick that hadn't quite made it back into her coat pocket. She opted for a brief nod at him before ascending the stairs. His gaze was burning into the back of her neck all the way up until the stairs doubled back and out of sight. For a moment, she heard the storm whistling away down there before the main door closed again and silence returned.

The four storeys had felt far easier to climb the last time she had been here. By the time she reached the door marked 'Lindström & Berger', she was ridiculously short of breath.

That was what the sign said.

Years after Freja Lindström had left Sam Berger and emigrated with the couple's twin boys, her name remained on the front door. Her name from back then – like a constant, masochistic reminder every single day. Now she had some French surname and had, according to Berger, been swallowed up by Parisian life.

Deer stood still for a while, exhaling. Then she took out the pick again and put it into the lock. This time it was easier – the lock was hardly worthy of a cop. Not even an ex-cop.

The door glided open, and Deer glided inside. She stood for a while in the dark hallway breathing in the atmosphere. Warm, moist, claustrophobic. Maybe she was imagining it, but was there an air of *abandonment* in the flat? The month that had elapsed since Berger had last been home could hardly have left its mark on the air she was breathing. That meant it was surely her imagination – the preconceived notions of her brain making their way into her impressions. But there was something else too. Another smell that she thought she recognised. The faint scent of antiseptic – as if the place had been cleaned less than a month ago. Possibly even disinfected.

The dark compelled Deer to switch on her torch, and she took another few steps down the hallway. For a split second, a nondescript woman in early middle age appeared to be about to attack her from the side – fortunately she quickly realised that it was a full-length mirror. Her heart pounding, she passed the closed bathroom door, glanced hastily to the left into Berger's dark bedroom and then spent a few moments looking to the right into the living room. The blinds there were also closed – everything was bathed in a sort of artificial darkness.

When had Berger last been here?

He would hardly have dared come here as a wanted man, and before that he hadn't had a clue that he'd be forced headlong into hiding. The roller blind in the bedroom was one thing, but why the blinds in the living room? Why the darkness? One possibility was that he actually lived his mediocre life in constant darkness – as soon as he got home, darkness closed in. But that didn't seem like the Sam Deer knew.

The second possibility was that he hadn't done it – someone else had put the flat into darkness. If so, why? Who? And when?

She stopped in her tracks a short way into the living room. The sofas, positioned in front of the last old-fashioned cathode-ray TV in Sweden, looked like they'd been sat upon until they fell to pieces. None of the whisky bottles on the drinks trolley contained more than a splash of liquid. The bookcase seemed to house more dust than books. And a chest of drawers by the door into the second bedroom – the one that had once belonged to the twins – had its bottom drawer open. She made her way towards it.

Just as she bent down, noticing that the drawer was empty, she heard a sound. The echo had already stopped resounding by the time the first thought coalesced in her suddenly empty head. Cutlery. Cutlery clashing together. A fork being dropped onto other forks. That kind of sound.

An unlikely sound.

Yet it had happened.

She could think of no natural explanation. She supposed a fork might have been balanced on the drying rack for the last month and might finally, at this very moment, have fallen onto the draining board. That was slightly too many coincidences not to draw her weapon.

Noiselessly, Deer prised out her pistol, the cool of the butt cutting through the stifling darkness like a knife. At the end of the dark corridor, unexpected light was seeping through the half-open crack of a door which – if she remembered correctly – led to the kitchen. Her weapon raised, she slipped along the corridor. The light ahead seemed dreamlike, faint, immobile, cold – there were no signs of movement in the otherwise obscured kitchen, no sounds whatsoever, no shadows. She passed a closed door, probably a closet, before peering through the crack. The door creaked gently as it opened.

Deer surveyed the kitchen. A faint glow from a nearby street light filtered through dirty windows, casting the most spartan of kitchen equipment in an irregular light. The sound must have come from the cutlery stand on the draining board, though it was impossible to discern how. Nothing could have fallen spontaneously. There were no other signs of life.

But . . .

She leaned forward, towards the window, and felt something. A difference. Perhaps it was a minimal change in pressure, perhaps it was a sound at a frequency that she couldn't really make out, perhaps it was a smell. Perhaps it was the very faint smell of antiseptic that made Deer crouch and turn round with a speed she didn't know she had in her. When her vision stabilised, she found her service weapon aimed straight at a figure.

The figure in its turn had a weapon trained on her.

A Mexican stand-off.

Behind the figure, the door to the closet was open. The guns were quivering ever so slightly, but there was no doubt that both were stable enough to fire lethal projectiles.

Time seemed to stand still.

A fluffy particle of dust came sailing through the faint beam of light from outside. It ran amok with Deer's peripheral vision. When it was gone, she spoke slightly hoarsely.

'Admit it: you haven't showered since you left the hospital.'

The body outside the kitchen door started slightly, without any noticeable change in the aim of the barrel.

'What?' said the figure.

'You've changed clothes,' said Deer, without lowering her gun. 'But you haven't showered. You still smell of hospital.'

'I've had a lot on,' said Molly Blom.

'What do you say to lowering that gun?' said Deer.

'You first,' said Blom.

'I don't know what you're up to,' said Deer, keeping her weapon trained.

'Yet you've sat by my bedside for days,' said Blom. 'Watching over me.'

'You weren't bloody awake then,' said Deer. 'You're not that good an actor.'

'You've got no idea how good an actor I am,' said Blom. 'But no, I read it in the ward security guard's records.'

'I thought the security guard spent most of his time sleeping,' said Deer, lowering her gun.

Molly Blom did the same.

They looked at each other.

'We ought to hug,' said Deer.

'Did you save me?' Blom asked, without holstering her weapon. 'Did you find that snowed-in cabin and save me?'

'You saved yourself,' said Deer, her gun also hanging by her side. 'We arrived a few minutes too late. But we called in an air ambulance and put you in it. I went with you. You got medical attention. You were in a coma. And then suddenly you were not only conscious, but sharp and mobile enough to swap places with a corpse by the name of Hanna Dunberg.'

'Hanna Dunberg?'

'That's what they say, yes. What happened?'

'I woke up. I realised I had to get out. I found an exit. Nothing more than that.'

'But you were in a coma – a respirator was breathing for you. You were teetering between life and death.'

'Don't we do that all the time?'

Deer stopped herself. She scrutinised Blom, trying to take in her entire being. New clothes, certainly. Shoes with chunky soles, a studded leather jacket, crazy goth clothing that didn't seem at all like Molly Blom. Bought recently, then? Hadn't she been home? Why? Because she was being pursued? Because she knew she was being pursued? So she remembered things. The question was how much. Deer weighed her words carefully.

'You saw the security guard's records,' she said. 'They were on the wall behind him. Did you see the medical records too?'

For the first time, Deer could make out emotion on Molly's face. A suddenly furrowed brow, scepticism, curiosity. Had she miscalculated?

'What are you saying?' said Blom.

'You know I visited you in hospital, but what do you know about your medical condition? Do you know how unwell you are?'

'Look, I woke up, felt fine, then I left.'

Deer exhaled deep inside herself. She hadn't said too much – she had calculated it just right. Blom wasn't aware of her own pregnancy. And now was hardly the time to provide her with that kind of life-changing news. Not right now.

'And now you're here,' she said instead, gesturing at the darkened flat and returning her pistol to its shoulder holster.

Blom looked at her for a few seconds and then did the same.

'Yes,' she said. 'Now I'm here.'

'In Sam Berger's flat,' said Deer. 'Why?'

'I did some googling,' said Blom. 'He's wanted. There's a national alert. He murdered the guy who tried to kill me.'

'You also know that he didn't do that.'

'Exactly,' said Blom. 'And that's why I'm here.'

'You want to find him?'

'Or at least understand what this is about.'

'Was it you who lowered the blinds?' Deer asked. 'Did you leave the flat in darkness and empty the drawers?'

'I was going to ask you the same thing.'

'Must be the Security Service, right?' Deer said with a deep sigh. 'That was what made the dropped fork so unexpected – why would they want to give themselves away?'

'It was a spoon,' said Blom, with a shadow of a smile.

'Internal Affairs have been questioning me for a couple of days,' said Deer. 'They wanted every last detail about what happened in the interior. But they weren't all that interested in Sam's location. Which makes me think that the Security Service has put a lid on it. You're one of them, Molly. You know what this is about.'

'What bothers me is that I ought to,' said Blom.

'And that's why you're here?'

'To try and find Sam, yes.'

'Me too,' said Deer. 'You got any other theories?'

For the first time, Molly Blom looked at Deer properly. It was a harsher gaze than Deer remembered it, but there was still a certain something in there.

'You really did your bloody all to find me,' said Blom.

'And we arrived just a few minutes too late, damn it.'

'But you didn't. You saved my life. I ought to thank you,

Desiré. I can do that – but I've got no intention of working with you.'

Deer nodded.

'Then we'll just have to go our separate ways,' she said. 'I assume you've had time to go through the flat more thoroughly than I have. Drawers emptied?'

'Most definitely,' said Blom. 'No toothbrush.'

Deer nodded again.

'Then at least he's alive,' she said. 'They gathered up his things without him being here – had he been, he would hardly have taken the lot. They lowered the blinds to avoid being seen. But why not put them back up again?'

'Because it didn't matter,' said Blom. 'They didn't leave any traces. There's nothing to find here. We're both here in vain, you and me, but you're welcome to keep looking. I'm going to sling my hook, and I assume you don't intend to try and stop me.'

No one moved. They looked at each other guardedly.

Eventually, Deer extended her arms. Blom responded in kind and they embraced briefly and not altogether comfortably. Yet it was somehow sincere.

In the end, Molly Blom made for the door. She stopped on the threshold, her hand on the door handle. For a moment, Deer got the impression she wanted to say something – something that couldn't quite be said – but then she blinked and was gone.

Deer allowed her gaze to linger for a few seconds before making for the chest of drawers by Sam Berger's kids' bedroom. She pulled out the three top drawers – the things that had been left behind were markedly female or childish in nature.

Then she peeked into the twins' room. There was no sign of madness there – it wasn't a crazy mausoleum, or obscure consecrated ground – but Deer still got the impression that the room was exactly as it had been the day the twins had left. She spotted something that looked like an eight-year-old boy's pyjama bottoms on the bottom bunk of the unmade bunk bed.

Sam Berger had simply closed the door and left it that way.

Deer stood there for a while before breaking the spell and sauntering back into the living room. She went over to the window and opened a crack in the blinds. The snowstorm continued to rage outside – it was hard to see much. When she finally managed to focus and spotted Molly Blom down on Ploggatan, she immediately let go of the slats.

Blom saw her.

Of course she saw her.

# 13

Molly Blom turned in the darkness and looked the abominable snowstorm in the eye. She had just turned up the studded collar of the leather jacket, and standing on Ploggatan she peered up to Sam Berger's flat.

She made out, ever so faintly, a crack in the blinds and met the gaze of Superintendent Desiré Rosenkvist, without truly being able to meet it. Then the crack vanished and Molly Blom set off.

She went round the block, taking an awkward route through the slushy snow towards the most neglected part of Bondegatan, where its main thoroughfare had already become Barnängsgatan but with a small side street to the left. Parked there, out of sight of the growing number of CCTV cameras across the city, was an old Volvo, looking abandoned in the wet snow.

Blom went over to it, glanced around furtively and then crouched. She fished out something oblong from under the car – something reminiscent of a metal ruler. She quickly angled it down inside the window slit in the driver-side door and yanked the lock open. Then she brushed the worst of the snow off her, got in and started the car by holding together two wires. It was lucky cars this old were still on the road.

Before putting it into first, she inserted her hand in the pocket of her leather jacket and felt around. She found it – against all the odds, it had remained dry. Molly Blom sat there for a while looking at the small envelope from Berger's flat, turning it over and over. It looked like an envelope for a greetings card, and it was sealed. Eventually, she shook her head and threw it unopened onto the passenger seat before pulling away.

She wove her way out to Nynäsvägen via all manner of back-streets, before heading south. The snowstorm that had come from the direction she was going began to dissipate, but it was probably still blowing a gale further north. Before long, neither the snow nor the wind was noticeable. She floored it through an increasingly mild evening.

The red mobile phone rang.

She looked at it for a while, then she picked up.

'Yes?'

She listened for a couple of seconds. She was speechless, and felt herself get paler.

Then time took on another form – an extremely purposeful one. She wondered what speed she could get out of a Volvo this old.

The accelerator was flat out now. Time was like a whip driving her forward. She got the car up to 180 kilometres an hour, refusing to release the pedal from the floor. The computerised cars on the motorway seemed to be static.

After many intense kilometres in gathering darkness, she wrenched the car onto a smaller road that eventually became even narrower before becoming nothing more than a pair of tyre tracks through the bare forest. She drove in a crazed rally style along the winding forest track, which appeared to continue indefinitely between trunks that looked dead in the ghostly sheen cast by the headlights. A deciduous forest without any leaves.

It was as if the wildly revving Volvo had passed through a wormhole and was driving through a completely different epoch. An archaic one. An epoch when tattered bodies hung from the dry branches of trees, ravens pecking out their eyes.

All she did was put her foot down. Accelerate, turn and grit her teeth so hard it felt like her jaw had locked in place.

Ahead of her was hell.

A clearing in the forest appeared. It grew wider and came to resemble a field, and that field looked as if it had once been a meadow. Beyond the field, the forest grew dense again, deciduous trees replaced by coniferous, and she was only just able to glimpse the facade of a house through the dense margin of the forest.

When she opened the door to the house, the darkness seemed to absorb her. It closed softly behind her, making the darkness absolute.

She pulled out her torch and switched it on, half stumbling down the steep stone staircase to the cellar.

It was no longer Molly Blom who was running.

It was no longer Molly Blom who felt fetid air washing over her, as if exhaled from the rotting mouth of a leper. She dived even deeper into the Middle Ages.

The being that was no longer Molly Blom crashed into an oppressive room. A new door, a new lock, a new rattling key. How could the cold be so damp? The door opened, creaking with an extraterrestrial rumble. The torch swept hopelessly across the stone walls. Nothing but darkness.

Black.

A new door, reinforced. The feel of a concrete floor at the threshold.

New key. New light as the door opened, a faint background light that was enough to reveal the absolute centre of focus in the underground chamber.

A seated figure.

She's there now. At the core.

In the very core of the darkness.

The figure is sitting on a rusty cast-iron chair bolted to the floor, completely still, a black hood over its head, arms behind the back, as if ties were still in place around the wrists. There is no more than a metre from the back of the chair to the wall with its irregular bricks, as if the bricklayer of two centuries ago had been a little tipsy at this point in his work.

She goes over. Grabs the black hood. Jerks it off.

The man's close-cut hair is reminiscent of iron filings around a magnet. And there is no longer any steel left in the grey eyes of August Steen, Head of the Intelligence Unit at the Security Service.

Only surprise.

'Molly?' he whispers.

Molly Blom pulls out her pistol and shoots him.

Neatly – three shots straight to the heart.

And what falls through the darkness is silence.

# 14

Sam Berger watched the video for the first time that day, but the fifteenth time overall. It ended, and he stared at the computer screen. Apart from a few marks that he couldn't account for, it was black. Were they fingerprints? Had he unconsciously touched the screen the day before? Sweat stains?

Smears of cold sweat?

It had been three miserable days since he'd parted ways from August Steen in the harbour at Nynäshamn.

That shot to the chest. From Berger's own Sig Sauer P226. Carsten had wanted to castrate him. Instead, the bastard had gone on to pick up his former boss August Steen and – silently, anonymously, without even a hint of explanation – tied him to a chair in a cellar.

Did any of this add up?

And why, in this incredibly precarious situation, did the Head of the Intelligence Unit at the Security Service turn to Sam Berger of all people? If Steen had the ability to communicate with the outside world about his position – emailing videos, albeit with terrible reception and via a micro camera – then why wasn't he shouting loudly for the top brass? Why wasn't he seeking to instigate a huge manhunt? Why wasn't he raising the alarm with the police, the army, the press – whatever? No, he'd prised that tiny camera from God knew which orifice and emailed the video to Sam Berger and Sam Berger alone. Sweden's most wanted, most isolated and thus least resourceful person. He'd sent it to an ousted and almost-castrated ex-cop. On God's earth, why?

What was going on?

Berger couldn't save him – Steen was surely fully aware of this. That meant that what Steen had to tell was *more important than his own life*. And it was to Berger in particular that he needed to tell it.

Or perhaps August Steen thought that Berger, and Berger alone, would actually be able to rescue him.

Either way, it was clearly of the utmost importance that this account reached him. And Sam Berger was really trying to understand why.

Right now, there was nothing in the account to motivate the addressee, nothing that seemed tailored to him in particular. It was a generalised story about the relationship between Steen, Gundersen and Pachachi, and Berger already knew most of it.

A very young Steen had recruited a young Gundersen –and Steen had moved Pachachi, saving him from the mole before the mole was identified. However, the mole had snatched Pachachi's daughter Aisha. He was presumably blackmailing Pachachi so that he would suppress his vast jihadist monitoring network throughout the Islamic world. In other words, there was currently a palpably elevated threat against Sweden, and 'the worst act of terrorism in all of Sweden's history' was clearly just round the corner.

If August Steen was as devoted to his country and his job as Berger thought, then he also realised what was at stake. Carsten's actions could kill masses of people in Sweden. Carsten had completely betrayed his country.

Something was brewing. And suddenly, the weird gunshot aimed at Berger's balls didn't seem as pathetic as it had done for a couple of days. Sam Berger was obviously playing a crucial role in a game of which he could only sense the contours. Steen had said that his video could only be delivered in small 'digital packets' – which probably meant the email client in the micro camera was incapable of sending large files, instead dividing the file into smaller pieces – and there was a possibility that these would arrive one by one as soon as the 3G or 4G in the cellar was strong enough. The uncertainty made his already strained existence on the windswept islet off Landsort even more tense.

Why had Berger been put there?

Where did he stand now, following Steen's kidnapping?

What was that bastard Carsten playing at?

And who was he?

Berger bent over the computer. At least he was now in – into the Security Service's internal network. With even a fraction of Molly's deft skills he ought to be able to identify Carsten and get to grips with who he actually was. And he might have a chance of saving August Steen. Because surely that video had been an appeal? A cry for help?

But why? Berger had never been near the Security Service. He'd been a regular detective inspector with the Stockholm police, albeit with 'special duties'. What the hell made him, of all people, so important to one of the Service's bigwigs?

Berger dived into the deeps of the Service, immediately finding himself in the mid-water.

He didn't know which way was up and which way was down, nor front nor back. In their previous two cases – if they could even be called 'cases' – it had always been Molly Blom who had handled the Security Service systems and archives. Now he had to learn to swim himself. Or at least work out which way was up and which way was down.

He exhaled a small bubble of air, following it with his gaze, getting himself onto an even keel, and took a few tentative movements. Eventually, he began to understand how it worked.

The system was very different from that used by the regular police, and when he finally managed to submit an appropriately formulated search it turned up nothing. The name Carsten didn't record even a single hit.

Okay, that wasn't entirely unexpected. Carsten had been part of August Steen's inner circle, his right-hand man, and it was no surprise that his identity was difficult to determine. Strictly speaking, Berger didn't even know whether Carsten was a first name or last name. And actually, wasn't it vaguely Danish?

After a few awkward manoeuvres, Berger found a way into a deeper layer of the intranet which contained a plethora of links to other hidden corners of the internet. He triggered a search, knowing it would take time.

Time for a summary.

Was there any way to find out where August Steen was being held captive? Hardly, from the footage – it was a cellar like any other. Except that it contained an iron chair bolted to the floor and shackles. And none of what Steen had said could be interpreted as subliminal clues. He had been snatched from outside police headquarters, woken up in the cellar and never glimpsed any of the kidnappers.

Dead end.

What about Carsten then? What did Berger know? He had met him a couple of times before he'd been unmasked as the Security Service mole. Impressions? The first was of those insanely thick lenses. Why were they left behind in the flat in

Tensta? Everything there had been a sign – deliberately discarded signs. Which meant Carsten had hardly *forgotten* his glasses. They might very well be an incitement to read, lying there on top of Shakespeare. But that seemed a little too banal. Obviously the Security Service would open the book, and blatant signs like that weren't Carsten's style. What was more, they were presumably expensive, specially customised glasses for a man with deteriorating eyesight as a result of RP. Those weren't the kind of thing you left behind just to signpost a book that would be opened, read and interpreted anyway.

It was possible that the glasses were pointing to themselves. Maybe Carsten wanted to say their time was over – he was shedding his glasses like a lizard shed its skin.

His blindness was much closer now.

But why would he want to say that?

Berger fumbled on through the wasteland of his short-term memory. He remembered a mad journey to Arlanda airport with Carsten in the passenger seat and Sam and Deer in the back. A highly focused Carsten who had sent further instructions to the two of them up in the interior. Who had done all he could from a distance to assist them in the release of Molly Blom.

And who had then gone up there and killed the killer with Sam Berger's former service weapon.

Berger tried to contain his anger and make it all add up.

It didn't add up.

♂ and ♀, that was what August Steen had said. What the fuck did that mean?

Next step. The flat in Tensta. Something that must have been a precisely positioned clue to lure them there. Everything perfectly timed. Even a few small bees buzzing around the flat at just the right moment to trigger Sam Berger's eye for detail. *To bee or not to bee.* Shit.

What about the rest of it? The envelope. The quote.

Shakespeare: 'Some say the bee stings: but I say, 'tis the bee's wax; for I did but seal once to a thing, and I was never mine own man since.'

Tableau.

That was the word he was looking for. The roof of the building had been a tableau. A stage on which something had unfolded that was put into perspective by the first quote: Carsten was no longer his own man. He had signed a contract that meant he was not free.

But what contract?

And what the hell did it have to do with Andalusian girls? 'Like the Andalusian girls'?

Andalusia. Southern Spain. The picture in Carsten's flat, the beehives, the yellow hillside, the donkeys, the Rock of Gibraltar in the distance. 'Like the Andalusian girls.'

Did Andalusia have some bearing on it all?

Berger grew tired of speculating wildly, got up abruptly and went to the bedroom. The storm was still raging – clods of water, seemingly raised straight from the depths of the sea, were being hurled indefatigably at the window. Each time the roar of the storm was amplified, it felt as if a loose shutter that he'd had to batten down at least ten times was on the brink of breaking loose again and being fired through the window like a projectile from outer space.

He looked out into the strange darkness of the December day. It was impossible to see more than a few metres ahead. He couldn't even see the sea – he could see no water except that being thrown at him, together with disparate bits of tree branch.

Yet it was very apparent that this was only the beginning.

The storm was rising before him like a wall, seemingly demonstrating his misery, how imprisoned he was. If the man who had put him here – the only one who knew he was here – was out of the game, then did that mean he'd been forgotten for good?

A couple of others from the Security Service had been mixed up in it, but the helicopter pilot was guaranteed not to know who he was, and the people who had emptied his flat into the four big moving boxes had probably had no idea where the items were destined to go.

No, only August Steen knew. And August Steen was out of the running.

Did that mean Sam Berger was a free man?

Free to escape?

Although where would he escape to? The moment he set foot in Nynäshamn, someone would recognise him and call the police. Perhaps the motorboat out in the boathouse would have enough fuel to get him to Estonia, perhaps he could go to ground in some empty house in Tallinn. But was there really any future in that? He had no money, and couldn't use his credit cards or ID. He would spend the rest of his life a penniless refugee.

That wasn't how he wanted to live the rest of his life.

Tail between his legs.

Claustrophobia struck at the same moment he turned his back on both the window and the storm. It was as if the walls were drawing in around him, pressing closer. For the last few years, solitude had been part of his life, but it had never been quite this *active* before. His head was his prison.

Berger returned to the living room. He glanced quickly at the display – the search continued unabated. Maybe, just maybe, Carsten was getting a little closer with each passing moment.

Then his eyes settled on the untouched moving boxes. He grimaced and made his way over to them. He surveyed their chaos. There were certainly artefacts from his life in there – not to mention artefacts from his lost family life, things that reminded him of Freja, Marcus and Oscar – but the disorder, as if the hand of chance had been running on high octane, made the objects seem remarkably unfamiliar.

He decided to reconquer them. Nevertheless, his patterns of movement as he began to remove things from the huge cardboard boxes were ambiguous. As if order entailed memories. And memories would hardly provide relief from the rising claustrophobia.

In the background, the search for the evasive Carsten continued.

Berger had rather clumsily begun to pick through the ruins of his past when the computer chimed.

An email had arrived.

# 15

*The greying man leans back against the rusty chair bolted to the floor, and his close-cut hair comes into focus. The only mumbled phrase discernible is one that is repeated.*

*'I won't talk, Sam.'*

*Then something seems to happen to August Steen. He looks up at the ceiling, his gaze seems to alter, his facial expression takes on a different cast. It's as if he catches himself.*

*Catches himself in a lie.*

*Something seems to be coursing through him – a silent rain that slowly but surely becomes a deluge washing away all untruths. His entire being gathers together what vitality remains. He begins to speak in a new voice.*

*'There's a watershed, Sam. A point that divides life in two. That point – that watershed – was William Larsson. He was Nils Gundersen's son.*

*'For seventeen years, my contact with Nils ticked over at a reserved distance. But when the professor who would become Ali Pachachi came into the picture, our ties grew closer. Nils and I were forced to maintain close contact in order to smuggle Pachachi into Sweden in the utmost secrecy. It was in connection with this that Nils Gundersen deviated from our strictly professional communications for the first time. He'd had a feeling – a feeling! – that as a result of his brief visit to Sweden*

seventeen years earlier, he'd become a father. He asked me to look into the matter.

'To cut a long story short, my enquiries with Stockholm's maternity units led me to one Stina Larsson, who lived in a flat in the centre of Helenelund in Sollentuna. She had a sixteen-year-old son with a facial deformity. I took a couple of photos that I passed on to Nils Gundersen. His reply was heart-rending. Nils had spent his entire childhood living with the fear that he might start to develop the same symptoms as his father: those of a terrible genetic facial deformity. It had never happened. Instead he had made himself hard as nails – but apparently the genes had skipped a generation and been passed on to his son.

'The more I shadowed the boy, the more I realised how bullied he was. His salvation lay in one overriding interest: clocks, clockwork, wristwatches. He seemed to have just one friend – a boy that I occasionally saw sneaking in through the main door at Stupvägen. It was only many years later that I realised that the boy was you, Sam. Otherwise, William's whole life was centred on avoiding a bunch of bullies.

'I was on the verge of taking them down, Sam. Scaring the shit out of them. But I controlled myself and consulted Nils. He thought more drastic measures were necessary – he wanted William to come and live at his home in Byblos in Lebanon. We could use the same human trafficking route we'd used to smuggle Pachachi into the country, just in reverse.

'Spring arrived and the plans slowly fell into place, but one day in early summer something happened that forced me to act sooner than expected. I found William in an appalling state. He'd been tied to the goalpost on a football pitch. He was unconscious and had been given the kind of beating that could no longer be called bullying. This was downright assault. His genitals were bleeding. I genuinely feared for his life.

'I took him to my pied-à-terre in town. The plans had to be brought forward. When William came to, he had no objections whatsoever to moving to live with a father he didn't know he had – he wanted to be as

*far away as possible. He asked only two things: that his mother be con-
sulted, and that he be allowed to bring his clocks.*

'I visited Stina Larsson in Helenelund. I had no idea how dreadful
her circumstances were. She was an alcoholic and under threat of evic-
tion. I forced through the purchase of the flat by the Service for use as a
safe house. Stina was permitted to live there as long as she wanted, and
with her blessing I smuggled William out of the country to his father.

'Nils had engaged some of the world's finest plastic surgeons, and I
received updates about William's transformation. He had begun to
work out, was studying diligently. As soon as the complex facial surger-
ies were done, he joined his father's mercenary army and became both a
successful soldier and an advanced computer technician.

'In short, he became a man who was useful to me.

'Stina didn't have the same luck. It didn't take more than a few
months for her alcoholism to well and truly break her. She went into
rehab, but even with that help, she passed away within the year.

'On the other hand, that freed up the Security Service safe house in
Helenelund. I'd received indications that the professor's new identity as
a pizzeria owner in Alby had begun to come under scrutiny. It was time
to give him a truly secure identity. He was given the name Ali Pachachi
and he and his family moved to Helenelund.

'That was how things remained for a number of years. The man
who was now known as Ali Pachachi retained his network and continued to supply the Service with the names of potential terrorists both
during al-Qaeda's days and later on in IS.

'Then, a rumour reached him about the notorious Albanian arms
dealer Isli Vrapi's crime syndicate. Vrapi himself had died in an infam-
ous brawl in a pub on Götgatsbacken in Stockholm, and it was unclear
whether what happened was related to his arms empire. It was now
apparent that an as-yet-unknown but definite successor had taken over.
This man was building up an arsenal – including high-capacity weapons,
suicide bombs, possibly even rocket launchers and missiles – to be*

distributed across a number of European countries, and was preparing to sell to IS. Or the highest bidder. It was a terrifying prospect.

'I contacted Nils Gundersen. He was very interested in this rumour and promised to look into the matter. He also said there were vague indications of a threat to Pachachi. They were a little too vague for my taste to necessitate the complicated process of changing identity again. The Pachachis remained the Pachachis.

'However, a bodyguard seemed advisable.

'That's how I saw things, Sam, and I told Nils, who immediately suggested his son. It didn't take many days for William Larsson to make his way to Sweden using the new identity Olle Nilsson. He was hired by the Security Service's technical subcontractor Wiborg Detaljist AB, but his actual assignment was to serve as bodyguard at the home of the Pachachis – who happened to live in his childhood home on Stupvägen in Helenelund. There was an advantage to him being very familiar with the flat, and Nils had guaranteed his son's undying professionalism.

'The Pachachis never really needed a bodyguard. It was me who needed William in place, unswervingly loyal, a soldier with a big debt of gratitude.

'Sam, it was on my orders that William Larsson kidnapped Aisha Pachachi.

'The assignment was directed by me and only me, and led to William eventually abducting seven girls.

'Perhaps you'll understand why I did it, Sam. Perhaps not.

'The fact is, I think you will, Sam. Despite everything that happened.

'Now I'm going to tell you. Ali Pachachi's network had –'

# 16

Sam Berger contemplated the flickering computer screen. That was where it ended. August Steen's second video stopped just as he was about to reach the heart of his story.

Only after an indeterminate amount of time could Berger bring himself to turn away from the migraine-inducing screen. His gaze fell on young Aisha Pachachi. That was what she had looked like as a fifteen-year-old. That was what she had looked like on the final day of school – the day when her compulsory schooling came to an end and she was off into the wide world to flex her wings. Twenty-three minutes after that photo had been taken, she had been kidnapped. By William Larsson.

On August Steen's orders.

The story ran amok in Berger's brain.

William Larsson was August Steen's man – that was new and disconcerting information. For reasons as yet undisclosed, he had been tasked with abducting Aisha Pachachi. It had made something misfire in the brain of the boy who had once been bullied so harshly, and he had continued kidnapping fifteen-year-old girls. Steen must have known at the time what William was up to, and he must have hoodwinked his protégée at the Security

Service, Molly Blom. He must have pretended to support her pursuit of William while in reality having his back. Even though he had kidnapped seven girls.

At some point during this, Steen's own right-hand man, Carsten, had started double-dealing. Carsten became a mole at the very heart of the Service, engaged by a foreign power to find Ali Pachachi, whom Steen had by then moved to an undisclosed safe house known only to him. Carsten's plan was to locate the kidnapped girls, snatch Aisha Pachachi from William's grasp, hide and wait for Pachachi to react – presumably by offering to sacrifice himself for his daughter.

That was where things stood right now.

What all parties involved in these cases seemed not to care about at all were the seven kidnapped girls. Frankly, that left Sam Berger fuming. Not that he himself was blameless.

On this desolate patch of gravel, the early summer feels ruthless, windless, the air matted with dust, the sun sharp and piercing.

There are two witnesses to the scene by the goalposts. Someone is slumped against the left one. That's the young William Larsson, tied up, bloodied.

One of the witnesses is sitting at a safe distance, in the shade of a tree. That's Sam Berger. He's fifteen years old and crying. He wipes the tears away with his bloody handkerchief, tasting William's blood.

But there is another witness, and when Sam spots the big, unfamiliar man approaching the goalposts he throws away the handkerchief and runs off.

The silence in the house on the small island in the archipelago was deafening. Berger was struggling to breathe. His guilt enveloped him like a dark, heavy cloud. He breathed in darkness. Moist darkness that was in the process of drowning him.

Like in the mid-water.

He stood up abruptly, slapping the big map of the archipelago with the palm of his hand, before turning his gaze to the white-board and fixing it on Aisha's portrait.

Carsten had snatched her around a month ago, and judging by everything, he had taken her just a few miserable kilometres from Helenelund to a soundproofed flat in Tensta. Neither the soundproofing in the flat nor the apiary on the roof were spur-of-the-moment interior design decisions, so it was likely that Carsten had had the flat for much longer – and perhaps the shed on the roof separately. The Security Service almost certainly already had at least four men in Tensta alone, but he still needed to check it out, now that he had finally gained access to their inner networks. Perhaps he'd even stumble on the investigators' own reports and get up to speed with the ongoing investigation. He sat down at the computer again, invigorated with new energy, and began to work his way through the system.

To his surprise, he quickly found a 'preliminary memo' from a civilian staff member addressed to someone called 'Agent Malmberg'. A further search for this unknown Malmberg turned up that he or she was leading the investigation and reporting directly to August Steen. A number of emails and phone calls to Steen during the course of the day suggested that Malmberg was unable to make contact with their boss.

The preliminary memo had today's date, giving Berger some insight into the very latest situation on the investigation. The flat in Tensta was a condominium that had been bought by someone called Johan Svensson two years earlier. However, the shed on the roof was owned by someone called Sven Johansson and had been for the last three years. Berger felt tired. The Security Service's fake identities, although untraceable, had a frankly ridiculous air to them. The fees to the housing co-op and the electricity and broadband bills were being paid from two different corporate bank accounts in two different countries. Two tax havens – Monaco and Gibraltar.

It could be a coincidence. The photo on the wall in the flat in Tensta, the Rock of Gibraltar in the distance, the idyllic Andalusian landscape. The note that said 'the Andalusian girls'.

Nope. Berger was reading too much into too little.

Everything was untraceable. The Security Service hadn't got any further than a Gibraltarian company called Big Exit Ltd, which could conceivably be related to Carsten's own grand exit from the Service.

Carsten was naturally an expert at avoiding the disclosure of any traces that might give the Security Service more clues than he wanted to. Did that mean he wanted to give them a clue about Andalusia? Why? However, there was nothing to suggest that Agent Malmberg was interested in finding out the answer.

Berger's thoughts returned to the living room in Tensta. The photograph of the Rock of Gibraltar, the beehives on the hillside. Two bees buzzing around the room. *To be, or not to be.* It was Berger who had spotted the connection – not Steen, not Roy, not Kent. Perhaps his way of thinking was more like Carsten's after all? Freer, bolder, wilder? Was it in fact the case that Carsten was trying to say something to Berger *in particular*? And once again, if so, why?

Intuition was nothing more than concentrated experience.

No. Stop. Enough. Once again: he was reading too much into too little. Time to move on.

Where was Carsten now? Where was he holed up with Aisha? And where had he taken August Steen?

Since criminal activity in Tensta had increased – rioting, cars set on fire, drug dealing, gang murders – the police had fitted more CCTV. There was weeks of footage to review. As yet, it hadn't got them anywhere, but Berger had the links. He could try himself – if for some reason he needed to make things on the desolate island feel even more claustrophobic . . .

He glanced out of the window. The sleet had at least stopped hammering the windows, but it was still falling in dense heavy drops that spattered this pasty archipelago day.

Back to the report. So far, no vehicle that had conveyed Carsten had been identified. Berger suspected he was fully aware of the locations of the CCTV cameras. No, the vehicle was not the right approach. What else was there? Opticians? Eye doctors? Where did Carsten get his thick specs? He'd left a pair in the flat, so he'd clearly got new ones somewhere else – presumably stronger ones. Where had they come from?

The beehives.

Where could you buy beehives? How did you get hold of bees?

According to the reports, the Security Service was already looking into these things in depth. Berger had no edge whatsoever in that regard.

However, he did have one advantage over the Service: he didn't have to obey the law; he didn't have to report to anyone. Not a soul. His intuition was telling him to take a look at Gibraltar, after all.

The bank in Gibraltar was called PPB, and its reputation was not entirely unblemished. According to a website bursting with conspiracy theories, PPB – apparently it stood for Plutus Private Bank – was one of the banks that the Calabrian mafia known as 'Ndrangheta used for money laundering purposes. Regardless of how truthful this was, it was a company permeated by secrecy, with tax evasion at the core of its very business concept. By definition, they didn't take chances. Berger worked slowly but surely on finding a number of bank employees and starting a bigger search – with a little luck, he'd turn something up.

He was free, bold, wild and needed nothing more than his little finger. While the search ran, he got up to stretch. He creaked rather worryingly. He had begun to stiffen up, but neither the weather nor the geography encouraged physical activity. He had walked around the island – a circuit of barely a kilometre that could not be run without breaking a leg. It would have to be a whisky instead. To his great but not entirely unmixed joy, there was a twelve-year-old Highland Park in the house. The discomfort at the fact that August Steen completely had his number was temporarily drowned out by the pure exultation of tasting it.

On the way back to the desk, it occurred to him quite how much of an obstacle course the half-unpacked boxes were. He had to remedy the matter – at any rate he had to filter out the unimportant things.

After all, those were the ruins of his life lying there, getting in the way.

When he returned to the computer, a little finger was beckoning from the screen.

Berger grasped it, certain he would be able to get the whole hand. A married middle manager at PPB appeared on a dating site, well concealed but revealed thanks to the decoding systems of the Security Service and FRA. In a conversation between two women, one expressly warned the other about this man, whose alias 'Makarenkov' was telling in itself. And promising. Valery Makarenkov was the world's most prolific documented rapist, who had celebrated every birthday by raping women and girls. The choice of this man's surname as an alias said a lot.

The two women's messages couldn't have made things much worse – it was clear that the middle manager was among the growing band of men who thought sexual harassment online was perfectly natural. His entire hand was ripe for the picking.

As Berger contemplated what kind of profile would convince

Makarenkov that he was desperate enough to contact both the man's wife and bank executives, his computer chimed. He switched windows and found Carsten staring at him from the display through his thick lenses.

Berger recoiled. It actually took him a couple of seconds to realise that it was just a photograph. He had finally found the mole in the very deepest and darkest corners of the Security Service.

Carsten's last name was apparently Boylan, and it said he'd been born in August 1974 in Stockholm. Unfortunately, almost all other information was conspicuous by its absence, and a quick google of the name turned up nothing. There was, however, a basic CV on record with the Security Service.

Carsten Boylan had been hired by the Service thirteen years earlier. After three years of what appeared to be regular desk duties – but presumably had been nothing of the sort – Carsten had been granted six months' leave and had then slowly but surely worked his way towards the inner circle, rising through the ranks while under the protection of August Steen.

There was no sign of any revelation that Carsten was a mole in the organisation.

Berger stared at the screen. The CV's seemingly deliberate thinness told its own tale. Carsten had by all appearances been thrown in at the deep end – three rough years that had probably ended with some kind of burnout, followed by six months' recovery. Then his career had gone like clockwork. First the years of drudgery, progressing through the baptism of fire, and then his reward.

It still wasn't enough information – not enough for any purpose. Berger hadn't got even a step closer to Carsten.

Without any great hope, he started a search that combined the names Carsten Boylan, Sven Johansson and Johan Svensson in various ways. Then he examined one thought a little further.

Why Tensta? Was there a connection? Childhood origins? 'Born in Stockholm' was Security Service lingo for anonymity, untraceability, and he could just as well be from Tensta as he could from Örkelljunga. There was no social security number, no hit in the population register, no address details. Carsten's life before joining the Service had been eradicated, and his life in the Service had been diluted to the point of meaninglessness. Nevertheless, Boylan was a pretty unusual name – there couldn't be many of them in Sweden. Would it be possible to track down a relative? Tensta in the seventies, an American or British immigrant family . . . even back then they wouldn't have been typical Tensta residents. But on the other hand they wouldn't have been remarkably atypical. In the shadow of various floods of refugees, English-speaking immigrants had always constituted a majority in Sweden. Berger couldn't get to grips with it – there was nothing to get his teeth into. He made a note of the few Boylans in Sweden and peered at the corner of the desk. It was where the untraceable satellite phone was – the one that belonged to a completely different life.

Which would be more stimulating? Calling a few scattered Boylans already weary of December – which the Security Service would surely already have done – or dialling the country code +350?

It was an easy choice – he had already entered the digits. A slightly out of breath man answered.

'Corby.'

Berger addressed him in English.

'Is that Roger Corby in Gibraltar?'

'Can this wait? I'm at the gym.'

'Strength Factory, I take it?' said Berger.

There was silence on the line. Then Roger Corby replied: 'Who's calling?'

'In principle, it could very well be serial rapist Valery Makarenkov himself. If he had permission to make phone calls from Petak Prison.'

The same silence, but more intense this time.

'I'm hanging up.'

'That would be a mistake,' said Berger. 'I'm looking at the full "Makarenkov" thread from the dating site All Heart right now. Including sound evidence that the person behind the alias is a married father of young children by the name of Roger Corby.'

Another silence. There was breathing to indicate that no reply was forthcoming.

'The person behind the alias "Lovebird", on the other hand, is my sister,' Berger continued. 'Would you like me to read out what you've written to my beloved little sister?'

'What do you want?' Corby said hoarsely.

'There's one, and only one, way that you can prevent this from reaching your wife and your bosses. Is that understood?'

'Yes,' Corby said, still hoarse, but more distinct now.

'Good. I'll call again tomorrow at 1600 hours. When I do, I want all the information you have on one Sven Johansson at a Gibraltar-registered company by the name of Big Exit Ltd, which is responsible for paying the bills for a shed on the roof of a block of flats in a Stockholm suburb called Tensta.'

'That might be tricky,' said Corby.

'Compare that with how tricky life might otherwise become for you,' Berger said before hanging up.

He looked at the satellite phone.

If there was one thing he hated, it was extortion, and the mere thought of leaking something to a betrayed partner was inherently alien to him. *Blabbing* was simply not the done thing – it wasn't in the realm of humanity.

It was in the realm of the devil.

He consoled himself with the thought that Corby had behaved badly – not to mention criminally – towards at least one woman, and that he ought to be in jail. The question was whether he was going to let the bastard off. It was not without some self-contempt that he pushed the phone away and met the gaze of fifteen-year-old Aisha Pachachi. For a fleeting moment, he thought she was nodding her silent assent.

However, it did little to drive away the restlessness that self-contempt so easily brought with it. The sleet outside the window had intensified again – outdoors felt even more claustrophobic than inside. It would have to be the moving boxes.

He went over to them and heard his own groan – it had the same sense of unfamiliarity that being woken by one's own snoring did. It looked like the moving boxes had exploded as a result of pressure within. He sorted through the remains for a while before spotting something that captured his interest. Earlier, it had mostly been a source of irritation – why the fuck did the Security Service bring old school yearbooks from his closet and think they mattered to him any more? But now the memory of the scene from the football pitch had given them a new, piercingly sharp focus. He grabbed them, refilled his whisky glass and threw himself onto the undeniably comfy sofa. Highland Park worked on his soft palate while he navigated his way through an archipelago he hadn't even seen in more than twenty years.

The yearbooks were from the Helenelund school in Sollentuna for the years 1991 and 1993. He put aside the former, when he had been in seventh grade, and focused on the one from ninth grade. That was when William Larsson had joined Sam Berger's class. He wondered if William was in the class photo. He had no memory of it.

He leafed through. He couldn't find his class – perhaps because he genuinely overlooked it, or perhaps because subconsciously he didn't want to find it. But eventually there it was. When he let his gaze drift towards the top left corner all other memories were blotted out. No memories except the angular, gnarled face that inevitably drew attention from the rest of the class. The chin was completely askew, a horn-like bulge stuck out of the side of his brow, and the right cheekbone was angled upwards while the left pointed down.

If looks could kill . . .

It was early summer again. The air thick with dust, the sun sharp and piercing. William hanging by the goalpost, the big man moving towards the bloodied figure. Fifteen-year-old Sam, sitting at a distance wiping his tears with a handkerchief tasting of William's blood, sees it all again – in flashes, him raising the towel and whipping, the girls' giggles fading, even the worst bully Anton disappearing, and eventually it being just Sam there alone with William's bloodied genitals bared for all to see. He whipped William because he saw a monstrous piece of clock-work, and the pain shot arrows across the decades, arrows that caught the convolutions of his brain and were sent to every nook, every cranny, every centimetre of his head, making his whole brain crackle with electricity until he had to turn back several pages.

Berger stares at the class photo without really seeing it. All the same, he can tell they're visibly younger, not by much, but it is palpable. An eighth-grade class – no deviation here. No one with edges, gnarls or horns on their face – just regular faces from the Swedish suburbs. Thirteen- and fourteen-year-olds. It's a comfort to sweep across this bafflingly homogeneous crowd of children on the brink of adulthood, his gaze caught by a face – a girl's face – and the wheels turn, and he sees her stuck there, he sees William in the background, and he realises that the Molly standing there with silver tape over her mouth is the same Molly that is now carrying his child, and he is completely captivated by her pure smile.

Molly.

The beginning of term. Her gaze should be clear and pure and unblemished, but there is something equivocal about it. Regardless, the resemblance is very clear, very like now, and while she might be in a coma and might be dying, Sam Berger can see unambiguously what his child will look like. He can see it with great clarity. And his eye is drawn down to the list of names below the class photo, and he sees the name Molly. It's there, for all to see. And his eye lingers because he doesn't want to read on, because something about what comes next is wrong. His still tender brain has decided not to read the rest, because it doesn't make sense.

It doesn't say Blom after Molly.

There's a different last name.

It says Steen.

It says Molly Steen.

# 17

The dead were all around her in the darkness, a silent but powerful presence. They were getting closer and closer – all that kept them at bay was the small, small light. As soon as its beam turned away, the distance between her and death shrank. And she couldn't shine the beam in every direction simultaneously. She felt the rotting, ice-cold breath of the dead getting ever closer to her face.

Come on, sober up. Get a grip. Calm down.

Molly Blom was walking through a cemetery. All that stood out in the darkness was the faint glow of her torch. The graves were fairly new, while the church was not in the slightest. When the torchlight swept across the facade, the tower didn't have a spire but was instead topped by a regular sloping roof. The stone facade was rough and crude. When she lowered the torch back towards the graves the full mass of the ancient church withdrew back into the expansive darkness.

She stood there for a while. Settled her breathing to a reasonable rhythm. Surveyed the tombstones. Ashes to ashes, dust to dust. Life. A brief, brief period on earth, a wildly darting will-o'-the-wisp that glimmers and then ceases to be.

But one which ought to be left to burn itself out in peace.

She closed her eyes. It made no great difference.

Then she meandered on through the small cemetery. She reached a church door that appeared to have been there since the beginning of time. She knew – given the many acts of criminality against church buildings these days – that the door ought to be locked, barred, hermetically sealed. She realised that it wouldn't be. She gripped the icy handle firmly and opened the door.

It opened into a darkness that was not absolute. A faint shimmer was discernible over what she thought might be known as the chancel where the pulpit, more deeply shrouded in darkness, rose up.

Molly Blom moved slowly forward through this longship. She saw the faint light but not its source; she saw the inner contours of the church fading away the higher up she looked. She saw nothing else. And then, only five or six pews ahead, she caught sight of something, a little to the left, where the light barely reached. The back of a male, slightly greying head. It was barely perceptible, and it was implacably still. Blom reduced her tempo, more tiptoeing than walking. Nevertheless, she checked herself.

A calm male voice spoke: 'Stop. Enter that row.'

She slipped along the pew in the row behind the man. She was stopped again a couple of seats away. She sank down onto the bench, studying the back of the head in front of her. The man was still sitting completely still.

'Meeting in a church?' said Molly Blom. 'Seriously?'

'I got the impression that you might need it,' the calm male voice said.

'The cliché?' said Blom.

'The church,' said the man. 'The serenity.'

He turned round briefly. All she made out in the darkness were his eyes – a neutral gaze without a face.

'The grace,' he said, turning back again.

Something compelled Blom's own gaze towards the suffering figure of Christ with his outstretched arms, crooked legs, blood pouring, face a picture of universal anguish. The crown of thorns. Perhaps grace really was what she needed.

The man continued:

'Herrestad is the oldest church in Sweden. Early Middle Ages – it almost crosses over into the Viking Age. The beams up in the roof have been dated to the year 1112 – that was long before the founding of Stockholm. Early Romanesque style, smooth limestone walls, an unadorned astringency. Perhaps this is the prototype for the soul of the Swedish people. Austere and barren. Dutiful.'

Blom leaned back and tried to allow the nine hundred years of holiness to envelop her. It wasn't really working.

'What do you want?' she asked.

'What do *you* want?' he replied.

Silence returned to the ancient church. Well, what did Molly Blom want? For this bloody place to make use of all its stored time and recast it a little – for it to become a time machine. For her to emerge in Sollentuna in 1978. To hear the adoption case-worker say:

*I'm afraid you're not suitable candidates to adopt a child.*

The man turned round again but he was still just a pair of eyes. Perhaps there was a warmth of sorts in the gaze this time, perhaps it was just in her imagination. In her wishes.

'Patricide isn't easy,' he said, turning away.

She closed her eyes.

August Steen. Not just her mentor.

Much more than her mentor.

It was as if the man were allowing the pain out. Just as it began to dissipate, he spoke again.

'This church is you, Molly Blom. It is filled with so many different eras, so many roles and disguises. Dolled up over the years, but in essence austere and barren. Dutiful.'

The man took a deep breath.

'You also know that it was necessary, Molly. They needed to see the body – it was a matter of extreme urgency, and we made it. The situation is under control. Thanks to you, we made it. The body has been dealt with and presented. On time.'

'Is that what you came to say?' Blom said in a stifled voice.

'I came to check on you,' the man said calmly. 'Patricide isn't easy, like I said. But if you were able to make your way out to the middle of nowhere, to this old, desolate farm community between Lakes Vättern and Tåkern, then presumably you're okay. Are you okay, Molly?'

'I'm okay,' Blom muttered.

'How were you able to wake up so quickly?'

Molly Blom blinked in the low light. It flickered for the first time. The man had presumably lit one or two candles somewhere to the rear of the pulpit. To make it atmospheric?

Atmospheric?

'What are you talking about?' she hissed.

'You were in a coma. Best case, you were going to wake up in a month or so and slowly claw your way back to life. Walking aids, physical rehab, legs giving way. As recently as the night before, the consulting physician declared your condition to be tragically unaltered. But you defied all the odds and were awake enough to extract yourself from a secure, well-guarded ward in the most resourceful of fashions. Do you have any idea what happened?'

Blom's mind was cast back to the hospital. The sudden wakefulness. As if new blood had been pumped through her veins. The white room, her memory blank, everything just white. A pounding headache, immense thirst, a drip stand, a needle in her arm, surgical tape. The door ajar, the contours of a trolley outside in the corridor, a bare white foot protruding from the folds of the sheet. Trying to understand the situation in that context. Trying to form a plan of action. Realising the situation without remembering. Understanding, the result of extensive professional training that was perhaps more akin to brainwashing. Yanking out the needle, gathering her strength, swapping places with the corpse in a state of grave dizziness, leaving the corpse on the toilet. Reading the security guard's records from under the sheet. Happening to touch somebody with her hand while in the lift. Being conveyed through hospital corridors. A mortuary, other trolleys, just one of the dead among many. Waiting, looking for an opportunity. But the trolley was constantly watched. Time seemed to escape from her, as if she were slowly but surely realising she had ended up in the right place. In the mortuary. All of a sudden, the two men disappeared and she was alone in the corridor, almost naked, wearing just thin hospital clothes. She emerged into a rear courtyard, found some steps, staggered down them, managed to pull herself together on the way to the bus. A number 3. She walked slowly, trying to look sober and with her wits about her, as best she could while wearing a hospital gown and no shoes. She begged and pleaded with the bus driver, who eventually let her on. She headed for the back and saw a woman getting closer and closer to the back of the bus. Saw her running closer. Heard the bus set off, felt it pull away, saw the woman get even closer. Shouting. Screaming. But the bus driver just sped up.

It was when her gaze met the big hazel eyes looking at her that Molly Blom returned to reality. When she realised that Deer was chasing her.

Although the entire memory sequence was really just there to conceal another one, from a dark cellar.

Always fucking cellars.

She shivered.

'Isn't every time we wake up a miracle of sorts?'

The man shrugged and replied calmly: 'Perhaps. Disconnected synapses that manage to reconnect the right way like magic. I know what you mean. But I still think it went a little too fast.'

'Thanks,' Molly Blom said morosely.

The man nodded slowly.

'If you're sure you're okay then we can move on. I realise this hasn't been easy for you, Molly.'

She said nothing. There was nothing to say.

Easy? No, it hadn't been easy.

She laughed. When the echo bounced back from the ancient church walls, it no longer sounded like a laugh.

'I asked you what you want,' the man said quietly. 'But I already know what you want.'

'For the last six weeks to be nothing but a fucking nightmare.'

'Ah, wishes and dreams.'

'Well, what do you think?'

'I think you want to find Sam Berger,' said the man.

Molly Blom fell silent. Her eyes swept past the faint light and deep into the darkness. Her gaze remained there for so long that she actually shuddered with astonishment when she realised the man had turned again and was looking at her. He had that most unusual of things – a black eye. Behind the bruising, his gaze was focused. But also warm.

'Why don't you find him yourself?' she replied.

'Who says I haven't?'

'Why haven't you brought him in then?'

'Are you sure you're okay?'

'What are you getting at?'

'If you were okay then you would know that I can't bring anyone in. I don't have any operational capacity. I have to draw on undercover operatives for that. And in that context, there's no one better than you, Molly.'

'Was that a compliment?'

'Beauty lies in the eye of the beholder,' the man said, turning away.

Herrestad church seemed to envelop her – its entire dark, medieval history pressing itself close to Molly Blom, like tubing around a cable. She inhaled and ate humble pie.

'So is it true that you've found him?'

# 18

Once upon a time, Deer had been good at this. This very thing.
She wasn't altogether certain she still had the skill to draw upon,
but she tried anyway.

The young man spoke.

'Are you sure it was today?'

'Absolutely sure,' Deer said. 'At nine fifteen.'

The young man glanced yet again at the brand-new clock on
the wall.

'There's still a couple of minutes to go.'

'But surely he's here?' Deer said with all the indignation she
could muster. 'The Head of Security Intelligence helped me to
find the right place. He knows what I'm talking about.'

The young man brandished the receiver at her, a ringing
sound audible.

'And I've been trying to get hold of Jonas for a couple of minutes. I really will need you to take a seat.'

'What exactly is the difference between the Security Intelligence Department and the Intelligence Unit?'

'You sure you're definitely a police officer?' the young man
asked, scrutinising her ID again.

'Superintendent Desiré Rosenkvist from the National Operations Department. NOA. It's right there in front of you. Are you definitely August Steen's private secretary?'

'Because if you were a police officer,' said the young man a little more tersely, 'you'd be aware of the difference between the Security Intelligence Department and the Intelligence Unit.'

'Like the fact that the head of unit, Mr Steen, has an office in police headquarters on Polhemsgatan even though the National Police Board and the Security Service are two completely different organisations these days?'

The young man blinked at her a couple of times.

'It's a relatively recent distinction. The move is a work-in-progress that has been taking place in phases. We'll soon have all the central elements of the Security Service with us here in Solna.'

Deer looked out of the window and saw railway tracks. Railway tracks and industrial buildings. She refrained from commenting. Instead, she stuck to her guns.

'Isn't the distinction that the "Intelligence Unit" simply doesn't exist? August Steen is going around telling everyone that he's Head of the Security Service Intelligence Unit, when there is no such thing.'

'It's a specialist unit,' the private secretary muttered.

'It's a quarter past,' Deer said, pointing.

'You're not in the diary – I need to get it confirmed.'

'And how's that going?' Deer asked, turning her index finger from the clock to the receiver.

The young man blinked again before hanging up.

'I'm trying to track Jonas down. In the meantime, take a seat. *Please.*'

Deer held out her hands in placation and ambled slowly towards the visitor sofas in the antechamber to August Steen's office at the Security Service's new digs in Solna. Her gaze did not leave the crack of the open door to the inner sanctum. With a little luck, the private secretary would get worked up enough to leave it unattended.

It was just as obvious that August Steen was not present as it was that there was something stressing the young man out to a disproportionate extent. She wondered what it was.

The private secretary departed, closing the door behind him. Deer opened it again to leave a small crack that would let in sound. Then she got to work.

Breaking into the office of a high-ranking Security Service officer was about the craziest thing a police detective who had recently been grilled by Internal Affairs could do. But she saw no alternative. The more she puzzled her way around it, the clearer it became that the Security Service had stashed Berger away in some safe house, and the only people who had been in contact with Berger and Blom of late had been August Steen and his men. What were their names again?

Deer had met a twosome called Kent and Roy, and she and Berger had been guided by someone called Carsten who had worked remotely to help them find the serial killer up north in the interior. Perhaps there was some trace of them in Steen's office.

Of course it might be alarmed. Of course there might be CCTV cameras following her every step. Of course there was a risk she wouldn't make it more than a metre or two into the office before the klaxon sounded and armed guards swarmed in.

August Steen's office was spacious but pared down. There was no superfluous paraphernalia, no bragging and no aesthetics. No doubt about it, it was bordering on a parody of masculinity. The expansive desk was a shade of green reminiscent of a well-kept football pitch, a computer standing in the centre as if it were a big screen for close-ups and replays. Adjacent to the desk was a wide, almost empty bookcase. On the side of this item of furniture was where the only adornment to the walls of the room was to be found. It appeared to be a very basic rota, with names and phone numbers added in pencil. Deer pulled out her mobile and snapped it. There were a few Post-its stuck around the sheet with indistinct notes scrawled on them. She photographed them too.

Then she looked at the computer and realised that she would have no chance of doing anything worthwhile with that, so instead she set about the desk. There were documents in practically every drawer, crumpled, stuffed in – possibly ignored, put away as quickly as possible. It was vital she make an extremely rapid yet well-chosen selection. She rifled through sheets of paper, stopping occasionally to listen, finding nothing useful – local updates, dreary memos, mobile phone bills, credit card statements, nothing out of the ordinary.

There were faint sounds coming from the corridor. In the distance there was a woman's laugh. Deer stopped while clutching a sheaf of papers, assessing. The man had gone to fetch another man, which ought not to involve a woman's voice, certainly not a laughing one. She took a chance and kept digging, eventually spreading out as many of the sheets of paper on the floor as she dared, and began taking photos. In the middle of the shoot, she heard the woman's voice again, this time so close that its source seemed to be right behind her. She froze. The voice said something about a bastard who'd groped her in the break area, then it grew fainter and fainter again.

Deer carried on, taking as many photos as she could. She photographed the rest of the office and began to return the sheets of paper, trying to remember their original order. Then she heard new sounds out in the corridor.

A little too close.

Footsteps, that was all. Two sets of footsteps.

With silent freneticism, she chucked everything into the desk drawers, closed the last one, surveyed it all. When she was relatively certain that everything looked as it had done when she'd entered, she put away her mobile and lunged for the door. She spotted a shadow out in the corridor through the crack in the door and just managed to throw herself onto the sofa, almost certain that the blatantly false smile on her lips gave an impression that was equal parts hopeful and courteous.

The private secretary was almost completely concealed by a burly, authoritative man in his prime. Deer stood up and proffered her hand. The man didn't take it.

'No, we've never met before.'

Deer lowered her hand and hoped that her face conveyed that she was confused rather than wounded.

'But . . .' she said.

*Now* the man proffered his own hand.

'Jonas Andersson, Head of the Security Intelligence Department and operational lead here at the Security Service. Superintendent Rosenkvist claims that *I* showed her in?'

'I thought that it was –'

'It was most definitely not,' Jonas Andersson interrupted. 'On the other hand, I am the man who will show you *out* of the building.'

He opened the door wide and gestured at Deer. She exited, Andersson slammed the door in the private secretary's face and began to make for the way out.

'Steen's not here today,' he said. 'Why did you want to see him?'

'I was hoping he might help me iron out a few question marks.'

'And so you lied about having an appointment? Why?'

'I didn't lie. I spoke to him just a couple of days ago. Very briefly.'

'And what question marks might these be?'

Deer paused for effect.

'Do you know who I am?'

Jonas Andersson contemplated her for the first time and then replied: 'Yes. The case in the interior. The serial killer. Good job.'

'With a little help from you lot, yes,' said Deer. 'Albeit that help was rather unclear. I need to know more.'

'Why?' asked Andersson.

'Professional curiosity isn't a good enough reason?'

'Most definitely not. Who showed you the way to Steen's office?'

'I thought it was you. He looked like you.'

'Hmm.'

They descended the same stairs that Deer had climbed a few minutes earlier. She had sat in the car outside and waited until someone professional-looking had appeared, then she had joined him, initiated conversation, made her way through reception with his assistance and been pointed in the right direction. Indeed, she confessed to herself, that might be thought of as using her feminine wiles. But there had to be some damn advantage to being a woman.

Reception again, then out the glass doors. Jonas Andersson proffered his hand again, but just as she was going to take it and say goodbye, he turned it ninety degrees. The palm of his hand facing up, urgent.

She looked at him in surprise. Although she looked more surprised than she felt. This wasn't wholly unexpected.

'Your mobile phone, please,' said the Security Service operational lead in a calm voice.

'What?' Deer exclaimed indignantly.

'You can wait while our people go through it – it should be ready in a couple of hours. Or I can have it sent over by courier when we're done. I'm also going to have a long chat with our receptionist and review the CCTV cameras in the foyer. There are a couple of well-trained heads that might roll as a result of your little trick. Your mobile.'

Deer groaned. Then she stuck her hand inside her winter coat and pulled the mobile out from her inside pocket. Jonas Andersson took it and nodded.

'I'll send it over by courier.'

She tried to conceal her lameness as she went down the steps into the car park. She found her car and unlocked it with a beep. Then she drove off. Her foot hurt.

She headed onto the E4 motorway briefly, exited at Hornsberg and pulled onto a side street off Lindhagensgatan, stopping as soon as she could. Then she bent down, removed her right trainer and prised out something that had been pressed into her arch for a little too long.

Her other mobile phone.

She only hoped she hadn't broken it.

# 19

Berger was sitting on the jetty, his legs dangling. It was at last possible to go outdoors again, and that was what he needed. To breathe fresh air. To oxygenate his brain. To combat the claustrophobia with order.

He stared out at the endless water, already able to make out the approach of twilight. Four small islets broke the line of the horizon, otherwise there was nothing but open sea. There was no wind, no rain, and the temperature couldn't make up its mind which side of freezing it wanted to be. In places, ice was forming, elsewhere it was melting, and he realised how few of the laws of physics he understood.

Physics? Well, surely how few of the laws of *life* he understood. How little he understood about anything. About this case. About Carsten. About Molly.

About Molly Steen.

August Steen's past was even more inaccessible than Carsten's – there was no chance of ascertaining whether Molly's original surname even had any connection with August Steen. It was hardly the most uncommon name in Sweden – around two thousand people in the country were called Steen with two e's, including at least ten or more in Sollentuna in the eighties and nineties. It didn't have to mean anything.

It didn't have to mean that the Head of the Intelligence Unit at the Security Service was Molly Blom's father.

But it seemed pretty bloody likely.

It didn't have to mean that she'd changed her name when she'd been recruited by the Service – she could have changed her name any time. It didn't have to have been as an adult. It could have been at any time after eighth grade, when she'd vanished from Berger's sight.

But it might also be the result of marriage.

He had searches running for both names. Berger was sick to the back teeth of all these searches.

He couldn't find her in sixth form, or after that either. That was not particularly strange. She had become an undercover agent with the Security Service – of course they'd erased everything they could find about her past. Anyway, it was all from a time before widespread digitisation; things simply weren't online. Unless you found some unusual routes to it – and that often took time.

Hadn't Molly said she'd been to drama school?

He tried to recollect the moment she'd said it – it hadn't been long ago – and what she'd actually said. And how. 'I'm a year younger than you, and I became a police officer two years before you did, and by then I already had an acting career behind me. While you were bumming about South East Asia and taking random courses at university.'

There were lots of places to study acting in Sweden – not to mention abroad – but surely the utterance that had suddenly sprung to mind suggested a *proper* drama school? In that case there was only one in Sweden.

Berger let his eyes wander towards the horizon. There was

nothing to see there apart from the Baltic's deepest trough, and there was truly nothing to be seen of the Landsort Deep; the fleeting sense of hidden depths that grazed against his consciousness came from within. He made his way back into the cottage, ploughed through the increasingly scattered contents of the boxes and began to google drama schools. It was not an entirely straightforward process.

Molly Steen had been born in 1978, and if she had become a police officer two years before Sam Berger then that would have been in 2003. If she'd done a three-year course in acting before that, she must have started no later than the turn of the millennium. In 2000, Molly had just turned twenty-two. How long did she give her acting career?

He searched for various terms: stage school, the Royal Dramatic Training Academy, theatre college, theatre training, acting training. He was running parallel searches. If there had been anything on Molly Blom or Molly Steen, it should have cropped up in the ongoing search by now.

It was becoming clear that the past of each newly hired undercover agent was erased as soon as they took up their job. If he was to circumvent the efforts of the Security Service IT Department, he would doubtless need to try more ingenious searches. And Berger wasn't sure he was among those people regarded as ingenious.

He was more of a champion, and this champion wasn't going to give up. Not yet.

It was on page 42 of his Google Image search that an old photo appeared. The first year at the National Academy of Dramatic Arts in Stockholm, taken in the months before the turn of the millennium. Among a group of around ten people, a blonde woman in the top row on the far right stood out. It was most definitely a young Molly Blom.

Although perhaps it wasn't. Perhaps it was a young Molly Steen.

Berger tried to click through to the website the photo was hosted on, but that didn't work. He ended up on a page saying it could not be found. There was no caption, no higher-resolution image, just the small thumbprint image available via Google. He initiated a facial recognition scan while at the same time focusing on the faces in the happy-looking acting class as best he could. He didn't recognise anyone. He launched more searches without quite knowing what he was looking for. The Academy of Dramatic Arts, 1999, actors, registered students, every combination he could think of in a true mishmash.

He scanned the nondescript searches page by page. He found a student roll. The year group who had enrolled in '99 had rather recklessly staged a production of *Hamlet* just under a year later. According to the reviewer from *DN*, Ophelia had been played as 'very brittle' by one Molly Sten. One e. There was even a picture – albeit in grainy low resolution. But it was definitely her. The blonde hair was much longer back then, and fanned across the stage as if in a flood of water. As Ophelia, Molly Blom was a natural star on that small stage.

Albeit a dead one.

Berger clicked a couple of random links elsewhere and ended up on a site with amateur photos of documents. Among these was a blurred overview of graduating students from the Academy of Dramatic Arts in 2002. Berger zoomed in, trying to read, fuming that he was unable to get directly to what was now the Stockholm University of the Arts at Vallhallavägen. But that kind of police work was confined to his past. Now it was a case of using super-slick skills, zooming in, trying to make out text in barely legible, terribly photographed documents.

After a great deal of difficulty, he managed to find what he was looking for. Molly Blom was among the actors to graduate in the summer of 2002. Not Molly Steen, whether with one e or two.

Okay. The person admitted to the institution had been Molly Steen. The one who had graduated had been Molly Blom. At some point during her drama-school days, between 2000 and 2002, she had changed her name. When? Where? How? Surely the most likely cause was marriage? Had she really got married as a young and promising thespian?

He was uncertain how advanced the digitisation of whole newspapers from 1999 to 2002 was. He managed to access the archive containing the country's biggest dailies, and started a search for old classifieds and wedding announcements. He saw them scroll past, one after the other, losing himself in their progress. He barely noticed when the screen changed to something else completely.

A barren coastline. A feeble but clear light, two islets on the horizon. A stony beach some twenty metres in length in front of the dark, rippling water where no ice had formed. There was a number 5 glowing in the corner.

Camera 5.

Berger recognised it. The seabirds. But right now he could see no signs of winged creatures.

Camera 5 was the one located furthest away on the far side of the island. He watched the image – darkness had begun to fall, the gentle wind lapping the surface of the water intermittently – and there was no way of telling what had triggered the alert. Probably a bird that had already made its getaway. The question was whether he dared take the risk of presuming that.

He opened the top desk drawer and pulled out his Security Service pistol. He checked the ammunition, removed the safety, put it back and left the drawer open. Then he surveyed the strip of coast again – there was nothing to be seen. Not any more, at any rate.

He changed windows on the computer and inspected his searches. They continued unabated. There was nothing to see there either.

Then it happened again.

The screen was replaced with a view that Berger hadn't seen before. In the top corner there was a 3. CCTV camera 3. In the early twilight, the camera mostly showed trees, but he couldn't make out where it was located – he had to find the map on the desk. Camera 3 was the middle camera in the centre of the island, perhaps some three hundred metres away. And there was nothing to be seen – the breeze was making the odd branch tremble, no more.

Two alerts in quick succession, closer and closer to the cottage. Not further out to sea – so probably not seabirds like before.

But it might also be a coincidence.

He grabbed the gun with one hand just as something came up in one of his searches. He saw it vaguely behind the unassuming CCTV footage, and he quickly swapped windows. It was a hit – a classified ad on microfiche from *Upsala Nya Tidning*. It was a very rudimentary text that had been abbreviated – clearly with the intent of making it as cheap as possible. It appeared under the heading 'Married'.

'C. Blom & M. Steen. 4 Nov 2000.'

Berger didn't have time – he really didn't have time. If there was an intruder out there then the individual in question was much too close. Nevertheless, he began to redirect his other newspaper searches to focus on 4 November in the year 2000.

Then he set off.

It was bare and grey outside; twilight was well under way. He looked around, aiming the weapon in every direction. Apart from the twilight growing ever darker, there was nothing to see out there. Nothing at all. He returned inside, closing the door behind him, and stood a little lamely next to the wine racks just by the doorway to the big living room. In the distance he saw the computer change screen again with a peculiar slowness.

To camera 1.

Where he had just been.

He lunged back towards the door, yanked it open, took aim, made out movement behind a dense copse of trees just five metres away. He had nothing to lose.

He fired.

Fired without asking questions, without any warning. Twice. Three times. The trees shuddered.

He went over, his weapon raised. The gun was trembling in his hand.

The silence following the gunshots was deafening. But he could hear something. Something that made the bleak tree branches sway. A body fell slowly down through the branches of a pine.

It fell towards him.

He shot the body again as it fell, heading for the ground. Only once it was lying there, stone dead, did he see that it wasn't a body. He got closer and quickly inspected it. It was a sack – a jute sack filled with grass and stones. It had been set on a rock and had slowly started to slide off. That was the movement that Berger had seen.

And then he'd shot the sack.

For two seconds he stood there completely paralysed. Then he turned back to the cottage. Twilight was fully upon the island.

The door was closed.

He hadn't shut it.

He staggered back to it. The gun was trembling ceaselessly.

When he reached the door, he grasped the handle and slowly opened it. There was a draught from inside the house – a cold draught that seemed to want to shut the door. He held on, thinking for a second, trying to be as ice cold as the draught itself.

Then he wrenched open the door and lunged passed the wine racks, emerging into the big living room with his weapon more than ready to fire.

The tiniest of instincts curtailed his trigger finger – the slightest impression held him back from shooting the figure sitting on his desk chair, shooting them in cold blood as they studied the monitor of his laptop. The figure turned round.

Patches of blonde had begun to make their way through the brown pageboy haircut.

'You're very trigger-happy all of a sudden,' said Molly Blom.

To his surprise, Berger didn't lower his weapon. He continued to keep it trained on Blom. But he was speechless.

Speechless.

He walked slowly towards her, stumbling a little. All manner of human emotions were coursing through him. The draught made the door to the outside slam loudly behind him.

'I opened the window,' said Blom, gesturing towards the bedroom. 'Rather than smash it.'

He wanted to hug her. He wanted to shoot her.

He wanted to do everything with her.

Except talk. He couldn't do that.

He got closer, finally lowering the pistol. He surveyed her face – it was serious, yet playful.

Playful?

She pointed to the monitor. Her expression was impenetrable.

'You've got a hit,' she said.

Berger stepped closer. He saw a photo on the screen – a

140

wedding photo of two smiling young people. The date was 4 November in the year 2000.

Berger stared at the photo of the newly-weds. It was 'C. Blom' and 'M. Blom' as she was now known. And there was absolutely no doubt that the young woman was Molly Blom. Berger turned his attention to the young man.

Perhaps it was the absence of glasses that meant Berger didn't recognise him straight away.

Perhaps that was why it took a couple of seconds for him to recognise the bridegroom: Carsten Blom.

# 20

'Taste good?' she asked.

'It's downright essential to life,' he replied.

He set aside the beer glass that had contained twelve-year-old Highland Park on the desk and felt his spirits returning to him.

They were sitting side by side in front of the desk. There was too much to be said. It was impossible to know where to begin.

'How did you find me?' he asked, though he didn't really care.

She shrugged.

'Don't forget my past in the Security Service.'

He settled for that. Really, he just needed to say something – anything – that didn't involve August Steen, Molly Steen, Molly Blom, Carsten Blom, Carsten Boylan.

'So you woke up?' he asked.

'Disconnected synapses managed to reconnect themselves properly in a seemingly magical way,' said Molly Blom with a grim smile.

'What?' said Berger.

'I don't know what happened. I woke up. Surprisingly clear-headed. I escaped. I decided to find Sweden's most wanted man. If nothing else, to thank you for what happened up in the interior.'

Berger's entire being seemed to be in a magnetic field. There were two strong poles. On the one hand there was emotional chaos, on the other cold rationality. For a split second, the latter was victorious.

'So you've talked to someone?' he said.

'What?' she said.

'You were unconscious when we found you in the snow. You remained unconscious in the air ambulance, in Falun, at the Southern Hospital. You woke up, you escaped. You not only know that I'm "Sweden's most wanted man", but that I "saved" you up in the interior. That means you've talked to someone since you woke up.'

'And you're not just a trigger-happy hermit on a desert island,' Blom said, smiling wryly.

It was a very attractive smile.

'Who did you talk to?' Berger said as coolly as he could.

'Desiré Rosenkvist,' said Blom. 'She was in your flat.'

'She was *in my flat*?'

'I was there too. We met. She told me.'

'Most of my flat is here,' said Berger, waving his hand towards the chaos reigning in much of the big living room. 'What was Deer doing in my flat?'

'Same thing I was,' said Blom. 'Albeit for different reasons.'

'Looking for me?'

'Yes,' said Blom.

Berger nodded. That would have to do. Once he felt the whisky taking hold of him, he could do likewise. Take hold of it. This.

'Carsten Blom?'

Molly Blom shook her head.

'It's a long story.'

Berger laughed.

'I'm feeling pretty receptive towards a long story.'

Blom laughed too and turned towards the computer. When it awoke from darkness, she minimised the picture of the happy couple with distaste.

'What do you want to know?'

'Everything!' Berger exclaimed. 'You've been in a coma, so if you've only spoken to Deer then you don't know that Carsten . . .'

'What?' said Blom.

Berger gave the single malt another few seconds to do its work, trying to get his thoughts in order.

'Okay. I've managed to work out that he's called Carsten Boylan. Not Carsten Blom. And you're Molly Steen, not Molly Blom.'

'I'm Molly Blom,' Blom said quietly. 'Blom by marriage.'

'But Carsten's called Boylan.'

'It was a young marriage. Neither of us was ready for it. We separated after three months. I kept the name Blom, but he changed his. But why would you be investigating Carsten? He's Security Service.'

'He was. And he helped to find you up in the interior. But carry on. You got married and then divorced right away?'

'Wait a second,' said Blom. 'He *was* Security Service? Since when hasn't he been?'

'Since he murdered the person who was planning to torture you to death and framed me for the deed.'

Berger thought he saw her get paler.

'Not Carsten,' she said in a faint voice.

'Yes,' Berger replied sharply. 'Very much Carsten.'

'But I saw him. The day before yesterday. He helped me to get hold of a weapon.'

Berger stopped himself and stared at her.

'You saw him *the day before yesterday*?' he said. 'The whole of the fucking Service is on the hunt for him. Full-time. No one knows where he is. He's wanted. And you *saw him*? Where the fuck did you see him?'

'In our old flat on Eolsgatan. I called him, he came there and handed over the gun. That was it. But even if it's true – why is the whole Service hunting him down just for one murder? Shouldn't the regular cops be handling that?'

'It's much worse than that,' Berger said, looking at her. 'We'll come back to it. How did you meet?'

Blom met his gaze, then turned away and shrugged.

'Some party somewhere. I don't remember. I was young – an aspiring actress, trying to erase the darkness of the past. I partied a lot. Carsten was there. He was at circus school. New circus. It might even have been Cirkus Cirkör. He was a hotshot when it came to climbing ropes and picking locks. An acrobat, an escape artist, a juggler, that kind of thing.'

'And that appealed to you?'

'Not particularly. But we had something else in common. The mutual literary idol of our youth. Joyce.'

'Joyce?'

'James Joyce. The writer. You must know him?'

'*Ulysses*,' Berger said to his own surprise.

Blom nodded with a furrowed brow.

'The classic novel published in 1922. The protagonist is called Leopold Bloom. The final chapter consists of his wife Molly's long internal monologue from bed.'

'Molly Bloom?' Berger said sceptically.

'Carsten thought there was something magical about the fact that I loved Joyce too, that I was called Molly Steen – with two e's – and he was called Blom. He talked about signs in the stars, messages from a world that made more sense than ours. If we married then I'd get as close to being Molly Bloom as was possible. He'd be my Leopold.'

'Shit,' said Berger.

'That's how it ended up,' said Blom. 'Shit. We gave each other a run for our money in terms of immaturity. We spent around a month in my flat on Eolsgatan by Riddarfjärden, but then I'd had enough. It was my flat, not his, and we divorced quickly. His revenge after being chucked out was to change his name to Boylan.'

'I don't understand . . .'

'In *Ulysses*, Molly Bloom's lover is called Blazes Boylan. He's a seducer, advertiser, boxing promoter, one of Molly's fellow singers. He crops up here and there in *Ulysses*, not least because Leopold *knows* that Boylan is going to sleep with his wife that very afternoon. Carsten took the name to mess with me. So that he could return as my lover, not my husband. Or so I assume . . .'

'But then the Security Service? Just like you?'

'It was actually Carsten who talked me into it. He got in touch all of a sudden and said that after 9/11 the Service had been searching high and low for undercover agents, and there were no better candidates than actors. I'd already started to lose my thespian convictions and was more interested in law and order.'

'He talked you into the place through your dad? August Steen?'

Blom stopped herself. She glanced at him grimly and said with the utmost clarity:

'He's not my father. It's just a coincidence of names.'

Their eyes met. They read each other.

Eventually Blom carried on.

'Why would Carsten have murdered that wretch and then framed you for it? What's going on?'

'What's going on doesn't actually have anything to do with that,' said Berger, striding over to the whiteboard. 'What's going on is *this*.'

He pointed to the portrait.

'Carsten is holding Aisha Pachachi. Seven minus one. He's the quisling in the Security Service, the one that Steen's been after for years. You know what I'm talking about.'

He watched her with the greatest of care. He saw her confusion, and had she not been Molly Blom he would have taken her in his arms. But right now he was faced with perhaps the sharpest undercover agent at the Security Service, the best actress, the woman who had pulled the wool over his eyes many times before. He laughed.

He thought to himself: *at least you don't know that you're carrying my child.*

What he actually said was:

'Because you must do. You and your ex Carsten both worked for years in immediate proximity to August Steen. You must have seen each other on a daily basis.'

'It doesn't work like that,' Blom muttered.

'How does it work then?'

'August Steen is good at compartmentalising operations. He divides everything up and the walls between those compartments are absolute. I don't know a thing about what Carsten is doing. Don't really know what Steen is up to either.'

'Carsten snatched Aisha from William to prevent her father from revealing when, where and how a terrorist attack is going to take place in Sweden. Your ex-husband is most likely working for Islamic State – the caliphate.'

Even on this occasion he could not determine how authentic her horror was. The question was whether he – if he managed to get out of this whole thing alive – would ever be able to avoid becoming a cynic. If he was to retain any faith whatsoever in genuine truth and sincerity.

When he spoke again, he could feel the distrust looming large in the cottage.

'You don't know a thing about Carsten – the man the whole Service is after – but you found me here, in a location known only to Steen. Something doesn't add up.'

'I'm not going to waste time explaining myself,' Blom said calmly. 'Either you trust me or you don't.'

'How did you find me?' Berger asked emphatically.

She gave him a very pungent look which indicated with the utmost clarity that she was going to say no more on the matter.

'My contact oversees Security Service helicopter sorties.'

Something hot and pervasive coursed through Berger. He pointed back to the photo.

'This is what we need to do. Find Aisha. Save her. Stop Carsten. We have to stop that arsehole at any cost. Our job isn't done.'

'But what are you supposed to be *doing* out here?' Blom asked, gesturing at the living room. 'You're just sitting here; there's not a whiff of your involvement having been sanctioned. Why is Steen keeping you away from the laws of justice? You're not even in the Service – you're an outsider.'

'I'm freelancing,' said Berger. 'That's why I'm here. Freelancing without having any clue what my role is. I'm *waiting*. But that's not enough for me. I've got to do more. I've rigged up your computer kits and I've accessed the Security Service archives. So let's get on with it. In the middle of our pursuit of William, when he'd just moved the seven kidnapped girls from Bålsta to the flat in Helenelund, Carsten found him, took Aisha – and none of the other girls – and made off to Tensta. He'd had a flat there for the last two years in the name of Johan Svensson. He also had a shed up on the roof of the same building – using the alias Sven Johansson through a Gibraltarian company called Big Exit Ltd – and he was keeping bees in it. Carsten baited a trap there for the Service just the other day – he lured us up to the roof, let his bees neutralise a couple of men – one of whom, your old partner Roy, died – and he'd rigged up my old service weapon to fire a shot at what should have been my crotch. My service weapon, which he'd already used to kill your kidnapper up in the interior. Then framed me for it.'

Blom stared at him and paled again. There appeared to be no blood left in her face.

'Carsten killed Roy?' she said slowly. 'I've worked with Kent and Roy for years.'

'With bees,' said Berger. 'With goddamn fucking bees! It's beyond comprehension. I was in the chopper with him after. He was in two pieces, Molly.'

Blom looked up at the ceiling. Berger thought to himself: the pale thing has limits. You can't fake it. No actor can go pale on command. This is for real. She didn't know that Roy was dead.

'And what about Kent?' she said finally, without removing her gaze from the ceiling.

'It looks like he's going to make it,' Berger said. 'But I haven't exactly got a hotline to the hospital.'

'And Carsten planned all this?' she said.

'Down to the smallest detail,' Berger said. 'Two men in the building on the roof. One badly attacked, the other less so. That meant the third could pretty much head on inside to get his cock blown off by his old service weapon.'

'You?'

'I don't think he likes me,' Berger concluded.

'If your cock's been blown off then you're hiding the pain well,' Blom said.

'Thank my lucky stars I crouched just before I opened the rigged drawer. I was wearing a bulletproof vest. I'm indebted to them.'

'The vest?'

'My lucky stars.'

'But how could he have known that you would take part in the raid on the apiary?' Molly Blom asked, a little colour returning to her cheeks.

'I've been grappling with that question,' said Berger. 'That's the only thing about Carsten's mission – the one he's presumably going to make a lot of blood money from – that doesn't make sense. And my conclusion is this: he simply sees me as a rival. It's *you* he wants, Molly. You're the opposite of replaceable. He wants you before he goes blind.'

'James Joyce went blind too,' said Blom with a grimace.

Berger nodded.

'Leopold Bloom hasn't got over his Molly.'

Molly Blom gazed into the darkness. Berger followed her line of sight.

'I think Carsten staged Tensta with pinpoint precision,' he said at last. 'I was to start by interpreting the clues, then open the drawer and have my balls blown off. His main rival castrated. That's not quite how it went.'

'Clues?' said Blom.

'In a small envelope,' Berger said, showing its size with his fingers in the air.

Blom seemed to disappear inside herself for a moment before speaking.

'What clues?'

'Two handwritten messages. One was a Shakespeare quote about bees that actually seems to be about some contract or other that means Carsten isn't a free man. The other was the words "like the Andalusian girls".'

'Oh Jesus,' said Blom.

'Oh Jesus?' said Berger.

'I know the Andalusian girls,' said Blom. 'It's from *Ulysses*. From Molly Bloom's internal monologue. I think I remember a few words of it. "Yes when I put the rose in my hair like the Andalusian girls used or shall I wear a red yes and how he kissed me under the Moorish wall." Something like that.'

'He really *is* talking to you, Molly,' Berger exclaimed, sensing a slight crack in the iciness between them.

'But can it be that convoluted?' Blom said at last. 'And that weird? Can he really be that fixated on me? After all these years?'

'Undoubtedly,' said Berger. 'But somehow, I still think there's more to this. The Andalusian reference isn't just to Joyce and you and your old connection. I think there's a stronger, more immediate tie to Spain and Andalusia. To Gibraltar. What time is it?'

Blom stared at him, blinking, then looked down at the desk. She found Berger's clock drawer, opened it and gestured towards the antique wristwatches.

'You choose.'

Berger picked his own, angling the old Patek Philippe on his wrist until he saw that it was just after four. Four o'clock in the afternoon. And it was already pitch-black outside.

'I've got to make a call,' he said, reaching for the satellite phone and starting the recording.

'Who to?'

Berger didn't reply. Instead he began to enter the dialling code of +350.

# 21

Deer moved ever so slowly out of the bedroom. A chasm-deep snort stopped her and she stood stock-still. The risk that the entire process would have to start again loomed large.

But then the snorting transitioned into abrupt snoring which in turn became the sound of a regular eight-year-old asleep. Deer was able to silently close Lykke's door from the outside.

It had been a struggle disguised as storytime. Who would emerge victorious from this bitter feud? If Mum fell asleep first, then Lykke would put the book to one side, sneak into the living room and start watching some of Liverpool's classic victories on YouTube at a low volume. If Lykke fell asleep first, then Mum would be able to sneak off to her study in the second garage of the terraced house where she would transform evening into night. After dozing off a couple of times and only just managing to catch Lykke at the threshold to the living room, Deer had emerged the winner – against all the odds.

Her husband Johnny worked shifts as an ambulance driver. He was working the back shift rather than the night shift, which meant that he would be home at around ten o'clock – probably knackered as always. And Deer would be able to work on.

Even though she was on leave.

She had been given ten days' paid leave for her work in the interior, but she hadn't told her own husband that. It was as if the double life had seeped into her bloodstream.

Before Deer headed off, she looked around the small terraced house in Skogås on Stockholm's outskirts. This was the flipside of the coin. Life – real life. The question was whether she had any chance of finding her way back to it.

Then she took her usual route through the first garage, which always smelled exactly like a garage – how was it possible for all garages to smell the same? – and then she reached garage number two. Which was not a garage at all – instead, it was the workspace of a classic workaholic. She no longer even bothered to conceal it – her work was her hobby. Not least since it had become both weird and complicated. Since it had become one long balancing act.

Her study was pared down. There were a number of printouts pinned to the whiteboard. She woke up the PC and carried on printing where she had been interrupted some hours before by Lykke's increasingly intrusive yelps of hunger from inside the house.

She pulled the old office chair in closer and examined the printouts from the mobile phone shots taken in August Steen's office. Up to now, most of them had been credit card bills and mobile phone bills. She compared, took notes, tried to draw conclusions.

About what? What exactly was she doing? She leaned back for a moment, trying to cool down, trying to interpret the bigger picture.

If the Security Service knew that Berger was innocent of the murder of that serial killer, why weren't they setting out the evidence to clear his name? It didn't seem as though their protection was about helping him – in fact, it seemed more akin to extortion. Something along the lines of: we'll protect you if you do something for us. And what kind of something could Berger do for the Service? Deer didn't know. She was searching for clues, and those clues were only to be found with August Steen, who she knew was Molly Blom's mentor. That meant she was looking for anything at all that might hint at where Steen had been, which might somehow correlate to where Berger was.

The mobile phone bills revealed a large number of mobile numbers and a few landlines too. She didn't recognise any of the numbers, but continued to diligently take notes. The credit card bills implied a certain pattern of movements that thus far did not extend much beyond the city limits of Stockholm. The combination of the two might give an indication of where Steen had been when he'd called one number or another, but on the whole that had to be written off as a bit of a long shot.

Her loud printer stopped abruptly. She spun round, went over to it, pulled out a wedge of papers and sat back down before leafing through them. Her eye was caught by what she had taken to be a rota – it was definitely designed by and for an older man. It was a printed monthly schedule, and new pencil marks covered the traces of older ones that had been rubbed out. The fact that it had been attached to the end of a bookcase, out of sight of visitors but still easily accessible, suggested there was an element of secrecy to it. Perhaps, hopefully, this was Steen's own rota for the dealings of his immediate team.

On the few occasions that text appeared, it consisted of coded, impenetrable combinations of letters, with the exception of a couple of rows at the bottom that consisted of two letters followed by combinations of numbers that were almost certainly mobile phone numbers. Among these five were RG and KD.

It was surely not impossible that this was a list of August Steen's external resources. And that RG and KD were Roy Grahn and Kent Döös. She called RG's number. After slightly too many rings for it to seem hopeful, someone actually picked up. But the voice was most definitely not Roy's – it was a woman's.

'Yes?' said the voice.

'Hello,' said Deer, caught on the back foot. 'Who's speaking?'

'This is Roy Grahn's phone.'

Deer stared at her spare mobile as if she'd never seen it before.

'Splendid. Is he there?'

'Well, yes. We've got the phone for safe keeping. I thought it was dead. It was in the drawer here in Reception.'

'I'm not sure I follow,' Deer said entirely genuinely. 'Who am I speaking to then?'

'Oh yes, sorry,' said the woman's voice. 'I'm Inger Stensson – an intensive care nurse at the Southern Hospital.'

Deer raised her eyebrows – more in hope than concern.

'Like I said, I'm looking for Roy Grahn. How's he doing?'

'Who am I speaking to?' the woman's voice said more professionally.

'I'm Lena Andersson,' Deer lied. 'Roy's a colleague.'

'I see,' said Inger Stensson. 'Your colleague is dead.'

Deer gulped, trying to stifle the feelings welling up inside her.

'Right,' she said. 'I wasn't quite up to speed on what happened.'

'Apart from the fact that the body was split in two, I've never seen someone with that many bee stings in my life.'

'Bee stings?'

'Bees. And nowadays considering so many bees have vanished off the face of the Earth . . .'

'What about Kent?' said Deer. 'Is he dead too?'

'Kent?' said Inger Stensson.

'His colleague,' said Deer.

'Ah,' said Stensson. 'Five three.'

'I beg your pardon?' said Deer.

'Kent Döös, ward 5, bed 3. He's alive.'

'Do you have visiting hours?' Deer asked.

She had a slightly guilty conscience, but not much more than that, although she had left her daughter alone in an empty house and left something as old-fashioned and inadequate as a note on the kitchen table. She consoled herself with the fact that Johnny was more than likely already home. He might not be overjoyed exactly, but he wouldn't be so angry he wanted a divorce either. And once Lykke was out for the count, she always slept soundly.

She looked up from the heavily bandaged man in the only bed in the room and felt the antiseptic odour grow even stronger, as if a draught from an unknown source was carrying with it the smells of all the disinfectant salves that covered his body under the layers of gauze.

Deer met the defensive gaze of Inger Stensson.

'Does he ever come to?'

'For short periods,' said Stensson. 'Kent's with us occasionally.'

'Is he sedated at the moment?'

'No, not sedated, but he's on some strong painkillers. It's been a long time since I saw someone in that much pain.'

'Do bee stings really hurt that much?' Deer asked, hoping for a more human reaction than the habitual script of the health profession.

'In that volume, yes,' said Stensson. 'The venom still hasn't left his body. We often think wasp stings are the most painful thing there is, and it's true that they can sting you more than once. A bee dies after it uses its sting, but its poison is ten times stronger than a wasp's and causes much worse symptoms. And the stinger itself is left in the skin afterwards, which is rarely the case with wasps. You wouldn't believe the number of stingers we've had to prise out of this body . . .'

No, Deer thought to herself. It wasn't easy to get Inger Stensson to say more than she ought to. But she had done so already – she'd said too much on the phone – so it wasn't impossible.

'I really do need a quick chat with him,' said Deer.

Inger Stensson shrugged.

'Morphine. He wakes up occasionally. You'll just have to be patient.'

Deer put a hand on Inger Stensson's arm and said very quietly and professionally:

'Do you think it's at all possible for me to have a word with him in private? It's about a sensitive case. It'd be best for you if you weren't a witness to it. It involves people who prefer there to be as few witnesses as possible.'

Stensson looked her up and down. Then she nodded her professional assent and strode back towards the nurses' station.

Deer waited. She surveyed Kent Döös. She took a seat, and she waited. Perhaps she nodded off, because when she next looked at Kent his eyes were open and his gaze was clear.

'Hello, Kent,' she said.

He merely looked at her. There was a sharpness to his gaze that she took to be mistrust. She pulled out her police ID, covered half her name with a practised hand and quickly put it away again.

'I'm Lena Andersson,' she said.

'From NOA?' he said hoarsely.

So he bloody noticed that, she thought to herself as she nodded.

'Has anyone spoken to you about what happened?'

'Of course not,' said Kent.

Deer tried to be agile in her thoughts – flexible. But it was late. Night had well and truly fallen.

'I know it was a Security Service operation, but that doesn't mean people haven't complained. Neighbours called the police. We have to look into it.'

'Several days later, in the middle of the night?' said Kent.

Yup, Deer thought to herself. He is most definitely awake. That forced her to get it together.

'I didn't know that bee stings were ten times worse than wasp stings,' she said, pulling out a notebook that she had no intention of making any notes in.

'I know that *now*,' Kent said thickly.

'Roy knows that too,' said Deer.

Kent's gaze wavered. He stared up at the ceiling. She saw grief pouring through him – pure, raw grief over the loss of a colleague. Possibly a friend.

'The course of events was witnessed from a distance,' she lied. 'Could you describe them in your own words?'

'The Security Service press department might be able to,' Kent said, tight-lipped.

'Different organisations, I know. Brand-new opportunities to keep secrets. The Service's power is constantly growing. More and more police work is becoming secret without any democratic oversight. We know all that. So what happened?'

'You're making a fool of yourself,' said Kent. 'Lena Andersson? Is that straight from the Service's handbook of fake names or what?'

She laughed. She couldn't help it. The odd thing was that he laughed too. The bandaged body rocked about, the clearly inadequate springs of the bed continuing to move for a while. She sighed.

'I'm Superintendent Desiré Rosenkvist.'

Kent nodded.

'Thought you might be,' he said. 'Deer, right?'

'I can see you've been involved with Sam Berger. How did you end up with so many bee stings? How did they kill Roy?'

'What is it you want?'

'To find Berger. But I'm guessing that August Steen is also missing. Does he usually go missing?'

'I'm an external operative,' Kent said, coughing alarmingly. 'I don't exactly keep tabs on the Security Service top brass.'

'The Head of the Security Service Intelligence Unit, that's right. Except there's no such thing as the Intelligence Unit.'

'Of course there is. And it's time for you to leave, before someone sees you.'

Deer looked around, raising her gaze. There were several indistinct junction boxes up on the ceiling.

'Give me something, Kent,' she said. 'Was Berger with you when you were attacked by the bees?'

'You don't want to pursue this. I promise you that much,' said Kent. 'Just go. As quickly and inconspicuously as possible.'

Deer stood up, beginning to realise the impossibility of the whole thing, and opted to beg.

'Anything, Kent. What does Steen want Berger for? Why is he shielding him from justice?'

Kent shook his head.

'Not so long ago there was an Intelligence Unit,' he said quietly. 'Now there's just August Steen.'

'But why does he have a special arrangement like that?'

'Why do you think? Time for you to go.'

'No. Tell me.'

'For fuck's sake, he's Hoover. Now get out!'

Deer left him, her brain in a spin. Hoover? She waved rather absent-mindedly through the glass window at the nurses' station where Inger Stensson's face was illuminated by a computer screen as she managed some half-hearted gesture of farewell in return.

Deer meandered through the labyrinthine corridors of the Southern Hospital, while indistinct thoughts ran through her head. She wondered whether she would ever find out with any clarity what had happened, where Sam was, and what this was all about. Perhaps it really would be best to drop it all and enjoy her week off. What had happened to Sam Berger had probably been his own fault – one way or another. The last time she'd got mixed up with the Berger and Blom duo, her own child had been threatened – her own Lykke. Nothing like that could ever be allowed to happen again.

Then a text message arrived – it was from Johnny. *Arrived home to an empty house. L was asleep and still is. When you read this I will be too. Don't stay out too late. Xx*

Without any warning, Deer's eyes filled with tears. She continued to walk for a while as if in a fog, through the hospital building's maze. She saw stripes on the floor change colour, and just when she had made up her mind to drop it all and to return to life as a completely ordinary public servant with a week's unexpected holiday, she was overcome by a strange feeling. She was all at sea. She looked around. She looked down. Up, to her left, to her right. Except there was no up, no down, no here, no there.

There was no direction whatsoever.

After an indeterminate amount of time she managed to regain some of her faculties, and realised where she was – where her seemingly aimless feet had led her. Her consciousness said one thing (drop the lot!) and her subconscious said something entirely different (get to the bottom of it!).

After all, Deer's job was her hobby.

She was a nerd, plain and simple.

There was no longer a dozing security guard inside the door, but far away at the end of the corridor she glimpsed a woman in a white uniform through another window, her face also illuminated by a computer screen. Deer rang the bell. No sound was audible, but the woman in the glass cage looked up and pushed her reading glasses onto her forehead. Exhibiting a languor that indicated boundless reluctance, she stood up and began to amble along the corridor. With remarkable tardiness, she grew bigger and bigger until she was right up by the door. Deer held her police credentials to the window. The woman in white screwed her eyes up momentarily before opening the door.

'Thanks,' said Deer, reading the woman's name badge.

It said: 'Vilma Lundh, night nurse'. In her hand she was clutching a book with the title *Gramática básica de la lengua española*.

'Spanish grammar?' said Deer.

'What do you want?' said Vilma Lundh gruffly, pushing her reading glasses even further up her brow.

'I've been here several times in the last few days to visit a patient – Molly Blom – if that rings any bells?'

Lundh once again squinted and nodded. Deer looked at her with interest, but no answer came.

'It was so odd,' Deer said instead. 'There were no signs of life at all, and suddenly the day before yesterday, she just came to and pulled off a sophisticated escape.'

'I did hear about that,' said Vilma Lundh. 'Surely it's a good thing that she's well?'

'Absolutely,' said Deer. 'Were you here that night, Vilma?'

The night nurse looked at her. When her eyes screwed up for the third time, Deer continued.

'Just tell me.'

Vilma Lundh fiddled with her textbook for a while. Then she appeared to reach a decision.

'Follow me.'

They walked down the corridor until they reached Blom's former room. They entered. Someone else was there – an elderly man, albeit with the same equipment surrounding him. A respirator producing deep, heavy breaths, while a tube ran from a drip stand into the man's arm.

The night nurse squeezed the drip bag held in the stand and tapped the flow regulator with her fingernail.

'The tube was swaying.'

'Sorry?' Deer said, slightly disorientated.

'It started with me hearing a window open and close somewhere on the ward,' said Lundh. 'I was certain I'd imagined it – none of the windows here open. When I looked in this room, the tube was swaying.'

'I see,' said Deer, suddenly a little more alert. 'But there were no other signs?'

'Nothing whatsoever,' said Lundh. 'Except . . .'

'Except?' Deer was even more alert.

'Well, I might just have missed it earlier that evening. Perhaps it came from a bouquet of flowers that had been thrown out, or a box of chocolates. It was hardly worth waking up the security guard and the on-calls for.'

Deer merely looked at her, scrutinising but waiting.

'Oh,' said Lundh, screwing up her eyes yet again. 'Bloody hell. Come on.'

They went to the nurses' station and entered. Deer saw a clock on the wall; it showed it was 10.23. Lundh opened a desk drawer and began to root around among the bric-a-brac inside. Finally, she pulled out an object, and with a guilty conscience writ large on her face she handed it to Deer.

Deer took it.

It was a small, sealed envelope of the kind that usually contained greetings cards.

# 22

Molly Blom held up a small, sealed envelope of the kind that usually contained greetings cards.

Berger was upright in bed. It wasn't that he'd drifted off – his laptop was *supposed* to be lying on the floor with half a page of qqqqq's at the end of his notes – but now he was wide awake.

She came in from the sofa bed in the living room wearing something that looked like loungewear, proffered the envelope and said:

'It was on the chest of drawers in your flat.'

'And you waited six hours to show it to me because . . .'

'You were so preoccupied with that Roger Corby guy in Gibraltar. We both were. Then I forgot about it.'

'Of course you didn't,' said Berger. 'I told you about the little envelope in the apiary in Tensta, with the Shakespeare and Joyce quotes inside it. The fact that you found one *just like it* in my flat should have made you show it to me right away. So you must have kept it secret for some specific reason.'

'Do you want it or not?'

'Is it unopened?'

'Sealed,' Blom confirmed. 'Should we open it?'

'Oh yes,' said Berger, looking at her. 'Are you cold?'

'Yes, it's freezing out there,' she said. 'Not enough blankets either.'

'I've got this double bed here,' said Berger, gesturing. 'There's room for you.'

She looked at him. He looked at her. Nothing happened. She handed him the envelope.

'Open it then.'

Berger took at the envelope and put it down. Then he reached for the computer on the floor. He had to reach a way out of the duvet.

Blom said: 'Don't tell me you sleep naked.'

'I'm not telling you anything,' he said, erasing the large number of q's before rereading what he had written.

Blom sighed and made for the other side of the bed. She settled down as far away as possible, and when she pulled the duvet around herself it almost slipped off him. They fought briefly over it. Perhaps there was a degree of playfulness to that struggle.

'Let's start by summing up our call to Gibraltar,' Berger said eventually. 'Our rather nervous friend Roger Corby had managed to turn up the fact that Sven Johansson's Gibraltarian company Big Exit Ltd was overseen by the Pantoja & Puerta law firm in Nerja, Andalusia. Big Exit's bank account at PPB, for which we now have a statement, has a balance of nearly forty thousand euros, but that's not exactly big bucks. If there's any real blood money then Big Exit Ltd must have a fatter bank account elsewhere.'

'Or he's waiting for the money,' said Blom. 'He might only get paid once Ali Pachachi is out of the game.'

'Also credible,' Berger said with a nod.

'What about the other name?' said Blom, wriggling a little closer. 'Johan Svensson's Monaco account?'

'No idea,' said Berger. 'We'll have to dig deeper into that too, but right now it feels like this law firm in Andalusia is where the irrefutable evidence will be. The rest was all a bit too obvious – Carsten would never have shown his hand.'

'Big Exit, you mean?' said Blom.

'Of course he may have cash in other corporations like the one in Monaco, for which I don't yet have a name, but it sounds like this is still about his *big exit* and that it's linked to Andalusia. Surely the fact that he's got a law firm on hand suggests there's some business going on?'

'And that contract you mentioned,' said Blom. 'The bee's wax that stings worse than the bees. The contract that means he's not a free man. That exudes business too. Rotten business.'

'There are plenty of luxury yachts in Puerto Banús,' said Berger. 'But you didn't really buy that?'

'It's not the Carsten I know,' said Blom. 'Of course, he might have changed his lifestyle, but if he's going blind I'm more inclined to think it's a property – something like a big villa in a great location with huge terraces in the sun. The kind of place he can enjoy without being able to see, and where he definitely doesn't need to rely on a skipper and crew.'

'So who is the Carsten you know?'

'A circus chimp, above all else,' said Blom. 'I don't think that ever leaves you. Everything about him was always quite affected, as if the audience was in the distance and he was testing out a new act and exaggerating it a bit. What was at first seductive and exciting soon became very annoying, because it never seemed genuine.'

'But he's a real quisling,' said Berger. 'A real mole in the Security Service. Your Security Service, Molly. How did it happen?'

Blom shook her head.

'I don't know,' she said at last. 'I haven't seen him for fifteen years. I really don't know.'

'You're right about the overacting,' said Berger. 'He's making a racket and showing off and really trying to mark his connection to you in an exaggerated way. Showing that he regards me as a rival, that he's playing a literary game with the Service, that he's going blind, that he's got a romantic tie to Andalusia. And with that bee performance, he wants to show how tied he is to a certain contract that will never let him be a free man again in this life, which also means he'll never stop. But is there anything that suggests where he is?'

Blom wriggled yet closer, stretching her arm across him and pointing towards the nightstand with her index finger. He sighed, nodded and picked up the envelope.

'Should we open it now then?' he said. 'What's in it? And above all, who is it for?'

'If I've got the right end of the stick with your story,' said Blom, 'the first envelope was put out for you in the seconds before you got shot in the balls, possibly fatally. So it wasn't really for you, it was for August Steen and the Service. Not for you, not for me, but for the Security Service. This envelope was in your flat, and since the Service had been there we know it was left there afterwards – hence fairly recently. There's presumably an order to be followed. The envelope in Tensta was meant to be found first. This should be a sequel with more information, and it should also be for the Security Service. I was in a coma, you had been gunned down – in Carsten's world we were both out of the game, perhaps for good. So why these games with the envelopes? Are we just being egocentric? Might this actually have nothing to do with either of us?'

'Good point,' said Berger, managing to make an opening in the envelope and inserting his index finger. 'Although I doubt it.'

'Open it now,' said Blom. 'No matter what's inside, we won't be able to do anything about it tonight. But we can sleep on it.'

'True,' said Berger, opening the envelope and adding, 'I bet this is for you.'

He prised out a small card and then described it.

'On the front of the card there's a 3 written in marker pen and circled. On the back, it says: ". . . but I don't know what kind of drawers he likes none I think didn't he say yes and half the girls in Gibraltar never wore them either naked as God made them that Andalusian singing her Manola she didn't make much secret of what she hadn't . . ."'

Molly Blom's eyes widened. She stared out of the window into the dark night. Berger waited. At last he spoke.

'Manola?'

'There's something about this,' Blom said instead of replying.

'Is it from *Ulysses*?'

'Yes, it's from Molly Bloom's monologue. It sounds like Manola is some kind of song or piece of music, but I wonder whether it's sexual too.'

'That's my general impression of it,' said Berger. 'Because surely "half the girls in Gibraltar never wore them either naked as God made them" must be referring to those drawers? As in underwear? And who is meant by "he" in this, as in "he likes none"? Blazes Boylan? Molly Bloom's lover? Is he the one who likes to be naked as God created him? Under his breeches?'

Blom laughed.

'Like you, really,' she said.

'You don't know that,' he said with a wry smile. 'Come on, does it refer to Boylan?'

'I think so – that's how I remember it. It's a very long time since I read *Ulysses*. But there really is something about it. Something that invokes some kind of memory I can't access right now.'

'Perhaps you should sleep on it?' said Berger.

'I don't know whether I *can* sleep,' said Blom. 'Maybe I need to think. Or at least digest it.'

'But I need to sleep,' said Berger, putting the computer back on the floor. 'Do you want to see the letter?'

He thought he made out Blom shaking her head. Then he felt his eyes closing. Very faintly, barely perceptibly, he felt her breathing against his shoulder. There was something exceptional about those breaths.

Emotions, he thought as he drifted into the incomprehensible domains of sleep. Being filled with them and unable to show them. Seeing her here without being able to let out the relief that she had survived, awoken, come back to life, become her former self. Not being able to say that she was carrying another life within her, a life that was presumably half his. Not even being able to turn over right now and embrace her, accept her, become part of her.

Life was still not complete – that much was obvious.

Halfway into the realm of sleep, he spoke.

'A 3 circled on this letter. It was a 1 in Tensta.'

Molly Blom's breathing suddenly became a small, icy breeze against his shoulder. Her voice was thick as it spoke.

'The 2's missing?'

He would never remember whether he managed to reply.


He realised with the very first vibration that it was an email. The lamp was on his side of the bed. It was off – he hadn't switched it off. The room was pitch-black except for his mobile. So she must have turned the light out.

He saw the email's sender, and ignored the light and vibrations for a while.

When he got out of the double bed, her arm came with him.

It bounced a few times on the mattress without rousing her. She appeared to be deeply asleep.

On the other hand, he had unfortunately learned that what was before his eyes did not always tally with reality.

He slipped into the bathroom, locked the door, didn't turn on the light, found the toilet seat in the dark, felt for the cable running out of his phone and inserted the earbuds into his ears. Then he opened the email and the bathroom was faintly illuminated.

Before he paused it, he heard August Steen say:

'Perhaps you'll understand why I did it, Sam. Perhaps not.'

Berger attempted to recollect the contents of the previous digital packet.

It wouldn't quite come to mind.

Instead, he focused on the frozen Steen. His age, fear, exhaustion – all the things that Berger had never before seen. There was no indication of when this had been recorded, but it was all part of the same long monologue, in which Steen increasingly found himself telling lies. Perhaps he would eventually reach the truth.

Perhaps he would die then.

Berger remembered what it was about. August Steen had just confessed that he had hired William Larsson – not as a bodyguard for the Pachachis as he had claimed, but to kidnap their daughter Aisha. But why Steen would need to steal the daughter of Sweden's leading resistance force against Islamism remained unclear.

Berger needed to pull himself together.

He pressed play.

# 23

'Perhaps you'll understand why I did it, Sam. Perhaps not.

'The fact is, I think you will, Sam. Despite everything that happened.

'Now I'm going to tell you. Ali Pachachi's network had intercepted chat about the deceased Albanian arms dealer Isli Vrapi's arms syndicate, which was now under new leadership. It was assembling huge arsenals in multiple European countries and preparing to sell these to the highest bidder. A year ago, we received unconfirmed reports that the venture had reached Sweden following two trial auctions in similarly sized countries. I realised then that we had a mole in the Security Service.

'It's probably best to think of us as a Triumvirate, Sam. A trio determining how to assess and manage the situation faced by Sweden's security services. Others didn't refer to us as a Triumvirate – they called us the Bermuda Triangle: anything falling into the force field between August Steen, Ali Pachachi and Nils Gundersen would disappear without trace.

'I still prefer the designation of Triumvirate. It has connections to the antique and classical period, hints of the Roman golden age, of Caesar, Crassus, Pompey. It has the essence of justice and civilisation, with an overtone of a balance of powers based on equal strength and mutual ambitions. If any form of disruption were to interfere in the *finely calibrated balancing act of the Triumvirate then we would all be ruined. And there was a clear risk that we would all be consumed by the dark magic of the Bermuda Triangle.*

'Our roles were clearly distributed. I was in the corridors of power at the Security Service, Nils was overseeing the Middle East, Ali was handling the flow of information. Our collaboration was perfect – just as long as the three of us wanted the same thing.

'But then something happened. On an official visit to Russia in April, I wanted to go shopping for gifts for my family and had been recommended a shopping centre on the outskirts of Moscow. He appeared out of nowhere and asked me to sit down on a bench in the crowded mall. I immediately made out three bodyguards who were sufficiently ill-hidden among the lingerie and toys for me to realise that I was meant to spot them. His English was faultless.

'What he had to say was far from faultless.

'He said there were grey zones, that you could sometimes do what was best for your country and make a fortune at the same time. He said "there's that magnificent mansion, after all". When I played ignorant, he told me I'd been out to the island of Möja three times to look at it. That was when I realised he meant business. They were going to make a genuine offer.

'I assume after all these years as a public servant I was essentially receptive. It was hardly the first time I'd been a target, and it had always been easy to resist before. But this was the first time it was so simple, so clear. He told me a figure, described a financial arrangement – a sophisticated, impenetrable ownership structure.

'"The Russian mafia," I said. "Give them your little finger and they'll eat up your entire family tree out to your second and third cousins."

'He shook his head and smiled wryly. "Not the mafia," he said. "Guaranteed," he said. He gave me his word that weapons would never be used on Swedish soil against Swedes.

'"We know that you are the handler responsible for the most

extensive network in the Muslim world. We also know of the impending arms auctions. But the arms dealer can't be got at – Isli Vrapi's successor is beyond reach. We want you to deal with it via your network. We want you to find a way to put a stop to the auction and give us exclusive rights."

'Before he left me sitting there in that ridiculous mall, he added:

' "We need your decision within the week."

'A brief pat on the shoulder and then he was gone. The bodyguards too.

'I travelled home and thought it over, exploring the terrain and trying to understand who had made contact with me. I got nowhere. My deadline, however, was approaching. Then Ali Pachachi got in touch. I met with him. By then he'd obtained the name of Isli Vrapi's heir and all of a sudden the organisation seemed much closer. Pachachi told me everything he had and I felt I could see a clear way in. Based on what my highly esteemed colleague in the Triumvirate told me, there was an opportunity to sow a seed.

'That was when I made my fateful decision. It was also at that moment that the balance of power in the Triumvirate shifted. I told Pachachi nothing. I claimed I would pass the information on to the ministry and get them to issue an international alert.

'Ali Pachachi believed me. Just as we always believed each other.

'Months passed, Pachachi grew impatient. Why weren't we striking against this arms dealer? I asked him to be patient. Told him this was what democracy looked like – slow. I realised I needed a "bodyguard" for Pachachi.

'Someone who could keep him in check.

'I turned to Nils Gundersen in Lebanon. When he sent me his recently reshaped son to serve as bodyguard for the "threatened" Pachachi, the imbalance in the Triumvirate was complete. Now I was lying to Nils too about his dear son whom we had saved from damnation together.

'William Larsson arrived, I gave him a cover job at the Security Service's technical contractor, and I issued him with his first secret orders. William was an obedient soldier. When Pachachi's son had disappeared, I saw signs that Ali was off kilter and I helped that along by ordering William to kidnap his daughter Aisha.

'I sent Ali Pachachi a threatening letter that appeared to come from within Isli Vrapi's organisation. I made it as unambiguous as I could: if Pachachi did anything further with his knowledge about the organisation then his daughter would die. That got him to toe the line – his interest in the arms dealer cooled off considerably.

'As soon as the police interviews about the disappearance were over, I took Ali and Tahera Pachachi to a secret location. And he kept quiet. He reported to me, and I disclosed nothing – that was our solemn promise to each other.

'The fact that William flipped due to events in his childhood didn't change much. Molly was on his track, as you know, Sam. She developed an odd but functional approach with an undercover identity and a bicycle.

'And Pachachi kept quiet. Now all that mattered was receiving the intel about the Swedish auction being in progress so that I could reap what I had sown.

'Instead came the shock.

'Just before the turn of the year I discovered that a mole had infiltrated the Security Service. I had no idea who it was, but the traces were unmistakable. Someone inside the firm was trying to find Ali Pachachi, Sweden's most secret man. I'd already moved the Pachachis and I took the opportunity to erase all trace of the Triumvirate from the archives. Then I set out in pursuit.

'But it didn't work – I couldn't track the insider. Everything seemed to go wrong. The mole was very skilful, that much was clear. The question was how much the bastard had found out.

'And as far as the network went, news about the arms auction was conspicuous by its absence. I began to suspect it had been cancelled and that it had all trickled away into the sand. I feared that I would soon have to pay the price for a long, wonderful summer with my extended family on Möja.

'In October, fifteen-year-old Ellen Savinger was abducted, and I realised – not least thanks to Molly's reports – that William was now accelerating his operations and that the shit was on the verge of hitting the fan. William wasn't after Aisha Pachachi as such, or Ellen, or any of the other girls. He was after you, Sam.

'Everyone seems to be after you.

'There were now two things of importance. Firstly that I manage to get on the trail of the mole. And secondly that I keep you alive, Sam. You were important to me. But Molly broke out, freed you, and you vanished off my radar. I could only hope that you and Molly were able to cope by yourselves.

'Then Carsten found his way to Helenelund and snatched Aisha from William's incomplete cell system. That was my first clue – clearly the person who had taken Aisha and none of the other six girls was my mole. I tied the kidnapping to a couple of other murders linked to your and Molly's hunt for William – murders committed with something as unexpected as a sock rammed down a throat. But it was only when I saw Carsten stuff a black sock into the mouth of another victim on film that I realised the gravity of the situation.

'The victim that you, Sam, had supposedly shot. The serial killer in the interior.

'It actually seemed as if you were guilty of the other sock murders, even if it was completely unclear why you would kill your old friend Sylvia Andersson. Presumably, Carsten killed her while she was being tortured to try and find out where Pachachi might be – she might have successfully found out by hacking the archives.

'And it's only now that I truly understand who sent Carsten into the system.

'Someone who wants in on the fight for the weapons arsenal.

'Someone who wants to know where the auction is going to take place.

'Someone who sensed that the Triumvirate was on its way to becoming the Bermuda Triangle. And who doesn't want to disappear inside it.

'It's not Islamic State that bought Carsten. We may all be quislings, but his treason doesn't quite take those dimensions. The arsenal contains unique prototypes of various robotic weapons – prototypes that any mercenary on the planet would not only kill for, but would die for.

'Shortly before then, news arrived from Pachachi. The auction was going ahead, the arsenal was in Sweden. It's here now – all these weapons that any terrorist would commit hara-kiri for. Sam, the weapons are on Swedish soil – right now.

'I received a time, a place, a plan. I passed on the information to my contacts and prepared to activate my own plan. Now I can't, Sam. I'm stuck here in this awful cellar in the hands of Carsten. I have no idea what's happening right now. I can't conceive of any other scenario except that I'm going to die here. I hope they don't take Möja from my family.

'You've already guessed, Sam, and you're spot on. Nils Gundersen turned Carsten – he'll be paid handsomely for extracting from Ali Pachachi where the auction is going to take place.

'You have to stop Carsten, Sam. You really do. Gundersen is only interested in the prototypes. He'll all too happily hand over the rest of the arms to Islamic State.

'I think I may have found a vital clue to where Carsten has taken Aisha. I found it just before he snatched me.

'The Triumvirate has fallen, Sam. We're all in the Bermuda Triangle.'

# 24

Berger didn't sleep any more that night. Not a wink. And as he lay there tossing and turning, it occurred to him that it was no surprise. He had been carpet-bombed. Explosion after explosion, distorting both his perceptions and his thoughts. Molly's marriage and spiritual connection to Carsten, August Steen's confession, William Larsson's new role, Carsten's shifted role. The only question was whether it was all true: Steen had proven himself to be a most fluent liar. Not exactly unexpectedly, given his position in the least truthful industry in the legal universe.

Which was also where Molly Blom had been schooled.

Sam Berger was here again, alone with her. She had broken his isolation, and he had listened to her breathing all night. It had seemed regular, low, honest. But perhaps that was just a matter of practice too. Everything could be false.

That was the terrible lesson. Everything could be false.

His own life too, by all means.

The truth had become something fleeting, something transitory that could constantly shift and be changed. It was a dreadful state of affairs. But right now, the situation seemed to be the following:

August Steen was a traitor to his country, just like Carsten, only he had been in the pay of another foreign power – it was unclear which, but perhaps the Russians. His pursuit of Carsten was clearly more the pursuit of a competing mole than a pursuit in the name of truth and justice. And Carsten was clearly working on behalf of the mercenary Nils Gundersen, who was also not sticking to his long-term Security Service assignment.

How rotten did it get?

August Steen had been about to reveal his clue about where Carsten and Aisha might be when the video had cut out.

That alone was enough to induce a sleepless night.

When he thought about it, he realised that Molly's breathing had changed a couple of times, and he was convinced that she'd also had some sleepless periods. He tried to make out whether she was awake while also pretending to be asleep himself. There were moments when he guessed that she was listening to him with just as much attentiveness.

Suddenly, there was a shudder beside him. He switched on the light and turned over. She had got out of bed and was standing there in her cosy loungewear, her expression hard to interpret.

'What is it?' he said, scratching his beard.

'Don't know,' she said. 'Something about Carsten's quote. A realisation that appeared and disappeared again: ". . . but I don't know what kind of drawers he likes none I think didn't he say yes and half the girls in Gibraltar never wore them either naked as God made them that Andalusian singing her Manola she didn't make much secret of what she hadn't . . ."'

'Okay,' said Berger. 'Did the two of you read it aloud or something?'

'No, or maybe . . .'

'At your flat? Elofsgatan?'

'Eolsgatan,' Blom corrected him. 'Eol, the god of wind, Aeolus. But no, that's the thing. I said "I don't know what kind of drawers he likes" and he said "none I think". That was when I realised he wasn't wearing any pants. Under his jeans.'

'Romantic,' said Berger.

'Strangely enough that's exactly what it was,' said Blom. 'But where?'

'A flat, a hotel room, a . . . theatre dressing room?'

'It's on the tip of my tongue. Talk about something else and perhaps it'll come to me.'

Talk about something else, Berger thought to himself. As if there were a shortage of topics of conversation. One of the many he had brooded upon in his night of sleeplessness came to mind.

'Have you ever been to Möja?'

'Not that I know of,' said Blom. 'What kind of question is that?'

'I thought you might have family there . . .?'

She merely shook her head and looked thoughtful.

'Envelope 3,' Berger said. 'Envelope 3, left at my home not long after the attack in Tensta where envelope 1 was. Letter 3 was hardly meant for me; I was already meant to be castrated. I'd say it was pretty clearly meant for *you*, Molly. But Carsten was involved when Deer and I were looking for you; he knew full well you were in a coma. So why direct it to you?'

'Yes,' Blom said. 'And solely to me, right? You were meant to be out of the picture, and if I'd woken up, I would be on my own. He wants *me alone* to pursue him.'

'I think that's how we have to interpret it,' said Berger. 'But Carsten surely can't be aware that I'm okay and that we have, if I may say so, been *reunited*.'

He didn't add:

'If Carsten hasn't already tortured that information out of August Steen, that is.'

He really found the art of holding his tongue incredibly difficult.

Right now, he couldn't mention Steen and his videos. Berger still didn't know whether he could trust Molly. How had she found this, the most secret of the Security Service's safe houses? Via a helicopter administrator? Really? How had she come round so quickly? What exactly was her role in the bigger picture?

A life of double-dealing really was a shitty life.

If there was an alternative ending to this that didn't involve death then Sam Berger would be forced to reform his life. He would live in the clear light of transparency. He'd finally be the what-you-see-is-what-you-get person that he had always thought he was.

His existential musings were interrupted by a claw-like grip around his biceps. He turned, and Molly Blom let go, staring into emptiness. He waited, pushing the pillow against the wall and raising himself to a seated position. He watched her.

'I remember,' she said at last.

'Okay . . .' he said.

'We were on an island in the archipelago,' she said. 'Our first trip together. A weekend on an island. Somewhere in the archipelago. The first seduction.'

'Another island in the archipelago? Which one?'

'We rented a little cottage, if I remember correctly. It must have been autumn – almost winter. It was incredibly desolate. There were only a few houses and they were all empty for the winter.'

'Am I to take it that this means you don't remember where it was?'

'I can't remember which island it was, no.'

'You need to trigger your memory,' Berger said, getting up.

He was just wearing just trunks. He dressed quickly.

'You didn't by any chance have a computer with you in that bloody sack, did you?'

'Sack?'

'The one you tried to give me a heart attack with out in the bushes. Come on, don't just lie around.'

'I've got a computer with me,' said Blom, pushing back the duvet. 'But not in any sack.'

'Great,' he said, grabbing her arm and dragging her into the living room to the map by the whiteboard. She stared at the muddle that constituted the Stockholm archipelago.

'See whether any of this inspires you,' he said, sitting down and turning on his own computer to search for lists of islands in the archipelago. He found a big one in alphabetical order with various subcategories.

Blom stared at the map of twenty-five thousand islands. It didn't look as if it was providing her with much inspiration at all.

'How did you and Carsten reach the island?' Berger asked. 'Car, bus, ferry, steamer?'

Blom shook her head.

'I just remember the house and the not-very-long walks.'

'And finding out he wasn't wearing any pants, I know. But you must remember more than that. Did Carsten have a car?'

'I don't remember.' Blom closed her eyes. Finally she said: 'No, we took a steamer. There weren't any cars on the island.'

'Good,' Berger said, clicking. The selection on the screen grew smaller, although it was still enormous.

'We didn't go north,' said Blom, producing a backpack that had been tucked behind the waste-paper basket under the desk. She pulled out her laptop and booted it up, settling down on the other chair.

Berger stood up and went over to the map of the archipelago.

'Was it a long way?' he asked. 'Could you see other islands?'

'Yes, several,' said Blom, copying the URL from Berger's computer. The same list appeared on her device.

'Was it a big island? Could you walk around it? Did the steamer stop there? Did the island have its own jetty for the steamer? Or did you have to transfer onto a smaller boat?'

'Fairly big island,' Blom said, nodding as she scrutinised the extensive list of island names. 'Odd name. And yes, the boat called there.'

'Odd name? And it was dead in late autumn? No year-round residents?'

'We were there for a weekend. I don't remember seeing anyone else.'

Berger stopped suddenly, freezing mid-movement and staring at her.

'And it wasn't Möja?' he said.

She stopped too and met his gaze. Then she shook her head and said:

'What is it you're not telling me?'

'Far less than *you're* not telling *me*,' said Berger.

Her gaze lingered on him as he returned to his computer and pulled up the map of the Waxholmsbolaget steamer network.

'Where did you catch the boat from? Stockholm? At Nybrokajen or Strömkajen? Or from Årsta havsbad? Dalarö? Nynäshamn?'

'It was from Strömkajen,' Blom said in a low voice.

'You remember more than you think,' said Berger, and perhaps he even sounded a little encouraging. He added: 'It may have been a long time ago, the routes may have changed over the years, but at least take a look at these timetables and see whether anything rings a bell.'

Blom wheeled over to him and scrolled down his screen. He

watched her and suddenly saw her brow furrow, her hand freeze on the mouse.

'Hmm,' she said.

'Hmm?' he said.

'Fjärdlång,' she said.

Berger immediately went over to the big map of the archipelago and found the island, making a rough calculation.

'Are you sure?' he asked.

'I think so. Odd name.'

'In the southern archipelago,' said Berger. 'East of Ornö, which is the biggest island. There are lots of islands nearby, but it's not far from the outer archipelago. And not that far from here. Something like fifty kilometres by boat, whatever that is in nautical miles. Zoom in on Fjärdlång on Google Maps.'

She did. They studied the satellite photo in detail.

'Some settlements to the north,' said Berger. 'Not much by the steamer jetty in the west. Some bits inland, including a deluxe house called the "Thielska Villa" that's a youth hostel in summer. A few cabins down in the south-east. What do you think?'

Blom nodded and pointed.

'I think that must have been where we stayed,' she said. 'In the south-east.'

'Then let's initiate a big search based on Fjärdlång right away. Everything we can find. Ownerships, rentals, distances, terrains. Find discrepancies and see whether we can locate the exact spot. It might very well be the house where you once upon a time realised you weren't wearing any underwear. That's where Carsten has Aisha.'

Blom obeyed without beating about the bush. Their keyboards rattled away in time with each other until one of them fell silent. After a while the other did too. Their eyes met.

'By boat?' said Blom.

'What?' said Berger.

'You said "fifty kilometres by boat". So you're saying you have a boat?'

Berger scratched his beard.

'It's a pretty awesome boat, as it happens.'

# 25

It was most definitely not the perfect weather for an outing by boat in the archipelago. It was growing dark, not only because twilight was just an hour away, but also because the sky was clouding over.

The angular stern was cutting through water that appeared to be boiling. It was hard to tell whether that was solely the result of the increasingly heavy drops of sleet or combined with the surface of the water beginning to freeze. The sleet slapped down onto the deck like rocky road mixture being dolloped onto a tray, a mess of crushed brown and grey pellets.

To her surprise, the occasional flake of snow was actually white.

The archipelago was a strange place at this time of year. There seemed to be a grey mist shrouding the infinite islets and skerries. Not a single archipelago-worshipping Stockholmer would dare to venture anywhere near the island kingdom in its present state. It would decimate forever their idyllic perception of a country with the second biggest number of islands in the whole world.

The person standing there, practically alone on the Waxholm steamer, was Deer. There wasn't another soul present.

At any rate, she was definitely the only person outdoors, albeit under cover. She pulled out the small envelope she had been given by the not altogether dutiful night nurse Vilma Lundh. She read it. It was clearly a clue. It was clearly right. But what would she find at the end of the rainbow? Something that would definitely justify being armed, she thought to herself as she hastily patted her chest.

As if a rainbow would appear on the horizon today, she thought to herself as she stared into the maddening curtain of mist ahead. It had become so common in Sweden to have these big fat snowflakes mixed with rain that 'sleet' no longer seemed to quite fit. They needed a new word . . .

And if Deer wasn't mistaken, it appeared there was a storm imminent.

The Waxholm steamer approached an island that looked effectively uninhabited. She eventually managed to make out the jetty along the barren west coast.

\*

No, it was not ideal weather for an outing by boat in the archipelago.

Berger looked up into the darkening sky and hoped that the storm of the day before was not spilling over into today. Increasingly heavy drops of snow mixed with rain perforated the sea, which was shades of grey and black, as Molly Blom's legendary navigation skills saw them avoid every single reef. She didn't check the GPS navigation on the iPad even once.

They had chosen to refrain from landing at the steamer jetty in case Carsten had set up CCTV at the most obvious mooring point on the island. Given that the high-powered speedboat was also noisy, they chose to make their way northwards, further out to sea, rounding the island of Bockholmen and trying to find a safe anchoring spot a kilometre or so north of the cabins on the south-eastern shore of Fjärdlång. Everything pointed to Carsten and Aisha being somewhere around those cabins.

'There are reefs around the middle of the island here,' Blom said without taking her eyes off the chart. 'Slow down.'

Berger obeyed unhesitatingly. He followed Blom's instructions, trying not to think about how bad it would be if they ran aground as he tracked the adjacent island heading north before turning west and seeing Fjärdlång looming ahead of him. The island had been inhabited for a millennium and rose to a respectable height.

There were several good natural harbours even on the island's west coast, and in the end Molly Blom made the decision that it was time. Berger lowered their speed to a minimum and allowed the boat to bob towards shore. The inhospitable rockiness of the coast made him extremely cautious. They slipped into an inlet that looked accommodating enough for mediocre skippers.

Everything went fine; Blom dropped the anchor at the right moment and jumped down onto the shore with ropes to make the boat fast.

There was just shy of a kilometre of rugged terrain ahead of them. Berger tugged the zip of his coat all the way up to his chin, taking care not to get his beard stuck. Then he nodded to Blom who patted her chest, and they set off, following his navigation system.

\*

In spite of the absence of cars on the island, the road was fairly wide. Deer ambled through the twilight, occasionally glancing at the map on her mobile, which was fortunately well charged. Increasingly, her phone was her only source of light.

It was insane living in a country where it got dark at half past two in the afternoon.

The sleet had by now been joined by a fairly strong wind. She thanked her lucky stars that she had wrapped up in layer after layer. Her outermost layer was something windproof that she didn't even have a name for.

The road suddenly narrowed, becoming no more than a footpath. Deer knew that before long it would peter out into nothing at all. Quite how she would make her way from there remained unclear. The rocky, wooded terrain didn't look particularly tempting to venture through, and the map was unable to show what the coastline was like. It was probably steep and impassable, and presumably she would need to go straight through the woods in spite of her reservations.

The path straightened somewhat. For the first time in a long while she saw the sea. She also saw a couple of lights glowing faintly in the distance, like a mirage. Then the path took another corner and the sea vanished from sight.

All light vanished, apart from that cast by her mobile phone.

And the storm intensified.

*

They pushed on through terrain that seemed mostly to consist of precipices. As if it weren't complicated enough traversing the unusually thick heather and the almost-impassable boulder fields, they realised another thing as they went on. Despite the fact that they were walking in woodland, they could tell that the wind had gained in intensity. The sleet wasn't coming down as hard now as it had been in the inlet, but instead the tree branches were flailing even more energetically, as if they really were out to get them. And the cold was biting ever more deeply into them.

Blom led the way, her torch beam catching the merciless branches. Nothing indicated that any end was in sight – whether to the woods, the darkness or the cold.

★

The trail ended without really being noticeable. Deer could have continued her hike straight into the icy cold waters of the archipelago without being aware of any great difference.

There was no sky.

She tried to follow the coastline with her gaze. It was impossible. Nevertheless, it felt better than heading into the woods. She made an attempt, ducking into the side when the black water broke across the rocks. She took a few faltering steps. The rocks were big, as slippery as anything, irregularly distributed by the ancient giant who had on a passing whim decided to sprinkle all these small islands across the sea separating Sweden and mysterious Finland. Deer gave up her hike heading towards Finland, switched on her phone torch again and forced herself into the woods instead.

★

There wasn't far to go. Berger was suddenly overcome by dizziness. It felt as if it had been an eternity since the kidnapping of Ellen Savinger had revealed a perpetrator who had spent two years snatching seven fifteen-year-old girls and holding them captive in a cellar. When they had been moved for the second time to a labyrinth in a flat, Berger and Blom were lying in wait and had saved six of them. Six out of seven.

And now they were here.

They were very close to rescuing the seventh and final hostage.

189

The one who had been the first.

The one it was all about – not that she had a clue about that.

And soon she would be legally an adult.

The storm was deafening. The sleet was striking them like poorly rolled snowballs through the dense canopy of branches.

Gradually, the woods began to thin out. The sea became visible. Small, faint lights from nearby islands were occasionally reflected in the frothing water. There were no other lights. The moon was gone. The stars were nowhere to be seen. Instead there were just two torch beams shining down at the ground.

To ensure that no one noticed anything.

The woods thinned out markedly. The rocks far ahead that led down to the sea were sleek, bare, glistening in the viscous precipitation. A number of cabins facing the sea were visible along the bare rocks.

There was no light from any of them,

Molly Blom crouched, her back to the sea, as if someone down there might be able to make out the glow of her mobile. She pulled up the map image. Around ten or so squares were scattered along the shore heading towards the steamer jetty. The furthermost one on the far side of the jetty had a drop-shaped marker blinking above it. It was definitely the most isolated and most secluded.

The small cottage had been rented for six months.

By one Johan Svensson.

Blom drew her weapon and scrutinised Berger closely. He drew his too. Then they nodded at each other and set off.

Blom slithered her way down a rocky ridge. She tensed her body, preparing for a hard landing, but it was instead soft. She slipped to the side, grasping something she thought was a branch.

Instead she found herself embracing a body.

*

After a few hundred metres in the woods, something happened. Deer thought the trees seemed to be thinning out, although she couldn't put her finger on why. She stopped. Exhaled. She aimed the beam of her torch, minimising it against the ground.

She hadn't been imagining things. There were houses down there.

There were houses to the left – several of them – some by a jetty at which there were no boats. But there was also a house to the right.

There were no lights on in any of them.

Deer pictured the moment in her mind's eye. She was in her study in the second garage at home in the terraced house in Skogås. Against every instinct, she had taken the small envelope all the way home from the Southern Hospital. Once she reached her study she had inserted a letter opener into the envelope, stopped herself for a moment, taken a deep breath – and then opened it.

All there was on what might actually *be* a greetings card was a circle with a number inside it. The number 2. Then she turned the card over and read the message.

It had led her here, but there was no information about which house might be the one, so she would have to check them one by one. She started from the right – the nearest one.

Beyond all the other houses, in the most isolated, most secluded spot, there was a small red cottage that was in no way remarkable. On the contrary, the fact that it was remarkably unremarkable was its defining feature.

Deer approached from diagonally above, where there were no windows. She turned off her torch. The rocks were steep and slippery. She crouched, slithering down through the storm. She was as silent as she could be. She reached the cabin. She pressed herself against the wall. Then she drew her weapon and clicked the safety off. She held it against her ribs, aiming it up past her face, waiting for her breathing to normalise, cleansing her mind, letting a minute elapse, listening. There was no noise. No light. She peeked round the corner of the house.

She glided slowly to the only window in the facade facing the sea. The curtains were drawn.

Deer moved even more slowly to the crack between the curtains. Just as she reached a position to peer inside, something happened. Without her really noticing, the snowfall had stopped. Now the wind died down, and the moon emerged from between clouds that had seemed impenetrable just minutes before. A few moonbeams arced through the window, illuminating the inside of the cabin.

And then she saw something else.

She saw the head.

*

Blom embraced the body a little too long, as if some part of her was clinging on for dear life. Then she let go and moved the beam of her torch up towards the man's face.

What was left of his eyes had run down his cheeks.

Blom recoiled quickly. This was definitely Carsten's handiwork. Presumably an inquisitive neighbour who had got a little too close.

'We're in the right place,' she said, crouching in the dark.

There was no doubt about it: it was the last house they were after – the one furthest away. Berger and Blom slipped past the preceding cabins. Both had their weapons drawn, both held their breath. The rocks were incredibly slippery as a result of the recent sleet and they had to ensure they kept their balance. Their interaction was intuitive by nature, and they reached the furthermost cabin simultaneously. There was a window, and they took up their positions fluidly – each pressed against the bitterly cold wooden wall on either side of the window, both with their guns raised. At that moment, the moon emerged from between clouds that had just minutes before seemed impenetrable. A few moonbeams arced through the window, illuminating the inside of the cabin.

What Berger and Blom saw inside turned the blood in their veins ice cold.

*

There had never been any doubt. The front door to the cottage was down towards the water, and the strength that Deer had built up not just on her walk across the island but throughout this peculiar case was more than enough to kick down the door.

It wasn't necessary. The door was open.

With her gun and torch raised as high as possible, she crashed into the small house. The sight from the window lingered in her from the moment she had seen it. She had a ringside seat.

She saw the decapitated head.

*

They came round the end of the house. Incredibly, the door was open – as if someone had kicked it down.

Berger stood on one side of the door, Blom on the other. Both were breathing through their nostrils, both could smell their weapons; their pistols were pressed close to their noses.

Then they crashed into the house.

Straight into the awfulness.

*

Deer's gaze was fixed on the decapitated head. It was so grotesque in this tiny little house. It must surely have been shot elsewhere.

Its antlers were majestic. Each had six tines – it was without doubt a solid twelve-pointer.

The elk head was mounted on the wall above the fireplace. There was something on the mantelpiece.

When Deer got closer, she saw that it was a small envelope.

The kind that usually contained a greetings card.

*

They tumbled into the small house. There was a fireplace, a mantelpiece. On the wall above there was a picture – a landscape photograph. The bewitching shimmer of sunset playing across a hillside of cypress and pine trees, a couple of white houses, a few donkeys with their heads bowed, a row of beehives climbing up the hill on terraces, and an expanse of butter-yellow flowers running down to where the glittering sea began. Far beyond, the Rock of Gibraltar extended into the sea.

But that wasn't what was awful. There was something on the mantelpiece.

It was another photo under the landscape photo.

Something as ordinary as a portrait.

It was a wedding photo. It was Carsten Blom and Molly Blom. And the bridal couple's eyes had been coloured in with luminous orange. Four fiery yellow circles around four eyes.

For a second or two they stood there by the mantelpiece, then they split up.

The living room included a primitive kitchen. There was no one there. Through one door there was an earth closet and a rather stale smell.

But there was another door. It was closed.

They gathered, positioning themselves either side of the door. It opened inwards – if it was locked, all they had to do was kick it down.

They exchanged a quick glance. Berger nodded. Blom pressed the door handle down and pushed.

There was a bedroom inside – a very small bedroom. It contained a bed. But there was more than just a bed.

There was a drip stand.

There was a tube.

There was a huddled shape under the covers.

The person lying there hugging a battered old teddy bear appeared to be asleep. It was a very thin woman, almost emaciated. When Blom pulled away the covers, there was no doubt that the tube ran via a needle straight into the young woman's arm.

There was no doubt about who it was: Aisha Pachachi.

Berger stared up at the ceiling without seeing anything. Blom heard a resounding, noisy groan.

She approached and put an ear to Aisha's mouth. She heard breathing. She nodded to Berger.

Berger felt his own head fall forwards. He closed his eyes.

Somewhere in the distance, he heard a boat engine start up.

# 26

The stolen old Volvo pulled into the abandoned industrial area. The weather gods were playing cat and mouse with them – the storm had withdrawn temporarily before cranking the stakes up a notch at the critical moment. But right now everything was dark and silent.

Dark as the grave.

Silent as the grave.

Berger was driving, and Blom was directing him from the back seat with Aisha Pachachi's head on her lap. The seventeen-year-old wasn't even whimpering – nothing other than tortured breathing crossed her lips. But she was clutching her teddy bear tightly.

She hadn't been conscious for even a second.

But they had found her.

For a long time out on Fjärdlång, that had been enough. They had found her alive – the seventh of the girls. No more seven minus one.

They had basked in the sweet realisation.

Perhaps they had basked a little too long, because afterwards, something bitter had cut through that sweetness – the multifaceted, sour realisation that Carsten had got away. That he might return at any moment, that the speedboat they had heard might not have been his.

Then the next question: why wasn't he there? Why hadn't he tried to stop them? Aisha was Judas's ticket to thirty pieces of silver. Why had he let her go so lightly?

And had he actually done that?

It had been Carsten himself who had provided Molly with the clue – he had wanted her to come there. But only her. There was naturally the possibility that he had fled when he'd seen that she wasn't alone – and if that were the case, how had he seen them?

But did that really sound like Carsten? The man who had killed another person in cold blood, someone tied up, simply to frame Berger for the murder . . . The man who had seemingly, without hesitation, stuck a knife in the eyes of an inquisitive neighbour?

If Carsten wanted to hang on to Aisha Pachachi at any cost, he would have done it. Something had happened. Something had changed his plans.

The wedding photo with the sinister orange around the eyes contradicted the idea that Carsten had dropped his fixation on Molly Blom. On the contrary, it seemed as active as ever. But he had given up Aisha. Did that mean he had also given up Molly?

They had wandered around the small house on Fjärdlång sinking into a quicksand of questions, unable to find any answers that satisfied them.

And in the meantime, the clock had been ticking.

They didn't know what condition Aisha was in. Had Carsten left her to die? Had he added poison to her drip? Had he found another, better route to Ali Pachachi and simply abandoned her? They didn't know how long she had been there – it could have been since the Sunday before, perhaps longer. When they got down to it, they didn't know when Carsten and Aisha had left Tensta.

There was, however, one question that overshadowed all the others: what were they supposed to do with Aisha? Call an air ambulance? Alert the rather mundane marine police? Or let the Security Service take over? Although in August Steen's absence, was there really anyone there who had even the slightest knowledge of her role in the Triumvirate's intrigue and who could offer her protection?

Berger had to bite his tongue before he said anything about that. He was obliged to keep the insights from Steen's videos to himself. There were too many questions around Molly's role in all of this. In purely practical terms, how had she managed to reach the small island where Berger had been? He had actually asked that question and received a reasonable answer in return – on a rubber dinghy with a silenced outboard motor from Landsort. But could he even trust her? At all?

It was like being in the mid-water.

The air bubble that set him on the right course was what Molly Blom said to him.

'We have to put Aisha first.'

Berger nodded, spreading his hands.

'Hospital?' he asked.

She nodded too, but in a very different way.

'That would expose her. There are too many powerful forces out to get her. She must presumably be in possession of a lot of information.'

'Am I to take that as meaning you have a solution?' asked Berger.

She made her call outside the cabin on the slick rocks – he caught fragments of syllables, not much more. Berger *had* to trust her – she was good at this and everything related to her past in the Security Service. Everything that took place in the shadows.

He was alone inside with Aisha, the girl who had not only been kidnapped first out of the seven hostages, but had also been held the longest and subjected to the violence of two different kidnappers. By now she had been deprived of freedom for two and a half years – the most crucial years of her adolescence. Yes, of course she possessed information. If she was still among the living.

He sat down on the edge of the bed, pushing the teddy a little closer to her. He gently caressed her cheek. Everything that made people good could also make them bad, he thought to himself. Everything tied to our freedom could so quickly be turned on its head.

Blom returned. She had initiated a plan and it would take a while. Berger was to fetch the boat alone. Blom would prepare Aisha for their departure and build a makeshift stretcher. Berger was to moor up by the empty jetty. Berger and Blom would carry Aisha to the boat. Blom would navigate while Berger captained them to Nynäshamn. Berger would drive Blom's stolen old Volvo to an abandoned industrial area outside Haninge.

And that was where they were now. At the appointed hour.

'Stay here,' said Blom from the back seat.

Berger stayed where he was, checking himself for a moment and then thinking with as much crystal clarity as he could muster. Obviously, Molly Blom could lead him straight to the doors of hell. A swift assassination – no one would ever find out. He would be counted as a fugitive from justice for decades before being written off. But no, he decided. No, it would never happen.

Molly would never be able to murder someone in cold blood.

That was where the line was.

Especially not someone she was close to.

The sky was dark and there was only the faintest light as they carried the stretcher through a battered door and entered a less dilapidated industrial unit. In fact, it simply looked abandoned – as if everything had been dropped mid-process. And it was all rather indistinct. What type of industrial activity had taken place here could not be determined, but the roof had the loftiness of a cathedral and there were chains and cables hanging from the bare roof trusses.

A man emerged from an almost invisible door. Just like that. The strange thing was that he was wearing surgical greens. He pulled on latex gloves, letting go of them with a snap, and then spoke.

'Do you have the drip with you?'

Berger merely stared at him. For his part, the man didn't even glance at Berger. Blom took the bag from the stretcher that they had set down on the concrete floor and handed it over. The man in surgical garb took it, examined the bag and then nodded curtly.

'Carry her inside.'

Then he vanished back through the unobtrusive door.

They picked up the stretcher and carried Aisha Pachachi into a small room that smelled of antiseptic. There was absolutely no doubt that the man dressed as a doctor, now bending over a small metal table of surgical instruments, had thoroughly disinfected the whole room. He was alone – there was no trace of any colleagues or nurses. Without looking up, he pointed to a folding bed in the centre of the room beside a couple of pieces of equipment that looked to be both high-tech and expensive.

'Put her there,' he said.

They did as they were told. Berger tried not to think about the impact that a certain type of determined male authority could have on the world. He briefly stroked Aisha Pachachi's hand.

'Wait outside,' the man said, picking up a spray bottle. He vanquished them from the room with a shower of disinfectant.

The door closed. They found themselves back in the huge industrial unit, looking at each other. Eventually it was Berger who spoke first.

'Now you have to explain this.'

Blom cleared her throat and made what Berger assessed as an authentic attempt to do so.

This doctor operated on the fringes of the law – that was effectively his job description. Molly Blom had encountered him several times during her undercover work, but on those occasions it had been he who had sought her out, without ever providing his name. He had done this in a variety of precarious circumstances.

Berger wondered what they might have been.

There was a fully concealed Molly Blom in there and he wondered whether he would ever find out more about her.

Discretion was at least a point of honour. The Doctor – that was what he was called, with a capital D – was apparently able to pitch his mobile clinic anywhere, at any time. When the right person got in touch. With the right budget.

There was a lot of Security Service business that Berger wanted to know no more about.

A long wait followed. Berger and Blom eyeballed each other. They looked for somewhere to sit down and rest. Eventually they settled for the floor. A couple of metres apart.

'The swimming trunks were a surprise,' Blom said at last. 'I hadn't predicted that.'

Berger laughed loudly. In fact, cheerily. It sounded shameless in the cathedral-like industrial building.

'What's going on around us, Molly?' he said, once the long and resounding echo had faded away. 'Has the world completely lost its senses?'

'This world has always existed,' said Blom. 'It's only now that people see it.'

'But people like you have always seen it?'

'People like me are a part of it.'

Berger nodded and then shook his head.

'What are we hoping? That she'll lead us to her father?'

Blom looked at him, clear-eyed. He liked that.

'It all depends on what happened when August Steen hurried the Pachachis away from Helenelund. Did Ali suggest somewhere? Or did Steen just show up and take them away?'

'August Steen is your father, right?' said Berger.

At that moment in time, Blom thought to herself: *No, he isn't my father.*

'Why is it so important to you?' she asked.

'There's a bit more at stake if he is,' was all he said. 'And the fact that he seems to have gone missing isn't a good sign.'

She avoided follow-up questions.

'If Aisha needs intensive care, what do we do? If she's okay, what do we do?'

'I'm thinking about it,' said Berger.

'I don't believe that for a second,' said Blom.

'My subconscious is thinking.'

'Sounds lethal.'

'I don't know how much the Security Service knows about my existence on that island,' said Berger. 'There was a helicopter pilot who dropped off my moving boxes. I can't imagine it being completely undetectable for anyone who was searching properly. *You* found me. Otherwise, it's a great place for reflection. No matter how much I hated it. Although I hated it alone, it would be completely different if . . .'

'. . . you, me and Aisha lived there?'

'I wouldn't exactly say we're talking about living . . .'

'There's another place too . . .' Blom said slowly.

'I've been thinking about the boathouse. But now we're a long way south of town.'

'As if distance has ever stopped us before.'

'Back then we had something better than a lousy old Volvo to work with.'

'Well then, what do you have to offer?'

'The real question is which is more secret: the Service's safe house on the island or the boathouse in Sollentuna. August Steen went to the boathouse and Carsten went with him. And the island is obviously more comfortable. It's like choosing between Ryanair or business class with Singapore Airlines.'

'A choice you're intimately familiar with, I suppose . . .'

'Knowing about Ryanair is enough.'

Blom nodded. 'So if we get the all-clear to take Aisha with us and subject her to in-depth questioning, you'd prefer the island?'

'I was put there for a reason,' said Berger. 'I'm still wondering what it might be.'

'What's Carsten up to?'

'My subconscious is giving it its full consideration. I'll consult it.'

'Either he's truly fixated on me,' said Blom, 'or he's using that impression for completely different ends.'

'I see what you mean,' said Berger. 'If he gets us hooked on that idea then it shuts out everything else. Do you think he's fixated on you? Should we be taking that wedding photo with the crazy orange eyes seriously?'

'I've had nothing but sporadic contact with him for a very long time. I don't know who he is now. I really have no idea.'

'But it was him of all people that you contacted when you needed a weapon. As soon as you came round from your coma, he was the first person you contacted.'

'You don't know that,' was all Blom said.

'Do you remember the pole of inaccessibility? Lake Kåbtåjaure in Padjelanta National Park in Lapland. Do you remember putting in cameras there?'

'Don't be daft. It was only a few weeks ago.'

'You *have* been in a coma.'

'Yes, I remember.'

'August Steen said that Carsten was one of the observers. He was sitting on the other side of the camera watching us. He saw you, saw me. In his report, Steen said there were hints of fixation on you. And hatred towards me.'

Blom nodded and fell silent. Berger fell silent too. Fatigue and lack of sleep had caught up with him. Eventually it was Molly Blom who spoke.

'As I see it, it's extremely important that we find Ali Pachachi. Although I'm not sure I fully understand why.'

Berger roused himself and scrutinised her. It was no longer just his subconscious that was at work. How much could he really say? And was she making the very same calculations? Surely that was what was hidden behind that endearing Molly Blom expression?

Eventually he decided to hedge his bets.

'Pachachi is the key. He has a network of sorts that is good at unmasking jihadis. Steen has been active on one end, Nils Gundersen on the other in the Middle East. If we can notify Ali Pachachi that his daughter is alive, he may tell us things that he is currently too afraid to reveal. Life-changing things – possible terrorist attacks in Sweden, perhaps things even bigger than that. We'll be removing his gag.'

Blom nodded slowly.

'Good,' she said. 'That means we're on the same wavelength.'

'It may be that Aisha – or her subconscious – knows where her father is after all. Or she might be able to give us a lead that we can enrich with our deductive precision.'

She laughed. Properly. An equilibrium descended on them, an equilibrium that made it possible to rest. Both watched the other slowly drifting off.

It was unclear how long they had been asleep, but it was clear that they had both woken up at the same time as a result of hands clapping together. Hands in sterile latex gloves.

'She's sleeping,' said the Doctor.

'No change then,' Berger said drowsily.

The Doctor looked at him as if he were something the cat had just dragged in.

'An erroneous conclusion,' he said sternly. 'She was unconscious before; now she is sleeping. The drip contains a nutrient solution and a mild hypnotic. She's malnourished but not lethally. There's some muscular wasting, but no trace of any brain damage or impact on her internal organs. On the other hand, she is *tired*. Exhausted. A fine balance of exercise, food and therapy should see her back on her feet in about a week. I've drawn up a schedule. She has good basic fitness. I've included a course of dietary supplements and basic medicines, including broad-spectrum antibiotics, and the new nutrient solution in the drip should be changed regularly in the early days. I'll email my invoice.'

As if to demonstrate that he'd said all he had to say, the Doctor handed them each a business card. Then he returned to the disinfected side room and began to pack up his equipment. He didn't cast them so much as a glance as they carried the stretcher holding the sleeping Aisha outside.

Back in the familiar darkness, Berger spoke.

'Hypnotics?'

'Sedative,' Blom clarified.

They carefully returned the stretcher to the old Volvo. Blom took her place on the back seat with Aisha's head resting on her lap, as before. Berger sat in the driver's seat, bent forward and held together a couple of wires. The engine coughed into life and he turned to Blom.

'Well then, are you ready for some nocturnal navigation in the archipelago?'

# 27

*Sunday 6 December, 07:49*

It was Sunday morning and Deer had been sitting at her desk in her study in the garage for several minutes. Before that she had been awake, tossing and turning, for at least a couple of hours.

In the end she had resigned herself to vacating the marital bed, crept out of the bedroom which was dominated to an astonishing extent by the snoring of her husband Johnny, and woken up properly as she crossed the icy cold floor of the first garage in her bare feet and reached the second.

At least it was warmer here.

In front of her on the desk were the things that had roused her and kept her awake. Two greetings cards.

On the left was the number 2, circled, nothing else. On the right was the number 4, also circled. She could tell from the numerals alone that it was the same handwriting.

Card 2 was from Molly Blom's hospital bedside, while card 4 was from the cabin with the elk head.

She turned number 2 over. The words revealed themselves in its familiar, small, precise handwriting.

'*For judgment I am come into this world, that they which see not might see, and that they which see might be made blind.*'

And underneath, slightly smaller and in parentheses, it said: '*(John 9:39)*'.

It was definitely a Bible quotation, although the very first words from the thirty-ninth verse of John's ninth chapter were missing. In full it reads: 'And Jesus said, "For judgment I am come into this world, that they which see not might see, and that they which see might be made blind." '

Deer remembered the deductions she had made the day before, which had led her to the island of Utö. The small handwriting had looked absurdly focused on precision, as if it had been created by a child, or someone illiterate, or someone visually impaired.

And what exactly did it mean? She had gone back a little in the ninth chapter, to where Jesus healed blindness. He spread a paste made with, among other things, his own spit onto a blind man's eyes, whereupon the man regained his sight. But what followed was odd. Jesus referred to himself as the 'Son of God' and said that he had come to the world to make the blind sighted and the sighted blind.

The sighted blind. What?

Okay, it was one thing for Jesus to cure the blind – that was clearly a good deed. But why would he do the opposite and strike down the sighted with blindness? She headed online to look for interpretations.

It seemed to be related to more metaphorical ways of perceiving sight and blindness. Spiritual sightedness, spiritual blindness. People who believed they could see were struck down with blindness, presumably so that they might begin to truly see. It seemed to be a double movement: from false sight and living one type of life to blindness and thus genuine sight – a life of truth.

This revealed nothing.

So Deer had looked at the context. The envelope with this

quote had been left on Molly Blom's nightstand in the Southern Hospital while she was in a coma. *Maybe* someone had performed an almighty acrobatic manoeuvre, climbing up the sheer facade of the hospital with the aid of some type of rope, and then hung outside in the dark to pick the lock on a window that was supposedly impossible to open from outside, before climbing in to leave this envelope containing what was quite frankly a pointless Bible quotation by her bedside. And then they had hastily left again, disappearing without a trace.

Surely it was more probable that the envelope had already been there? That it had been left behind after an accompanying bunch of flowers had wilted? And had it not been for letter 4, Deer might by now have bought the explanation that some half-witted Salvationist had done a good deed for a solitary lost soul in a wretched single bed in a miserable hospital ward.

But letter 4 existed.

Deer recalled all this very clearly, and with a degree of complacency. She had looked more closely at the text and had a thought. If the writer wasn't a dimwit but was actually intelligent then he or she *wouldn't have* noted the source. Bible quotations were easily checked online, and writing 'John 9:39' was frankly overdoing it. At any rate, it made a rather unintelligent impression on the reader.

If someone had really climbed up to Blom's room, got the right window in the dark, and gone to all that bother, then said person with their meticulous handwriting would surely have written with the utmost consideration. She dismissed the Salvation Army hypothesis for a moment and googled 'John 9:39'.

As expected, the quotation appeared in all sorts of languages. The number of Bible sites online was apparently never-ending. But she didn't give up. Not until page 30 when there was no longer any trace of 'John 9:39'. Instead, she switched to an image search for 'John 9:39'. What appeared was a collage of religious imagery of text excerpts, from sixteenth-century German Bibles to the logo for the Word of Life megachurch, from God's light emerging from a cloud to floating doves of peace clutching olive branches in their beaks, from adverts that said 'Take care of the body God gave you' to stills from the feature film *The Emigrants*. And there was one more thing, a long, long way down: a map with squares drawn over a stretch of coastline and further inland.

With a sigh she had clicked on the image and saw the abbreviations noted inside each square.

One of them was '9:39'.

A cadastral designation. A reference to a plot of land.

But what about 'John' then? Well, above the large plot it really did say 'John' as a heading of sorts. She had pulled up the website hosting the map image. It was from a local homeowners' association on an island out in the archipelago.

The area in question was known as Johamn. Which meant that 'John 9:39' referred to plot 9:39 in Johamn. A cluster of cabins on the island of Utö.

There was a Waxholm boat to Utö departing from Årsta havsbad in around an hour. She could drive there from Skogås in twenty minutes and she'd have time to do a little research.

She had looked up the owner – one Slobodan Ivanović – and attempted to get in touch with him. All she got was an answerphone at a cab company she hadn't heard of. She looked up neighbours nearby and called them. One picked up. She wasn't on the island just then, but she knew that Slobodan had gone to Belgrade for the winter. He could 'no longer hack the Swedish winters'.

In the car on the way to the ferry, she understood exactly what Slobodan meant, and her sympathy intensified on board the more or less deserted Waxholm steamer as it slogged through the increasingly heavy sleet.

At Slobodan Ivanović's cabin – located at plot 'John 9:39' – she had found an elk's head and a small envelope. Inside the small envelope there was a small card with a 4 circled on one side. It was now lying before her next to its sister card. Deer turned it over and read the words that had left her sleepless.

'*I am but mad north-north-west. When the wind is southerly, I know a hawk from a handsaw.*'

*Hamlet.* That much she had turned up. Hamlet feigning insanity. Shakespeare and the Bible on two greeting cards with the same meticulous handwriting. But what the hell did the letter writer mean to say by this? It was impossible to extract anything meaningful from these solitary lines. It was a real anticlimax after her direct hit on Utö.

A real let-down.

Perhaps that was the whole point.

Letters 1 and 3 had to be somewhere. Perhaps there was something in them that might cast light on letter 4. But it didn't really make any difference. Someone had accessed the room containing the unconscious Molly Blom in order to send someone, possibly Blom herself, to the wintery end of nowhere on Utö.

Who would go to those lengths just to troll someone?

Deer pondered whether Blom had enjoyed any more success in her pursuit of Berger than she had. She had better resources at any rate. Perhaps they were already reunited.

She sat there for a while staring into space, which meant the windowless garage walls of her study. Perhaps it was time she gave up and went back to the house, back to bed beside snoring Johnny, inserted the earplugs again and waited for Lykke's tripping footsteps when she woke up. She decided it really was time.

She pulled out the top desk drawer and shoved the envelopes

and cards inside. They ended up in a stack of papers. She stopped herself, removed the sheaf of papers and examined the printouts of the bills from August Steen's office in Solna. She had gone over them before without finding anything of note. Perhaps it was worth a second attempt – to drill down to the smallest details.

She sighed and hoped that her family would be having a long lie-in.

She got down on the floor and spread out the mobile phone bills on her right, the credit card statements on her left. Then she got to work. First the credit cards.

Then the phone rang, with an unfamiliar tone.

Her mobile was somewhere – Lykke must have messed about with the ringtones. It was a nerve-racking, psychotic sound that some jaded engineer had added to the electronics.

Eventually she found it. Her hackles rose – though she managed not to swear – as she retrieved it from stacks of paper. When she looked at it, it resembled an alien artefact.

Deer forced herself to be rational. She had three mobile phones. A personal phone, a work phone and the new one.

The one she was holding right now wasn't her personal mobile. Nor was it her work phone. It was her new phone. The pay-as-you-go with the photos taken at the Security Service headquarters. No one had ever called it before.

It said 'unknown number' on the display.

She let it ring for another beat. She pulled herself together. She was too curious not to answer.

Too much of a geek.

'Yes?' she said into the phone.

'Is this Desiré Rosenkvist?' said a man's voice authoritatively.

'Who is this?' Deer asked, but she thought she recognised the voice. She just couldn't place it. It was probably because it definitely shouldn't be coming out of that phone.

'This is Jonas Andersson,' said the voice.

He didn't have to add that he was Head of the Security Intelligence Department and operational lead at the Security Service.

'This is a private number,' Deer said hesitantly. 'It's a pay-as-you-go phone and the number isn't listed anywhere.'

'I'm sorry about that,' said Jonas Andersson. 'And I must apologise for calling like this on a Sunday morning.'

'I never did get my work phone back,' said Deer. 'This is a rather unexpected time to try and return it . . .'

'We did try,' said Andersson. 'You weren't at police headquarters. I gather you're on holiday. But I'm sure you'll understand that's not why I'm calling.'

Deer felt as if she needed to amuse herself. She could at least act as if she were nonchalant.

'It's impossible that you could have this number.'

'We know a bit more than you think,' said Andersson in the same level voice. 'And I must applaud you for that. An extra mobile phone wasn't something I would have suspected. But when our techie reviewed the CCTV footage from the building during the small hours of his shift, I dare say you know what he found, Superintendent.'

Shit, Deer thought to herself.

'What do you want?' she asked.

'We need to meet,' he said.

Just like that.

'I agree,' she said. 'I've got a number of unanswered questions.'

The Security Service's operational lead laughed. Then he cleared his throat before he replied.

'It's eight twenty-two right now. I propose we meet on neutral territory at ten o'clock.'

'And what do you mean by "neutral territory"?'

'I thought Tössebageriet might suit.'

*A bakery? What on earth . . .*

'Okay.'

She was just about to hang up when she heard him add:

'Oh, and Superintendent . . . Bring the mobile.'

'If you bring mine,' said Deer, hanging up.

# 28

It was no worse than business class on Singapore Airlines, but all planes were a little on the cramped side. A safe house with just one bedroom was hardly suitable for the future. On the other hand, the future was already behind them.

Berger had slept on the floor, although the word 'slept' wasn't really appropriate. Blom had taken the sofa again with a couple of extra blankets from the boat, and he guessed she had slept more than he had. In the end.

But now they were up and already sipping coffee after breakfast. They moved as quietly as they could. Berger sat down at the computer. Blom nudged the bedroom door ajar, peered in, and then left the door like that before returning and taking the seat next to him.

'Her breathing is more regular,' she whispered.

He nodded, leaning towards the screen.

'The Security Service investigation into Tensta,' he whispered in reply. 'I'm trying to find out the latest.'

She leaned in too and took a sip of coffee.

'Do you know an "Agent Malmberg"?' Berger asked.

'Hmm,' said Blom. 'Sanna?'

'No idea.'

'For sure. Sanna Malmberg is good. Young but good. But has she got anything to work with?'

'She mostly seems to be trying to reach August Steen.'

Blom nodded. Berger thought he saw a shadow cross her face. But it was probably just his imagination.

'Nothing else?' she said.

Berger read carefully. His head bobbed.

'No one seems to be working on the ownership at Tensta. There are just a few general remarks about Big Exit Ltd. No one seems to be even close to the Pantoja & Puerta in Nerja, Andalusia.'

'Your extortion racket . . .'

'Sometimes you have to swallow your pride,' Berger said. 'I certainly won't be blowing Roger Corby's secret for him, and he's probably just been taught the lesson of his life. But I'm going to check that he toes the line.'

'What do we do about the law firm?' Blom asked.

'Carsten has hardly gone to Spain,' said Berger. 'He's still after Ali Pachachi. He needs to complete his mission if he's going to get his dollars.'

'Is he really working for Islamic State?'

Berger shook his head.

'Why don't we take a look at what Agent Sanna Malmberg has to say? Here we are. I quote: "At present, investigation gives rise to no real hypotheses about Q's paymaster. The finance desk in Intelligence Collection has been brought in and is surveying the international situation." What utter mumbo-jumbo.'

'Q?' said Blom.

'They refer to him as Q. Q as in quisling.'

'I see.'

A soft creaking made them turn towards the bedroom door. She was like a ghost. And yet not quite. The figure standing in the doorway in a vest and shorts trailing the drip stand and clutching a battered teddy bear was very much human. But she was pale and thin – and extremely bewildered.

'Where am I?' Aisha Pachachi asked. 'Who are you?'

*Well, yes*, Berger thought to himself. *Who are we?*

It was too bad that the first thing Aisha heard in her newly won freedom would be a lie. Berger chickened out and said nothing, letting Blom do it.

'We're police officers,' she lied. 'I'm Molly; this is Sam. We freed you yesterday, and there's still a threat to you. That's why we're currently at a secret location in the Stockholm archipelago. How are you feeling, Aisha?'

She stared at them, gripping the drip stand. Berger stood up and went over. Blom followed. They carefully took hold of one of her arms each and began to lead her back to bed.

They tucked her in, looking at her bird-like face. The smooth skin was stretched across prominent facial bones, her gaze wandering but the eyes crystal clear. And the passing of the years had transformed her long black hair into a bird's nest.

'Try and take it easy, Aisha. You're safe now,' said Blom in her most gentle tone.

It had some effect – her gaze stopped wavering and focused on Blom. Berger pulled up two chairs so that they could sit next to the bed. At the same time, he started the recorder on his mobile phone.

'Where's my family?' Aisha asked.

Blom took Aisha's hand, delaying her reply. Aisha let her, but didn't avert her gaze.

'Your mother and father are safe,' said Blom. 'It's just that no one knows where they are. You saw your second kidnapper, didn't you? You weren't unconscious all the time?'

'Carsten?' said Aisha.

Berger and Blom quickly exchanged glances.

'Yes, Carsten,' said Blom. 'Did Carsten ask where your father is?'

'Did he ask *me*?'

'Yes. Was he unkind to you?'

Aisha shook her head.

'No, never. He was . . . kind . . . Weird but kind.'

'But he asked?'

'He asked. I didn't answer. I never answered. He did the talking. He was completely different. William was something else.'

'We really need to find your mother and father – it's rather urgent. Do you have any idea where they might be?'

Aisha shook her head again. She closed her eyes.

Blom took her hand with her other hand too, squeezing it.

'If you want to tell us more about your years in captivity then we'd obviously be happy to listen. But we'd also understand if you don't feel up to it. Once everything has calmed down, you'll get to talk to some real professionals – psychologists, therapists – but it might help if you start by telling us. We're good listeners. And perhaps you'll think of something that might help us to find your family. Then we'll be able to reunite you in safety.'

'He was our bodyguard,' Aisha said suddenly. 'I couldn't understand why we needed a bodyguard.'

'Who are you talking about?' Blom asked.

'William, obviously.'

'How did he come into your lives?'

'He showed up all of a sudden, he was at ours for ages, stayed with us, slept on the sofa, watched over us. He escorted me to school.'

'Every day?'

'Yes. But he couldn't watch over us all the time. Yazid still went missing.'

'Your brother?'

'Yes.'

'But William stayed?'

'Yes, for a month or so after Yazid did a bunk. Mum and Dad were shattered. It really did seem as if he might have gone to Syria to fight for IS. But it was so weird. Yazid wasn't the slightest bit religious.'

'Did you contact the police?'

'We couldn't. Not if he had gone there. That made him a criminal.'

'You kept going to school as usual?'

'Yes. And William kept watching over me.'

'Then it was the end of the school year . . .'

'Yes. And he was waiting for me when we came out. But this time it was different. He said that we needed to keep out of the way for a while.'

'Keep out of the way?'

'It sounded weird, but I'd started to trust him, so I went with him. While we were in the car, he asked to borrow my mobile phone. I let him. We went to a house in Märsta.'

'He borrowed your mobile phone?'

'Inside the house, he gave it back to me. But I couldn't call my parents – he'd taken the SIM card. I asked why. He said that right then I shouldn't contact anyone. It could all be traced.'

'Did he say who it could be traced to?'

'No. I pretty quickly cottoned on to the fact that something was up. When I stood up to leave, I got a needle in my arm. I woke up in a cell.'

'Do you know where the cell was?'

'It must have been in the cellar. I was tied to a mattress. With one of these fuckers in my arm.'

Aisha slapped the drip stand, almost making the bag tumble down onto her head.

'I'm so fucking sick of drips!' she shouted.

'I know just what you mean,' said Blom, squeezing her hand a little tighter. 'This is just a nutrient solution until you start eating again. Would you like to try some food? Or would you like to stop? We can take a break.'

Aisha shook her head.

'No,' she said. 'I want to carry on. I've got to get through this shit.'

'Are you sure? You mustn't overdo it.'

'I bloody *want* to overdo it. I want to be alive. I want to be free to do whatever I fucking want.'

Berger and Blom exchanged an uncertain look. Aisha had certainly received a thorough examination from the doctor – and not just any doctor – but they were still dealing with a seriously traumatised kidnap victim. Were they even doing the right thing? Shouldn't she have been handed over for immediate physical and mental assessment? On the other hand, she didn't seem too bad. There was a lot to suggest that Carsten had treated her far better than William had. And she wanted to do it – she wanted to tell them. She had clearly been longing for a real conversation, to tell her own story. And they needed her brain ticking over, they needed to open it up to memories and associations that might possibly lead them to Carsten Boylan and/or Ali Pachachi. The end of that look said *yes, we should do it.*

*We should carry on.*

'You *are* free, Aisha,' said Blom. 'No one can get you here.'

'It feels like I've been kidnapped a third fucking time.'

Berger leaned in a little.

'It's really very simple,' he said. 'We need to find your mother and father before Carsten does. And I guarantee that you *haven't* been kidnapped. We're on an island in the archipelago. It's a protected island that belongs to the Security Service, and you're welcome to go for a walk just as soon as you're feeling up to it. It's an unexpectedly fine day today. The sun's shining for the first time in weeks.'

Aisha looked at him with a shimmer in her eyes.

'I'd love to take a walk,' she said. 'But first I want to talk.'

Berger nodded, smiled and leaned back in his chair.

It felt as if it had been weeks since he'd smiled.

'You were tied up in the cellar,' said Blom. 'Attached to a drip.'

'Yes,' said Aisha. 'It was a cramped cell, and the concrete walls seemed fresh. There was soundproofing. Not much light. I never worked out where it came from. There was the feeling of never truly being awake. My clothes were gone and I was wearing some weird grey pyjamas. There was the mattress, the sweat, the toilet bucket, the drip stand. Disgusting food. After a few days, I ripped the cannula out of my arm. William showed up almost straight away, put the needle back and told me I didn't have to be tied up, but I had to leave the needle alone. Days passed. Weeks. He started to become a different person. He never said a word, his eyes changed, his clothes got sloppier, he smelled different.'

'Did you manage to keep track of how long this was?'

'More or less. Eventually I heard the whimpering.'

'Whimpering?'

'How do you stay strong?'

'What do you mean, Aisha?'

'How do you stay strong when you're cast into hell just when you've never been happier in life? I'd graduated from ninth grade. The world was my oyster. And instead this. What the fuck are you meant to do?'

'You have to keep moving,' Blom said slightly awkwardly.

'I couldn't stand being tied down. So I had to obey, couldn't pull out the cannula. There was probably a fucking alarm on it or something. My grandpa was in Abu Ghraib.'

224

'The prison? In Baghdad?'

'My mum told me. The worst thing a person can imagine. Grandpa said two things before he died. The first was: never lie completely still, you'll atrophy. So I tried to come up with my own workout programme – one I could do with the needle in my arm. The second thing Grandpa said was: keep track of time. But if there's no difference between night and day then how do you keep track of time?'

'I don't actually know . . .'

'Periods!' Aisha exclaimed.

'What?' said Blom.

'Obviously it stopped later on. I haven't had a period in forever. But I did then. I could count the months at least. And I'd had five periods when I heard the whimpering.'

'Right,' said Blom, nodding. 'Of course. You're a clever girl, Aisha.'

'The roof was soundproofed, perhaps the outer walls too,' said Aisha. 'But not the inside walls. There had to be other cells. And the whimpering was coming from the right-hand wall. I put my ear to it and waited. Then I heard it again – it was a short sob being stifled. I called out. Once, twice, three times. Eventually there was an answer. I was no longer alone in the cellar.'

She fell silent, disappearing into herself. Blom let her.

'Are they dead?'

Blom stroked her arm and said with the utmost clarity:

'No one is dead, Aisha. Everyone survived. All seven.'

Aisha looked at her. Tears flowed noiselessly.

These were two and a half years of repressed teenage tears. Time that could never be recovered but could be *taken* again. It was such an infinitely gripping, almost beautiful sight. Blom turned to Berger. When she saw him slowly close his eyes, she could no longer contain herself. It washed over her. Molly Blom dropped her mask for a moment.

What was happening in this cottage on a small island in the archipelago was a simple mercy. A moment of grace when all the rotten double-dealing lies and falseness disappeared. Dissolved away. They let it linger for as long as they could.

The one to break the enchantment was Aisha Pachachi.

'It was you, wasn't it?'

Berger opened his eyes. He saw Blom do the same, wiping them as quickly and imperceptibly as she could. He heard her slightly cracked voice reply.

'Us?'

'Who freed them? It was, wasn't it?'

'It doesn't matter,' said Blom. 'What does matter is that they're all free and alive.'

Berger saw the bed shaking violently as Aisha jumped backwards, raising herself to a seated position with her back to the wall.

'It fucking well *was* you who freed them,' she shouted. 'You're fucking heroes.'

Berger laughed. He couldn't help it. The sight of life effectively being *pumped* into her pumped life into him too.

The lifeless one.

Blom gave him a sideways look – but she couldn't completely conceal her own wry smile.

Aisha wrenched the cannula out of her arm.

'Right, I want to go outside and see the sea. But first lablabi. Tepsi. Khouzi. Bloody hell, I need some batata harra.'

When they simply stared at her, she gestured at them in frustration.

'Oh come on! Don't tell me you haven't sorted out any grub!'

# 29

Once upon a time in the late nineteenth century, Dean Pontus Persson of Dalsland welcomed a little girl into the world. He and his wife decided to christen the child Helga. After completing her schooling, Helga moved to Uppsala to train to be a home economics teacher. She married and became Helga Södermark, and at around the age of thirty she acquired a property on Stockholm's Karlavägen. There she founded a bakery, and she named it after the village in Dalsland where she was raised: Tösse.

Not only is Tössebageriet still on the same site to this day, but it also retains many of its original interior features. Deer spotted a few ceiling roses and a number of ceramic tiles in the window recesses that appeared to have been there since day one.

Sitting at an inconspicuous table towards the back was the Security Service's operational lead and Head of the Security Intelligence Department. And he wasn't alone.

Jonas Andersson stood up to greet her. He started by introducing her to the woman at his side, who could have been no more than thirty.

'Superintendent Rosenkvist, meet Sanna Malmberg.'

Deer greeted the young woman with a degree of surprise. She had difficulty understanding what role she had. No explanation was forthcoming. Before she'd even had time to settle herself, Jonas Andersson got straight to the point.

'The mobile, if you please.'

'Why don't we swap?' said Deer.

Wordlessly, Sanna Malmberg handed over Deer's work phone and received her spare in return.

'I want that back,' said Deer.

Sanna Malmberg still didn't say a word. She grabbed the mobile and was immediately engrossed.

'I took the liberty of buying you a coffee,' Jonas Andersson said with a gesture towards a cup on the table.

'Just the way I like it, of course,' said Deer. 'A nice but rather unsubtle marker.'

Jonas Andersson laughed briefly.

'Marker of what?' he asked.

Deer took a sip. Naturally it was exactly to her liking. As a matter of fact, it was downright delicious.

'Why did you want to meet?' she asked instead of answering.

Andersson had no trouble with rapid changes of subject. He nodded at the mobile.

'That was part of it. But also for the simple purpose of establishing what you're up to on your bonus holiday. Trespassing in the office of a high-ranking Security Service officer is obviously a serious crime. The minimum sentence is two years in prison.'

*Shit*, Deer thought to herself.

'If you were going to arrest me we'd hardly be meeting on "neutral territory".'

Jonas Andersson smiled joylessly.

'I can take you down wherever and whenever I like. I promise you that.'

'So what do you want?'

'Why are you looking for August Steen?'

Deer smiled, but only to herself. It was a smile of confirmation.

'Because his disappearance seems to have pulled down someone close to me. Someone without whose assistance I wouldn't have been able to solve the case that gave me ten days of extra holiday.'

'Berger, yes.' Andersson nodded. 'As it happens, I don't know a thing about Sam Berger.'

'The worst of it is that I don't think you know anything about August Steen either. And yet you're his boss.'

Jonas Andersson laughed. There was no trace of joy in this laugh either.

'It's a question of definition,' he said.

'I gather that,' said Deer. 'It's been claimed that August Steen is like Hoover. J. Edgar Hoover spent almost half a century at the top of the FBI and was untouchable – he had kompromat on every single American politician. Is Steen like that? What, for instance, does he have on you?'

'Attack is the best form of defence,' Andersson said coolly. 'So I understand your strategy, Superintendent Rosenkvist. If Steen has anything then it isn't on me, I promise you that.'

'But it's on someone. Someone high up. Otherwise he wouldn't be allowed to run his parallel operation. The Intelligence Unit doesn't even bloody exist.'

'That is another question of definition. And any secret service worth its salt is obviously home to agents with independence. August Steen's role incorporates a great deal of freedom.'

'What is it he has?'

Jonas Andersson glanced hastily towards Sanna Malmberg, still engrossed in the mobile phone.

'I'm sure even you understand that I can't say,' he said. 'Let's settle for the fact that he has access to something absolutely fundamental to the Swedish Security Service.'

'The Bermuda Triangle,' said Sanna Malmberg, without looking up from the phone.

'What?' said Deer, although she recognised that Malmberg was unlikely to have said too much – doubtless they had a script. Her role was to deliver her first line – that one – at that particular moment.

*The Bermuda Triangle.*

'Some people call it that,' said Andersson. 'People and things in proximity to August Steen tend to disappear. Berger seems to have ended up in the Bermuda Triangle.'

'What do you mean "disappear"?'

'They disappear, but they also resurface. Transformed. Upgraded. In new roles . . .'

'I really don't understand . . .'

'I've got it,' Sanna Malmberg said, holding up the mobile to show it to Andersson while keeping it out of sight of Deer.

'Good,' said Andersson. 'Zap it over.'

'All of it? Must be at least thirty pictures.'

'Yes, I want it. Copy all of it. And delete everything off that phone.'

'Come on, you really have to give me something,' said Deer from across the table.

'We don't have to do anything,' said Jonas Andersson, watching his own phone. Eventually it chimed. He zoomed in on a photo and nodded in satisfaction.

Then he leaned forward.

'Listen to me carefully, Superintendent Rosenkvist. Highly specialised circumstances are required to get away with what you did. And thanks to this handover, you've at least made a start on fulfilling that requirement. We're not satisfied yet, but you've taken a few steps away from Hinseberg. Do you understand what I'm saying?'

'I understand what you're saying, but I could probably offer you more assistance if I knew what you were talking about.'

Jonas Andersson fixed his gaze on her.

'Look, all things considered it appears that Berger and Blom did a good job up north in the interior, even if most of the case has vanished into the Bermuda Triangle. That's why there's a bit of leeway for you – because you did such a good job on our account. And that's why I'm going to let you in just a bit. But only a bit.'

'Looks like I've pulled,' said Deer, regretting it immediately.

Andersson raised an eyebrow, cleared his throat and placed his mobile phone face down on the table.

'The fact that our techie found the CCTV footage with you in it was a fluke. He was actually looking for something completely different – footage from the night before. August Steen's office was subject to a more regular break-in, but there was no footage. Somehow, the intruder had managed to neutralise the camera. All we had was the result of the break-in – a missing computer and missing notes. We've got backups of the computer, so we know exactly what went missing – and it ought to be sufficiently password-protected to prevent intrusions. But in terms of the missing notes, we had nothing more than the private secretary's vague memory. Now we've got it.'

Jonas Andersson flipped his mobile phone over. The rota on the end of August Steen's bookcase was visible – the one that had helped Deer to locate Roy and Kent. There were a number of Post-its of various colours around the rota.

The Security Service's operational lead swiped the photo off the screen. A new, almost identical picture replaced it.

'No Post-its,' said Andersson, pointing. 'Now we know what they said and why they were worth stealing.'

'Thanks to me,' said Deer, cursing herself for not looking more closely at that picture in particular.

'Thanks to your criminal actions,' Andersson corrected her. 'Now we've done our duty, seized your photographs and erased them from your phone. Any backup copies that you may have made are beyond our remit.'

Deer digested those words.

'Am I to take it that you want my help?'

'If you do happen to have copies then you're naturally welcome to take a look at those Post-its too, but I dare say the Security Service's cumulative analytical power is more efficient in that context. However, I would like to know more about you and Berger and your collaboration in the interior that led to the rescue of our former colleague Molly Blom. For instance, how did you know where to find her?'

'Ah,' said Deer. 'I see.'

'Oh?'

'The Security Service helped us. August Steen, through a man by the name of Carsten.'

'Hmm,' said Jonas Andersson. 'And how exactly did that work?'

'Long story,' said Deer. 'Is Carsten important?'

'I want your long story, Desiré. I want it in writing, completely truthful and with every single detail. And I want it yesterday.'

Deer looked at him in astonishment.

'Are you being serious?' she asked.

'That I want your story? Most definitely.'

'That you "want it yesterday"? That's what some poxy corporate middle manager says, not the operational lead at the Security Service.'

Andersson laughed. Sanna Malmberg, on the other hand, didn't bat an eyelid. Andersson leaned forward and pushed a business card across the table.

'Get your story to Sanna within two hours – before twelve o'clock. And it had better be a decided improvement on the one you supplied to Internal Affairs. Leif Eskilsson may have been satisfied with you, but I think you pulled the wool over the eyes of the lot of them.'

Deer contemplated the young woman, who was most remarkable for her conspicuous detachment from the conversation.

'I thought this might be a little more cooperative. I thought you'd update me on the investigation into August Steen's disappearance.'

Jonas Andersson sighed audibly.

'I'm afraid that's what we've just done.'

With a vaguely guilty conscience, Deer parked down the street. Then she walked towards the house, slipping through the side door into the garage. From there she could clearly hear the sound of a football match. Presumably Liverpool's 2009 four-nil massacre of Everton. The vaguely guilty conscience grew heavier as she crept through the first garage, and showed its true colours in the second one: it dissolved entirely upon sight of her desk. Deer walked the tightrope between the printouts scattered across the floor, and rifled through the stack of papers still on the desk. Eventually, she found the photograph of the rota with the Post-its dispersed around it like motley satellites.

She pulled out a magnifying glass and peered through it at the Post-its, transcribing them. All of them were in pencil. Three were worthless – shopping lists and cinema times. Two were mobile numbers with no further comments, one contained nothing but incomprehensible abbreviations, and one – it was pink – said 'Remember: mo. o. 1234'. That was what caught Deer's interest.

It was without doubt August Steen's handwriting – it matched all the other pencil scribbles – and he'd needed to remember something. It might mean Monday – he was meant to remember something on a Monday. Or perhaps 1234 was a code, a time, a sum of money, or just plain gobbledegook. Because what the hell did 'o' mean?

'Remember: mo. o. 1234'.

She surveyed her notes – everything that had been on the Post-its. Overall, it made a rather futile impression on her. As usual, it was best not to get bogged down but to let the brain process it in the subconscious – which meant it was best to do something else.

She turned her gaze towards the floor. All the photographs of the printouts she had taken on her new mobile in August Steen's office at the Security Service in Solna were there. The mobile phone bills were to the right of her desk, the credit card statements to the left. She sighed deeply, got down on the floor and set to work.

First the credit cards. The bills were all from the last year, and clearly issued after the Security Service had formally changed its address from Kungsholmen to Solna. She had gone through them before, month by month. She did so again, even more thoroughly.

If there was any part of police work that was by definition hopeless, it was this: drearily threshing through material, carrying out dubious double checks and dumb comparisons of figures.

Although there were in fact two bills from September.

And the comparisons of figures weren't quite so dumb, the threshing through not quite so dreary. When she looked more closely, she saw that one of the September bills had a different credit card number attached to it. Surely it was a typo or some careless mistake? But no. It was the same name – August Steen – with a different number.

Okay, she thought to herself. Nothing strange about that. Of course a man like Steen had multiple cards. The statements for one of these were, however, not kept at the office. Apart from this one that had slipped through. Why was that?

It was a little strange that she had overlooked this before, but there were only a few figures that were different. A corporate card registered to Steen's home address in Äppelviken, Bromma, but with the Security Service listed as the billing address. It was that handful of figures in the card number that differed.

And where the withdrawals had been made.

There were no card payments – just four ATM withdrawals. One per week. And they had taken place in different locations across Uppland county.

Deer faltered. Uppland? Exactly where was Uppland?

Feeling a little ashamed of her own ignorance, she noted that the withdrawals had taken place in Enköping, Rimbo, Gimo and Östervåla. She got up from the floor, pulled up a map on the computer and highlighted the locations, inspecting the constellation they formed. She ruminated.

There you had it. Four cash withdrawals of five thousand kronor apiece in different corners of Uppland county during the month of September. Twenty thousand in cash in a month, with a regularity that suggested that this was not just a September thing but presumably common to both the months before and after September.

She compared it to the statements of the other card. There it had been used a little more liberally in the way one might expect, for all manner of purchases ranging from wine to petrol and trips to the supermarket. Granted, there were rather a lot of purchases of wine. But it looked like a perfectly ordinary credit card statement.

Not the other card, though.

She pushed back her desk chair and got down on her knees again to look at the mobile phone bills. There were three different numbers – hardly a surprise for a man in August Steen's profession. She compared the dates, finding a couple that correlated with the withdrawals. She circled several mobile numbers before quickly realising they were probably irrelevant. Nevertheless, there was some sort of connection that she couldn't quite get to grips with.

She raised her gaze. She reflected on exactly what it was that she was doing.

The basic mission, admittedly one she had assigned to herself, was to find Sam Berger, who might very well be staying under the radar of his own volition. Regardless, there were clear signs that the Security Service was protecting him and keeping him in hiding. The only senior officer at the Service that Berger had been in contact with was Molly Blom's old boss, August Steen.

Further investigations showed that Steen was also missing. There had to be a connection between the two. Steen had an extra credit card that was potentially being used by him in various corners of Uppland county.

Could it be a woman? A secret mistress? A lover who wasn't a mistress . . . Perhaps Steen, who was the stable breadwinner for his family in Äppelviken as far as Deer knew, went on an erotic outing to different locations in Uppland once a week. Although – Uppland? Really? He stayed in hotels, paid cash to avoid the risk of discovery and had a great time. If so, then one of the mobile numbers was surely that of a mistress. And wouldn't that be the ideal place to hide someone? Someone like Sam Berger? If August Steen was – what was it that Jonas Andersson had said? – an agent with a 'great deal of freedom', then a mistress's home would be the perfect place to keep Berger off the radar.

The Bermuda Triangle? What the hell was that? Was that

where Berger had disappeared? In the Bermuda Triangle . . . in Uppland?

Deer scanned mobile number after mobile number. There were a couple she recognised. Roy's and Kent's. There were at least another four she didn't know but which appeared frequently. None of them matched the numbers on the Post-its, but perhaps it was the thought of these bloody notes that drew her gaze to a particular call among the reams of bills. Perhaps it was the figures – the timecode. And that it was a Monday. To one of Steen's mobiles.

The time was twelve thirty-four.

The call had lasted for some three minutes, a couple of Mondays previously in November. August Steen had made a note to remember it.

'Remember: mo. o. 1234'.

What he hadn't remembered was to remove the Post-it from the bookcase in his office.

Unless it was something recurrent that he needed to remember. Unless that was somehow what 'o' meant.

O as in odd? As opposed to E for even?

Deer searched the list and found a pattern. While different numbers were used, every second Monday in odd weeks at twelve thirty-four on the dot there was an incoming call. She put the bills in order and found another pattern too. The calls came from the same number for two of those Mondays, before switching to a new one. Presumably a new pay-as-you-go phone once a month. She went to the latest mobile bill – the number for Mondays on that one had only been used once. It was presumably still live. She circled it.

That was the number she had to focus on.

Her knees ached. She got up. She inspected the map on the computer monitor. She had an idea and rooted through a drawer, digging up a set of folded maps. She rubbed her knees as she unfolded one of the maps, got back down again and studied it. She marked the four locations where the ATM withdrawals had taken place using a thick marker pen. Enköping, Rimbo, Gimo and Östervåla. They seemed to form a circle. She drew it – a circle across Uppland county. In the centre of that circle there was a town. A big town. Uppsala.

Deer expanded her gaze, moving south past Stockholm and into the islands of the archipelago. The southern archipelago. Utö.

There was a ruler on the desk. She got up, grabbed it and went back down onto her knees – she really did need to get some bloody kneelers – and put the ruler on the map. Then she drew a straight line from Utö to the centre of the circle. To Uppsala.

There was no doubt about the direction. About the point on the compass.

It was north-north-west.

She got up again and opened the desk drawer, removing both greetings cards. She turned over the one marked with a 4. There she read Hamlet's words:

*'I am but mad north-north-west. When the wind is southerly, I know a hawk from a handsaw.'*

*This has started to get really bloody complicated.*

At that point her mobile rang. A neutral male voice was on the other end.

'I just want to remind you that you've got fifteen minutes left.'

'What?' Deer exclaimed in alarm.

'You've got a statement to write,' said the Security Service's operational lead.

# 30

The sun was really shining. It illuminated the small islets and made the bands of still sea between them sparkle as if there were ribbons of gold in the water. And the sunshine along the shoreline felt like the very last traces of summer for the year.

Aisha Pachachi tilted her head back and drank in the rays of sunshine, closing her eyes and breathing in the oxygen-rich archipelago air. Berger and Blom could almost *see* the life seeping back into her slender body. She'd eaten and then some. They'd had to stop her in the end, in an attempt to stick to the doctor's schedule, as well as trying to subdue her desire to spontaneously run and skip.

She had survived. Two and a half years of captivity and she had survived. She had actually made it through that hell.

She looked down again at the old teddy bear sitting on her lap.

'I couldn't believe you had both khouzi and batata harra in the fridge.'

'That was Molly,' said Berger truthfully. 'There was a takeaway en route.'

'Although I don't know whether it was Iraqi,' said Blom.

Aisha merely smiled and stared out to sea.

'There,' said Berger. 'If you follow the line of my index finger between the skerries, just there, on the horizon, is the deepest point in the whole of the Baltic Sea. The Landsort Deep – half a kilometre straight down into the abyss. It's hard to imagine.'

Aisha smiled.

'I've been down there.'

Berger laughed.

'I haven't even been halfway,' he said. 'But it was cold and dark where I ended up.'

'Shall we go back inside?' said Blom, looking at Aisha.

The young woman nodded, still smiling.

'I want to see Mum and Dad.'

'We're working on it,' Berger said in a low voice.

They began to stroll slowly back across the island. Aisha was wearing the spare clothes from the safe house, and although they were baggy and slightly oversized, they suited her surprisingly well. On the way, they passed Blom's rubber dinghy – now deflated – which had been pulled up into some bushes, its small motor hanging there limply like a tragic appendage.

They kept to the shoreline as much as possible. It really was a splendid day. There was a purity in the air that was soporific. It was like being massaged to the ground by freshness.

They saw the jetty and the boathouse and then they reached the cottage, entering by the wine racks and emerging into the big living room.

'Do you want to go back to bed, Aisha?' Blom asked.

Aisha shook her head.

'It feels like I've done my time there.'

She and Berger sat down on the sofa while Blom remained on her feet.

'Would you like a cup of tea?' she asked. 'Or coffee?'

'I've never had coffee,' said Aisha. 'But I'd like to try it.'

Two and a half years in ruins, Berger thought to himself. The two and a half years when you usually – among other things – started to appreciate coffee.

'I'll make some tea just in case,' said Blom, heading to the kitchen.

Berger turned on the recording on his mobile, met Aisha's piercing, vivacious eyes and thought about time. How the passing of time removed vitality. Then he thought something that was a sure sign of ageing.

He thought: *youth is wasted on the young*.

'Do you want to tell us any more?' he asked.

'I don't know if I want to go back there,' said Aisha.

'How did Carsten treat you? You said he was . . . kind?'

'Only compared to William, though,' Aisha said. 'But he thought I was way more out of it than I was. I played up to that. As if my brain had gone to mush during all that time as William's hostage. Which meant he didn't care that much about whether I would understand. And I didn't talk. I pretended to be a bit of a vegetable – that made it much easier. So it was basically just him who did the talking. He talked a lot about a world that was being snuffed out. How his body and mind were in tip-top condition, how he needed help to see. And he quoted from Shakespeare. Something called . . . *Macbess*.'

Berger found himself chuckling, not entirely convincingly.

'We're talking about the flat in Tensta now, right?'

'I've no idea where we were. But yes, it was a flat. The blinds in the flat were almost always down, but the few times they weren't I saw other blocks of flats.'

'Did he tie you up?'

'No, but he locked me in my room when he went out. There weren't any windows in there. And there was no chance of screaming for help or escaping.'

'Were there bees?'

'Were there *what*?'

'Bees. The animal – the insect. You know, bees. Were there any?'

'Well, there was a picture of beehives.'

'And a sunset, cypress and pine trees, white houses, donkeys, yellow flowers, the sea, the Rock of Gibraltar. And a big thick book of Shakespeare's collected works in English next to the reading chair.'

'You've been there?'

'I have. Not long after Carsten took you away from there. He's moved you quite a lot, Aisha.'

'William moved us a couple of times. Carsten also moved me more than once. And you've moved me too. I've been a hostage in six places.'

Berger nodded, counting on his fingers.

'Märsta, Bålsta, Helenelund, Tensta, Fjärdlång and now here. Although you're not a hostage here.'

'Prove it,' said Aisha Pachachi.

Berger smiled.

He couldn't.

Not least because it was entirely possible that it was true.

Perhaps she was their hostage.

Blom returned with various steaming cups on a tray. Aisha reached out and sniffed the nearest coffee cup. She wrinkled her nose.

'I think you'll want milk,' said Blom, adding plenty.

Aisha sipped a little coffee before wrinkling her nose again. She drank a little more. She made an expression of surprise. Then took another gulp.

'Nice,' she said.

'Do you remember anything else?' Berger asked.

'It was uneventful. Carsten was gone a lot. Working. When he was out, I was locked in. I thought I might be able to get out of the room, but it was very securely locked.'

'But then something happened a few days ago . . .'

'Yes, he locked me in while he was in the flat – he hadn't done that before. I heard him pottering about outside. Then he came into my room and sat down on the chair next to the bed. He looked sort of different – I realised afterwards that it was because of the glasses.'

'Glasses?'

'He had new glasses. Thicker ones.'

'He sat next to the bed to talk to you?'

'Yes, he said we had to move and that it would be for the best if I were asleep while we did that.'

'And you were?'

'The last thing I remember before falling asleep is him getting out a syringe. Then I woke up in another bed. There was a drip.'

'Where was that bed?'

'I don't know. But Hagar came with me. I think he realised that I would have died without her.'

'Hagar?'

Aisha held up the old teddy bear.

'Hello, Hagar,' Berger said a little self-consciously.

'Hagar says hi,' said Aisha. 'But she wonders who you are.'

Berger laughed.

'Me too. What else happened once you were in the new place?'

'He didn't let me get up any more,' said Aisha. 'So I spent almost all my time sleeping. But it was dead – there was no one nearby. That kind of insane silence that you only find in the countryside. I went to the country a few times when I was a kid. It was so bloody quiet at my mum's uncle's house. No blocks of flats. I peeked out of the window a couple of times and all I saw was water. It was cold pretty much constantly and I thought the water might freeze. But it never did – it never froze. I want to see my mum.'

Berger looked at Blom. She looked back. He nodded briefly.

Blom said: 'We're going to get to your mother. To Tahera. But we have to sit tight here for now. While you're remembering things, can you describe your childhood?'

Aisha looked at her. After a while, she replied.

'It was good. In Helenelund. On Stupvägen.'

Molly Blom smiled.

'I know. Would you believe us if I told you that both Sam and I grew up in Helenelund?'

'The fuck? Come on!' Aisha shouted excitedly. 'Where?'

'We both went to Helenelund School,' said Blom. 'A year apart.'

'I grew up in a small house on a street called Tallvägen,' said Berger. 'What about you, Molly?'

Vile. Petty. Low. But all he got in reply was an indulgent but wry look from Blom.

'Edsviken.'

'Shit,' said Aisha. 'Latchkey kids. You're proper Swedes.'

'I'm sure we were,' Blom said calmly. 'But I had loads of friends on both Pilvägen and Stupvägen. What about you, Aisha? Many friends?'

'Bloody loads,' said Aisha, bouncing up and down on the sofa. 'I wonder where they are now.'

'You'll be a hero when you get home,' said Blom. 'You'll be in the papers. Your old friends will flock to you. No one has forgotten you, Aisha. I promise.'

'Hope so. I've really been missing Rakel and Nabila. Jonna and Millan too.'

'It's great having so many friends,' said Blom with what

sounded like real enthusiasm. 'Did your family have them too? Did you visit a lot of friends or relatives of your parents?'

'Not really,' said Aisha. 'But quite a lot of people came to ours. Mostly men. Single men. Neither Yazid nor I met them. We realised it was something secret. They would sit in the kitchen with Dad and talk.'

'But you rarely went away together as a family?'

'Barely at all. A few times when we were really careful. I really wanted to meet my cousins, but Mum and Dad said we couldn't – it was too difficult. But we did a few times. And Great-Uncle Salem, of course. Out in the country where it was so quiet. Although that was even more difficult.'

'Tell us more about your cousins.'

'It was in Alby. They weren't real cousins. Before Mum and Dad moved to Helenelund, when Yazid was just a baby, they lived in Alby. Dad had worked for a while in a pizzeria with someone called Mukhtar, and they were like brothers. Mukhtar had loads of kids – we called them cousins even though they weren't. But we couldn't see them as often as Yazid and me wanted to.'

'Do you remember where in Alby?'

Berger left his mobile on the table and crept away, waking up the computer and searching for Mukhtar, pizzeria, Alby.

'Just some block of flats,' said Aisha. 'They had a big balcony. I think they were at the top. You could see all the way down to the lake.'

Berger nodded as he sat by the computer, clicking away.

'What was your dad's relationship with Mukhtar like?' Blom asked. 'As secret as the ones with the men who came to visit?'

Aisha thought about this.

'Hmm, no, it was getting there that was the secret bit. We parked really far away and stuff. But Dad and Mukhtar were more like mates, I think. It was fun but a bit weird – so different from all the other men. Mukhtar made lush food. I really could imagine him as a pizza guy – but not Dad. He really can't cook. It's all terrible.'

'Do you know what your dad's job was?'

'He worked from home. He was always at home. Something to do with data. He had his own company.'

Berger kept clicking.

Under Alby, he'd found a pizzeria owner by the name of Mukhtar Nadhim. He had, however, sold the pizzeria four years earlier and there was now no trace of him. That was suggestive. On the other hand, it was possible to locate where Muktar Nadhim's family *had* lived. Berger pulled up a satellite image and zoomed in. The balcony was undeniably very big, and there was no doubt that you could see all the way to Lake Albysjön.

He pulled up details for the current occupant – one Amjad Sulaka, who had two mobile phone numbers.

It was at least theoretically possible that Amjad Sulaka was Ali Pachachi who was the Baghdadi professor. Or perhaps Sulaka was Steen's man and was hiding the Pachachis. There was definitely logic to the fact that Steen had chosen to keep Pachachi as far as possible from all the Security Service's usual safe houses.

It was without doubt better to delve back into the past for something that had never been put on paper.

Berger got out the old satellite phone and slipped into the bedroom.

Blom asked: 'How are you feeling?'

'I'm free,' said Aisha. 'Everything feels great.'

Berger returned, shaking his head.

'I just spoke to Amjad Sulaka in Alby. He lives in Mukhtar's old flat. And unfortunately he appears to be the worst sort of career criminal. Drug dealer, hard man.'

'I suppose that's a good cover,' said Blom.

'Although hardly . . .'

Blom grimaced and seemed to remember something.

'But didn't you say something else, Aisha? About the country-side. The silence. An uncle?'

'Uncle Salem, yeah.'

'And you said that it was even harder to visit him. How come?'

'He lived out of the way in a little house in the countryside. It was always quiet there. Dad would park really far away. There was a track to get there, basically through the woods. Although we only ever went there a few times.'

'Do you know where it was?'

'I'm trying to remember. He'd moved from some flat in the suburbs not that far away, and he was so chuffed about his house. And I think he was actually Mum's real uncle, even though he was ancient. Like, he had wrinkles. He had family photos show-ing Mum as a girl in Iraq. With Hagar. I inherited Hagar from Mum. She was a cute kid.'

'Hagar?'

'Hagar's the fucking teddy bear. She's never been a kid. What's wrong with you?'

'Your mum then,' said Blom. 'Your mum was really cute as a child. And you know that because you saw a photo at the house of your mother's old uncle?'

'Yeah, Salem,' said Aisha, looking insulted.

'Does Salem have a last name?'

'I don't know. It was all top secret. And Uncle Salem was pretty weird. It was a lot more fun in Alby.'

'More fun than where?'

'I'm trying!'

'Just take it easy,' said Blom diplomatically. 'We've got time.'

Aisha's furrowed brow suddenly smoothed out.

'Sunnersta,' she said.

Berger and Blom looked at each other. After a while both of them shook their heads. Berger sighed gently and got up to go to the computer. He was stopped in his tracks by Aisha.

'I think I'd be able to find it from the flats.'

'Perfect,' Blom said, stroking her hand. 'Do you remember the street name?'

'I think so . . .' said Aisha. 'But . . .'

'Come on, Aisha, you can do this.'

Aisha Pachachi closed her eyes. Screwed them even tighter. Eventually, her face returned to normal.

'Gottsunda.'

Yet again Berger and Blom exchanged glances. But this time there was a different meaning in them.

'Gottsunda,' said Blom. 'You mean . . .'

'Yeah,' said Aisha. 'Uppsala.'

# 31

The peculiar calm. The obligatory waiting. The conviction.

A route he had not found. Let them work. Better them than him. Better, not smarter. Just better at this.

The stillness of the flashing red dot on the screen. No real movement since it arrived at that little island.

One of the classic strategies. Feign weakness. Pretend to have lost. Encourage superiority and cockiness. Create a false sense of security. And then wait. Wait until the red dot moved.

Carsten was in an anonymous hotel room at the intersection of two motorways. He was waiting.

As he had done for so many meaningless years. The good had been there, and he hadn't managed to keep hold of it. It had simply slipped out of his grasp.

Not it. *Her.*

♀.

*Youth is wasted on the young.*

A quick divorce, then emptiness. A mature man who caught him amid his desolate wanderings, who somehow saw something in him. A man who seemed to scan the terrain and use radar precision to locate those directionless talents. The man had probably come to the circus school in pursuit of physical perfection. He'd found it in his adopted daughter's ex-husband, who was floating around like a loose cannon. August Steen, the ex-wife's adoptive father whom she wasn't close to at all. Yet another incident that appeared to have intent behind it. Steen, who had thrown him, without warning, into a world where he was expected to climb, slither and open what could not be opened.

But that was only part of it. A negligible part.

Carsten had become an infiltrator and was cast straight into the hideous maelstrom of trafficking, dealing in sex slaves who – right under the nose of the humanitarian superpower that is Sweden – were used up within a couple of years and then scrapped. That was actually how the Albanian mafia described it. Scrapped. All the death he saw, all the suffering. He was drained of what little faith in humanity was left inside him, of every shadow of hope, and he let that void be filled with drugs. The Albanians received short Swedish sentences, and went straight back to work in a perpetual cycle that it cost the earth to break into, but could never be disrupted for long. The memories of detoxification. The sapping emptiness that replaced the junk. Wanting to die. The journey. How the emptiness was filled – at least enough that he wanted to keep on living – by Andalusia, by his faithful bees. And by August Steen, who once again took him under his wing. The years of loyalty, true loyalty to Steen, his role model, his saviour when in need. He wondered where he'd gone.

Why wasn't Steen working harder to track him down?

The years of dutifulness. The enhanced training in ultra-violence. A necessary skill, even for a humanitarian superpower. Daily working life was hardly grey, but it was homogeneous – it was increasingly tangible. Carsten was not exactly living, but he was professional, a physically accomplished shell around the realisation that life had already passed him by. He'd had his chance; he hadn't taken it. But the shell survived, the shell around that emptiness, and he climbed the ranks of the Security Service.

His career was all he had when he got the news.

Steen let him stay despite the obvious progression of his eye condition. He was given dispensation to wear thick glasses while on duty. And then came the offer he couldn't resist.

*Se vende.*

The villa above the beehives – for sale.

The villa with the big terrace.

The surveillance on ♂ and ♀ in the interior. The disgust when he saw their intimacy. The betrayal. Only giving a marriage three months. The opportunity presenting itself. ♀ would become his eyes. And ♂ would die.

To love and hate simultaneously – was it even possible? To want to be with someone and become engrossed in them and also want to harm them. Poison. How sick did one have to be to harbour such double-sided emotions?

Something happened. A change in atmosphere that interrupted his dark philosophising and rooted him fast to the hotel-room floor.

The red dot on the display was moving – slowly but surely.

Carsten smiled self-confidently. He had predicted it all. There was no possibility of anything unexpected happening. Everything was going to go just as he had planned.

There was no possibility of any dark horse emerging.

Everything was predestined.

There was presumably a name for it. He'd never heard it. She hadn't talked much. But it surely had a name.

Surely that battered old teddy bear was called something.

# 32

They hadn't made it much north of Stockholm when the weather took a turn for the worse. They had already lost the mild archipelago sun while on the boat ride to Nynäshamn, and just a few kilometres further on the old Volvo had been enveloped in a truly horrid squall comprising shades of brown and grey sleet. Under these conditions they were obliged to battle their way through the languid Sunday traffic in the capital before they got onto the E4 motorway heading for Uppsala. The weather changed again somewhere around Arlanda airport. All of a sudden, it was minus four, and thick white snow covered everything around the road; every expanse of water they passed was crowned with a layer of ice. After Arlanda, the traffic eased up too, and they were able to think about more important things.

Berger was driving, while Blom was in the back seat with Aisha. She had the battered old teddy bear with her as always.

'So we're going to Gottsunda first?' said Berger. 'You think you know the way from there, Aisha?'

'That's what I said,' said Aisha Pachachi.

'It was a long time ago,' said Berger. 'And it's dark out there.'

'It was dark then too.'

Berger fell silent. Snow began to sail down from the sky in big flakes that were illuminated as they neared the car, pirouetting along its chassis and quickly being engulfed by the darkness. After a period that seemed to defy the passage of time, a delicate nimbus began to glow in the sky ahead. It took a while for them to realise it was Uppsala.

The lights of Uppsala.

They exited the motorway by the village of Danmark and made their way in towards the biggest town in Uppland county. A main road took them south of the town centre, past Valsätra and into Gottsunda, one of the country's most deprived areas and home to unusually high levels of crime, gang shootings, religious extremism and an impotent justice system.

But the present wasn't what mattered. This was a journey into the past, into the childhood memories of Aisha Pachachi.

She seemed remarkably untroubled – it was as if the terrible years in captivity had brought her closer to her childhood, as if the past had been all that she had had to cling on to. She directed the car in a practised fashion through the centre of the post-war social housing project. Groups of young men were sloping about in coats that were clearly too heavy. Not even something as romantic as snowfall managed to cast them in a romantic light.

Eventually Aisha spoke.

'We go along here.'

She pointed towards a road that ran south, out of the blocks of flats into a more suburban cluster of houses. After a while, a road sign told them they were passing into Sunnersta.

Aisha hesitated sometimes at a crossroads, but she always managed to find the right way in her mind's eye. On one stretch of road where the distance between the houses increased and the street lights disappeared, she told Berger to stop the car.

'This is where we parked.'

They did so too. Berger and Blom adjusted their weapons and trudged behind Aisha through the snow-covered landscape recollected from her childhood visits, hoping that not too many new houses had been built around here and that the lie of the land remained recognisable. Aisha found a small side road leading in among the houses, and it soon became labyrinthine. As the houses began to thin out, Berger spotted the old Flottsundsbron bridge over the Fyrisån river in the distance. It was just before Uppsala's legendary river emptied out into Lake Ekoln.

Big snowflakes continued to whirl around them as Aisha stopped and looked around.

'Ah, yes,' she said, pointing at the narrower of the two roads leading away from the crossroads where they stood. 'It's up there. At the edge of the woods.'

It wasn't much of a hill, and not much of a house. They approached slowly through the darkness. There was no moon or stars to guide their way, and the street lights had stopped at least fifty metres before.

The small house was tucked away in a grove of trees. The untouched snow seemed to have pushed it further back into obscurity. After a while, they saw a garage, but the driveway leading to it was also covered in snow. There were no indications of human life. Not even a lamp in the window.

Everything lay in dense darkness.

The fence was interrupted by a gate. Berger put a hand on the gate handle and pressed it down. They went along a gravel path, crouching slightly, in the assumption that they were approaching the house, but it was impossible to be sure. Everything was shrouded in snow. Any hope of not leaving a trace was in vain.

The gravel path reached some steps, which were slippery. Aisha skidded, dropped her teddy and let out a shriek. It was only a brief exclamation, but it was enough to be audible from inside the house.

If there was in fact someone waiting for them.

Berger pushed closer to the house and climbed up onto the porch. Then he stopped by the front door, crouched and peered at the lock mechanism. He signalled to Blom, who prised out her weapon, taking the safety off. Berger pulled out his skeleton key and inserted it into the lock as quietly as he could, feeling for invisible tags and spikes. The key caught, and he heard a faint click. Then he too took out his pistol.

The snow continued to fall unceasingly.

Berger and Blom took up their positions on either side of the door. They had it covered. They kept Aisha at a distance. Then Berger pushed down the handle and carefully opened the door.

Then everything went very quickly.

Yet at the same time it went so very slowly.

The first thing they saw in the darkness inside the house were two figures – nothing more than contours. Then they realised they were staring right into the oversized muzzle of a shotgun. The crack was incomprehensibly powerful, deafening them. Berger saw the shotgun lift as if through a huge recoil, but then it continued up towards the ceiling and flew backwards into the room, and from the corner of his eye he saw a small puff of smoke rising from Molly Blom's pistol.

The two figures let out a cry of woe that quickly transformed to jubilation, and then Berger was able to make out a woman's shriek through the whistling of his tinnitus.

'Aisha. My Aisha.'

Aisha Pachachi pushed her way past Berger and Blom and rushed towards the couple who were in the living room directly ahead of them. Aisha threw herself at them, the twig-like contours of her slender figure being absorbed by the woman's embrace. The man quickly glanced at his swelling hand but then he turned to look at Berger and Blom.

A little hoarser than usual, Berger managed to speak.

'Ali Pachachi?'

The man eyeballed him and decided that the situation was under control after all, before turning to his wife and daughter. He hugged them, tears streaming from his eyes. They resembled a group sculpture as emotion poured out of them.

Berger took a few more steps inside, looking appreciatively at Blom, who was looking at her pistol in surprise. There was a moment's silence, which was only broken by the sound of scraping from the still-open front door. That made Berger turn on his heel.

There was a man standing there – a big, dark silhouette. And he was aiming a large-calibre firearm at them.

'Weapons on the floor, please,' Carsten said mildly, pushing the thick spectacles up to the bridge of his nose.

They had no choice. Both Berger and Blom obeyed, the double clatter of their guns hitting the floor like the pointless little cry of death itself.

Carsten shut the door behind him and then, without taking his aim off them for even a second, he spoke.

'I must thank you, ladies and gentleman, for leading me here. I would never have been able to do it without you. Or that teddy bear.'

He smiled broadly.

'The teddy bear?' Berger said numbly.

'Electronically tagged,' Carsten said in a bored voice, indicating that Berger and Blom should move to the other end of the room. They did so, moving sideways, without taking their eyes off the gun. Carsten approached the Pachachis. He waved the women away towards Berger and Blom. Aisha was still clutching her teddy bear to her. Tahera Pachachi was sobbing ceaselessly. Carsten shushed her and bent over Ali Pachachi.

He whispered a few words, and received a few whispers in return. This quiet exchange of words went on for a minute or so. Then Carsten nodded and took a few steps back towards the front door. He once again brandished the gun and herded the group together, five humiliated people against the far wall of the living room.

Berger saw Carsten's gaze seek out Blom's. Once upon a time, in their youth, they had been married, lovers. And it was quite clear in his eyes that nothing had changed. What radiated from behind his thick lenses was unmistakably love. And just as recognisably there was hate.

Even though he had tried to get her here *alone* to be reunited with her, there was other human trash that had come along too, changing his plans completely.

Trash like Berger.

Carsten spoke quietly.

'Very well, my friends. Time to die.'

Berger heard shrieks and bellowing around him, but that made no difference whatsoever. He could tell that it was true. There was nothing to be done.

When he flew, Sam Berger often imagined how he would react if the plane was about to crash. Would he be panic-stricken or would he accept the inevitable and try to gather his thoughts? Would he focus them on the things that had meaning in his life?

Now he closed his eyes and saw the twins before him. He saw Marcus and Oscar with the utmost clarity, and he felt ready.

Ready to die.

Time to die.

When the first shot was unleashed, the sound was oddly

muffled. Berger knew he was first – he was at the top of Carsten's death list. He wondered with a degree of paradoxical curiosity where the bullet had caught him. The second shot was much louder and brought him back to reality. He didn't want to open his eyes. He expected to see dead bodies at his side.

He would have liked to save Molly.

He would have liked to save their child.

But he was incapable of it. Too weak, too unstable. Too impotent.

Yet when he opened his eyes, he saw Carsten's gun flying across the room. He saw the man put a hand to his thigh with a growl; he saw the pale trouser leg slowly turning red. Carsten hurled himself towards the open front door, lunging past the small figure standing there.

As he passed by, he hissed: 'Dark horse.'

The woman in the doorway tracked him outside with the barrel of her pistol, although she didn't take a third shot.

Then she turned back and Berger was staring straight into a pair of enormous doe eyes.

He met Deer's astonished gaze and froze.

He froze to ice.

Life seemed to be on pause. He recognised the feeling from that time up north in the interior – the sensation that he no longer functioned. He felt himself shaking violently and terms like *post-traumatic psychosis* and *acute reactive psychosis* crossed his mind. The thoughts moved incredibly slowly.

He knew that brushes with death always opened a void in time, and a small, small part of him spoke up: *Not a panic attack. Not just at this moment.*

But he couldn't move.

He managed to turn his gaze towards Molly. When he saw

that she was in more or less the same state as him, he had to overcome his own inertia.

*Overcome*, he thought to himself slowly.

*Myself*, he thought with a little more vigour.

Sound returned to him in fragments. Aisha and Tahera Pachachi crying, Ali Pachachi groaning. Molly Blom quiet, stunned.

One single person talking.

In the doorway, Deer spoke quietly and in amazement.

'I shot him.'

Berger saw his hand trembling as he bent down to retrieve his weapon. He stopped momentarily at the door to caress Deer's cheek. Then he made his way out into the winter night in pursuit of Carsten.

It was still snowing, the snowflakes drifting, dancing, seemingly singing. Carsten was nowhere to be seen, but Berger finally spotted his first trace down by the gate. A red trace. The trace grew more obvious after that – he had no difficulty tracking Carsten's blood trail through the snow. Surely he ought to be impeded by the gunshot wound to his thigh? Surely Berger ought to be able to catch up with him?

But 'surely' was no longer dependable.

After far too long, he reached the road. There too it was impossible to miss the red stains. With his weapon fully raised, Berger staggered along the road. Snow whirled around him, enveloping, snaring him.

Given all the gunshots that had been fired in the idyllic suburb, Sunnersta was strangely desolate. Not a soul was visible anywhere, let alone Carsten.

Just as Berger caught sight of the confluence of Fyrisån into Lake Ekoln, he had to stop. He was shaking violently. He gritted his teeth. Damn it, he was a pro – this kind of thing couldn't happen.

At the very end of the river where it merged into the lake, there was a slight bubbling in the water, but the further up the river he looked, the more frozen it became. And when in the distance he made out the old Flottsundsbron bridge, he saw that the ice had been covered in a layer of snow.

The blood trail was thicker. Berger staggered along the road beside the river, but he still saw not so much as a whisper of Carsten anywhere around him. He was absolutely nowhere to be seen.

Eventually, it was obvious that the trail led to the bridge.

Cutting along Åmynningsvägen, the road became more and more slippery. Berger was increasingly struggling to stay on his feet when he should have been running.

After what felt like too long, he reached the bridge. He found a clear bloodstain on the way up. Big, fat, fresh – there couldn't be much blood left in Carsten Boylan's body, rotten to the core as it was. Berger followed the trail onto the bridge, where he clearly saw further patches of blood leading wildly into the desolate, white-speckled winter's night.

Then suddenly there was no blood any more.

It simply came to an end.

Berger hesitated for a moment on the bridge, his gun at the ready. His reactions were a little too slow. His thoughts were a little too slow.

Where the blood trail ended there was one final stain. On the balustrade itself.

Berger heaved himself to the patch of red, peering over the edge of the rail, gazing down some five metres to the snow-covered ice of the river.

Just below the bloodstain on the balustrade there was a dark hole in the ice.

Berger sank to his knees, breathing heavily, staring down at the hole where Carsten had disappeared into the icy cold waters of the river, sucked under the ice.

It took a while for Sam Berger to realise that the strange sound resonating through the whirling white winter darkness was that of his own sobs.

# 33

*Sunday 6 December, 17:57*

With faint surprise, Berger realised the scene that lay before him reminded him of a nativity.

In the living room, Aisha Pachachi was lying on the floor with a pillow under her head. Two women were crouching by her – Molly Blom holding one of her hands, Tahera Pachachi crying and holding the other. In an adjacent armchair sat Ali Pachachi, pale-faced, staring at the group. And Deer had sunk down in the doorway between the hall and living room. She was squatting with her head down and her gun pointing at the floor.

Berger paused, allowing the tableau to sink in.

From her position in the living room, Molly Blom raised her face towards him.

'Carsten?'

'Dead,' said Berger.

He went to the doorway and crouched down beside Deer. Eventually she met his gaze.

He was ashamed to find himself thinking of doe eyes.

'How on earth did you find us?' he asked.

Deer shook her head.

'A slightly too long story.'

'I want your long story,' said Berger.

She laughed, seemingly without reason.

'Soon,' she said. 'Let's do it soon.'

Berger nodded. Then he caressed her cheek. He received a sad smile in reply.

'Your efforts saved the lives of five people,' said Berger. 'Including me. I'll always be indebted to you, Deer. For the rest of my life.'

Her head sank forward again. Then she produced something from the inside pocket of her coat and passed it to him.

He looked at the two small envelopes of the kind often used for greetings cards. He stood up, sighing. Then he walked further into the room, deeper into the midst of the nativity.

It was the evening of the second Sunday in Advent.

'We ought to scarper,' he said to Blom. 'Why aren't there any police here yet?'

Blom stood up from Aisha's makeshift bed and held up her mobile phone.

'I stopped them,' she said. 'We've got a bit of time to think this over.'

Berger nodded. Then he directed that same nod towards Aisha.

'Is she okay?'

Blom examined a small electronic chip and also nodded.

'And even the teddy is intact,' she said.

'What is that?'

'As far as I can tell, it's an RFID tag. Radio frequency identification. Carsten transformed Hagar the bear into a radio transmitter, so he could follow us to Fjärdlång. He knew she'd never let it out of her sight.'

'Not "us",' said Berger.

'What?' said Blom.

'Not *us*, it was *you*. He followed you to Fjärdlång, not me.'

'Right . . .'

'And here, tonight,' Berger added, 'Carsten probably planned to kill the rest of us, but not you. He would have liked you here alone so that he could have taken you with him. He would absolutely have shot all the Pachachis. Not to mention me.'

Blom nodded slowly.

'Is he definitely dead?'

Berger grimaced.

'Admittedly, there's no body. But he fell off a bridge, right through the ice. I promise you, no one could get out of that hole – especially not someone losing blood at the rate he was.'

'I really would have liked a body,' Blom said stubbornly.

Berger leaned towards her, grasping her upper arms and fixing her with his gaze before saying slowly and emphatically:

'I promise you that Carsten Boylan is dead. That's a promise.'

Blom shook her head in silence.

They stood there like that for a while. Wills locked in combat. Strong wills.

Eventually, Berger wrested himself free and produced a couple of small envelopes from his coat pocket. He united them with the two he had just been given by Deer. Then he handed all four of them to Blom. She looked at them for a good while, casting a grim glance at him, and then she went to the nearby coffee table. She began to open the envelopes, distributing the greetings cards across the table surface.

Berger turned to Aisha and Tahera. He crouched beside them.

'You're as brave as ever, Aisha.'

She smiled from the floor.

'I'm home.'

Mother and daughter looked at each. The obvious affection

between them warmed Berger's own blood. It had been a long time since he'd missed his own twins that much.

He turned towards Ali Pachachi in the armchair. A clear brightness emanated from his pale, furrowed face.

'Thank you,' he said.

'We'll need to have a longer conversation very soon, Ali. You'll have to make sure to thank the right people then.'

As Ali Pachachi slid out of his armchair to join the rest of the family on the floor, Berger went over to the table. The cards were laid out in order, from the circled number 1 to the circled number 4. Blom turned them over one by one. In the right order, they read:

1: *'Some say the bee stings: but I say, 'tis the bee's wax; for I did but seal once to a thing, and I was never mine own man since.' / 'like the Andalusian girls'.*
2: *'For judgment I am come into this world, that they which see not might see, and that they which see might be made blind. (John 9:39)'.*
3: *'. . . but I don't know what kind of drawers he likes none I think didn't he say yes and half the girls in Gibraltar never wore them either naked as God made them that Andalusian singing her Manola she didn't make much secret of what she hadn't . . .'*
4: *'I am but mad north-north-west. When the wind is southerly, I know a hawk from a handsaw.'*

'Bloody hell,' Berger said. 'If you didn't know better, you'd think this was an out-and-out madman. Not just in the north-north-west.'

'It really is all about luring me to him,' said Blom. 'Even if I don't quite understand all the details.'

Berger turned to the hallway, but Deer had already crept over.

She was standing next to them looking down at the cards on the table. She pointed to number 2.

'That one was on your nightstand at the Southern Hospital, Molly. While you were in your coma. There's a lot to suggest that overnight from Tuesday to Wednesday, someone climbed up the wall outside, jimmied their way in through the window and left the letter next to you.'

'Carsten used to be a circus performer,' said Blom with a wry smile.

'But what is the Bible quote all about?' said Berger. 'He was going blind – it has to be related to that.'

'It's Jesus speaking,' said Deer. 'He says he's going to make the blind sighted and the sighted blind.'

'I was going to be his eyes,' said Blom.

She fell silent. Deer and Berger looked at her. Berger nodded slowly before Deer continued.

'Although that wasn't the important bit. The important bit was "John 9:39", which was a cadastral designation for a plot on Utö. The fourth letter was in the house there.'

Berger couldn't help but laugh mirthlessly.

'All that bloody trouble,' he said. 'And for what? To drown in Fyrisån?'

'There's something Shakespearean about it all,' said Blom. 'The eternal fickleness of life, the complete meaninglessness of all our efforts.'

'Everything's just one big fucking tragedy,' Berger muttered. 'Is that *Hamlet* at the end?'

Deer nodded.

'Hamlet's words when he's acting crazy. It pointed me in this direction – north-north-west – from Utö. But it was the mobile number that led me to this specific address. Someone was in phone contact with August Steen every other Monday. They changed phones monthly, but this one was still live. I got NOA to help me triangulate the mobile. It's almost certainly right there in Ali Pachachi's pocket.'

'Impressive,' said Berger. 'Carsten must already have known *roughly* where Ali Pachachi was – north-north-west – but needed help finding the exact address.'

'And he got that help from us,' Blom muttered. 'From Hagar the teddy bear. What I don't understand, Desiré, is why *you* were searching for August Steen.'

'As I told you at Sam's flat, I was looking for Sam,' said Deer. 'I realised that he was being protected by the Security Service for some reason. All I had was Steen as Sam's contact – I guessed there was something going on between them. And then it turned out that August Steen had gone missing too. But there really is a whole bunch of stuff that I just don't get. Who is Carsten actually? What did he want?'

Berger and Blom exchanged a quick glance.

'It's too complicated to explain it now,' said Berger. 'The short story is that Carsten was a traitor, a quisling, a mole in the Service. He was after vital information that he was going to sell to a foreign power.'

'Jesus,' said Deer. 'It was him.'

'What?' said Berger.

'Someone broke into August Steen's office last night. It must have been Carsten.'

'How the hell do you know that?' said Berger.

'I've had some contact with the Security Service, oddly enough,' said Deer.

'You've had contact with the Security Service?' Blom asked sharply. 'Who with?'

'Jonas Andersson,' said Deer, who seemed rather astonished too. 'Head of the Security Intelligence Department and operational lead at the Security Service.'

'Hmm,' was all Blom said, but she didn't seem all that excited.

Deer regarded her for a few moments, then she turned and pointed to cards 1 and 3.

'And these?'

Berger angled the cards slightly more towards himself.

'The first is Shakespeare and it's about a contract that Carsten signed that meant he wasn't a free man. And "like the Andalusian girls" is a quote from Joyce that directly ties his past to Molly's. The third is also from Joyce and led us indirectly to the house on the island of Fjärdlång where Aisha was.'

'With a bugged teddy bear.' Deer nodded. 'So that you could lead Carsten here. I'm with you so far. But I'm still missing a fuckload of pieces from the jigsaw.'

'We'll go over it later, Deer. Right now we need to get out of this situation.'

He lowered his voice before continuing.

'The Pachachi family have been reunited, which is all very well, but the question is, how safe are they here? We know that the Security Service has been leaking like a sieve, and I think we ought to keep Ali as far away from them as possible.'

'The Bermuda Triangle,' said Deer.

Berger stopped, stared at her, glanced at Blom, but said nothing.

It was almost impossible. How on God's earth could Deer know anything about the Bermuda Triangle, aka the Triumvirate? And what did Blom know? He hadn't told her anything about August Steen's videos – he still didn't know whether he could fully trust her. Fortunately, she hadn't particularly reacted to the term 'Bermuda Triangle'. But then she was a first-class actress.

Berger opted to change the focus slightly.

'And where is August Steen?'

No one replied.

'Back to the original question in that case,' said Berger. 'If we daren't trust the Security Service, what do we do with the Pachachis? It's absolutely essential that Ali doesn't talk to anyone and doesn't have the chance to do so. That means my answer has to be you, Deer.'

'Me?'

'You. You've got no formal connection whatsoever to any of this. If we're going to keep the Pachachi family anonymous then it has to be you who hides them. You basically have to take the three of them with you *right now* to a secure location.'

Deer gaped at him.

'Some distant relative who doesn't use their place in the country in December? A house that's been empty for ages awaiting sale? There can't be any ties to NOA either. This has to be kept completely off the books.'

'But I . . .' said Deer.

'Give it some thought,' said Berger. 'Take Mum and daughter out into the hallway now. We'll help you. We need to have a word with Dad.'

When they came to move Aisha and Tahera Pachachi, Aisha stood up under her own steam and took a few determined steps towards the hall. There was no doubt that she was going to manage this just fine.

Berger and Blom shifted towards Ali Pachachi who had once again sat down in the armchair. As he crossed the room, Berger's secure mobile phone buzzed. He stopped to pull it out of his pocket. An email had arrived. With an attachment.

A video attachment.

From August Steen.

It would have to wait. He would have to wait to find out what came next without giving the game away in the meantime. Blom looked at him quizzically, and he merely shook his head – playing for time as he sought to rack his brain.

Berger would have preferred to speak to Ali Pachachi alone, but he couldn't think of any explanation that would convince Blom.

She definitely wanted to be present.

'Incredible shot,' was the first thing Pachachi said.

Blom looked at him and managed to reply: 'Thanks.'

'It takes real talent to shoot a shotgun out of a man's hands without injuring him. Although my hand is a little sore . . .'

'We need to discuss that whisper,' said Berger.

He would have liked to ask about so many other things – Steen, the Triumvirate, Nils Gundersen – but all that would have to wait. Right now, there was only one thing that was very pressing – that, and the issue of whether it could reach Molly Blom's ears.

'I understand,' said Ali Pachachi.

'Carsten whispered something to you,' said Berger, 'and you whispered something back. We need to know what that was about.'

Ali Pachachi looked thoughtful.

'I don't know what you know of the background,' he said.

'You can give us the background too,' said Berger.

'I'm not so sure,' Pachachi said with a degree of hesitation. 'I've been under threat for so long – the threat that my daughter would die if I said anything.'

'Your daughter is with us now,' said Berger. 'You'll be taken to a secure location – safe from all threats.'

Pachachi nodded.

'In recent years, the world's most powerful illegal arms

syndicate, a gang led by an Albanian called Isli Vrapi, have begun to sell huge, advanced arsenals to the highest bidders, such as IS – and all manner of other terrorist organisations. These weapons caches are very well suited for use in attacks, and also include some prototypes of new, revolutionary weapons systems. There are plenty of interested parties – that much we do know.'

'Auctions?' said Blom.

Berger looked at her closely when she said that.

Pachachi nodded.

'There have already been a couple. One in Ireland, another in Austria, and no one noticed a thing. Those arms are already on the market, and the threat level has been raised dramatically in those countries. It's claimed that the third auction will be the biggest to date, and that it's going to take place in Sweden. And soon.'

'What does "soon" mean?' Blom asked.

'That was what I whispered to that man so that he wouldn't shoot my daughter.'

'What exactly did you whisper?'

'Where and when the auction is going to take place. And the identity of the new leader of the organisation, who has succeeded Isli Vrapi. He died not so long ago in Sweden.'

'Okay,' Blom said with a deep sigh. 'Go on.'

'Do you know Landsort?'

'Landsort?' Berger exclaimed, as it started to dawn on him. An icy cold sensation ran down his spine.

That was why August Steen had put him on that island off Landsort. Sam Berger was going to play some kind of decisive role during the arms auction on Landsort.

'The island isn't actually formally called Landsort,' Ali Pachachi continued. 'It's the lighthouse that's called that. But increasingly, people call the island Landsort instead of its real name, which is Öja. That's where the auction is going to take place. The organisation have used decoys to ensure that most of Öja will be effectively deserted the day after tomorrow – Tuesday 8 December. There's a youth hostel at the southern end of the island called Sista Utkiken, which is where the auction will take place. No one knows where the arsenal itself is, but it must be somewhere nearby. All the stakeholders will be present – right now it looks like there will be at least three buyers. All of them killers. The auction itself will probably be run by professionals – lawyers – with mercenaries armed to the teeth on the scene. Over the course of a few hours, Öja will become a heavily militarised zone.'

Berger and Blom didn't just glance at each other. They stared at each other wide-eyed. Trying to find the words, to find the questions. Eventually, it was Berger who spoke.

'And what time does it start?'

'The auction starts the day after tomorrow at 1300 hours,' said Pachachi. 'In the best-case scenario, it'll be an orderly affair. In the worst case . . . it will be something entirely different.'

'Islamic State on Landsort?' said Blom. 'Seriously?'

'On Öja,' Pachachi corrected her. 'And yes, very seriously. Primarily their legal representatives, but naturally there will also be a few heavies for security.'

'There's something else, isn't there?' said Berger, his hand clasped to his brow as if to keep his wildly oscillating thoughts in place.

'Something else?' said Pachachi.

'The arms dealer,' said Berger. 'Who is the arms dealer?'

Pachachi nodded.

'Oh yes, of course. The name I've uncovered is Jean Babineaux.'

# 34

The man quickly leans back on the chair, his close-cut hair reminiscent of iron filings around a magnet. Then he continues his monologue.

'I think I may have found a vital clue to where Carsten has taken Aisha. I found it just before he snatched me.

'The Triumvirate has fallen, Sam. We're all in the Bermuda Triangle.'

'I don't know how much of a shock this is going to be, but I really have no idea how much time I have. There's no more time to waste on lies. As I say, I don't know how much of a shock it will be when I tell you that I have three children and four grandchildren. They often come to visit me on the island in Möja. In the big summer house. Two of the children, anyway. All the grandchildren. It's my youngest daughter who rarely comes. She was adopted. She grew up as Molly Steen when our family was living in Edsviken in Sollentuna. She changed her last name because of a rash marriage to a man called Carsten Blom when she was very young. A few months later they divorced, and he changed his last name to become Carsten Boylan. Later on, I employed both of them – they were two superb intelligence agents.

'I've been a good spy, Sam. I have an eye for talent. I saw it in you from an early stage. That's why I don't think I'm overestimating you when I say that you probably already know all this. I expect you've already managed to sniff it out. Perhaps you've even found the place where Molly and Carsten had one of their romantic encounters. I received indications immediately prior to being snatched by Carsten that it was likely he had taken Aisha there. It's a cabin on the south-eastern shore of Fjärdlång island, out in the archipelago.

'Always having to conceal one's emotions, Sam, is one of the worst parts of this job. Not so long ago you wrote a text in the snow including the sign *M*, a struck-through M. I assume you now realise with the benefit of hindsight all the emotions that flooded through me then. We met in the boathouse, you got me to help out with the rescue mission in the interior, and I put my best man on it – not least because I knew he had direct connections to Molly, our struck-through M. Presumably he was highly driven to help you rescue her.

'That man was Carsten.

'As I understand it, he did help to rescue Molly, but she ended up in a coma. At the same time, I realised that Carsten was the mole in the Security Service. The quisling. The traitor to his country. It was almost too bitter a pill to swallow.

'But you see, Sam, the thing about family, loved ones, kids, all that stuff – it's what you'll remember when you're on your deathbed. It's so precious, so delicate. Not least in our line of work.

'I don't know whether Molly has come round from her state of unconsciousness – I can only hope she has. She may have been adopted, but she is my daughter, Sam, and it's your duty to watch over her a damn sight better than I've been able to. She's carrying your child, and if I die in this godforsaken cellar and if she never wakes up then I take it as read that you, Sam Berger, will look after Molly's child, my grand-child, just as you have cared for your own children.

'No, better.

'Much better, Sam. Much better than you've taken care of your twins, Marcus and Oscar.

'The frontman for Isli Vrapi's arms syndicate is a French lawyer called Jean Babineaux. He's a highly energetic and eloquent corporate lawyer who has made his fortune representing the most dubious organisations you can imagine. As a result, he keeps a very low public profile.

'But who is he actually?

'Who is Jean Babineaux?

'After much detailed research, I caught a glimpse of a very intimate part of his life, which could be useful. My Russian friends would be satisfied, I would get my house on Möja, and before long I'd be able to retire and enjoy my incredibly privileged life.

'You see, it transpires that Babineaux's family is Swedish. He met a Swedish woman and took on her children, twins. Only later on did I realise that the abandoned Swedish partner and father of those children was a police officer.

'It was your family, Sam. What was once your family.

'Through you, I would gain direct access to Jean Babineaux's personal life. Sam, you were the seed that I planted.

'I assume I have your attention now.

'I also assume that you'd like me to continue.

'The Babineaux family have remained constantly off the radar in Paris. No one knows where they are.

'I'm going to tell you what my plan was. It was an exquisite plan, although how it's going now with me stuck in this cellar is in the lap of the gods.

'It would be impossible to get at the Babineaux family before the auction – they are too well hidden, too well guarded – but it would be possible during the auction itself. Jean Babineaux always travels with an entourage made up of the best bodyguards on earth – practised experts, presumably drawn from the Foreign Legion. In total, there are always five, and no one – absolutely no one – can get near him. All the same, the auctions themselves seem to be very orderly affairs.

'However, according to one of our sources, one new thing has cropped up for this Swedish auction. It seems that Babineaux's entourage is going to be expanded in Sweden compared to the first two auctions in Ireland and Austria.

'There will no longer be five – instead there will be eight.

'You see, Sam, the rest of the Babineaux family will also be on Landsort. I have no idea why Jean would bring his family to the auction. It seems a little peculiar. Perhaps he suspects them, perhaps he wants to keep an eye on them, perhaps he doesn't fully trust them.

'Anyway, Jean Babineaux's entourage is no longer five-strong, but comprises eight people instead.

'Five plus three.

'And that's why you're on that island, Sam. You see, I had a way in. You were going to contact your twins, lure them to your side, and get them to leave the hostel on Landsort just as the auction began – when they would probably be left alone inside. You were going to be completely convinced that you were there to save them. Instead, I would be there. I would grab your twins right in front of you and kill you. And then I would make it known that you were mixed up in the auction and that you were a spy, Sam.

'During the auction, word would reach Babineaux that his family had been kidnapped. The auction would be interrupted. A direct negotiation with my Russian contacts on site – the lawyer from Moscow – would be able to proceed. And I would be in safety with your family.

'Who would naturally not be permitted to live.

'That was the plan. You were to be my sacrificial lamb, Sam. You and your family. A family of sacrificial lambs.

'What will actually happen on Landsort without me, well, I have no idea. But I fear that it may be a bloodbath. And I very much doubt your family will get out alive.

'Those are my parting words to you, Sam.

'Your family is under a death sentence.

'Oscar is dead. Marcus is dead. Freja is dead.'

*For a moment, the man with the steely grey hair looks childishly sat-*
*isfied. He leans back in the chair and smiles a smile that in any other*
*context would have looked fatherly, caring and empathetic.*

*But then he turns quickly to the side, and appears to be listening for*
*a moment. Then he hisses:*

*'Shit.'*

*His hand is raised to the camera, becoming enormous. He grabs the*
*camera, and the image bounces around the cellar, showing the ceiling,*
*the walls, the floor. Everything moves very quickly.*

*Then the camera is switched off.*

*And everything goes black.*

# 35

The winter weather which had joined them from Uppsala lingered on across Stockholm, spreading a white blanket of snow across the Skogskyrkogården cemetery and obstinately remaining present as they passed Farsta, Trångsund and Länna before starting to ease up in Jordbro and disappearing altogether at Häringe Castle. At Björsta, the sleet took over and everything looked just as it had before as they got into the boat in Nynäshamn. The storm obligingly refrained from unleashing itself until they had reached the big living room and poured themselves a glass of Barolo each, but well before bedtime it was exerting its full force, hurling objects as big as snowballs at the windows.

Yet it wasn't the storm that woke Molly Blom, it was the howling.

Throughout the journey it had been as if Berger were paralysed. Blom had left him alone.

Jean Babineaux.

She couldn't and didn't want to say anything.

She had to let him digest it on his own terms. In his own way.

Deer had at least managed to think of a possible hiding place. Her husband Johnny's aunt was a widow and always spent her winters on Gran Canaria, which meant that her house on the outskirts of Strängnäs was empty. And it was in a secluded spot. After filling the car with necessities from an Uppsala supermarket, Deer had immediately driven the Pachachi family to Aunt Sofia's house. Word had reached the island off Landsort that everything was under control. Ali Pachachi had even brought the shotgun with him from Sunnersta – it turned out it was still in one piece. And Aisha was okay.

But it was the howling that woke Molly Blom.

Before Berger and Blom had left Uppsala, they had driven to the Flottsundsbron bridge. Despite his somewhat paralysed state, Berger had managed to brush away the deepening snow to show a trail of blood. He was particularly careful with the bloodstain on the balustrade. A thin layer of ice was forming over the hole into the black river waters. Eventually, a snowplough appeared and shunted all trace into the Fyrisån river.

'Carsten's dead,' Blom said as the Piemonte made her taste buds dance.

'That's what I said,' said Berger, leaning back on the sofa. In another context, he might have looked relaxed.

Blom scrutinised him.

'Don't we need to talk about Jean Babineaux at least a bit?'

Berger shook his head. His slightly paralysed state didn't seem to want to let go of him.

Blom was already feeling dead tired, and there was really very little preventing her from getting an early night. Very little except Berger's behaviour.

'I can't talk about it now,' he said. 'I think we'll have to leave it for first thing tomorrow.'

Without any further discussion, they lay down on either side of the bed in the bedroom. Blom dropped off unexpectedly quickly, but Berger remained awake.

As soon as he heard her breathing assume a more regular rhythm, he began to fiddle with his mobile phone.

Should he wait? Wouldn't it be best to get a full night's sleep before the Landsort story unleashed its full force? In his current state could he even deal with another of August Steen's toxic videos?

Somewhere amid this tossing and turning, he drifted off. He woke with a start just after half past four. He was still holding the mobile in his hand in a grip that had been so vice-like that he had to prise loose his own fingers using his other hand.

He lay there for a few minutes waiting for the onset of weariness. But there was no doubt about it any longer. He had to.

He made his way into the living room.


Molly Blom was woken by a howling at four forty-five. Her first thought was that a wolf had somehow managed to swim across from the mainland. Then she understood.

Without understanding.

She crept into the living room. It was dark. At the far end of the room, a faint light illuminated a face with a cold blue hue. Berger was staring down at his mobile. He was amazingly pale and his face was contorted. The inhuman howling rose again, although it sounded more like it was coming from somewhere else in the room.

She went over to him, crouched down and brushed his arm.

'My God, what's the matter?'

He stared at her as if she were the spawn of the devil. She reached for the mobile and he pulled it away.

'But you've got to tell me what's happened,' she said with as much restraint as she could.

He stared at her with an even more crazed look. But there was also a wild energy in it.

'My family have been sentenced to death,' he said in a faint voice.

'What on earth do you mean?' she exclaimed.

'Marcus, Oscar, Freja. They're going to be murdered. My twins are dead. Marcus. Oscar.'

'No,' she said.

'Yes,' he said. Then he shouted: 'Yes. Your bloody dad has sent them to their graves. All three are dead. Do you understand what I'm saying?'

'My dad?'

'August fucking Steen.'

'No,' she said again.

'Why are you saying no? For fuck's sake, I *know* that bastard has –'

'What is it you've got?' she interrupted him, reaching for his mobile. 'Can I see?'

He stopped himself, petrified. He held the mobile away from him, staring at it. Then he calmed down a little and shook his head.

'No,' he said. 'No, I can't.'

'Why not?' said Blom. 'What are you keeping secret from me?'

'I don't care about anything now,' said Berger, feeling as though he were floating away and out of the room, vaporised. 'That bastard has killed my kids. There's nothing else to say. There's no life after that. It's all over.'

Blom took the mobile from him and put it on the table without looking at it. Then she grasped his hands, squeezed them and fixed her gaze on his flickering eyes, managing with great inner power to steady them.

Outside the window, the harsh archipelago storm continued at full throttle.

They sat there like that for a while. Just like that. In some kind of paradoxical understanding. Perhaps there was even a trust that exceeded and briefly overcame their mutual mistrust.

'No,' Molly said at last. 'They're not dead.'

'This is no fucking time for a pep talk,' Sam said, tears running from his bloodshot eyes.

'This isn't a pep talk. This is fact.'

'Then you'll have to make yourself clearer.'

'August Steen was going to go to Landsort to kill your children? Is that right?'

Berger raised his gaze, meeting Blom's, holding it fast.

'You can't know anything about that,' he said in a hollow voice.

'But what if that's just what I do know?' said Blom. 'If that's just my thing? If I tell you that I was there in that cellar? If I tell you that I made sure he couldn't make it to Landsort?'

Berger was silent. He was stagnating. Life was stagnating within him. And somewhere amid all that hideous decay, *hope* reared its ugly head.

'How could you be there?' he asked. 'It was Carsten who kidnapped him.'

Blom shook her head slowly.

'No,' she said. 'It was me.'

'But why?' Berger exclaimed.

She looked him in the eyes.

'Did he send you videos?'

'With the truth,' Berger confirmed. 'He eventually got to the truth. It didn't come naturally to him.'

Blom nodded.

'Yes,' she said. 'I understand. He had a camera. He must have dropped it on the floor, then recorded a video that got uploaded in chunks and was sent to you. And now you've received the last bit? Is that right?'

Berger nodded slowly.

'You have to promise – really promise – that what you're telling me now is true,' he said with great clarity. 'The whole of the rest of my life is at stake.'

'It's true,' said Molly Blom.

He exhaled. She saw kilos of anxiety dissipate. His shoulders settled, his neck straightened out.

'But why did you kidnap your own father?' he said.

'There's a lot of this bloody mess left,' was all she said.

'And where is he?' Berger asked. 'The whole of the Security Service is looking for him.'

'Exactly where I left him,' Blom said quietly.

Berger looked puzzled.

'There's something about this that's wrong. Why did you kidnap your own father? Why did you kidnap one of the Service's top brass?'

'He was rotten to the core.'

' "Was"?'

'Is. He's still rotten to the core. And I snatched him for personal reasons. You won't get any more out of me. Not right now.'

'Then I'll settle for that,' said Berger. 'But fuck me, you've taken family drama to the next level.'

Blom laughed – it was a low laugh that emerged from unknown darkness.

'I can't help thinking that it's you who's taking family drama to the next level,' she said slowly. 'I'm thinking of the name that Pachachi mentioned. I'm thinking of Jean Babineaux.'

Berger was silent. He stared grimly into space.

Blom remained insistent.

'There's more in the videos about Babineaux?' she asked.

'It's all in the videos,' said Berger.

Blom pointed to his mobile on the table.

'Videos I'm not allowed to watch. Because there's a secret in them.'

'I just wanted to spare you . . .' said Berger.

'I . . . kidnapped my own adoptive father,' said Blom. 'What secret could possibly be worse than that?'

'Are you sure you want to know?' Berger asked, fixing his gaze on her.

'Yes,' said Blom. 'I'm sure.'

'You're pregnant,' said Berger.

There was silence in the room.

Outside the window, it was as if the wind had gained new strength; the storm shrieked as if it wanted to get inside – as if staying outside wasn't enough. It wanted to be inside. Indoors. Inside them.

Molly Blom stared vacantly into space.

'I have a vague memory from up north,' said Berger. 'From the weeks when I was unconscious and drugged up. It's like a dream, a wild dream, and I had a lot of those. But in one of them, I clearly see a star-shaped birthmark just under your right breast, as we make love.'

'You saw me in the shower,' Blom said tonelessly.

Berger stopped himself, looking at her, seeing the empty gaze, trying to interpret it.

'Are you in denial? Who's the father in that case?'

Blom put a hand on her belly on the outside of her absurd pyjamas. She said nothing.

'No, I never saw you in the shower,' said Berger. 'I saw you half naked in the house up by the pole of inaccessibility. But you were wearing a sports bra. It happened to cover that particular area. I saw nothing. Not then.'

Blom's eyes were closed. Then she undid the top button of her pyjama top. And the next one, and the one after that.

Berger sat still, watching her.

Eventually, the top was fully open, both sides hanging straight down. She pulled them apart, widening the gap.

Sam took her in and tried to capture everything in it. He saw the star-shaped birthmark under her right breast.

Something gave way.

He slipped over to her, placing his head between her breasts, his ear straight to her heart. It was beating fast, much too fast. But then he heard it slow down as some kind of calm descended. Molly put her hand to his cheek, and he felt her face press against his hair.

Then he felt her very quietly begin to sob.

And still the storm roared outside the window, shut out.

# 36

He was lying on his side of the bed looking at her. She was sitting propped up against the wall with earbuds pressed into her ears, and unless he was mistaken this was the third time she had watched August Steen's suite of films.

It was an exceptional sight. For every tiny, interactive mechanism across the body and consciousness to be able to result in something so miraculous was simply amazing.

In the end, she removed the earbuds and blinked a few times. She met his gaze, smiled briefly but sadly and then shook her head.

'Well,' she said.

'Well,' he said.

She plumped the pillow behind her back a little. He did the same.

'Thanks for tonight,' said Berger.

'Thank you too,' said Blom.

It was the first time she had smiled that kind of smile.

After a few seconds it morphed into something more like her usual one. She pointed at the laptop on her knee.

'I know I denied our family ties – August and me. There was a good reason why. And we're not related. I found out when I was fifteen that I was adopted. And he was hardly an active dad.'

'Is it true that your siblings and nieces and nephews have spent a couple of summers in the house on Möja?'

'I guess so,' said Blom.

'You haven't been so often, but you have been, right?'

'Yeah, I've been.'

'And what would you value it at?'

'The value?'

'You know. The value of the property. What did the bloody thing cost?'

'He mentioned an inheritance. Mum mentioned a different inheritance. Put together it was enough.'

'No, really . . . What did that pile on Möja cost? At a reasonable guess?'

'But I haven't a clue,' said Blom.

'Are you in denial?' said Berger icily.

She laughed cheerily.

'Probably at least thirty million.'

'I know you, Molly,' said Berger. 'At any rate, I know you're intelligent. And I can't imagine your siblings being radically more stupid than you. Presumably their spouses aren't either. And no one in this bright clan questioned whether it was possible to procure a house worth thirty million on a government salary?'

'And two legacies,' Blom said.

'I can see your face right now, Molly. What did you really think?'

Blom groaned, gathering her thoughts.

'I always saw him as honourable to a T – bordering on square,' she said. 'He was hardly there during my childhood – an absent father. It was clear as bloody anything that he had no clue what

William was up to with me in the boathouse. He would barely have reacted had I been missing an arm. So I never drew that conclusion. I never drew the conclusion that he might have been turned – that he might have ended up in what he referred to himself as a grey zone. The sort that are so black it's practically impossible. So it never occurred to me that Möja might be linked to illegal activity. He was a Security Service boss, he was *my* boss, and he would never betray his country to some weird Russian mafia outfit.'

'Sometimes in life you just get that offer you can't refuse,' said Berger.

'But not him,' said Blom. 'Not August fucking Steen.'

'The more of a moral absolutist you are, the more at risk you are. He was sick of himself, his own squareness. Somehow, the Russians knew there was an open goal there. He was nothing but one big dollop of receptivity. It's the moral relativists that are tricky to pin down. The ones that don't sit on any high horses.'

'I assume you're referring to yourself here?'

'Perhaps,' said Berger.

'But the alternative story is even crazier. I don't know whether we can rely on a word he says. Contacted by a Russian attorney in a shopping mall outside Moscow? Seriously?'

Berger stared out of the window. The worst of the weather seemed to have moved on. It had stopped raining – and was that a hint of sunshine he discerned?

Molly Blom suddenly looked thoughtful, as if she were remembering something.

'There is one thing,' she said.

'One thing?' said Berger.

'August Steen says something in the final instalment that's stuck with me. He says: "frontman".'

'What do you mean?'

' "The frontman for Isli Vrapi's arms syndicate is a French law-yer called Jean Babineaux." He doesn't expressly say that *Babineaux* is the new leader of the world's biggest arms syndi-cate. He's a *frontman* for it. Just as he has been so often in the past in his role as a corporate lawyer – he's represented all manner of crooks. Been their frontman.'

Berger raised his eyebrows.

'What did Ali Pachachi say about it?' he asked, directing the question at both himself and Blom.

'I've been trying to remember that. I think he said: "The name I've uncovered is Jean Babineaux." '

'Again, he didn't expressly say that Babineaux is the undis-puted leader of the organisation. What does this mean?'

Blom shrugged.

'Don't know,' she said. 'It might not mean much. Babineaux is *going* to be there with his family; he's in all likelihood *going* to run the auction like he did in Ireland and Austria. It's just that he might not be top of the pecking order.'

'Interesting,' said Berger. 'But it changes nothing as far as we're concerned, does it? Where do we even take this? We need to make a decision on that. Do we get the Security Service involved or not?'

Blom sighed. She shook her head.

'If I've understood these videos correctly, your most import-ant task is to somehow get Marcus and Oscar out of the building they'll be staying in, which will presumably be the youth hostel that Pachachi mentioned – Sista Utkiken. You have to make con-tact with the twins, make it to Öja and be ready to free them. Although I've got no idea how that'll work.'

'And Freja,' said Berger.

'Okay,' said Blom. 'Perhaps. Although she actually made her own decision. The twins didn't.'

'But won't the whole of Öja be a hornets' nest? Not just Babineaux and his bodyguards, but an unknown number of representatives for various terrorist organisations and all that shit will be there. Islamic State will be there; those bloody Russians will be there.'

'But not Nils Gundersen, right?'

'The uncrowned king of mercenaries,' Berger said bitterly. 'The fallen third column of the Triumvirate.'

'In the third video August Steen says that it was Gundersen who turned Carsten and that Carsten's mission was to get out of Ali Pachachi when and where the auction was going to take place. There's a troubling window of time there.'

'Window of time?'

'You know what I mean.'

'Not quite,' said Berger.

'Sunnersta,' said Blom.

'Ah,' said Berger.

'Yes. Between when Desiré shot Carsten and when he fell into the river. He was injured, shot in the thigh, bleeding so profusely that an artery was probably clipped. It's possible that all he did was stagger on, dying, in blind flight. But it's also possible that in the meantime, he made a call on his mobile phone.'

'To Nils Gundersen?'

'Not that it would change circumstances all that radically. But it would mean that we have to count on another would-be arms buyer at Landsort. Nils Gundersen himself.'

'I wonder if there's any CCTV on Åmynningsvägen,' said Berger. 'Perhaps there was a camera near to the Flottsundsbron bridge. I'll ask Deer about it. She might be able to run it through NOA.'

He paused.

'Steen said that he had a "way in". I assume he meant a way in to Marcus or Oscar or Freja?'

'But you can't trust a word the man said.'

'The man is still your father,' said Berger.

'What could he have meant? What *way in*?'

'No idea.'

'Perhaps we don't have any chance of finding *his* way in, but you must have your own, Sam.'

'I knew that bastard Jean was some kind of lawyer, and that he might be under threat somehow – a target. I googled. I searched for traces online every single day. There was never anything. Except . . .'

'Except?'

Berger halted, reflecting.

'But it meant nothing,' he said. 'I discounted it. It was *my sign*. It gave me unreasonable hope.'

'There are so many elements to what you're saying right now that are beyond comprehension,' said Blom.

Berger picked up his laptop from the floor and began to search, scrolling frenetically.

'Facebook,' he said. 'Oscar suddenly had a Facebook profile. It was just the other day. Then it vanished again. He was lying on a bunk bed doing *my sign*. Double V's.'

'Double?'

'Quadruple, really. Using both your hands and feet. It's a work of art. I took screenshots. But there was nothing there. It looked like a regular profile of any eleven-year-old. Although I got it into my head that the V-signs were for me. Then the profile was gone again.'

Blom nodded, sliding over to Berger's side of the bed to take a look at the screenshots.

None of the posts offered anything, but there were other possible ways in. Firstly, there were twelve friends, of which the majority were probably still on Facebook. Secondly, there were two – just two – pictures of value: Oscar's profile picture as a fully fledged hip-hop artist and the photo from the messy boys' room with someone lying under the covers in the lower bunk of a bunk bed, extending their hands and feet and showing the V-sign with all of them.

'Divide it up?' said Blom.

'I'll take the photos,' said Berger.

'Then I'll take the friends,' said Blom. 'Send me the screenshots.'

They set to work. Before Berger had even had time to zoom in on the photos, he heard the clatter of Blom's keyboard. Then he zoomed in on the first photo, the profile picture. The first thing he was struck by was how little Oscar had changed. Granted, he was imitating a hip-hop artist, and sure, he was markedly older than the little boy – number two, always number two – that he had helped out of a ditch filled with coltsfoot in the spring a couple of years earlier. That was the last photo taken of the twins in Sweden, at least to Berger's knowledge. And it hit him all over again. How he had just given up on the twins, transforming them into some kind of unattainable ideal, a refined dream. The truth wanted to get into him; it was hacking away at him. And the deeper inside him it went, the more merciless it was.

Was that really how he was happiest? Keeping them at a distance like ghosts – ethereal figures without their own lives? Without any drama, without any solidity? Had he burrowed into the role of victim, finding his own security there? The twins were the fixed point in his life. The polar star, the still point of the turning world. Everything emanated from there – yet at the greatest distance possible. Was that so that he could really enjoy his suffering and innocence without having to make an effort?

This was something else. This was about proximity, about

getting close to them as people – living people whom he had the chance to save and also reconquer and bring back into his life, real life. Not the life of the figments of his imagination.

He didn't want to think like this. But he couldn't help it. The closer he got to Oscar's face, the closer he got to himself. And he didn't like what he saw – which, upon further reflection, was also a victim's role of a kind. Enough. Enough!

Behind hip-hop Oscar there was a wall and little else. The wall was the same colour as the wall in the boys' bedroom, so it was likely the photo had been taken in that room. The edge of a frame protruded into shot and Berger zoomed in on it. There was text inside the frame but no picture – most likely it was a certificate or something like that. Under a fragment of French text there was a signature without any printed name underneath. The fragment hinted at some achievement, but it was impossible to determine more. The signature was essentially illegible, but nevertheless he took a screenshot of the clearest zoomed-in view he could get.

Then there was the bedroom itself. The bunk bed looked pretty expensive – this was no IKEA bed – and the sheets looked luxurious too, perhaps Egyptian cotton or Belgian linen. But that told him nothing. Berger zoomed in on the fingers, moving on to the parted toes. The two biggest toes were clearly more widely spread than even he could manage. The twins had apparently kept practising the noble art of separating toes. That told him something at least, something that warmed his heart. Even if the photo wasn't directly aimed at their father, it was indirectly – the memory of him hadn't been completely eradicated.

On a table diagonally in front of the bunk bed there was a heap of books and papers, while to the left were the edges of a window. It was daylight outside, and Berger zoomed in. Was that a church spire he could make out a few blocks away? He took a screenshot of that too, and prepared to review photos of every church in Paris. Then he shifted his focus to the table.

He hadn't noticed that the pattering of Blom's keyboard had ceased, but now he heard through the crack in the door to the kitchen and living room snatched phrases that resembled fluent French, at least to his untrained ear. She was on the phone. He ignored that, focusing on the table by the bunk bed, trying to find any paper with legible text. He panned past a number of well-drawn superheroes, his eye briefly caught by the bright spine of *Harry Potter et la Chambre des Secrets*, before reaching a half-scrunched-up piece of paper that looked like some message or other from a school. He tried to zoom in on the school logo, but there was a shadow on the paper just there, so all he could really make out were the words 'Collège Privé', which was admittedly a plausible line to pursue. At the other end of the paper there was the fully legible name Marcus Babineaux. Berger worked his way down the page millimetre by millimetre, and reached a sharp crease at the point where the address should have been. Below the crease there was a postal code.

It said '75116 Paris'.

Outside the door, Molly Blom spoke in a hearty voice.

'*Bonjour, Madame, voici commissaire Eva Lundström de la police suédoise.*'

Berger would have liked to ask her about it – she seemed at home in France, and indeed Paris. But instead he opted to google. Paris was *département* 75 in France, hence the first numbers in the postcode. The rest was based on the *arrondissement*, the numbered areas of Paris ranging from one to twenty, with a zero in between. However, just one *arrondissement* had a one in the middle. It was a special postcode for the sixteenth *arrondissement*, which was split into 75016 (south) and 75116 (north).

Blom fell silent on the other side of the door. He stopped and looked up. She came in clutching her mobile, her brow slightly furrowed. In her other hand, she had a note that appeared to have been taken from Berger's whiteboard.

He said with some intensity: 'They live in the northern part of the posh sixteenth *arrondissement* of Paris. The twins go to a private school whose name begins with "Collège Privé". Outside the window, there's a church with relatively distinctive characteristics in the distance. I think we can start to narrow down where their home is.'

Blom nodded quietly and thoughtfully..

'And how did you get on?' Berger said.

She looked at him. 'I've got a phone number.'

Berger stood up. 'A phone number?'

'For Marcus Babineaux,' said Molly Blom.

# 37

Even though there was an A3 printer in the Security Service safe house, they'd had to make use of sticky tape. Four sheets of A3 stuck together formed one sheet of A1, which showed the whole of the island of Öja fitted into eighty-four by fifty-nine centimetres. That ought to be enough.

It wasn't a regular map, or even a regular nautical chart. It was a satellite image. Every single tiny outbuilding was included in the picture.

It was lying on the floor of the big living room. Blom was sitting in an enviable cobbler pose scribbling on the map. She straightened her back, gathered her thoughts and pointed to it.

'Okay, there's less than twenty-four hours to go until the auction. My guess is that the island is already empty. What few inhabitants there are have been paid handsomely to stay away for a couple of days. All tourism has been cancelled on the quiet. Something tells me that the ferry from Ankarudden up here in the north will also be taken out of service for repairs for a couple of days. The various bidders have presumably already begun to gather. Unfortunately, I can't find any fully up-to-date satellite pictures of Landsort.'

'We'll have to work with hypotheses,' said Berger.

Blom nodded before continuing.

'Apart from the small cabins, there are two places on the island where you can stay – both in the south. The north of the island is mostly wooded areas and heathland. The first is Landsort's only youth hostel, sometimes referred to as "Sista Utkiken", which is in the shadow of the lighthouse and has thirty-four beds in several buildings. There's also a modest function room there, where I would imagine the auction will take place in the event of bad weather. Otherwise I should think it'll take place outdoors in the garden. But there's also another, more unusual place to stay. There's a peculiar tower, the Lotstorn tower, which was built in the sixties and looks like an anorexic version of a block of flats from the Stockholm suburbs. It's been refurbished and features six modern double bedrooms, one per floor. Once again, this is just a guess . . .'

'Hypothesis,' Berger suggested hopefully.

'. . . and my guess is that the lawyers will be staying in the Lotstorn tower. As in, the people who will be doing the bidding. The clients are unlikely to be present – they would never risk that – but the lawyers will almost certainly have bodyguards. That should make it possible for Jean Babineaux to take the main building of the hostel for himself, his family and his bodyguards.'

'Five plus three,' said Berger.

'By all accounts, yes,' said Blom.

Berger tried to adjust his legs but couldn't find a comfortable position on the floor.

'We've already noted that you're better at this kind of thing than I am,' he said. 'So how have they got there? How are they moving around the island? The ferry pier up here is at least three or four kilometres away from the hostel down here in the south.'

Blom sat up straight.

'They've got their own boats. There are lots of natural harbours along the coast of Öja. The lawyers and their bodyguards need to be able to move about freely and leave at a moment's notice.'

'No vehicles on the island?'

Blom pointed to an approximately north–south line in the centre of the elongated island.

'There's only one road,' she said. 'But there are lots of well-hidden mooring spots along the rocky coastline. No, they've come by boat. I bet the bidders' representatives are already there. All . . . three . . .?'

'Everything depends on whether Carsten managed to share the information before he disappeared under the ice,' said Berger. 'If so, Nils Gundersen's team will be there too. Otherwise it's presumably just Islamic State and the Russians. But there might be others.'

'Mad Russians,' said Blom. 'Russian lawyer, anabolic financial muscle. I don't even want to think about who is hiding behind that.'

'There will hardly be anyone else there except a team of mafia attorneys,' said Berger.

They stopped, looking at each other. Then their eyes went simultaneously to the satellite phone on the floor.

'So Marcus's number was "secret"?' Berger said at last.

'As I said, I spoke to his friend Olivier,' said Blom. 'According to him, the twins are "weird", keep themselves to themselves, are picked up from school by a chauffeur every day, and those friends they have are kept at arm's length – at least publicly. But in that small friendship group – the one on Facebook – things are different. They persuaded Oscar to create a Facebook profile even though he "wasn't allowed". And one of them bought a *secret* pay-as-you-go phone for Marcus so they could covertly stay in touch. All seems pretty logical if you look at it through the eyes of a middle-grader.'

'And contacting the pay-as-you-go phone now would be too risky,' Berger said. 'Any reply from your contact?'

'Not yet,' said Blom, checking the time. 'I hope that doesn't mean he's struggling to run the triangulation, which might indicate that Marcus's mobile is switched off.'

Berger closed his eyes.

'And that's our only possible point of contact,' he said.

'Yes,' said Blom, 'I'm trying to come up with a plan B. But right now we're running with plan A. Step one?'

It felt like there were arrows shooting through Berger's brain. Something was bugging him. He tried to work out what it was. Possibly all of it.

'I'm grateful that you're helping me to rescue my children,' he said. 'And I know it's impossible to predict what will happen to the auction if Jean Babineaux's family disappears shortly beforehand. Best case, he'll panic and we'll end up with a full-scale shootout on Landsort. If so, the cops might manage to pick up a few of them. Worst case, the auction proceeds according to plan and IS or the Russians or Gundersen get the weapons. For me, the most important thing is to rescue my kids, but is it really something that you can stomach as a former Security Service operative?'

Blom looked at him.

'The key word there is "former". I'm not in the Service any longer.'

'But shouldn't we have somehow put them on standby?'

She shook her head slowly.

'It doesn't work like that,' she said. 'Not in the world where you have to obey the law and follow protocol – the world that we're still trying to defend. Our focus right now is on your kids and nothing else, and that means that the law and protocol don't matter. So, plan A. Let's hear your version.'

Berger looked at the large satellite image and pointed to a couple of islets along the north of Öja's coastline.

'We inflate your rubber dinghy. If we're right, the silent motor will be enough to get the speedboat to this skerry. From there, I'll send a carefully drafted message to Marcus's mobile just before the auction begins, hoping that he and Oscar and Freja can – and *want* to – make their way down to the eastern shore, unseen. I'll pick them up from there in the rubber dinghy, I'll return to the skerry and we'll leave in the speedboat. While you . . . do your own thing . . . which *sounds* remarkable, but also sounds very dangerous. Are you absolutely certain?'

'What I'm not quite sure about is whether you should take Freja with you.'

Berger grimaced.

'I know she's living with a criminal,' he said. 'And we've no idea whether she has voluntarily assumed the role of a gangster's wife. It's likely she had no idea of who he really was when she met him, but she married him and has lived with him for three years. She might not want to lose her position. She might not want to lose her kids. I know all that. On the other hand, Jean Babineaux is pretty definitely a dangerous man. He's brought the family to this gangster auction because he doesn't trust them. Freja may want out.'

'In that case she could simply go to the twins' school any day she pleased, pick them up and go to the police. If that was what she wanted, she would have done it long ago. No, she's made peace with her role as a gangster's wife– and if she reads your text message then we're screwed.'

'He's brought my bloody family to a life-threatening professional engagement,' said Berger. 'That's a sign of the opposite. They're captives – I can't just leave her there.'

'That's nostalgia, Sam. You're remembering the good times with her. But you've forgotten that she left you in a pretty brutal way. Unless you'd treated her like shit. Had you, Sam? Were you a wife beater?'

'Is this an interrogation?' Berger exclaimed. 'Is that what we've gone back to?'

'Interesting reaction,' Blom said to the wall.

Berger was quiet, staring at the opposite wall.

'I have to know,' Blom said at last. 'It's crucial to the outcome of this operation.'

'"The outcome of this operation" . . .' Berger parroted.

'All I know about is Arlanda,' said Blom. 'You followed your family when they were due to fly to Paris. You turned violent with the staff at security and the police were called. Were you violent the rest of the time too? Was that why she was so easily able to fall for a handsome Frenchman?'

'I wasn't a wife beater,' Berger said softly. 'Not even Steen says anything like that in the videos.'

'You can't trust a word that man says,' Blom said, just as softly.

'And that's why you kidnapped him, I know,' said Berger. 'It sounds completely insane.'

'I kidnapped him,' said Blom. 'Then I killed him.'

Silence descended on the floor of the big living room. On the entire cottage.

Silent as the grave.

When Berger next spoke, his voice was hoarse.

'You killed your own father?'

Blom stared at the floor. It was as if she were struggling to suppress a maelstrom of emotions.

'I can't right now,' she said in a stifled voice. 'I can't deal with this right now.'

'But I think you have to,' said Berger. 'I need to know whether I can trust you. I really do. Are you . . . a murderer? You killed your father?'

'You have to rely on me to keep it together,' Blom whispered. 'Otherwise you can't rely on me at all. I've got to keep it together. At least for another twenty-four hours or so. After that it doesn't matter. Then I can have a breakdown.'

'But did you have to kill him?'

'There was a very specific reason. It was extremely urgent. I had to make a life or death decision.'

'But why was it so urgent? What is it you're not telling me, Molly?'

'You don't need to know any more right now,' said Blom. 'But I promise that you can trust me. We're going to free your family.'

Berger looked at her for a good while.

'Are you sure I don't need to know any more?'

Her gaze seemed very naked.

'I don't actually know whether my family will be in safe hands. You might not have kidnapped Steen at all. His plan might still be going ahead. You want to keep Möja too. You're his assistant, just as so often in the past. All you want is my trust, my grati-tude, so that I'm there on Landsort. To fulfil your father's plan. And so that I die there together with my twins. August Steen is somewhere behind the scenes controlling everything.'

She stared at him.

'Would I lie about having killed my own father?'

'Well, you lie about everything else,' said Berger. 'For instance, what's this?'

He dug something out of his pocket and dropped it in the centre of Öja with a thud.

It was a childish-looking bright red mobile phone.

302

Blom reached out for it, took it and blinked hard.

'You've been going through my things?' she said. 'Again?'

'And yet you'd hidden it so bloody well,' he said. 'Explain yourself. What's this mobile phone?'

'Tell me you haven't done anything with it,' said Blom, examining the red phone.

'It's locked. I can't do anything with it. But I came damn close to chucking it into the sea. After smashing it on the rocks.'

Berger looked at her caressing it as if it were a tiny mouse in the tender hand of a child.

'That would have been a terrible mistake,' was all she said.

'Then you have to tell me what it is,' he said. 'What is it that's exploding all around me?'

'I guarantee that this phone has nothing to do with you. It's something else.'

'Private?' Berger said, his voice dripping with irony. 'Something private that has nothing to do with our professional relationship?'

She sighed deeply.

'I'm not very well,' she said. 'But we have to get through this now. And I *have* to ask you to trust me. In spite of everything.'

A lot happened in the silence that followed. Entire dramas unfolded in the quiet, ghosts danced, ghouls bellowed, the very air seemed to quiver.

They sat there like that for a while. Everything had to have its moment and at last find peace.

Then Blom spoke.

'I want you on Landsort because you're going to rescue your twins. That's it. I need you in one piece. Regardless of what happens between you and me, my unborn child needs a functioning father.'

'I was a useless partner,' said Berger. 'Lame. Completely

inattentive. Insensitive. Egotistical. Immature. A failure. But I wasn't a wife beater.'

'But I'm a father killer,' said Blom. 'Sometime I might tell you what it was about. But not now.'

Berger looked up. He knew how questioning his own gaze was.

'He had to be dead,' she added.

Berger stared at her.

Silence returned. It descended, pervading everything.

It would have to be enough.

They sat in it until time no longer existed.

Then the red phone rang.

# 38

The sun set between the small skerries, seeming to melt into the sea, pouring sideways like sluggish lava flows from an unusually leisurely volcano. The horizon gleamed in shades of orange and gold, and it was as if there had never been any sleet in the archipelago, no awful, freezing sodden wet storms, no icy shivers between the shoulder blades.

Everything was calm, beautiful, peaceful.

The calm before the storm.

The bounty of gold was reflected in Molly's eyes as she sat beside Sam on a rock at the shoreline. Her pupils were fixed on the spot where the sun had been. The blue of her irises was divided by a golden horizon that parted sky and sea within her.

They were in each other's arms. For real.

The rubber dinghy lay between them and the sea. It had just been inflated. Hopefully it would take four people.

Or perhaps three.

In the worst case, only one.

The speedboat was anchored just out of sight. Berger was glad it wasn't visible. He squeezed Blom's shoulder a little. It was intended as a vague gesture of tenderness – but the gold line in her eyes was suddenly overshadowed by darkness. She pulled away and vomited noisily.

'I really don't feel very well,' she said.

'Morning sickness,' Berger said. 'I recognise it.'

'I don't know . . . I've never felt anything like it.'

'You've never been pregnant before.'

'What would you know about that?'

Berger laughed and tried to hug her awkwardly. In the end, she pulled herself upright again and leaned against him.

She actually leaned against him.

The sea's orange glow transitioned to a darker red, then it slowly went out and was consumed by the inevitable darkness.

'I know you'll keep it together,' said Berger. 'You grit your teeth and get on with it. And we're in this together. If you want. Even if you have a breakdown, we're in that together.'

It was her turn to laugh. They waited in silence for darkness to conquer everything, just as darkness always did. Until light returned and became the victor. And so on, forever more.

Once it was fully dark, Berger spoke.

'So you gave your contact the number for the red phone?'

'I had a momentary blackout,' Blom said. 'I forgot the number for my regular mobile. I decided it was harmless to give him the other number.'

'You never forget anything,' said Berger.

'I know,' said Blom. 'Should I be worried?'

'After everything you've been through? I don't think so.'

'But it was good news at least. Plan A is on.'

'I almost choked when it rang,' said Berger. 'Have you got tabs on Marcus's mobile now?'

'Not only that it's switched on, but its precise location.'

She held up her regular mobile. It showed a satellite image of the southern half of Öja. Two tall buildings were clear to see:

Landsort lighthouse and the Lotstorn tower. Not far from the lighthouse there was a small red marker flashing. When Blom zoomed in, a cluster of buildings came into sight, and the flashing was confined to the biggest of these. It appeared that Marcus and Oscar Babineaux were there with their secret mobile phone.

'Good,' said Berger.

'The interesting thing is that we can tell whether it's active,' said Blom. 'And it is. Since the phone arrived on Öja, eight text messages have been sent and eleven received. All to and from Paris.'

'And that in turn indicates that Marcus and Oscar have got it both charged and hidden so that they can stay in touch with their friends in Paris by text without their stepfather or their bodyguards knowing. It's unlikely their mother knows about it either, but it's harder to be certain about that.'

'That's the likely interpretation,' said Blom. 'Which raises the question of whether it's best to contact the twins in advance and see what they think about it. Try and prepare them.'

Berger nodded.

'I know,' he said. 'But it can't be too early, because that will mean two eleven-year-olds have to keep a secret for almost twenty-four hours, which is probably impossible. And I have to be certain that it's them answering rather than some bodyguard who's armed to the teeth.'

'Have you thought of a question that only Marcus and Oscar know the answer to?'

'Yes, I think I have. When should I put it to them, though?.'

'Don't leave it *too* late. We need time for a reply. We need confirmation of their interaction.'

' "Confirmation of their interaction",' Berger echoed.

Blom put her head back and stared straight into the almost pitch-black sky. Venus, the evening star, was already visible. Soon the dark archipelago sky would be bursting with points of light.

We can gather our thoughts and try to think as rationally as possible,' she said. 'Or we can let go of all thoughts and all direction and lose ourselves in a sea of nostalgia and bleeding hearts. Which would you prefer?'

'The night sky,' said Berger, following her gaze. It looked the same as it had for the people who had lived in caves by the inland glaciers, people who had painted their dream visions onto the rocky walls by the faint glow of their oil lamps.

'Then let's do that,' said Blom.

They laughed softly.

Berger tried again. He squeezed Blom's shoulder a little in a vague gesture of tenderness. This time she didn't throw up.

Berger was overwhelmed. He stared into the darkness and felt a strong and indisputable bond with the past. They were sitting by the campfire staring up towards a huge wall of ice. Despite the fire, its flames rising several metres towards the mysterious starry sky, it would soon be too cold to stay outdoors. Far back in the cave, mammoth skins, reindeer skins and the warmth of each other awaited them. Someone would be sleepless, refusing to put out the oil lamp and instead insisting on drawing on the cave wall. We would belong together, try to survive together, struggle against defeat, we would warm each other.

We would succeed in warming each other.

Molly pressed herself a little closer to him. The stars began to materialise out of the darkness, one by one. Berger knew most of them were dead. All that remained of them was their light.

The reflection of something that had long since died, lingering on.

Then Molly Blom drew away from him ever so slowly, slipping along the stone until it was no longer possible for them to touch each other. Instead they looked at each other.

'You know that you have to take me to Nynäshamn now,' she said.

'Already?' he said.

'There are a few things to sort out.'

He nodded. He edged forward, caressing her belly.

'There are going to be a lot of people who matter to me out on Landsort. Five people that I love one way or another.'

She said nothing. As she stood up, she held his gaze, directly and without subterfuge. The stars shone from her irises.

'Not two of my children,' said Berger. 'Three. Promise me you'll take a little more care than usual.'

She smiled. She leaned slowly towards him.

Then she quickly turned aside to vomit.

# 39

At half past twelve on the dot, rays of sunshine were reflecting dazzlingly off the lawyer's computer. It didn't matter; it was time. He closed the laptop, putting the glaring white screen out of sight, then he stood up from the desk, and went over to the window. He stroked his bare crown. Everything was ready, the instructions clear, the strategy firm but flexible. He had been in this game for too long to feel worried. The stakes were always life and death – it had become habit. He would have preferred to retire, but his house in Lugano was not yet big enough for him to step back from the fray. Anyway, he would miss the constant taste of blood in his mouth.

He took a few sips of energy drink and chewed through a protein bar, while he surveyed the archipelago-scape from the highest point on the island. Then he shook his head. What kind of crazy Norse god had concocted an inland sea with twenty-five thousand islands sticking out of its shallow water?

But it was a splendid winter's day in this cold country. Ice had begun to form, and the sun was being reflected in different ways from different parts of the sea. The road all the way to Sweden's oldest lighthouse was bathed in unusually clear winter sunlight. That was where he was going.

The lawyer turned on his heel and consulted the mirror. Once again he ran a hand over his newly shaved head, then he straightened his printed silk tie, adjusted his R. Jewels Diamond Edition jacket, put on his vicuna coat and slipped his MacBook Pro into a grosgrain Valextra briefcase. Then he looked in the mirror again, gazing deep into his own eyes before he spoke.

'Showtime.'

He took the stairs. A floor below, he encountered a man just as well dressed. They nodded curtly to each other without recognition. There was no doubt that the man was Russian. Nor did the lawyer recognise either of the two unremarkable gentlemen who appeared from the door on the next floor. At any rate, not personally, but they were undoubtedly jurists too.

There were too many of them – they were all dispensable.

They were legion.

And very few of them were interested in the spirit of the law.

His two colleagues were waiting for him on the bottom floor. Two other similar teams were in place. Younger, slightly sweatier. No women – only men. Wordlessly, the lawyer glided out of the front door, took a few brisk steps along the track and then stopped to look up at the strange tower where he had spent the night. It looked like a block of flats that had escaped from the Stockholm suburbs.

'The Lotstorn tower,' he said to his puzzled team, who had just caught up with him. Then he set off again.

It was a walk of a couple of hundred metres, just enough to oxygenate the blood. He had taken the same route the day before to get a grip on the geography and locations, trying to understand roughly where the competition and hosts were accommodated.

There was a main building, the hostel itself, and there were plenty of nearby outbuildings.

The lawyer and his team passed the old lighthouse, the south-ernmost outpost of the Stockholm archipelago, and approached the youth hostel, sometimes known as 'Sista Utkiken'. Before long, the meagre garden outside it came into sight. Tables had been set out in the sunshine, well separated and with a clear head table parallel to the facade of the hostel.

It was still empty, but two of the side tables were rather less empty.

Sitting at one of them were three enormous men wearing coats that were far too heavy. The lawyer could but guess what kind of arsenal was concealed beneath those coats. It was a little clearer where they hailed from. Rarely had the lawyer seen such clear Slavic features in three faces – he even wondered whether they might be brothers. What was beyond all doubt was that his Russian lawyer colleague, whose footsteps had echoed behind him all the way from the Lotstorn tower, would set a course for that table.

The presence of Russians was not entirely surprising. It was the other table that drew the lawyer's attention. The three sol-diers were very austerely dressed and they all had East Asian features.

Seriously? North Koreans? How the hell had they found their way into this?

There was no doubt about it: this was going to be a tough auc-tion. Very clearly the toughest to date.

The lawyer looked at his Patek Philippe Grand Complications Sky Moon Tourbillon and knew that his bodyguards would emerge from their own cabin in precisely two minutes' time. He sat down at a table. One of his associates sat down next to him, the younger man casting glances that were slightly too uncertain towards one of the clusters of cabins. Had it not been for the necessity of a united front, he would have given him a slap.

After exactly two minutes, the lawyer's bodyguards appeared as expected. Four rock-hard Arabs with beards like the Prophet's. Various weapons were protruding from under their khaki military jackets.

He'd had them with him in Austria and Ireland and knew exactly what the score was with them. They weren't your usual drug-addled petty criminals from Europe's ghettos – they were former elite soldiers from the Iraqi army. The toughest guys in existence.

They took their positions around him, in formation, effortlessly managing to look relaxed despite the fact that their eyes were covertly taking in the three Russian maybe-brothers and the North Koreans. Four versus three in both cases. That was always something.

The angry game, the lawyer thought to himself, snorting. It had been a very long time since his laugh had been remotely related to anything joyful. As a matter of fact, joy was something he merely remembered. Although he remembered less and less of it.

He pictured himself as a young man at Le Rosey in Switzerland – the world's most exclusive private school. He remembered a form of ecstasy at the great freedom of simply being alive. He saw himself as if from above, and tried to imagine that little towhead as the lawyer and representative of Islamic State.

No, he was never going to feel any more joy in his life.

Money, on the other hand. That was something he could still feel.

He detected movement at the kitchen door of the hostel. Then three women strode out balancing well-filled trays. They were wearing waiting uniforms that looked like something out of the nineteenth century, and they were ready to serve everything from champagne to coffee. The lawyer saw them approach a table each. One of them came closer to him, closer to his team.

At that point, another person appeared from behind the hill, down towards the sea. Although whether he was actually a person was unclear. It was almost as if Jesus himself had come strolling up the rocks. Not because the person in question was good and self-sacrificing – rather, it was because he was almost as mythical. The lawyer had never thought he'd see this man in the flesh. For the first time in a very long while, emotion actually permeated him.

In a group of four stone faces, this man was the toughest of all. It was like seeing a Titan climb Olympus. The other stone faces were his silly little flapping cherubs. Hummingbirds around an eagle.

He was the inimitable idol of every mercenary. The one that everyone dreamed of having as their commander.

It was Nils Gundersen. In the flesh.

And he had brought no lawyers with him. He was apparently going to bid himself. Surrounded by his mercenaries and without laying down the sniper rifle slung over his shoulder, Gundersen went to an empty table. He stopped there and looked around. If looks could kill, his gaze would have felled everyone to the ground. Then he smiled and sat down. He pulled out a mobile phone and began to casually tap away on it as if he were on the subway.

As if he were calmly composing a text message.

The lawyer hadn't quite managed to collect his thoughts when he looked up into the clear blue eyes of the smiling waitress. She had blonde hair with traces of brown dye. It was in a pageboy style.

'What would you like to drink?' Molly Blom asked in English.

*

Sam Berger was sitting in the rubber dinghy when he sent the text message that he had composed long before. The rocks of the skerry blocked his view of Öja, and the dinghy was moored to the larger speedboat. He watched the clock ticking on his mobile. This was the agreed time. He could taste his own cold sweat at the corners of his mouth. He tapped the number for Marcus's secret mobile into the recipient field. According to the app, it was on. He looked up at the unexpectedly blue sky and then read over his carefully thought-through text message.

*Dear Marcus & Oscar, this is your dad. I've missed you so much. But right now you're in danger. Your stepfather Jean is about to leave through the front door of the inn. His bodyguards will go with him. Be prepared. The next time I contact you, you should go straight out of the back door and head directly eastwards towards the water. I'll pick you up there. Hugs from Dad. PS It's up to you whether you ask your mother. If you're in, then reply straight away with the full number of V-signs!*

Then he sent it.

Everything depended on whether he got an answer.

Absolutely everything.

Everything in his life.

Every passing second was dreadful. Time dragged, dripping as slowly as tar. Disappearing mercilessly. Driving him closer and closer to downright despair.

He closed his eyes. Breathed less and less. Was prepared to stop breathing. To cease to be.

Then there was a chime – a crystal-clear chime.

It might say 'zero' in the message. It might say 'hahaha'. It might say 'nice try, mate'.

It didn't say that.

It said '12'.

Not only were the twins in, Freja was too.

Three times four V-signs.

Sam Berger inhaled. He inhaled all the oxygen in the Stockholm archipelago.

*

Together with the other waitresses, Molly Blom withdrew to the kitchen door. She surveyed the garden of the hostel, trying to make out the distribution. At this point, there were four groups: Arabs, Russians, possibly Koreans, and Nils Gundersen and his mercenaries. She most certainly recognised the hard-boiled old man from various pictures. There was even a resemblance to his son, William Larsson. William, whom she – Molly Blom and no one else – had killed.

At that moment, the four groups became five.

Five men came out of the main entrance. Four of them were extremely powerful and reminded her of Foreign Legion soldiers. Between them walked a tall, thin, very well-dressed man. Blom hadn't got near to the family when she had been brought in with the other staff that morning – watertight bulkheads had been established in the hostel – but there was no doubt whatsoever that this was Jean Babineaux. Together with his four bodyguards.

Five. And three inside the house. The rest of the Babineaux family.

Five plus three.

The five men stopped for a while to survey the garden. They

scrutinised the four tables. Just before the so-called housekeeper, a woman in her fifties and tough as flint, appeared to withdraw her waitresses into the building, Blom saw Babineaux preparing to speak. She craftily inserted her hand into the pocket of the house-keeper's voluminous pinafore, before managing to give her the slip by sneaking upstairs. Through a window on the stairs above a flowerpot she was able to look straight out into the garden.

'Welcome to the Stockholm archipelago. It's very gratifying to see so many prospective buyers in attendance, and I'm certain this will be a tough but honourable encounter. What distinguishes today's auction from the two previous editions is the significantly higher quality and volume of the arsenal in question, which means that we are joined today by our organisation's leader.'

From her position on the stairs, Blom tried to understand what she was hearing. She had clearly guessed correctly. Babineaux was just a frontman, a representative. The new boss of the arms syndicate was apparently present. But where? Inside? Were there people down there behind the sealed-off door, together with Marcus, Oscar and Freja?

But that wasn't what happened. No one emerged from the hostel building. Instead, a man rose from one of the tables and began to slowly move towards Babineaux.

There was complete silence outside as Nils Gundersen's mighty figure strode closer to the hostel.

Blom was overcome by nausea. She closed her eyes and tried at all costs to suppress the urge to vomit. And to understand what she was seeing.

Isli Vrapi's illegal arms trading organisation – indisputably the biggest in the world – was now led by Nils Gundersen.

Jean Babineaux was nothing more than Nils Gundersen's lawyer.

She processed this. Did it actually change anything?

Babineaux's four men were still outside. No one was left inside. It oughtn't to change anything. Marcus, Oscar and Freja ought to be alone downstairs.

Everything suggested that escape was an option.

Escape now.

Molly bent forward, dug in the flowerpot and pulled out a plastic bag from which she retrieved a childish-looking red mobile phone. She could feel her hands trembling, her entire being trembling, as she sent the short, pithy message: *Now!*

*

Berger's phone rattled. He read the message.

*Now!*

At that same instant he sent exactly the same message to Marcus and Oscar: *Now!*

Then he started the silent outboard motor and allowed the rubber dinghy to float around the small skerry. Öja was close, and Landsort lighthouse loomed up on the island. He maxed out the motor for speed as he tracked the rocky coastline. The sun glittered on the thin layer of ice that seemed to threaten the inflated rubber hull. He almost seemed to float across the ice, soaring.

He placed his weapon on the floor of the dinghy. He held out his hand, cupped it. It was empty.

What he held in it was life.

Nothing. And everything.

*

Diagonally below her, Molly Blom saw Nils Gundersen – the rifle still slung over his shoulder – reach Jean Babineaux and his entourage. Throughout his majestic amble through the garden, his gaze had remained trained on his mobile. Then he made a joking and theatrical gesture, as if sending a text message. And then he looked up at his honoured would-be arms buyers with a broad smile.

*

Berger's phone rattled again. It shouldn't have. He lowered his speed, letting the rubber boat float freely. If it was a text from Marcus's mobile then it could only mean trouble.

But it wasn't from Marcus. It was from a withheld number.

Berger took a deep breath and then read it.

*Dear Sam Berger, I gather that in your childhood you were the sole friend of my beloved son. I have also gathered that the way in which you betrayed him was frightful. In front of an audience of girls, you whipped his genitals with a towel until they bled. And many years later you shot him dead in exactly the same way – through his penis. The extent of your perversion impresses even me – and I have seen it all. Absolutely everything. And if you haven't already understood that I've brought my mediocre lawyer's beloved family here to kill them in circumstances that surpass those circumstances in which you killed my son William then you are hardly a worthy opponent, Sam. Please feel free to drop in and watch as I torture your twins to death with the utmost slowness. Kind regards, Nils Gundersen.*

Berger threw up with such force that the vomit seemed to turn to steam and rise into the clear air of the archipelago.

His face white, he returned to max speed.

*

It was time to check the situation. To make sure that the twins had got away as expected. Blom put her hand into the pocket of her pinafore and pulled out the housekeeper's keys. She slowly descended the stairs and stood by the door separating the service quarters from the rest of the hostel. Where the Babineauxs should no longer be.

She inserted the key in the door, turned it, stepped inside and found another door. She pushed it ajar. She saw a rear-facing room with a glass door at the end. But that wasn't what caught her attention. It was the five people.

Sitting between two heavily armed mercenaries were a pale woman and a couple of clearly confused eleven-year-old boys who looked very alike.

They also looked very like Sam Berger.

Her heart in her mouth, Blom curtsied low just as the house-keeper had shown her, and asked in a vivacious voice:

'Would the lady or gentlemen like anything to drink?'

The mercenaries made a dismissive gesture as if waving away a fly, but one of the boys spoke in a hoarse voice:

'I'd like a cola.'

'Me too,' the other boy echoed.

The pale woman said nothing. Meeting her gaze was like looking straight into death itself.

Blom looked quizzically at the mercenaries and received a vague affirmation in reply.

'I will be back in a moment,' she said, vivacious again.

She left the room swiftly, half closing the door. Then she hurled herself up the stairs, dug in the flowerpot, found the plastic bag with the red mobile phone, kept digging and found another plastic bag. It contained two objects. Her hand trembling, she attached the first to the second and took the safety off the newly silenced pistol.

The one she had already used to kill her own adoptive father. And to shoot the shotgun out of Ali Pachachi's hand.

Although then there had been no silencer.

She concealed it in her pinafore pocket, then made quickly for the kitchen, searched for cans of cola, received various glances from the other girls, managed to avoid the housekeeper, found a tray, turned up two cola cans in a fridge, and set off again.

She stopped herself outside the second door and stood completely still, realising with great clarity exactly what was at stake. Then she opened the door with her foot.

Smiling widely, she entered the room. She received a pair of sharp, suspicious looks from the mercenaries. But nothing more. There was no rattle of weapons.

Molly Blom let go of the tray. For a brief moment, it seemed to hover, soaring in the emptiness, as if gravity were gone. Then it fell to the floor.

As her tray fell, Blom pulled out the gun and shot the left-hand mercenary in the forehead completely silently. The right-hand one had already grabbed his automatic when she emptied the magazine into his body.

She put her hand to her mouth, index finger to her lips. She made a hushing gesture. The twins and the woman stared at her. It was as if they would never utter a sound again.

'Smart asking for the cola,' she said, gesturing to the glass door. 'You know where to go. Get out of here now.'

She stood there watching them disappear into the woods on unsteady legs. As she turned round, her nausea rose. Standing in the doorway, her mouth gaping but silent, was the housekeeper. Blom took a step closer. The housekeeper turned on her heel and stumbled towards the main entrance to the hostel. Through the window, Blom saw her emerge and totter towards Babineaux to warn him. But not a sound passed her lips.

Through the window, Blom saw Babineaux recoil. Everything was noiseless, as if in a silent film. She saw a movement from the corner of her eye, over by the Russians. The biggest of the brothers reacted on impulse, a bodyguard on speed. With astonishing rapidity, he produced something that looked like a classic Kalashnikov from his coat. The housekeeper had almost reached Jean Babineaux when the Russian bodyguard fired a precision shot at her throat. She collapsed onto Babineaux with blood spurting from her throat like a fountain, and managed to whisper something. He fell backwards with the housekeeper on top of him. Then she died in Jean Babineaux's arms.

Babineaux crawled out from under the body in disgust. Gundersen stood there with his hand raised authoritatively, managing to prevent any further gunfire. When he was certain that calm had been restored, he stepped forward to Babineaux, who finally managed to say something to him. Gundersen shook his head as if galvanising a frozen brain, and gestured to one of the men around him. He issued a clear order.

Molly Blom saw the bodyguard lurch away. As he ran past her, he pulled out his weapon – she thought she glimpsed a proper sharpshooter emerge from his Foreign Legion jacket.

He ran eastwards towards the water.

Blom ran up the stairs, dug in the confounded flowerpot, got out the plastic bag, unwrapped the red mobile phone, tried to dial a number. Everything was shaking. She felt like she couldn't do it – she lunged towards the flowerpot in the window and vomited wildly. She wiped her mouth, completed the number.

She really did not feel well.

There was an answer. She spoke in Swedish.

'Family out now.'

'Thanks,' said a man's voice calmly on the other end. Just before she hung up, she heard the same voice shout:

'Snipers ready!'

*

Berger had already reached the shoreline when he heard the shot. One single, very distinctive shot. Like a warning shot.

Or an execution.

He ran the rubber dinghy up to the water's edge, jumped out and pulled it fully ashore. Then he turned round and paused briefly. He retrieved his gun from the bottom of the boat. He took the first steps towards the place where his beloved twins were to be ritualistically murdered by a remorseless mercenary thirsty for revenge.

Had the shot been aimed at what had once been his family? At those who would always be his children? Even if they died on Öja.

But then he saw something. The seconds before he realised what he was seeing seemed to last an eternity. He saw what was pushing through the bushes by the rocks heading down to the sea. He saw the branch move forward before ricocheting backwards in a kind of absurd slow motion, before it slapped the boy right in the face.

The one at the front was already racing towards him. He immediately recognised Marcus, his elder son. His expression was pained, but he was still smiling. The smile of recognition in the middle of mortal anguish. Marcus was eleven years old and running as if possessed. He jumped into the boat. Berger immediately pushed it into the water.

Then he saw Oscar. His younger son was rubbing his face across his eyes where the recoiling branch had just struck him. He also tumbled into the boat. Despite the scarcity of time, the trio were united in a heartfelt embrace. That was all Berger wanted. That was all he wanted in the whole wide world. Yet he still managed to keep the boat at the shore just long enough to glance across the heads of his twins.

She was there. Freja was there. She stumbled out of the grove of trees last, staggering towards the boat. Their eyes met, Sam and Freja, mother and father, and she smiled slightly. But it wasn't the smile he had seen for so many years. It was different. How many plastic surgeons had put their knives into Freja Babineaux? He didn't care – he smiled at her, and she was about to step into the dinghy when there was a rustling in the trees fifty metres to the north.

A man appeared. A big man. He looked like a soldier – a soldier in the French Foreign Legion. The gun he slowly but surely raised to his eye looked ominously like a sniper rifle.

'Get out of here,' Freja shouted. 'Save them. Go as far as you can, capsize the boat. Dive.'

She threw a kiss through the air to them just as the shot was fired.

It echoed fatefully over Landsort.

Berger saw it in Freja's eyes, thought he could see her gaze go out.

It was an automatic – they wouldn't stand a chance. Berger hugged his twins a little tighter. He prayed they would come with him into the next, hopefully better world.

They had to.

He raised his gaze to the spot where Freja ought to have fallen.

She hadn't fallen. Her gaze hadn't gone out. In fact, it looked extremely surprised.

The Foreign Legion soldier had, however, fallen to his knees. The barrel of his sniper rifle was pressed down into the half-frozen ground and it continued to sink until it stopped. He fell forward over the butt, and ended up hanging there as if rigged up, with his arms hanging by his sides.

Behind him, a man appeared. He was holding a smoking gun in his hand. His hair was chalk white, and what little of his skin was visible was almost as white. He gestured at them urgently.

Berger understood none of it. But he got the silent outboard going, Freja hopped aboard and they made haste towards the skerry where the speedboat was waiting. They exchanged glances – astonished, confused glances.

The tall, thin, chalk-white man stood on the shoreline beside the body. Rather unexpectedly, he saluted them.

He stood there until they disappeared from sight.

Then they heard a third shot. A fourth.

And then all hell broke loose.

It was as if all of Landsort, all of Öja, exploded into unhinged, depraved fireworks.

\*

Molly Blom was lying on the stairs. It felt as if life was draining out of her body. It was a shot that brought her back to life – a pistol shot in the distance.

She got to her feet, staggered down the stairs, and exited through the kitchen door together with another waitress. She saw a very pale Jean Babineaux pressed up against the facade of the hostel in between three closely packed bodyguards; she saw the mercenaries rush to cover Nils Gundersen.

'The auction is temporarily suspended,' Gundersen said in a powerful, level voice. 'I must ask for your patience for a few minutes. Everyone lower your weapons. Now!'

After a few glances in different directions, the assembled forces did as they had been ordered. But one man decided to protest.

The Islamic State lawyer stood up. The sun was reflected off his shiny pate. Speaking in a loud, clear and unemotional voice, he said: 'I think we must postpone this spectacle.'

Then his clean-shaven head exploded.

Somewhere, a memory appeared of an ecstasy-filled boy in the shadows of a Swiss chateau, looking up to the sky, holding out his arms and receiving the gifts of life.

Then it was gone.

The IS soldiers react on instinct. One of them immediately shoots one of Gundersen's mercenaries in the head. Gundersen himself raises his sniper rifle to a firing position with incredible speed, taking out one of the Russian brothers while he is still fumbling for his Kalashnikov. The biggest Russian's attention is elsewhere – his Kalashnikov is already raised and he quickly takes out two of the North Koreans, while the third deftly shoots two of Babineaux's bodyguards. Even though his immediate neighbours in the meat cage around Jean Babineaux fall, a third bodyguard shoots the biggest Russian without hesitation.

Babineaux only has one bodyguard left now, while Gundersen is fully covered behind his two remaining men.

Babineaux's bodyguard protects him with his own body, moving sideways in front of him along the outer wall of the building towards the main entrance. The remainder of the IS soldiers and Gundersen's mercenaries open fire on each other, the last North Korean being hit by a stray bullet. Tables have been toppled, but they provide no proper protection from guns with boundless firepower.

There is only one of the IS soldiers left. He rises from behind the shattered table and sets his sights on Babineaux. The bodyguard takes the bullet with his body. He falls forward at the same moment his killer takes a long-range shot to the head. When he tumbles to the ground, half his head is gone.

Blom sees two well-aimed long-range shots strike Nils

Gundersen's two bodyguards, but when his defensive wall topples, Gundersen is no longer behind them. He is gone.

Shortly after the penultimate long-range shot is heard, taking out the Russian lawyer, the final one strikes Jean Babineaux's shoulder, tearing away half his arm. He slowly slumps against the wall of the youth hostel, leaving a red slug's trail behind him on the facade. That is where he remains lying as they pour in.

The first wave are black-clad. They're the ones with sniper rifles and automatics. They secure the few people still moving. A few of the survivors still have their wits about them, but not many.

Molly Blom sees all this. She sits down on the kitchen step next to a waitress who has passed out, and sees it all as if through a filter. A filter showing the collective madness of everything. She sees it with crystal clarity.

Then she throws up.

The second wave are in civilian attire. She can't bring herself to count their number. But she recognises a man.

He had tousled grey hair, was rather thin, wore jeans and a padded jacket. He still had a black eye.

He stopped in the middle of the garden, one hand clutching a pistol, and began to slowly spin round, scanning the battle site. Constantly shaking his head.

'Europe.'

As he began to approach Molly Blom, he called out to a Mediterranean-looking man nearby.

'Angelos! Have we got eyes on Arto?'

From the hill to the east of the island, a tall, thin, chalk-white man appeared. He returned his pistol to his shoulder holster before speaking.

'I'm here.'

The grey-haired man stopped briefly and turned to him.

'Was it a success?' he asked.

The white-haired man nodded.

'It was a success.'

The grey-haired man smiled briefly.

'You should conceal that black eye,' the white-haired man added. 'It's beneath you.'

The grey-haired man approached Blom, crouching beside her. She felt like she was at an angle; she felt her perception of existence itself was skewed.

'Are you okay, Molly?' he asked calmly.

'I wouldn't exactly say that,' she said. 'Gundersen is gone.'

The man with the black eye gestured quickly and barked an order in English. All the strangers took cover. The man quickly pulled Blom and the passed-out waitress inside.

'We would never have found this without you. I owe you a big debt of gratitude, Molly. It's getting a lot bloody harder to defend democracy these days. In the end you have to wonder whether that's even what we're defending.'

She looked at him. Her eyes were strangely microscopic. She saw everything down to the smallest, tiniest pore. She could make out a change in the skin just under the black eye – a red swelling.

A pimple.

The man with the black eye and pimple stood up again, and headed outside where he crouched over Jean Babineaux's fallen but still gasping body. He spoke to him in English.

'The coordinates, Jean.'

Babineaux's face, previously so picture-perfect, was contorted.

'*Va te faire foutre,*' he replied.

The grey-haired man shook his head slowly and sympathetically.

'We know that you have them somewhere on your computer or phone,' he said. 'The problem is that you'll have time to die if

I have to look for them. If you tell me now then you'll survive. It's that simple.'

Babineaux stared at him with a broken gaze.

'Europol,' he panted. 'Fuck off.'

'Life or death, Jean? I'll count down from three. I'm going to start now. Three. Two. O—'

That was when Jean Babineaux's head exploded.

The grey-haired man threw himself behind the fallen body. One of the men in black yelled:

'Edge of the trees, north-west!'

Then they set off.

'Bloody hell,' the man said, prising Babineaux's mobile from his jacket and withdrawing inside the building again. Back to Molly Blom's side.

'Gundersen?' she asked.

The man grimaced.

'He might be as old as Satan, our friend Nils, but he's still one hell of a sharpshooter.'

'But why did he shoot Babineaux?'

'He probably wanted to shoot this thing,' said the grey-haired man, holding up the mobile phone. 'This has the coordinates for the massive arsenal. Now I just have to find them.'

He began to work his way through the mobile. A peculiar minute or two elapsed. Time was no longer a function in Blom's head. She felt incredibly nauseous.

Eventually, the man nodded and smiled.

'No harder than that,' he said. 'Dumb starts with the same letter as destiny.'

He took a screenshot and sent it off before passing the phone to Molly Blom.

'What?' she said. 'What am I meant to do with this? You lot sorted everything out.'

'Us?' said the grey-haired man. 'We were never here.'

Blom began to laugh. She really wasn't feeling well, but she couldn't help laughing. She laughed for so long that the grey-haired man couldn't help joining in, at least a little at the end.

'Give me a hand up,' she said.

He did. Another man in civilian garb appeared and proffered his hand. She took it in surprise. He was shorter than her and South American in appearance.

'Incredible work,' he said in Swedish. 'Thank you.'

And then he was gone before she had time to reply.

She stared in the direction he'd gone.

'Who was that?'

'Jorge,' said the grey-haired man. 'Nothing to concern yourself with.'

Although it was obvious he was very much concerned.

They reached the hill. The sea appeared beneath them, half covered in ice, glittering in the early twilight. She stopped, crouched, waited. The man crouched beside her.

'Sweden's second oldest church, tomorrow. Got to have some variety in life in order to survive. How about one o'clock? You've earned a lie-in, Molly.'

She merely shook her head. Then she heard it.

She heard the speedboat engine start.

She closed her eyes. She could feel herself smiling.

Because that was all this shitshow was about.

# IV

# 40

A lone ship glided through the night. From a modest distance, it could have been a ghost ship.

All was dark: the archipelago was dark, the ship was dark. All was dark and cold. The black night corroded it.

But when the ship passed a remote island, there was suddenly light. A brightly illuminated area reminiscent of an ancient sacrificial site. White-clad Druids moved across the lit stage in angular patterns.

Upon closer examination, they were forensics specialists.

The floodlights that had been rigged up at the Landsort youth hostel were tremendously powerful but focused in their angling. There was little sidelight leaking to the wider world. A satellite might have been capable of capturing the scene from above, but there were no satellites in proximity.

Just the ship.

There were a number of people on deck. In the darkness, one of them spoke.

'Are you sure you want to do this?'

The man he had been addressing nodded. Unlike the Druids, he wore black and his clothing hugged his body unusually tightly.

His entire life was contained on the deck of the ghost ship. And it was still there.

Everything was still there.

He cupped his hand. It was empty. What he held in it was life. Nothing.

And everything.

In a heated area of the deck twin boys and their mother sat huddled close together, well guarded by unmistakable Security Service agents. Closer to the balustrade were other black-clad Security Service agents surrounding a small group. Apart from himself and the man who had spoken, there were also two women. Both had pageboy haircuts; one was brunette and the other blonde, albeit with brown patches.

In the distance, the illuminated area disappeared, the sacrificial site dissolved, the Druids evaporated.

With a nod towards the last fading light from the island, the man who had spoken before said:

'More than twenty dead. Unique on Swedish soil.'

He was Jonas Andersson, Head of the Security Intelligence Department and operational lead at the Security Service. There was silence.

Then a few seconds later Superintendent Desiré Rosenkvist from the National Operations Department said:

'More than twenty? Seriously?'

'And that's not counting August Steen's murder,' Andersson said. 'And I take it as read that you all know this remains unreservedly top secret. For all involved parties,' Andersson added, with a significant nod towards Marcus, Oscar and Freja.

Silence fell again. But then Deer couldn't contain herself.

'But more than twenty dead . . . Why isn't the whole island swarming with members of the foreign press?'

'It's equivalent to a few months' gang activity in the Swedish suburbs,' Andersson said cynically, with a shrug. 'And it seems to be the same phenomenon too: killer kills killer.'

'But the media ought to be there,' Deer said stubbornly.

'Nothing has got out to the wider world,' said Andersson. 'Just a few minor complaints from a couple of ladies about their dogs being upset by early New Year fireworks. Nothing else.'

'But there must have been people living there?'

'They'd emptied the island,' said the man in the close-fitting black clothes. 'This is a unique opportunity for the Security Service to operate without any media involvement.'

'We could have done with weeks in that respect,' Andersson muttered. 'It seems the residents are coming back first thing tomorrow. Unless we find some low-key way of stopping them.'

'So there are no witnesses at all?' Deer asked.

'Two waitresses,' said Andersson. 'One fainted, the other hid in a wardrobe. They don't have anything to say about the incident itself except that it was bloody noisy. But they *do* know that it took place.'

'If they hadn't been there then the Security Service would have been able to cover it all up,' said the man in the tight black clothes. 'And the question is whether you can gag a couple of waitresses.'

Jonas Andersson looked at him.

'Sam Berger, you weren't even there. But Molly Blom saw everything. She knows *exactly* what happened. In the same way that I now know *exactly* what happened up north in the interior, thanks to Superintendent Rosenkvist's concise written statement – an exemplary piece of work. You really are joined at the hips as a trio, aren't you?'

'A real triumvirate,' Berger murmured, glancing sidelong at Deer, who was beginning to blush.

'So let's put all our cards on the table now,' said Andersson. 'You know *exactly* what happened on Öja, don't you, Molly?'

'I'm really not feeling well,' said Molly Blom.

'You said that,' Andersson said coldly. 'And you are quite seriously claiming to have been unconscious the whole time?'

Blom nodded in the dark.

'I'm sorry,' she said. 'But you've got enough to go on anyway.'

'And your hypothesis is that Carsten Boylan, who is now dead, kidnapped and murdered August Steen? In order to extract from Ali Pachachi when and where the arms auction was going to take place, before providing that information to North Korea? Ali Pachachi, the man with the network, who thanks to Superintendent Rosenkvist is now formally in the hands of the Security Service?'

'That's what must have happened,' said Blom. 'It must have been North Korea that Carsten cut his deal with. "Some say the bee stings: but I say, 'tis the bee's wax" –'

'*Thanks to me* is overegging it,' Deer interrupted. 'It was Sam and Molly who –'

'You've got the video footage,' Berger cut in. 'Your job now is to ensure that no more corrupt power structures coagulate inside the Security Service, like the Triumvirate. All that happens when they do are Bermuda Triangles.'

'The Bermuda Triangle,' Andersson said with a nod. 'That was always the rumour about August Steen. That he knew things no one else did. That he could do pretty much as he liked. He was untouchable, even by me.'

Jonas Andersson was quiet as he thought, then he pointed in the direction where Landsort had long since been swallowed by the darkness.

'We'll have to go back there after all,' he said. 'Naturally I'll be questioning the three of you, but right now I need the basics.'

'Well, ask a question then,' said Berger.

Jonas Andersson laughed and then immediately turned serious.

'The arms auction. Tell me about it in a few sentences.'

'Isli Vrapi's successor in the world's biggest illegal arms organisation had assembled arsenals to be sold in Europe, on the grounds that a year or so ago Islamic State seemed unassailable and had just said they were going to carry out attacks in the West. That meant a new arms market had taken shape. However, other prospective buyers came out of the woodwork and the successor decided to hold regular auctions to secure the greatest possible profit. The one on Landsort was the third and definitely the biggest so far. Four groups of bidders had gathered. Something made them shoot each other dead. Everyone there was an exceptional shot.'

'And you claim that Isli Vrapi's successor was the mercenary Nils Gundersen? And that he was represented by an attorney called Jean Babineaux?'

'Yes,' said Berger.

'But Gundersen's body isn't up there. He's missing. Jean Babineaux was found dead, on the other hand.'

Berger gestured towards his family, where they sat in the heated section of the deck.

'I gathered that. And my family has been freed. I hope you'll be able to protect them from Nils Gundersen.'

'I should think it's probable they'll be given new identities,' said Andersson. 'Perhaps you too, Sam. But how was Nils Gundersen able to escape?'

Berger and Blom had looked each other in the eye so much of late that it was not necessary on this occasion. Both remained silent.

At that moment, the regular rhythm of the ship changed. The engines fell silent, the anchor chain began to run out, and the crew appeared on deck and begun to tug at thick ropes.

Molly Blom took out a mobile that wasn't hers. She pulled up a screenshot. Berger looked at the GPS on his own phone. The figures matched.

They had arrived.

An authoritative-looking man in his fifties appeared at their side – a real seadog. In a predictable whisky voice, he said:

'It's effectively the same coordinates as the Deep.'

They looked at him. No one said anything.

'A degree of caution is recommended,' said the skipper.

'The Landsort Deep?' said Berger. 'The deepest point in the Baltic?'

'Good lad. A crescent-shaped fault fissure, half a kilometre deep. Straight down into the bloody abyss. Your whatsit must be right on the edge of the Deep. Are you ready? We need four anchor points.'

Berger nodded. He quite honestly had no idea what he was nodding in response to.

He handed over his mobile to Blom and adjusted the wetsuit, pulling on neoprene gloves. Then a group of divers approached him. They began attaching things to his body. While the lead diver whispered instructions into his ear, Berger waved the twins over to him. With some hesitation, they approached. Heavily burdened, he lowered himself to his knees beside them.

Marcus and Oscar. Their faces so close. Their gazes, their expressions. So similar, yet so different. They would always be the fixed point in his life. But they would no longer be his heaven, not even a polar star. They would no longer be an unattainable ideal. They would be people, and they would be nearby. He reached out to caress their faces but they recoiled from the touch of the gloves. Instead he drew them close, cheek against cheek against cheek. Their warmth spread through him.

No words now. No words to make this banal. This would have to do.

He went to the balustrade. He briefly took Molly Blom's hand. She mouthed, 'Are you absolutely sure?' and he nodded.

The lead diver came over. He tugged at all the straps, adjusted everything, and closed the lid on the strange metal basket at Berger's chest.

'There are four metal plates with transmitters here,' the lead diver said. 'Don't lose them. We haven't got any more.'

'Okay,' said Berger.

The lead diver stopped for a moment, fixing his gaze on him.

'You know there are four professionals here, right? You really don't have to do this.'

'Yes,' said Berger. 'I do. There's something I need to confront.'

'What?'

'The mid-water.'

He pulled on his fins, and the last thing he did before they lowered him into the icy cold water was to bite hard on the rubber mouthpiece.

He was lowered on a small lift on the outside of the hull and was quickly overwhelmed by the shock of the cold. It seeped into the wetsuit, electrifying his skin. Nothing new under the sun. He lay there a while, floating beside the dark ghost ship. Then the floodlights came on, one at a time. At first above the water, then beneath it. He switched on his own dive light, which was attached to his wrist with a strap. It was astonishingly powerful. When he aimed it up into the night sky, it seemed to illuminate the stars.

Then he descended.

The underwater floodlights lit the darkness. Suddenly there was life here – movement. He saw bubbles, small creatures, floating fragments of seaweed and algae. A colourless school of fish flitted past. Then he saw a big deep. And that was only a fraction of what the earth had to offer in this hidden place – its biggest and most secret part.

He allowed himself to float for a while. His breathing was calm and measured. Then he made his way down.

He found the big container almost immediately. It was far inside a crevice beside a bigger deep. It couldn't possibly have been chosen at random. No regular echo sounder in the whole wide world would have had a chance of finding it, and it was also painted in a camouflage design. It lay at the point where the light from the underwater floodlights began to fade out. While engaging in his precision work, he would need his own light.

He swam closer. He let his gloved hand glide along the green-grey metal. He tried not to think about what was inside. Calm and collected, he made himself float right there in the moment. His movements were precise as he opened the strange basket strapped to his chest. He pulled out the first transmitter plate, twisting and turning it, removing the protective film and feeling the plate being drawn to the metal, sucked magnetically until it thudded against the container and didn't move. He let go. It was attached.

Then he swam round the corner. He repeated the same procedure – without issue. The plate was drawn forcefully towards the grey-green metal wall. It stayed there. Then round the next corner and the same again. The same process. Basket opened, plate out, film off, bang – in place. Three out of four. Child's play.

At the very moment he thought that, just as he thought 'child's play', he realised that he couldn't think like that. There was a side of the container still to go. He mustn't count his chickens.

He came round the last corner of the large cuboid. He clung to it. Close. He was on the side that was in shadow. He only had his own light to rely on. That made it harder to open the basket at his chest. But he still managed to do it using one hand. He held on to the metal plate containing the transmitter and all sorts of other arcane electronics.

Everything that had been so easy previously, so painless, was suddenly almost impossible. Removing the protective film forced him to let go of the dive light. It drifted away from him, extending to the full length of the strap. In the wavering light, he fumbled for the film, unable to find the tab. For the first time, he felt clumsy. He fumbled again. Got hold of the tab. Let go with his other hand. Suddenly he was floating there with just the protective film in his hand. He grabbed the light and turned it downwards to see the metal plate sailing down towards the seabed. It was far further down than it ought to have been. He made after it. He saw it falling down there in the weak glow of the light. He saw it silently hit the bottom, disappearing in a cloud of sand.

He waited, managing to have enough patience to allow the cloud of sand to settle. He saw the plate wedged between a couple of rocks. He made for it, using the diving lamp to light his way. He grasped the plate, prised it loose and looked up.

He saw something that appeared to be a ravine. Crescent-shaped. It opened downwards, towards the centre of the Earth. Berger turned his gaze upwards towards the container balanced on the ledge above in the crevice between the rocks. He knew he ought to go back up there – just straight up, to attach the final plate. Instead, his gaze sought out the ravine. He realised what it was.

It was the Landsort Deep.

The deepest point in the Baltic Sea. Half a kilometre down. An opening into a completely different world.

A bottomless world.

He turned off his dive light and saw the edges of the ravine in the faint residual glow from the floodlights on the ship. There was something magical about it.

He swam towards it. Against all his instincts, he swam towards the edge. He stopped just shy of it. He was clutching the final metal plate so tightly that his almost-frozen hand had begun to seize up.

He felt the draw of the abyss. He moved a little closer.

And then a being shot out of the huge gulf.

Berger's heart almost stopped. And did seem to stop as the dark figure reflected his own. The other diver took a final kick towards him.

He saw the knife – the enormous diving knife – and saw it swing. The knife moved with as much speed as the water resistance would allow. Berger deliberately aimed his chest with the metal basket at the attacker and raised the hand holding the metal plate.

The knife struck the plate, sliding off it and missing its target. Instead, the attacker's head came towards him. There was no more than an inch or two between their masks.

Diving mask versus diving mask.

The hatred in Nils Gundersen's icy grey eyes was unmistakable.

Berger wrenched himself free, ducked to one side and swam straight down into the Landsort Deep. He finned rapidly before turning round. He saw Gundersen's toned body also turning round, larvae-like. The ship's floodlights barely made it this far, and it was almost completely dark around him. The walls of the ravine seemed to draw in, pressing against him. He saw Gundersen get closer, the big knife once again raised.

And then he was on him again.

Berger raised the metal plate, the basket across his chest keeping Gundersen's torso at a distance, but not his arms, and not the knife that was approaching with peculiar languor through the dark waters of the Landsort Deep. The knife was heading for his throat.

He ducked, twisting his head towards his right shoulder, the knife passing straight by the side of his face. He felt it graze his wetsuit. He felt the cold forming like a stain on his left shoulder. He saw a red cloud escaping into the water. His own blood.

The knife must have struck his shoulder – not stabbing but cutting. It had cut a long wound. He couldn't tell how deep it was. But now the knife was at liberty again. Berger saw it raised. He tucked his legs up under the basket and managed to pull off a double kick despite his weightlessness. Both his fins struck Gundersen's ribs, and the aged warrior tumbled backwards.

It was an unexpectedly good strike. It must have taken a couple of ribs with it.

Not that this affected Gundersen. He attacked with the fury of a twenty-year-old, with no hesitation. This time, it was clear that he was aiming for Berger's air tube with the knife. Berger raised his left hand with the light and shone it directly into Gundersen's eyes. Dazzled, he missed badly in his lunge with the knife and Berger finned wildly upwards towards the opening above in the underwater ravine, switching off his dive light and slipping behind the container. He peeked out and saw Gundersen glide up from the Landsort Deep in a pirouette that implied far greater diving experience than his own.

This man had meant to kill his two boys.

He still meant to.

There was no doubt about it.

Berger peered upwards. He saw his own air bubbles. Saw that Gundersen saw them. However, he could see Gundersen's bubbles. He realised that neither of them would be able to hide behind the container. No ambush was possible.

His energy was running out. This was the tightest of tight corners. He had to do something. He had to think. Think seriously. He had to find just a little space in which to think.

From round the corner of the container, he saw Gundersen approaching, saw his gaze tracking the bubbles up towards the surface. Berger moved away from him, sideways, towards the next corner.

Gundersen reached the container. Knife raised, he peered round the corner. No one was there. The bubbles had moved sideways and seemed to be diagonally across the cuboid. Gundersen rounded the next corner. Now the bubbles were beyond the next corner. It was like dancing in circles.

This continued for a while, Berger constantly ensuring he was as far away from Gundersen's bubbles as he could be.

Gundersen stopped. He watched. On the far side of the container, Berger also stopped. Once again. Cat and mouse. Gundersen moved slowly down the long side of the container. He watched to see whether the bubbles followed, as they had in the last two laps of their dance.

They didn't.

The bubbles stayed still.

Gundersen gathered his considerable strength. He held his breath, stopping the bubbles. He checked that the knife was positioned perfectly in his hand, as it had been on so many occasions during his long life as an assassin. He had his son's killer right there, on the other side of that bloody corner. He was ready to execute him, to slaughter him like a pig.

He took an extra deep breath. He lunged round the corner of the container.

Lying on the seabed was an air cylinder. Bubbles trickled out of the unattached mouthpiece.

It took a half-second too long to react. Perhaps he was just too old. He didn't have time to spin round in the opposite direction to the dance – not all the way. Nevertheless, he turned enough to see the figure coming towards him. He felt a sharp blow to his head, his field of vision shattered and he was suddenly breathing in brackish seawater.

With all his might, Berger yanked the tube out of Gundersen's air bottle.

Then Berger struck him again as hard as he could. And he hit him in the same spot on his ribcage. Another blow, and then he had to return to his abandoned air cylinder. As he gratefully took in air, he saw Gundersen's lifeless body moving towards the edge of the Landsort Deep. Behind him, Gundersen's large hunting knife drifted for a moment in the great nothingness, before gravity took hold.

Berger took another deep breath and then let go of the mouthpiece. He caught the knife and finned out over the edge. With all his might, he stabbed the floating figure between the shoulder blades.

The knife stayed there.

Then Sam Berger pushed Nils Gundersen down into the Landsort Deep. He saw the bleeding, lifeless body captured by gravity and ever so slowly pirouette down into the precipice.

The body left behind a red spiral of blood.

Before long that too was consumed by the sea.

By the abyss in which Nils Gundersen belonged.

# 41

Gundersen was gone. Below Berger was nothing but the infinite chasm of the Landsort Deep. If it was indeed below.

He needed to get back to his air cylinder quickly and take that breath of life that his lungs were screaming for. He turned round. Everything looked the same in that direction. He turned his gaze upwards.

Although perhaps it wasn't up at all.

Out of breath and unable to breathe.

Berger spun round. His gaze darted in every direction. It all looked the same.

It felt as if his lungs were going to burst.

He grasped the dive light and shone it around him. It made no difference whatsoever.

He looked down, he looked up, he looked to his left, he looked to his right. Except there was no up, no down, no here, no there. There was no direction whatsoever.

He felt the panic spreading through his body like unfamiliar blood in his veins.

He was in the mid-water and he couldn't breathe. He felt his brain shutting down. He felt every single cell bellowing for oxygen. The realisation was almost liberating.

He was going to die here.

Sam Berger was dying in the mid-water.

There was nothing left in him that could think. Panic had paralysed his body. He saw it as if from a distance, saw its movements slowly abate.

His lungs were pure pain.

It was at that moment he gave up.

He gave up.

But a tiny, tiny part of his consciousness didn't want to. Refused. That part made him shine the light around him one last time. Once more.

There were no bubbles.

Last time in the mid-water, he'd been saved by the bubbles. He'd had an air cylinder and been able to use the bubbles to set him right. But not even that salvation remained.

The tiny, tiny part of his consciousness said:

*You have to create your own bubble.*

He had no air left in his lungs. Yet he managed to exhale – the one breath he had saved up as his last. It was a single bubble.

One tiny little bubble.

It seemed to dribble down his mask and continue down his immobile body. He managed to turn and see it float downwards.

The way he had perceived to be downwards.

It was actually upwards.

With strength he didn't really have, he followed the little bubble. His limbs were strangely tenacious. His blood seemed to flow so slowly.

He saw the bubble disappear above. Past an edge.

He reached the edge. His brain was about to explode.

But the edge was there, and beyond it lay his air bottle.

Just ten or so metres. It was lying next to the container like a mirage.

He lunged towards it. Except he didn't have the strength to lunge. His vision was blurring, it was disappearing. He tried to fin forward. He couldn't.

His body was one, single exposed nerve.

Something somewhere thought: *Not here. Don't die here. Not so close to the air.* This something lifted his hands, arms, legs. He gathered what little remained within him for a single movement, and that generated one more. And one more.

His lungs were bursting. He was quite certain. He could feel it.

In what remained of his vision, he saw the regulator wafting about like a sickly piece of coral. He thought he could see air bubbles trickling out. He didn't know how long he had left. He saw his hand reach for the mouthpiece, saw bubbles trickling out as if in a dance of death. Then he grasped it.

The time that passed before he actually managed to insert the mouthpiece between his teeth was indescribable.

And the first breath was pure rebirth.

His lungs whistled, they screamed. They hadn't ruptured, but now they were close to bursting in an explosion of happiness. He managed to master his breathing – not breathing in a panic, not losing his presence of mind.

He lay there for so long, just floating, that his increasingly normalised breathing was like paradise itself. It was as if he'd died and arisen in a better world.

A world where it was possible to breathe.

It was an illustrative existence.

He simply existed, and he loved existing.

He put a hand to the cold surface of the container and let himself simply exist. He applied the final metal plate with a caress.

Then he glided slowly upwards. He saw the surface. Reached the surface. Grabbed hold of the lift on the side of the hull, slowly removed his mask, breathed freely. He was brought up, saw the balustrade, saw the people beyond it. Saw four divers standing by, but also saw something much more important. He saw Deer smiling at him, he saw Freja nodding, he saw the twins rushing towards him, he saw Molly coming to meet him.

Sam Berger existed.

He was.

And everything was good.

For a very long time everything was very good. Simply good.

He would wait a while to explain about Nils Gundersen and the mid-water. He couldn't do it now.

'You're bleeding,' said Molly, touching his shoulder.

'Things were a bit rowdy down there,' was all he said.

A man pulled away from the group of Security Service men and approached the small cluster.

'Want to see?'

Berger looked up into Jonas Andersson's face. The four divers were already gone. A long girder had been unfolded from the ship and a winch lowered.

Berger followed the Security Service's operational lead. The twins came along, so did Deer, so did Molly.

Camera footage rather like an X-ray was visible on a screen on the ship's bridge. It depicted a cuboid. The plates that Berger had attached to the container's sides made it transparent. They could see inside.

'It's completely watertight,' said Jonas Andersson.

They saw a seemingly unlimited arsenal. They saw pistols, automatics, hand grenades, bazookas. They saw ballistic weapons, rocket launchers, they saw a whole platoon of suicide vests, they saw weapons they had never seen before.

Using an underwater camera of the more classic type, they watched on a parallel screen as the four divers attached chains under and around the container and connected the whole thing to a huge hook hanging down over them. All the chains were brought together there.

Then the container was lifted. It was released from the crevice where it had been hidden. It seemed to float, bobbing away over the seabed. Until it reached the edge of the ravine. Until it was perched on the brink of the Landsort Deep.

There the container hung.

Berger looked at the Security Service's operational lead. He could tell Jonas Andersson was puzzled. Andersson briefly closed his eyes and nodded at the old seadog, who was clutching a joystick. He nudged it.

And the hook let go.

The container tumbled down into the Landsort Deep, striking the cliff face as it went, spinning around, going end over end. Then, far below, Sam Berger sensed an explosion, a bright light shooting out of the depths, multiplying.

But by then, the container was already too far gone into the abyss for it to matter. Soon it would be reunited with Nils Gundersen's body.

The remains of the arsenal tumbled on and out of sight.

It meant nothing now.

# 42

The dead were all around her, but they were shrouded in a thick blanket of snow. She couldn't feel even the slightest whiff of their rotten, ice-cold breath.

Molly Blom was walking through a cemetery. The light was very bright, and the crisp cold harshly caressed her cheeks.

Fortunately, the path had been shovelled and she could follow its narrow course through the metre-thick whiteness. A narrow path towards Sweden's second oldest church.

But she didn't feel particularly well.

There was a powerful and brutal logic to the fact that the old Alnö church was on an island in an archipelago. Slightly less logical was the fact that it was four hundred kilometres north of Stockholm. When she allowed the hire car to carry her across the bridge that had been Sweden's longest until the building of the Öland bridge, she became uncertain for the first time whether she was in the right place.

When she reached the door, that uncertainty was vanquished. She could tell she was in the right place. Just like that. She could feel it.

On the other side of the wall was the new church – bigger and more impressive despite clearly being less remarkable. The old one was white and seemed somehow compressed, and when she entered the small porch, it felt even more like a miniature building or a playhouse. She strode into the nave and was overwhelmed by the way the medieval painted vaults, walls and ceilings seemed to be so close. Yet there was a peculiar sense of space.

A grey head towered in solitary majesty in one of the front pews on the left-hand side. She made her way slowly towards it, slipping into the pew behind.

She said: 'You're just sightseeing.'

The man chuckled gently.

'If I'm honest, I didn't even know where Sweden's second oldest church was. But it seemed somehow fitting. Far away on the fringes.'

He shrugged.

'Call it nostalgia. I never come to Sweden these days.'

'Am I free now?' Molly Blom asked.

He turned round and scrutinised her.

'You've always been free, Molly,' he said.

She gestured towards his face.

'The black eye's gone,' she said.

'Make-up,' he said with a smile. 'It was beneath me.'

She laughed, shaking her head.

'I've taken up boxing,' he added. 'A moronic sign of ageing, I know, but it's tremendous fun.'

They fell silent, letting the small church ruminate. Without a word, Blom handed Jean Babineaux's mobile to the man. He took it, nodded his curt thanks and pointed towards the altar and font.

'The choir originates from the twelfth century,' he said. 'It's in original condition. According to legend, twelve local farmers began work to build the church immediately upon converting to Christianity. The second in a country that was not yet Sweden.'

Blom swept her gaze across the stunning church paintings. She tried to be filled with something other than eternal exhaustion and increasingly recurrent nausea.

'The island of Alnö has been inhabited since time immemorial. There are a number of pagan cult sites across the island, and in the fifth century there was a sacrificial site right here. There's a lot to suggest they built the church on the old pagan sacrificial site to signal that the days of Odin and Thor were over.'

He stopped. When he continued, it was with a slightly changed voice.

'I assume that's how to build a culture. On the ruins of another one. Since the cognitive revolution, the history of humankind has been about power and violence and victory. But there has always been another aspect: that of human feeling, art, music, dreams, learning, thought. In spite of everything, that's kept us away from the abyss. And over the course of the last half-century, we've managed to maintain peace in Europe, even if we haven't been perfect. We've been able to think about other things – more valuable things than war and suffering. And no matter how you look at it, yesterday made not only Sweden but the whole of Europe a much safer place.'

'Are you trying to convince me or yourself?' Blom asked.

'Both, I suppose,' the man said, smiling.

'More than twenty people died,' said Molly Blom.

'More than twenty murderers murdered each other,' said the man,

'That's not true. The housekeeper got shot – she was innocent. And there were long-range gunshots too.'

'You were out cold the whole time. That's what you told the Security Service's operational lead in questioning.'

'You can't know anything about that.'

The man laughed.

'I know; I guessed.'

Molly Blom shook her head. She really didn't feel well.

'Nils Gundersen?' was all she said.

'Vanished,' the man said with an apologetic expression.

She smiled briefly.

'Yes. Vanished into the Landsort Deep.'

For the first time she saw an expression of surprise appear on the man's calm face.

'Just what is it you're saying?' he said.

'His body will never be recovered. But if it were, there would be a knife between his shoulder blades. Put there by Sam Berger.'

The man looked at her with significant interest.

'Can we be absolutely assured of that?' he said.

'Absolutely,' she said.

He nodded.

'Nice work by Berger. There will be power struggles in the organisation. Far fewer weapons on the market and a focus on putting their own house in order. No one will care about Freja and Marcus and Oscar.'

The man turned round and shifted tone.

'Listen to me, Molly. When I recruited you, I had no idea it would be this complicated. You'll have to take my word for it. It's over now – you have no further obligations. Enjoy life and the baby growing inside you. You'll be able to afford plenty of time off. Build something new. And you'll always have my gratitude.'

'Your gratitude?' Blom said softly. 'You don't even exist. None of you exist.'

The man shrugged and met her gaze. There was palpable warmth in his blue eyes. She would have liked to be well enough to appreciate it.

'It's true that we're still secret,' he said. 'I'd expected that time to have been over by now, but Europe is in a miserable state.'

Molly Blom stared up at the fabulous church ceiling. Medieval figures moved across it. The circle was broken; they were so close. They began to spin, dance, getting ever closer. The medieval age got ever closer.

She felt a hand on her shoulder. He was standing there, quite still, looking at her.

'Best we don't leave together,' he said. 'Wait a few minutes.'

Then he was gone.

Molly Blom was alone with the spinning medieval age. If this was morning sickness then she couldn't comprehend how any woman in the world ever contemplated having children, and she was hardier than most. She couldn't stand up, nor could she throw up inside the beautiful old church.

Medieval angels in pale colours appeared to spread their wings across the vaults. The suffering faces of monks loomed large, the expressions of pain on their bluish faces enhanced. Nuns' blessed smiles were contorted into expressions of sexual pleasure, the shrieks of rapture merging into each other. Saints raised their ever-larger, ever-greedier hands towards the skies, and God emerged as a form of healing light spreading from vault to vault, and behind each vault, infinite. The angels swept forth as if clutching wands, transforming the flow of ethereal light, turning it red, and blood seemed to consume the lowering sky, monk after monk pushing his head up through the pagan sacrificial bloodbath, seeming to gasp for breath, while the nuns grew angular, lopsided, contorted, their body parts enlarged, then diminished as they continued to scream in a constantly renewed orgasm. A monk developed a giant nose, the individual hairs visible on what was increasingly reminiscent of a pig's snout, while another pushed forward his chin, his mouth over-filled with blood, and a third's eyes grew enormous, came closer and scrutinised her as if through very thick glasses.

★

Late in the afternoon, the verger came to conduct his daily inspection of the old Alnö church. He knew his church inside out, and could tell immediately that someone had been there. That was admittedly gratifying – there were rarely visitors in winter – but despite the inadequate maintenance, they shouldn't have been able to get in. The pastor must have made a mistake. He'd probably lent the key to someone, as he often did.

He strolled through the nave, his eyes turned up towards the vaults – he loved them so, these paintings from a time when life was close and intense. The corporeal life, anyway.

It was only when he had almost reached the old choir that he spotted something. On the third pew to the left. He approached it.

There was a small envelope lying there – the kind that usually contained greetings cards.

# 43

Berger was no longer under house arrest.

Strictly speaking, he never had been, but as soon as the arms dump had toppled into the Landsort Deep, he, Molly and Deer had parted ways. From Nynäshamn, they had been conveyed in separate cars to Security Service headquarters in Solna.

They had been placed in an interview room each. A doctor had appeared to sew up Berger's bleeding shoulder before the questioning had begun.

Presumably the Security Service had deployed its very best interrogators on them – keeping them alone to ensure they couldn't coordinate their stories. Jonas Andersson, Head of the Security Intelligence Department and operational lead for the full Service, had occasionally turned up to interject with the odd question that was presumably tied to whatever Deer or Molly had just let slip in their own, isolated interview rooms.

Berger had never been as tired as he was in that interrogation. It had been as if the last week or so of madness was rocking him to sleep. Perhaps that had contributed to his letting his guard down. He had been longing for the twins and felt safer, calmer and more relaxed than in – well, years. The mere sensation of no longer having to watch his tongue, not having to polish the truth, not having to lie . . . it had been unparalleled.

And it had naturally been a lie.

He had said nothing about the extortion of the banker in Gibraltar, nothing about the tall, thin, chalk-white man who had shot his family's would-be killer, and obviously he had said nothing about Molly's act of patricide. Truth be told, he had lied rather freely.

As night had approached, Andersson had resurfaced and informed him that they'd managed to access the backup of August Steen's computer, and had found – among many other things that would take months to process – a video.

The video showed Carsten Boylan shooting dead the serial killer up north in the interior.

And with that, Sam Berger was no longer Sweden's most wanted man.

Jonas Andersson announced that he was free to go – which didn't mean he was actually free. He would be placed under surveillance for an initial twenty-four-hour period, during which time his ability to contact Deer and Molly would be blocked. Via all channels. The Security Service would need at least a day to work through their witness statements. During that time, they would have to remain incommunicado.

A black car from the Security Service fleet with a tight-lipped man at the wheel had driven him home.

Home.

Ploggatan in Södermalm. For the first time in three years, he wouldn't be alone there. What had once been his family would be there.

And a couple of Security Service heavies would be in the stairwell.

It might just as well have been described as house arrest.

The twins had been waiting for him. He had raised the blinds to let in the light. It had been a fantastic day – his stunted fatherhood was inflated *ad absurdum*. There had been so much to talk about, to take joy in, to mourn, to say. He had laughed a lot, cried a lot, engaged with an entire emotional spectrum that had been lost along with the twins.

He had become a new person. His true self.

Despite the fact that the flat was rather empty – the promised delivery from the Security Service safe house on the islet off Landsort was taking a while – they had found plenty of old games, including video games that were by now more nostalgic than current. The twins clearly played those ironically.

When either of them won, he would still instinctively do the V-signs.

Using all his fingers and toes.

It was hard to uncover much about their time in Paris, and he didn't want to push them. Nevertheless, it didn't seem to have been a particularly traumatic time – all that had been a little unusual was the constant isolation, and the strangely limited life. But they had been nine, then ten, then eleven years old and endlessly flexible. Everything that had happened was normal. They had adapted and moved on. What was clear was that Jean Babineaux hadn't been much of a father – rather he had been a form of pure absence. Whether Freja Babineaux had been a better mother was something he never got an answer to.

Perhaps because he didn't ask.

Freja had kept out of the way, barely showing her face. On the few occasions she had emerged from what had once been their shared bedroom, he had been incapable of interpreting her looks, not least because he barely recognised her face. Why all that plastic surgery? And was that shame burning so brightly in her eyes? Guilt? Anger? Indifference? Desire? Fatigue? Grief? He didn't know. He really didn't know.

At some point in the night, in the middle of a video game, Berger had fallen asleep between the boys on the sofa. At another time in the night, the two had returned to their old bedroom and the feeling of separation had never been stronger.

Berger hadn't woken until the mobile phone rang. When he had looked at it, he had seen the time was seven o'clock on the dot. And that it was an 'withheld number'. He had picked up.

Jonas Andersson had informed him that his quarantine was at an end and that he was permitted to speak to Molly and Deer if necessary. Nothing about the shooting on Öja had reached the media. The population of Landsort had returned to the island. Without any outcry. Berger had sensed that how long the Security Service gag on the two waitresses would keep them in check was in the lap of the gods. And it was unclear how effective the Service's masking of the large volume of bullet holes really was.

He had staggered to the bathroom and taken a quick shower. Wearing the same rather grubby clothes, he had made his way a little more confidently to the kitchen.

That was where he stood now. He was looking at Freja. She was at the kitchen table, staring out of the window. She didn't even turn to him when she spoke.

'They questioned us the evening before last. You know that, right?'

He nodded, poured himself coffee and took a seat.

'How did it go?' he asked.

'I said I couldn't explain how we survived. That everything after the moment when I jumped into the boat was just a massive, incomprehensible mess.'

Berger said nothing.

'I don't know how I feel,' Freja said at last.

'I've had that impression,' said Berger. 'But I assume that Marcus and Oscar gave you a choice. You made a quick decision.'

'I didn't know he was a criminal,' said Freja.

'Almost three years, Freja. You were married to him for three years.'

'I know,' she said. 'Long story.'

'I'm feeling decidedly receptive to a long story.'

She sighed, meeting his gaze for the first time.

'I'm not,' was all she said.

Their gazes remained locked together.

'No,' he said at last. 'I don't suppose we're ready for anything proper as yet. But you're obviously welcome to stay for as long as you like. It'll take a while to get things sorted.'

'They mentioned witness protection,' said Freja.

'It's a possibility,' said Sam. 'They need to prepare a full risk assessment. That takes time.'

She pulled an ambiguous grimace at the same moment that Berger's phone rang again. It was Deer. He stepped out of the kitchen.

'I think you ought to come here,' she said.

'Has something happened?' he asked.

'No, no,' she said. 'But we need to talk.'

'I'll drive over right away,' he said. 'Are you at home?'

'In my study,' she said.

Berger looked into the kitchen through the door. Freja was once again staring out at the rather grey skies, though her gaze reached far, far beyond the sky.

He was struck by the peculiarity of such a posthumous atmosphere prevailing in a home that had once simmered with life. And that once again simmered with life in the boys' room.

In the car on the way to Skogås, he called Molly Blom's number. He got no reply. She probably didn't feel very well. He hoped she was at home on Stenbocksgatan catching up on her sleep. Before long, her nausea would presumably be replaced by a delightful sense of appetite warped by pregnancy.

On his way to Skogås, the skies began to darken. The snowfall intensified but by the time he pulled onto Deer's driveway, the snow had once again turned to sleet.

He stepped through the side door into the garage, emerged into the first garage, gently brushed past Deer's familiar work car and then knocked on the door to the second garage.

She opened the door, smiled at him, admitted him and gave him a hug.

But wasn't there something strange about that smile?

'Has something happened? Has something happened to Aisha?'

Deer shook her head.

'No, no. Aisha Pachachi is fine. It's as if her time in captivity has enabled her to heal quite quickly, both mentally and physically. The Security Service has placed them in an undisclosed location with new names.'

'The Triumvirate has been shattered. One man does not a Bermuda Triangle make.'

She laughed.

'As far as I've understood it, Jonas Andersson is personally taking over as Ali Pachachi's handler.'

Berger nodded. Then he gestured towards the door.

'No heavies from the Security Service?'

'I don't suppose I'm regarded as being as much of a security risk as you.'

He regarded his former colleague and then frowned.

'Something has happened.'

'I've got to confess that I would have preferred to be shot of you for a few weeks,' she said, holding out her hands. 'For the sake of my mental health. But yes, something has happened. Your sharp-wittedness knows no bounds.'

'You're a poor actress,' said Berger. 'And I mean that as praise.'

Deer went over to the desk and sat down at the computer.

'You remember we sent a query through NOA?' she said. 'About a potential CCTV camera?'

It suddenly felt as if the blood was pumping a little more slowly around Berger's body. A bad premonition was just the start. He didn't reply, instead leaning towards the computer where Deer had just set off a video sequence.

Berger recognised it immediately.

The camera must have been on a lamp post on the far side of the Flottsundsbron bridge in Sunnersta, outside of Uppsala. The perspective was high up. Before long, a man entered shot, limping badly. Even from this distance the large bloodstain was visible on his light-coloured trousers. With some effort, the thick glasses could also be made out. It was without doubt Carsten on his way up the bridge from the far side. But then he stopped. Looked to the side. Caught sight of something. He bent down with great effort and picked something up. Only when he reached the centre of the bridge was it possible to see that it was a large rock, so large that he was barely able to lift it. Nevertheless, he dragged it along, putting it down at around the middle point, smearing blood on the balustrade and pulling some kind of emergency bandage from his coat pocket to apply to his bleeding wound. Then he pushed the stone into the river. And he seemed to fall with it towards the ice.

No more than a minute later, another man staggered onto the bridge. Berger vaguely recognised himself. He reached the same spot and peered over the edge, falling to his knees and breathing heavily while staring down at the hole into which Carsten had apparently disappeared. Then he cried.

Sam and Deer eventually saw the Sam Berger on tape leave the bridge. He disappeared from sight.

Then something happened.

With the deft movements of an acrobat, Carsten Boylan swung back up onto the bridge and lay there, completely exhausted, covered in his own blood. Then he stood up and staggered back, following his own footprints.

'Bloody hell,' Berger said. 'He was ice cold.'

'He must have been hanging under the bridge,' said Deer.

'He was a circus performer,' said Berger.

'I'm afraid that's not all,' said Deer. 'Just before I called you, I received an email from Reidar Korsvik.'

'What on earth are you talking about?'

'Reidar Korsvik is the verger on the island of Alnö.'

'Alnö? In the archipelago?'

'Yes, but not our archipelago. A much smaller one outside Sundsvall. Reidar is verger for both the new and the old churches on Alnö. This was found on a pew in the old church.'

A poor-quality photo appeared on Deer's computer monitor. It showed a small envelope of the kind that usually contained greetings cards. On it, it said: 'To Sam Berger! NB important! Email to desire.rosenkvist@polisen.se.'

'Why to you?' Berger exclaimed.

'As you said: no Security Service presence. Carsten saw us together in the interior. He realised how close we were.'

'And the contents?'

Deer looked at her former boss, trying to determine how he would react. Then she swiped on to the next poor-quality photo. It was the card itself. There was a circled five.

Letter 5.

'Shit,' said Berger.

Deer waited a few moments before clicking on to the next picture. It was on the reverse of the card.

Written in pedantic-looking miniature text, it said:

'*Gibraltar as a girl where I was a Flower of the mountain yes when I put the rose in my hair like the Andalusian girls used or shall I wear a red yes and how he kissed me under the Moorish wall and I thought well as well him as another and then I asked him with my eyes to ask again yes and then he asked me would I yes to say yes my mountain flower and first I put my arms around him yes and drew down to me so he could feel my breasts all perfume yes and his heart was going like mad and yes I said yes I will Yes.*'

'Fuck,' Berger howled.

His blood felt as if it had completely ceased to circulate through his veins.

'Anyway, I'm missing a lot of pieces in this jigsaw,' said Deer. 'But I discern a southerly breeze.'

'What are you saying?' Berger bellowed.

'Where he's well,' said Deer. 'Or at least capable of telling the difference between a hawk and a handsaw.'

'What?'

Deer clarified.

'*Hamlet.* "I am but mad north-north-west. When the wind is southerly, I know a hawk from a handsaw." "Like the Andalusian girls" was in a previous envelope, and I've found out from Google that those are the final words of James Joyce's novel *Ulysses.* In Molly Bloom's internal monologue.'

Berger began to wander around Deer's study. It was as if he wanted to get out of his own head.

'We should have understood this,' he hissed. 'The North Koreans. They couldn't have found Landsort if Carsten hadn't notified them where and when it was taking place.'

'As noted, he might have called in on his way to the bridge before he supposedly died. You can't blame yourself for this, Sam. The action, however . . .'

'The auction?'

'No, the action. Your future action. What you do next. It's on you, and you have to take it on now. Right now. Stop whining and act.'

Berger stopped. He realised how dizzyingly right she was. He forced the meaningless spinning of his brain to stop. He ended up where he ought to end up.

There was no longer any doubt that Carsten had Molly.

'The law firm Pantoja & Puerta,' he said. 'Are you willing to travel south, Deer?'

She pointed to the door.

There was a small suitcase next to it.

'*When the wind is southerly,*' she said.

# 44

The Balcony of Europe, they called it.

It was wonderful in the afternoon sun.

Europe's last outpost. An enormous terrace above a sheer rock face. Below, large rocks jutted out of the sea, still azure despite it being December. Even now, reckless youths still cast themselves off the cliffs, vaulting, pirouetting. Beyond, there was nothing but sea.

And Africa.

Every second counted. Yet they couldn't quite resist the view from this balcony.

They sat there for a while in the sun, gathering their strength. This was Europe too. Berger couldn't help thinking: the *real* Europe.

That had been his first conscious thought after landing at Malaga airport, when he had realised that Nerja was out of his way. They had set a course along Spain's southern coast, heading east, away from the Rock of Gibraltar. But there wasn't much that could be done about that.

Deer closed her eyes for a moment, accepting the gift of the sun. If she didn't die down here, she might stay a couple of days.

Take a December dip. Brag to Lykke and Johnny by sending them some pictures. She allowed herself to linger on that thought for a couple of seconds. Then she spoke.

'Don't we need to think about *why* Carsten wrote letter number 5 and addressed it to you in particular? It's not long since he tried to shoot off key parts of your body . . .'

'Aren't all the letters just him showing off?' Berger muttered, looking down at his mobile. 'He wants to show how clever he is; he wants an audience. He wants someone to think he's intelligent.'

'Or he's notifying his rival that the game is over. He's won. You've lost.'

'Also plausible,' said Berger, still focusing fully on his phone.

Deer grew tired of his semi-presence.

'Okay, what exactly are you up to?'

Berger read from the mobile.

'According to the Doctor, it doesn't sound like morning sickness. Carsten is likely to have *poisoned* Molly. It may have happened at the hospital when he dropped off the envelope. Perhaps he added something to the drip.'

'Jesus,' said Deer. 'The tube was swaying . . .'

'But she saw him another time, alone, face-to-face, and he gave her a pistol. It might also have been covered with some form of slow-acting poison. The Doctor offers a few suggestions.'

'She really wasn't feeling well,' said Deer.

'I want you to wait for me, Deer,' Berger said, his tone slightly altered. 'Get settled in a bar, have a coffee.'

Deer stared at him. Berger stood up.

'You're planning to go to the lawyers *alone*? Don't forget that I'm the only one here with genuine Swedish police credentials.'

'Believe me when I say you really don't want to come with me. You want to keep your job. See you later.'

Deer saw him leave. He didn't walk with Sam Berger's usual

gait. It was completely different. Something she had never seen before.

She called after him although it was too late:

'Who the hell is the Doctor?'

She shook her head and began to amble through the old town of Nerja. It was magnificent. The sunlight illuminated every alley and side street.

After a while, she consulted her phone. Not a whisper, not a peep. She really *didn't* want to know what Sam Berger was doing at the offices of Pantoja & Puerta.

And yet, at this particular moment in time there were very few things she would rather have known.

She had the address. She looked down at her phone, following the map and pretending to saunter. There was no person alive who could saunter with such intent.

She found the building, saw the plaque, worked out the office was a couple of storeys up and realised she couldn't spy without being spotted. Instead, she opted to settle herself at a table outside the bar across the street. Nothing was happening. The waiter appeared, and the sixteen-year-old within her said 'Sangria' without even remembering what it was. A glass of red liquid containing a floating slice of orange appeared. It tasted of something sweet, red wine, perhaps some spirit, water, cinnamon. It was nice. But she was losing her mind.

Deer had consumed the full contents of the glass by the time Berger stumbled out of the building. She stopped him. He stared at her as if he had no idea who she was. That went on for slightly too long.

'You smell of sangria,' he said. Then: 'The hills above Estepona.'

Deer did some rapid mental arithmetic. It was probably 150 kilometres from Nerja to Estepona. Past both Malaga and Marbella. But it was motorway all the way. Although this was where Deer was going to spend the remainder of her holiday. In Nerja. She'd already made up her mind.

If she survived, that is.

They ran towards the hire car, hoping it hadn't been towed. Deer glanced down at the endless sea. She could already make out the very first hints of the majestic Andalusian twilight.

*

Molly Blom really didn't feel well.

Her field of vision was dark. She was sitting on a chair on a terrace, staring straight up into the clear blue sky without really being able to see it. She wasn't bound, and was in no other way constrained except that she could barely move.

Her limbs would not obey her. They would not obey.

She raised her hand, managed to tilt her head down and looked at her hand. She clenched it, slowly but surely.

It was all about willpower.

Sheer willpower.

Molly Blom thought about the life inside her – the other life. There was no movement in there, there hadn't been so far, and it was impossible to tell what the situation was. But for the sake of this tiny thing, she intended to fight until the last. Fight like she'd never fought. And she'd fought her fair share.

She forced her gaze over towards the terrace balustrade.

He was standing there, staring out to sea.

Her hatred was more focused than she had ever experienced.

*

In any other circumstances, the pain following the gunshot wound to his thigh would have been devasting. But now, he barely felt it.

370

Carsten saw the majestic Andalusian twilight drawing near, without assistance. He saw too, with his own eyes, his own dream terrace, projecting one hundred square metres towards the sea, which wasn't green but glittered gold. He was able to make out every colour of the rainbow, and then some. ROYGBIV at the very least.

That was more than poor vision could have picked out.

Far, far in the distance, he could also see the Rock of Gibraltar rising like a giant shark's fin from the deeps of the sea.

And the beehives, his own apiary on the hillsides. He'd had them for so much longer than the house. The house he had spent years glancing at – the one that had been an unattainable dream.

And now it had been realised. It was simply that he would never see it.

Unless he had help.

All the bees buzzing away – even now in December – and all the control he could exercise over them! All he could do with them. The bees were like his own family – they did everything he asked them to.

Except getting him out of a contract.

But that was done now. No more North Koreans in his life.

The fact was that all the bills had been paid, all the documents signed, all matters temporal resolved. The rest of his life would be spiritual. As of now, everything was spiritual. Surely the two glasses of well-chilled white wine on the table between the two chairs, the glasses beaded with moisture, belonged to the spiritual domain?

Just like the motionless Molly Blom.

And her vision.

That was on its way to becoming his.

*

She saw Carsten approach from the balustrade of the large terrace. The lopsidedness of the former circus performer's ordinarily smart footwork indicated not only that his leg was incredibly painful, but also that he could barely see any more. Except for the boundaries – the boundaries that he had so clearly laid out for the terrace. Safe zone, unsafe zone. She wondered what it meant. She didn't stop thinking about it, even though he was so close now.

He crouched beside her. Since she had been drugged during the flight, this was the first time he was truly speaking to her.

'I wonder if you can understand,' he said, without really fixing his gaze on her. 'I wonder if you, Molly Blom, can seriously understand what it means to simultaneously love and hate a person. Truly simultaneously. Truly both.'

She tried her very hardest to find a voice, to find words, amid the slow-motion swarm of chaos that was within her.

'What have you done to me?' she asked hoarsely.

He smiled as he replied.

'You know what we spies are like. Dyed-in-the-wool geeks who seek out the latest stuff. In this case, two drugs that suit us perfectly. You and me. Together.'

'Drugs,' Molly hissed.

Carsten's self-assured smile was deeply frightening.

'It was me who woke you up, Molly,' he said. 'Without me, you would at best have been hunched over a walking frame by this stage.'

She merely stared at him. She couldn't summon the words.

'Zolpidem,' he added.

'What?'

'It was originally intended to deal with insomnia,' said Carsten. 'Powerful sleeping tablets. But it transpired that Zolpidem has the reverse effect on people in comas. They can wake up. But they can also die. I took a calculated risk when I added it to your

372

drip at the Southern Hospital. I overdosed you pretty heavily, as it happens. You're no use in a coma. Fortunately, you reacted positively. You were back on your feet quicker than I'd expected. You called me to say you needed a weapon. That opened an unexpected door and initiated phase two of our joint project.'

'Carsten, what do you mean?' Blom said, panting.

'A slow-acting poison applied to your gun. The one I passed to you at your flat on Eolsgatan. You know how particular I am about my gloves.'

He carefully adjusted the thin leather gloves before continuing.

'Very slow-acting. I was counting on its being about a week before it was time to come here. By then, the drowsiness would have taken hold, albeit and unfortunately via a transitionary phase of nausea.'

'Drowsiness?'

Carsten stroked her cheek slowly.

'I believed in Shakespeare for a long time. The relationship between Macbeth and Lady Macbeth. How she lures him into the fringes of morality and is then unable to cope with it herself. But then I realised that there was really only one place where one can understand what it means to love and hate a person simultaneously.'

'The monologue,' Molly whispered.

'You see how similarly we think,' Carsten exclaimed with a wide smile. 'Molly Bloom's monologue, of course. In James Joyce's *Ulysses*. A passive-aggressive masterpiece. The male control of the free woman's stream of consciousness. But you know all that, Molly. It was you who taught it to me.'

'We were married,' Molly snapped, short of breath. 'And you know why it ended.'

'Remind me,' said Carsten, producing his hunting knife. He slowly let it glide along Molly's cheek.

Neither her body nor her words obeyed her. She felt the cold steel approaching her left eye and couldn't even force herself to close it. The knife edge rose up the lower part of her field of vision like a sunset.

'You weren't stable, Carsten,' she said with restraint.

'Feel free to elaborate,' he said, slowly pressing the knife a little closer. She thought she felt it touch her cornea.

'You need my eyes,' she said, now so numb that she didn't even sound panic-stricken.

'I only really need one,' Carsten said with a smile.

'Your inferiority complex, Carsten,' said Molly. 'The sense that you might explode at any moment because you felt that you weren't worth anything. Because you always felt like I was better than you. At everything.'

Carsten nodded slowly and seemingly thoughtfully.

'My own value was in the mastery of my own body,' said Carsten. 'You know I could keep eight balls in the air at once, don't you?'

'And five knives,' Molly whispered. 'But you wouldn't let any-one rain on your parade.'

'It was dangerous to try,' said Carsten. 'It still is.'

He removed the knife from her eye. Stood up. Stared at the stunningly beautiful landscape. An unexpectedly cold breeze whistled up from the Mediterranean below.

Carsten spoke to this beautiful scene.

'I could be blind at any moment, Molly. You're going to see for me. You're going to stay in bed, just like Molly Bloom, and you'll be my eyes. You're going to open my eyes like you did then. Before you left me. You're going to lie there, still, and tell me what you see, and we'll be together for all eternity.'

Molly looked up at him. His face was melting into the orange of the setting sun.

'You've poisoned me,' she said. 'I'm going to die. There won't be an eternity together.'

'The poison can be counteracted,' said Carsten, crouching down again. 'Now it's you and me for eternity, Molly. I want to hear your inner monologue, now. While we wait.'

\*

Berger slammed on the brake when they saw the house. They saw it from far enough away that the skid wouldn't be heard. They got out and slipped over a hill, and a tremendous view unfolded before their eyes.

The bewitching shimmer of the setting sun, no more than hinted at, played across a hillside of cypress and pine trees, a couple of small white houses, a few donkeys with their heads bowed, a line of beehives rising on terraces up the hill and an expanse of butter-yellow flowers reaching down to the glittering sea. Far beyond, the Rock of Gibraltar extended into the sea.

It was like a still photograph.

Not far above the beehives was a large white villa – it was exactly at the point where the photograph on the wall in Tensta had stopped. High up along the facade, Berger and Deer spotted a terrace facing diagonally in the other direction, directly towards the glittering, golden sea.

Thus far, the only trace of life was something that looked like a puffing cloud of smoke above the beehives.

It was the bees.

It was as if they were waiting for something, circling, holding back.

Berger and Deer made their way up the side road leading to the house and the front door. They crouched as they slowly approached. It was further than they expected.

The terrace disappeared from view. So did the sun. The closer they got, the more deeply in shadow they were.

Off the radar.

Then they were outside the heavy front door of the villa. It looked fortified.

Berger pulled out his old skeleton keys – the whole bunch. When he pulled them from his pocket, there was a jangle.

There shouldn't have been a jangle.

\*

Carsten Boylan awoke from his lifetime's dream. A soft jangle brought him back to ice-cold reality. To the impending world of blindness. The one that he had to fight at all costs. He smiled.

He bent slowly forward over the table between the two chairs. He took one of the glasses of white wine, putting the other into Molly Blom's hand. He clinked glasses with her. He made out two pale surfaces, shades of yellow and green, bobbing about as he heard the clink. Otherwise, he saw little else.

He really did need someone to see for him.

He could listen by himself.

He could act by himself.

\*

Sam and Deer made their way into the house. The entire interior was decked out in marble. They followed an internal map towards the balustrade they had caught a glimpse of outside. They moved completely noiselessly, covering each other, taking the initial steps up the winding staircase.

Spiral stairs were the most difficult thing in existence.

They were sitting ducks.

They wound their way up the stairs. An odd chill seemed to rise from all the marble. As if it were all soulless.

They might be shot at any moment.

They reached the top. Alive.

Some kind of living room, thick curtains closed, facing towards what had to be the terrace. There was no crack at all in the curtains, only darkness. They made their way to the window, crouching low.

Their breathing was rapid.

They stood either side of the curtains leading out to the terrace as they fluttered gently in the breeze. Moved slowly. They couldn't make them flutter any differently.

Berger inspected his hands. The pistol in his right hand was quivering in a familiar, regular rhythm, while the left was making its way to the sealed opening in the curtains at a completely different pace. He felt like nothing more than an assortment of interconnected body parts.

Deer covered him as he yanked apart the curtains and without pausing for breath leapt out onto the terrace.

It was deserted, completely deserted. And much smaller than he had imagined.

There was no one there.

He crouched against the balustrade beyond the main wall. He peered forward a little.

He heard a shot.

Felt pain at the corner of his eye.

Looked up through a stream of blood. Beyond the wall, one storey below, he made out another terrace, much larger in size.

They were on the wrong bloody terrace.

There was another one – a bigger one.

Berger saw the corner of the wall, the concrete shot away, the blood on the wall. He withdrew, gingerly touching his eye. He managed to keep his mouth shut.

'Fragments,' Deer hissed, peering around the same corner.

The sound of another gunshot.

*

Carsten fired a second shot. He took a step back. He had his clearly established boundaries. He was prepared to expend the last of his sight on this. He knew he was out of sight and out of firing range. Safe zone, unsafe zone. He smiled wryly. He peered out again. He briefly saw the shot-damaged corner of the wall above, saw the blood slowly running down the wall, discerned the balustrade on the smaller terrace. Which of them would come down? Who would look out next?

He also had a full view of the door. No one would make it through the thick curtains without being shot. He was in control.

Full control.

He wondered whom he had shot.

Half of him was Leopold Bloom, meekly waiting; half was Blazes Boylan, impatient, horny and wild. He was both. He was whole. He was Bloom, he was Boylan. He was everything.

He was everything in the whole world.

And he was here with his Molly Bloom.

So much perfection, so much perversion.

He turned towards Molly Blom's chair. He was sure she was sitting there in the same state of drowsiness as Molly Bloom. That was how he wanted her.

Except she wasn't sitting there.

The chair was empty.

*

Molly had seen it all. All of Carsten's movements. How he had marked out his boundaries with great and practised calm. Safe zone, unsafe zone. He had positioned himself in exactly the right place.

The willpower it took to leave the chair was stratospheric. That required for what followed was even greater.

With a kind of incomprehensible slowness, she saw him turn his gaze towards the chair. Despite the fact that she had no more than a split second, time seemed to trickle, running so slowly, like congealed blood oozing down a wall.

Before his darkened gaze found her, she lunged, and at that moment, she saw clearly that Carsten Boylan became clinically blind.

The gaze that met hers was no longer a gaze.

Then she tackled him.

Rained on his parade.

She felt how weak the tackle was, she knew how dead she and her baby would be if it wasn't enough to push him over the invisible boundary.

But he staggered and took the step.

She stayed low, her head going straight to his hip. Felt the pain in his shot leg. Felt it clearly. Felt it tip the scale.

Carsten stumbled into the open, his pistol already aimed at her when the shot hit his back. He could have fired but he didn't. The next shot came without even a blink of the eye.

As Molly fell to the marble floor, she glanced up at the other terrace. Deer stepped out and took another shot.

When Berger lunged through the curtains with blood gushing down his face, he made no secret of where he was aiming.

Blom was lying on the floor vomiting as Carsten – with three shots to the back – tottered past her, aiming his vacant gaze at Berger. And Berger shot him with another two bullets.

One to each eye.

Through the thick glasses.

As Carsten fell, a swarm of bees rose up to the large terrace and massed for a while around his already dead body. He lay there, and it looked like the bees were trying to capture his soul. Then they coalesced into a plume rising into the heavens, forming for just a moment the only cloud to be seen in the reddening Andalusian sky.

\*

Deer forced her way through the curtains and tried to digest the scene before her. The first thing she saw was Carsten's thick glasses lying smashed and bloodied on the marble floor of the terrace. Then she saw Berger kneeling by Blom, hugging her.

Her closed eyes opened. The pupils seemed to reflect the sea, sinking like the sun into a shimmering ocean of gold, red and fiery yellow tints.

Tints of gold.

Deer contemplated them for a while. They were like a sculpture. And she recognised that there was something eternal about it.

She turned towards the Mediterranean. She saw the faintly illuminated horizon fading, and she saw the sun sinking below it. She saw the incomprehensibly magnificent light glowing at the edge of the Mediterranean, and she saw all of Andalusia mirrored in the incomprehensibly majestic sunset.

Then the sun disappeared.

# 45

The feeble rays of an eldritch sun filtered through the leafless branches of the poplar trees and the dirty windowpanes, gilding the inside of the boathouse with a faint and luminous light. There hadn't even been time for a proper layer of dust to form over the old clockwork with its cogs, pinions and mainsprings, pendulums and weights. Nor on the collection of stranded buoys and patinated anchors, the ropes, lanyards and sails.

It was the Feast of St Lucy.

The bay at Edsviken should have been covered with ice. Instead, the sun shone. It reflected off everything, dazzlingly.

'Fifty days on the dot since this began,' said Berger.

'And this little rascal is a month on the dot,' said Blom, stroking her stomach.

Berger opened the door to the boathouse, but he wasn't the first inside. Marcus and Oscar went in first. The twins made guttural sounds of impressed astonishment as they moved among the fascinating artefacts of the past.

Berger and Blom sat on the carpenter's bench and watched them. All the life that was within them. And all the life in her.

Even in him, a little. Despite the large bandage across his face.

'I bought the boathouse yesterday,' said Berger.

Blom stiffened and stared at him.

He continued with an apologetic gesture.

'The other buyers pulled out. I got it for a song.'

'And you did this while I was in hospital?'

'While you and our child were getting a clean bill of health, yes. You were right about Carsten having an antidote.'

'He hinted at it,' said Blom. 'But according to the doctors, it was an extremely potent poison. He'd brushed it onto the pistol that he gave me, while he wore his bloody leather gloves.'

'And it was a slow-acting poison?'

'But fortunately harmless to the foetus, yes.'

'We can't call it "the foetus". That sounds inhuman.'

Fresh silence.

The twins opened the door to the jetty and rushed out.

Molly Blom said: 'I don't know whether *we* should call anything anything. I don't know what *we* are.'

'Nor do I,' said Berger. 'But the boathouse is mine. And yours too, if you want in.'

Her long shake of the head was followed by a nod towards the jetty, where the twins had got hold of stones that they were dropping through the increasingly frozen surface of the water.

'How are things with the family?' she asked.

'They're still in the flat. I'm sleeping on the sofa. Everything remains unresolved.'

'Between you and Freja too?'

'To a great extent,' he said. 'And it'll remain unresolved. There's nothing left between us. She's alive and trying to understand herself. If there's no need for witness protection then we'll share custody. Otherwise it'll be complicated.'

'You might lose them?'

'She still has custody. If they go into witness protection then they'll end up in some small town in the sticks and I won't ever find out where. Then they'll be gone for real.'

He closed his eyes. Then he shook it all off.

'By the way, did you know Deer has joined Instagram? Nothing but pictures of sun and sea. In her most recent picture, she's jumping off the highest cliff in Nerja. Given that she posted the photo, I assume she's still alive.'

'Although who took the picture?' Blom said with a smile.

'She refuses to answer that particular question,' said Berger. 'Taken from the Balcony of Europe. She must have given her mobile to someone to use from a distance – someone who might just have run off with the phone. Who would you trust that much?'

'It doesn't have to be like that,' said Blom. 'Someone might have sent her the photo.'

'You're thinking like a detective,' said Berger. 'That's good. Good for the future.'

'You mean to say that we're going to kit out the boathouse and start some kind of detective agency?'

'I really do. On one condition.'

'Which is?'

'That we can trust each other.'

She didn't reply. She sat in silence. He watched her.

'There's been a lot of mistrust between us,' he said in the end. 'And I still don't know whether I can trust you. There are still some questions.'

She remained quiet. A great darkness descended upon her.

'Are there still any secrets, Molly? Surely there wasn't any helicopter administrator at the Security Service, for instance? How did you find me on that tiny island off Landsort?'

She sat in silence, staring into space. She pictured two ancient churches in her mind's eye.

'Someone saved us,' Berger continued. 'The twins were in the rubber dinghy, Freja was on her way down. A tall, thin, pale man saved us. And then he saluted us – right there on the shoreline of Öja. He wasn't in your report. But you must have seen him.'

Molly Blom pulled a protracted grimace before she finally spoke.

'There were friends on the island.'

'Friends?' Berger exclaimed. 'What friends?'

'There are a couple of old artillery pieces on Landsort. There are subterranean rooms underneath them. They were hiding there. That was where August Steen had planned to hide and snatch your children.'

'But friends from where?'

'Europe,' Blom said with a faint smile.

Berger stared at her in frank astonishment.

'And these "friends" knew about the auction because . . .'

'. . . because I told them about it. Yes.'

Berger had no words left. He was completely speechless.

'They had intel that there was not just *one* mole in the Security Service but actually *two*. I kidnapped August Steen because he was the second of them – the mole chasing a mole. They had eyes on Steen, but not Carsten. I didn't know about Carsten's betrayal when I came round, otherwise I would never have turned to him for a gun. And our friends needed to get at Ali Pachachi's information. About Jean Babineaux. About the auction. So that they could be there to derail the auction, stop the huge arms sale, get to the arsenal and arrest representatives from multiple criminal organisations. Although no one knew that Nils Gundersen had taken over the entire operation.'

'But you didn't have to kill your father.'

'He wasn't my father,' said Blom, looking out towards the jetty. The twins were still busy.

Leading the fast life.

'Fine, your adoptive father. You didn't have to kill him.'

'Yes, I did,' said Blom. 'He was a traitor.'

'But that's no bloody excuse! We don't have the death penalty in this country.'

Molly Blom sighed.

'The Europeans have an undercover agent who was in contact with the arms dealer without really knowing who it was. I met him on Öja. His name's Jorge. Only now do I realise that it was Gundersen who had recognised that August Steen was doing his own thing. He needed to see that Steen was dead, and he wouldn't settle for Jorge's word. He needed to see a body, and there was a deadline. A very tight deadline. It was urgent. Extremely urgent. Without Steen's body, the whole operation would have gone tits up. It was that critical.'

'You killed your own father to salvage the operation?'

'Yes,' said Blom. 'We had to make a quick decision. We weighed up the pros and cons. As we're forced to do in this world that you don't want to know anything about. The one that exists whether you like it or not.'

Berger stared at her.

'You are and remain an ocean of secrets,' he said.

'What about you?' said Blom. 'Who fought Nils Gundersen in the mid-water and then killed him?'

'At least he wasn't my bloody father,' Berger muttered.

'At any rate, it's over now,' said Blom. 'No more secrets. Everything's in the open.'

'What you see is what you get,' said Berger, smiling.

'Let's not exaggerate,' said Blom, smiling in return.

They sat there for a while. Then Berger said:

'What about the pale man? The one who saved my family?'

'One of the Europeans.'

More silence.

'August Steen was already dead when he spoke to me? When I watched the videos, he'd already died?'

'All of them except the first one,' Blom clarified.

Berger shook his head. He had spent far too long listening to the words of a dead man.

'Are you sure that was the last secret?' he asked at last.

Blom nodded slowly. Berger stared out at the winter sun reflected sharply off the waters of Edsviken. He stared, allowing himself to be dazzled. He felt almost blind when he next spoke, a faint smile on his face.

'I suppose this is amazing. What a superb network of contacts we'd have as freelancers! Europe. The Swedish Security Service, actually cleaned up. The National Operations Department through Deer. Molly, we'd be worth our weight in gold.'

'Although we'd be resources for unofficial operations, according to Deer. We'd be spies. And I don't know whether I feel up to flying under the radar any more.'

'Then you're in the wrong line of work,' said Berger.

'That's also a possibility,' Blom said grimly. 'I might want to do something completely different. Now that I'm going to be a mother.'

Berger nodded slowly.

'It'll take some time to get the boathouse sorted,' he said. 'We don't have to decide anything now.'

They looked at each other.

'Sometimes I ask myself the simple question: where does all evil come from?' said Berger, looking towards the jetty.

'Do you have an answer?' Blom asked.

'Not really,' said Berger.

'I'm a father killer,' said Blom in a low voice. 'Would you really be able to live with that?'

At that moment, the twins came in through the door from the jetty. It was apparent from their expressions that they still belonged in a magical world. Berger wondered how long it would last.

'Yes,' Berger said to Blom, getting down onto his knees and opening his arms to his sons.

As he hugged them, he looked up at Blom.

'Yes. I can live with that.'

The ice began to form, thick and strong.

# More From Arne Dahl

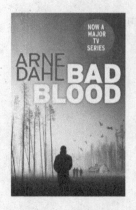

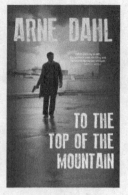

VINTAGE